'A vivid, unusual and intelligent fantasy in a style reminiscent of *Cloud Atlas*, supporting many elements of genuine folklore in a fascinating, well-characterised, historical mix. Gerald Killingworth writes about the fairyland of Hy Brazil as if he'd actually been there.'

Herbie Brennan, bestselling author of *The Faerie Wars* series

'From the chance-driven, incalculable Elizabethan world of Walter Raleigh and Edmund Spenser, in an Ireland promising fabulous realms beyond barely-imagined horizons, Gerald Killingworth has fashioned an engrossing fictional universe that Shakespeare would call 'fantastical' and I loved every moment of my voyage across it.'

Jonathan Keates, prizewinning biographer and novelist, Fellow of the Royal Society of Literature

'If you like fantasy and history, *Hy Brazil* will transport you to a world which is rich, strange and bewitching.'

Sue Limb, author of the best-selling *Jess Jordan* series and *Gloomsbury*, a comic series for Radio 4

'It is an intensely well-crafted literary novel, deeply felt, with incredibly persuasive evocations of time and place.'

Michael Bracewell, novelist and Turner Prize judge

'The best high fantasy story I have read to date…ever. I absolutely loved this story. If you like epic fantasy, this is a must read.'

Andrew Baker, reviewer at *http://FanboysAnonymous.com/*

Gerald Killingworth read English at Cambridge and was an English teacher for many years, including four very sunny years in Athens where he also spoke one line in a film and recorded a song.

He is now a full-time writer of (mostly fantasy) novels for adults and children as well as completing a PhD on the notorious Elizabethan writer Robert Greene. The folk music and folklore of the British Isles are a particular love of Gerald's and he is an enthusiastic morris dancer and folk singer, but still very much a shy novice on the tin whistle.

Gerald enjoys learning languages and numbers Irish, Modern Greek and Portuguese amongst those in which he is partially proficient.

www.geraldkillingworth.co.uk

Twitter: @geraldkillingwo

HY BRAZIL

The Elven Wars trilogy
Book One

Gerald Killingworth

Matador
9 Priory Business Park,
Wistow Road, Kibworth Beauchamp,
Leicestershire. LE8 0RX
Tel: 0116 279 2299
Fax: 0116 279 2277
Email: books@troubador.co.uk
Web: www.troubador.co.uk/matador

ISBN 978 1784620 066

British Library Cataloguing in Publication Data.
A catalogue record for this book is available from the British Library.

Typeset by Troubador Publishing Ltd, Leicester, UK
Printed and bound in the UK by TJ International Ltd, Padstow, Cornwall

Matador is an imprint of Troubador Publishing Ltd

I shall not begin my tale with the words *My Master.* Master Edmund Spenser has the glory of my enterprise, but I have the full knowledge of it and the hatred of the Elvenfolk everlasting. No, I myself, Edward Harry, am the only begetter and so *I* shall be the first word of all in the telling.

PROLOGUE

I was born I know not when; where and from what parents no soul has ever thought fit to inform me. My age and even my name are quite my own invention, one plucked from an almanac and the other from the annals of kings. I am inordinately proud of both and would defend both stoutly.

My earliest recollection is of the ancient dame who had charge of me and whom I called grandmother out of convenience rather than truth. 'You were left in my care,' was all she would ever say in response to my enquiries and, since she appeared to take this care as a solemn trust, I ceased to bother her with questions soon after I was six or seven.

We inhabited a modest cottage in a village a few miles from Peterborough. I have, since those days, seen the palaces of the mighty and so I am able to judge of luxury and extravagance. For warmth and a general sense of tranquillity, this building at a lane's end could set itself against any of these splendours, but I knew I was destined to leave it as soon as ever I could. We always had good sheets, they were the envy of our neighbours, and I never had to complain of a scarcity of food on the table. There was beef or fish whenever we had a mind to eat them and I developed a notion that if I questioned their origin too fiercely we should soon dine on cabbage stalks or, at best, gruel. So I held my peace and ate my fill.

The question of my name remained unanswered until well after I was old enough to roam the fields far beyond our village. Grandmother called me 'Child' and then 'Boy', but I did not find this grand enough for the conversations I had when I met villagers or travellers in my roamings. It belittled me to answer 'Boy' when I had spent a companionable hour in someone's company and he ruffled my hair and sent me on my way. I had too strong a sense of my own worth to accept such vagueness.

'I wish to have a name of my very own, grandmother, and to be christened in the church,' I asserted, handing her the collection of sheep's wool, plantain leaves and bird feathers I had gathered by way of a bribe.

'And what might that name be?' she replied making three separate piles of my offerings. I felt that I had chosen the gifts well and pleased her so I moved a step forwards and set my hands on my hips.

1

'I want a name that will bring me respect. It is not to be a name that men laugh at.'

I had heard the villagers call her 'Granny Windmill', but I suspected they drew this name from the mound at the back of our cottage where a stock mill had stood until a quarter of a century before. I rejected all country names; I was no John Blacksmith or Peter Thatcher.

'What name would you like?' she asked me as if my demand had been the most natural in the world.

'What was our last great king's name?'

'King Harry, but you are rising above yourself if you think I shall have you christened with his name in church. What think you of John Windmill?'

'I will not have it!' I stormed, seizing the edge of the table and bouncing it so that all her feathers took flight.

'What *will* you have?' She picked the beads of dung from the sheep's wool as if my rage had never burst out at her.

'Give me the name of another king.'

'Edward. He was a boy when he died.'

'You shall call me Edward then. *I* shall live to be very old.'

'Will you?'

'I shall. You will see.'

'Edward Windmill.'

'Edward Harry!'

'Edward Harry, then, if the parson will have it.'

He did have it and so, on Midsummer's Day, I was given a proper name of my very own. I announced it to the whole village whether they inquired or no. It rang proudly from my lips and I never grew tired of giving it voice or scratching it on any surface that would take a mark. I decided that my baptsimal day should be my birthday too and, with the two sets of half-hearted godparents the parson found for me, I felt that I had advanced in importance in a way that the world could not fail to notice and bow to.

From this time that I bore a name which marked me out from all others, the parson began to take my education in hand. I was called to his house and made to correct all the eccentricities of reading and writing that my grandmother had impressed upon me. She was by no means a foolish woman and I knew that when she fingered her way through our prayer book at least half of what she recited was actually there on the page before her and not her own invention. What was invented, the parson swiftly whipped out of me. My sharpness was a constant amazement to him and a lesson that had begun with the lash often ended with an apple or a sweetmeat. His plan, and mine, was that I should be made ready for the King's Grammar School in Peterborough. He, no doubt, imagined that I would make an usher in such a school myself, an industrious, sensible fellow grateful for his escape from Windmill Lane. My own ambitions over-topped his ten-fold I should think. I had often stood beside The Great North Road which ran two miles or so beyond our home. I was forbidden to do this because of the stream of human scurviness and knavery which flowed north and south along the road, but I watched disobediently from the hedgerow and thought my *One day* thoughts, of the day when I should set foot on the road and march towards the glories that I knew awaited me.

I duly learnt my declensions and a suitable measure of humility and was soon thought fit to be enrolled at the Grammar School. Money was always to be found for my clothing and shoes from a source that my grandmother and I never discussed although we spent many an evening by the light of a taper talking over my experiences at school and the families of my schoolfellows. On holidays or at the time of the city horse fair I always had a few coins to jingle and squander and more than once another boy was moved to conjecture that I must be the Devil's whelp or the bastard issue of a gentleman with a conscience. As a matter of course I thrashed those who spoke of me in this way, not because I felt the offence, but because it gave me the excuse to practise those fighting skills I was sure would be as necessary as my Latin. I studied hard and was respected, although I made no close friendships. Boys were alarmed that I would turn with equal ferocity on one who considered me an ally for some trivial slight as I would on those older rascals who sought to make the school their own little kingdom. They were not to know, as I never told them, that all such exercises of my brawn were no more than that, mere flexing of the sinews against some day when greatness would hang on a string before me and I should seize it. I progressed through the school without a swagger. I avoided unfairness and, at times, defended the puny. Master and scholar alike found me a strange fish, an oddity who grew tall and strong and who could construe a hexameter better than the best of them. The parson regarded me as his creation, although I knew in my heart that I myself had created all I was. He enjoyed my company at his table and gave me some of his papers to manage. It was thus that I began to gain some notion of *The World*, that great vanity whose empire began where the small fields of our village ended and The Great North Road beckoned.

As I have said, my grandmother and I never talked of the source of our income, I would not call it wealth, but we shared the knowledge of where small stores of it were hidden about the cottage. There were three or four coins here and there, behind a brick near the fireplace, in a small pouch in the thatch, 'In case that day ever comes,' as grandmother said. What that day was neither of us troubled to put into words. For her it was, perhaps, that dark day when our benefactor, or the Devil himself, closed his coffers to us. For me it was clearly the day when my restlessness got the better of me and a cottage at the end of a lane could contain me no longer.

When I was sixteen, or in what I had chosen to call my sixteenth year, my grandmother began to decline in health. Her last months ran side by side with my last year of school imparting a taste of sadness to our lives although neither of us stumbled under the burden of what we knew would happen soon. There was money for possets and potions to lessen the sharp pains which beset her from time to time and I was usually within call. The parson took it upon himself to try to ease her with a vision of myself first at the university and then, suitably drably garbed, in his own place in the village pulpit. His words certainly eased her but only in providing the one cause for mirth as she died. She knew that if I were ever close to a pulpit with any regularity then I was surely being denounced from it.

'You have done very well,' she said to me. 'But has any day of your life given you pleasure?'

'Pleasure is in the future, grandmother,' I said confident that this was the truth. 'I have been preparing myself.'

This was the nearest I ever came to sharing my heart with her.

'Promise me you have not lost your reason with all that Latin,' was all she said.

'I will certainly promise you that but do not ask me to promise any other thing.'

A schoolfellow had been made to promise his dying father that he would cherish his many brothers and sisters to the extent of his own harm if need be. I intended to be shackled in no way by her who had her foot already in the next world. I would have broken all promises in any case, but I did not choose to begin my life's great adventure on a raft of broken undertakings to the dead.

A woman from the village tended my grandmother towards the end. She obliged all those needs of the failing body that I shied away from. We watched grandmother slip deeper and deeper into wherever it is that we shall all come at last. In my best scholar's voice, I read her favourite prayers as bubbles formed on her lips and her hands froze in their final grip on the sheets of which she was so proud. The parson came and went, leaving me with the corpse. I had dismissed the nurse saying that I wished to keep a vigil, to take my farewell alone. She had possibly never loved me and I had never truly loved her, but she had done her best. Here I was, educated and hale and about to begin my most important journey just as she was about to begin hers. As I chose and packed my clothing, I made observations to her, explaining why I chose this garment or discarded that. If any part of her still lingered, I deemed that she would like to be informed what I was about. I explained that I would leave her burial money in a purse on the parson's doorstep. The rest, taken from all our secret places and more than I anticipated, would see me on my way. At dawn I closed the cottage door and clenched my fingers around the head of my cudgel. I had on my strongest shoes and all the possessions I had chosen to take with me were folded neatly in a satchel. The coins were distributed at sundry points about my body. If a villain found one, then he might overlook the rest, or so I reasoned. My hopes were high and the day promised well. I delivered the purse of coins in secret to the parson's doorstep and then, with an unspoken 'God be with us both', I strode southwards. The adventure that awaited me was far far stranger than even I, with my sense of destiny, could have envisioned.

CHAPTER ONE

'I am your man, Sir Walter!'

I had learnt from my employer, a Master Byfield of Clerkenwell, that the great man would visit the Drapers' Hall on a particular Wednesday. Master Byfield, who dealt in expensive cloths, was in a state beyond excitement at the thought of being invited to the same feast as one of England's noblest sons. He conducted his business very poorly for the entire week before that Wednesday and many times observed that he thought he should perish with joy. I offered my services as his companion to Drapers' Hall, as his protector, leaning post, whatever he willed. I was immediately refused but, having set my heart on the scheme, I persisted. It was finally agreed that I should, in the name of Byfield family pride, accompany him to the door of the Hall and await his re-appearance however many hours later. I preened and combed myself and set off some discreet paces behind my master, my mind full of what I should say if Fortune granted me the interview I intended. For the occasion Master Byfield had loaned me a better suit of clothes than, as his man, I usually wore. The higher quality of cloth and tailoring increased my self-esteem to a degree the poor fellow was now bitterly regretting.

'I am your man, Sir Walter!'

London is a city of swaggering and pretension. Every abject Jack Slop at his master's back door dreams of clean hands and a splendid livery and, eventually, a household of his own. But who was trimmed with more ambition than myself? I had fetched up on Master Byfield's doorstep a handful of years before and clever-worded my way into my present position as his secretary and Edward-of-all-errands. Now, in a far corner of the great hall, amongst those as worthy and yet as insignificant as himself, unhappy Master Byfield wrung his hands and silently disowned me for my forwardness.

I had easily found my way into the Hall, Thomas Cromwell's former mansion and a building that cried, 'I have arrived and I matter.' I understood perfectly the words the building spoke, just as I remembered that the builder now slept headless having failed his master the king grievously.

Sober and presentable as I was, I experienced little difficulty in flitting here and there until I was so near to Sir Walter Raleigh that I could have tweaked his ear had I so wished. He looked a little angrily at me and placed his hand where the hilt of his dagger should have been. The wine was to flow freely and all weapons had been forbidden. I made a bow and swept my hands back to show that I carried no dangerous blade. Master Byfield was not alone in thinking me forward. There was I at the heart of the gathering, well brushed over-all and intelligent of face, although wearing the dowdiest of plumages in comparison with the peacock magnificoes all about me. But my song was a chirrup they should all hear.

'You are no man of mine,' said Sir Walter and held his own hands in front of him as if I meant to spring.

'I am come to offer my services to you,' I answered. 'I am strong, willing and I have been to the king's own Grammar School.'

'Have you by God? And so has many a fellow who has swung at a rope's end before now.'

'I offer you devotion and the finest handwriting you will see.' This mixture of talents seemed comical, even to me, and I joined in the laughter. Against my expectation, Sir Walter decided to play with me a while, like a handful of nuts or radishes taken to sharpen the appetite before dinner.

'Would you sail with me to heathen shores?' he demanded.

'I would sir.'

'Would you let the savage's arrow strike your own breast rather than mine?'

'All that, and I could make a poultice from the hedgerow or compose you a stanza in Latin.'

There was more laughter. I smiled too and held myself up straight. Many eyes were appraising me and I intended that Edward Harry should impress them. In truth, I believed that the nuts and radishes were done and that I should be kicked back down to my proper place outside such a gathering. Sir Walter's mood was the mood of us all and we waited as he mused on thoughts we could not guess. Eventually he said, 'Would you be willing to be given to my friend?'

Here was the rub. Should I be saucy now or a man without esteem? I chose sauciness.

'I would gladly be your servant sir, but I am in no man's gift.'

'Well said. So you would be my man but not my dog?'

He turned to a companion who had barely joined in the laughter, a man of my own height with a high, clear brow and a sharp, disapproving nose. My words had not entertained this man, I was well aware, and I half expected him to order me a beating for my presumption.

'And what is your opinion of this youth who has been to the king's own Grammar School?' Sir Walter asked his friend.

'I think he should look to his manners.'

'But he has sworn to present his own breast to the arrow of the savage.'

Sir Walter was disposed to continue his quipping although a shuffling round about suggested that others were growing tired of the interview. Had I failed? I spoke out again.

'Sir,' to Master Disapproval, 'I promise nothing I cannot discharge. This is neither the time nor the place for me to pen you a paragraph but you seem a gentleman who could test the truth of my Latin.'

Let him find this a challenge if he felt so minded. If he could not test me in the authors then I was the better scholar and I could be kicked from the Hall knowing this.

Of a sudden he said, nay whispered, '*Tu calamos inflare levis, ego dicere versus. Hic corylis mixtas inter consedimus ulmos?*'

I was expected to fall on my arse here. His eyes were gimlets and the circle of amusement closed around me. I drew in a breath and looked directly back at him.

'*You are skilled in blowing the light reed pipe and I in composing verses. Shall we sit here together where the nut trees commingle with the beeches?*'

There was applause and Sir Walter struck me on the arm.

'*Hazels and elm trees,*' said his friend. I stood corrected.

But thus it was that I became the secretary and copyist of Mr Edmund Spenser, Clerk to the Council of Munster, Sheriff of the city of Cork and a poet who composed verses beneath trees of all kinds while I wrote down his lines in a hand which far excelled that of anyone I have ever known. There were savages and heathens too as Sir Walter had suggested for we were all to sail for Ireland within the month. Master Byfield suddenly discovered that I was a most valuable member of his household and he underwent near-fatal excesses of joy when he was asked graciously to release me by Sir Walter himself. This joy did not extend to letting me keep the better suit of clothes despite my asking directly for it. Mistress Byfield refused to believe that I would survive my Irish experience. She said that every night she dreamt of my defiled corpse sliding into an Irish marsh while the rain teemed and the wild natives cackled.

We sailed in April 1591, not All-Fools' Day, although it might just as well have been so for the weather was poor even for the Irish Sea. In many ways, however, I was more uncomfortable when we first set sail and were still able to stand on deck and gaze at a flat, unruffled horizon. Master Spenser had engaged me somewhat precipitately, barely interrogating me and trusting mostly to the good opinions of Master Byfield and Sir Walter Raleigh himself. To pass the time, as Bristol disappeared behind us, my new master asked me questions about my family and early life. He had quickly established that my Latin was as good as I claimed it was and now set himself to learn more of this young man he had so recently taken on. I was reluctant to begin my service with him with a set of falsehoods, but, on certain aspects of my life, I was obliged to do so if I wished him to pay me the respect I craved. I answered each of his enquiries brightly and he would never have guessed what I was about.

'My father was an honest man of little learning and less religion,' I said to diminish any interest Master Spenser might have had in him. 'He died and left me in the care of my grandmother. I have my name from him, my manners from the aged dame who managed me and my first steps in Latin from our local parson. He made me ready for the King's Grammar School and no doubt thought I should grow up to be an industrious, sensible fellow fit to be an usher in such a school myself.'

'And *are* you fit for such a post?'

'I prefer where I find myself now, sir. An usher's place is mostly to thrash unruly boys and I should soon grow tired of that.'

'To be sure.'

It was a long voyage as we were tossed off our course with every exhalation of the gale that dogged us. I truly believe it was the breath of disapproval puffed out by Hibernia herself to deter us from ever setting foot there. Sir Walter laughed at our discomfort which was unkind as Master Spenser all but died from his puking. My first true service in his employ was to wipe the vomit that liberally sprayed his breeches and mine. We were a sorry, stinking pair by the time the wind dropped and the coast of Ireland slid into view. Our first port of call was Youghal on the Blackwater River, Sir Walter's town, where the harbour walls shut out the rough seas like an oaken door. My new master and I lay on the floor of his cabin too wrecked by the voyage to enjoy the quiet. We had both called for death any number of times while Sir Walter guffawed and told us that such outcries were the worst kind of ill-luck. We said goodbye to him and continued our journey along the coast to the city of Cork. We pulled into the channel and made our way through the marsh-fringed waterways that lead to this strongly-walled outpost of England.

'There is a kern with his javelin aimed at our hearts behind every clump of reeds that you see,' said Master Spenser. 'Never be so seduced by the beauties of this land that you forget this.'

These were not the sentiments I wished to hear as we sailed in our hardy ship towards a city that looked as resolute as I imagined a city could. I had helped him into a new shirt and an expensive suit of clothes slashed with several shades of green as it would not do for a man of his significance and Her Majesty's newest pensioner to arrive home looking as wretched as we still both felt. I had washed my face and chewed an apple to sweeten my mouth but my breeches were in a sorry way. As soon as we had tied up, I found myself too busy to worry about my appearance or to wonder whether I should hear the whistle of an unfriendly javelin. I had offered myself as secretary and young man of all work and now I had to fulfil that promise. Struggling ashore with the chest of books and writing materials which I had been told were my main concern, I had no time to think, *So now I am in Ireland, the more fool I.*

It fell to me to supervise the safe unloading of all my master's effects. I am by nature the sort of person who takes to authority with great readiness and I soon had all the chests and bags on a cart. Master Spenser barely noticed, for I was merely performing that function for which he paid me, but I was enormously impressed with myself. In as resonant voice as I could manage, the actor's boom I had admired in the London playhouse, I commanded the boy with the cart to proceed ahead of us, carefully and with a proper sense of the value of our possessions. As he turned to grasp the handles with either arm I caught the first of so many expressions of hatred that are daily writ large on the faces of that ungrateful race.

'Get on with you,' I said, 'or I shall beat the surliness out of you.'

At last my master smiled at my efforts and I spat on the ground both to clear my teeth and to show what I thought about those who refused to bend to Queen Elizabeth's authority.

'We sleep tonight in Skiddy's Castle,' my master said. 'That will put two sets of walls between our beds and this barbarian nation. Tomorrow, at first light, we start for Kilcolman Castle where I trust my Muse awaits me.'

I was more concerned with becoming acquainted with the city of Cork than I was with his Muse although Sir Walter regularly dubbed him a 'Prince of Poets' and his chronicles of *The Faerie Queene* were the talk of London I gathered. I am a city man, one drawn to the varied lives of its inhabitants and I was anxious to make the most of my dubious adventure.

Cork was a mere herringbone I had noticed, a pattern of streets like a rib cage and hardly bigger than Peterborough but it had quays and ships and I wished to explore it if only to prove that I had not committed a grievous error in allowing myself to be transported there. If I arose before dawn there might be time to hasten the length of its backbone, The Queen's Majesty's Street, a grand name for a thoroughfare which stretched for little more than a quarter of a mile. In the lanes that were its ribs, Master Spenser had said there were the fashionable residences of wealthy merchants. Did 'fashionable' and 'wealthy' have the same meanings as in London, I wondered. I fancied they did not and it was perhaps as well that all my time was taken up with preparations for our departure on the morrow. Too severe a disappointment with the grandest city in that corner of Ireland might have led me to stow away aboard any ship sailing to any port in England. I was not to see the city again for several months by which time I had become, as it were, an unwilling native.

That first night I had perforce to content myself with the composition in my head of a letter to the parson in my grandmother's village. The only purpose of my letter was to give my address as 'The most venerable castle in the noble city of Cork'. I had no news to impart and only the barest good wishes. That life seemed so distant now, a child's history from a time long gone. Perhaps London had spoiled me. It certainly had made me restless and willing to see my destiny written in the bravest, boldest letters.

I felt neither brave nor bold that very first night I spent in Ireland.

Composing my ungracious letter to Parson Fitzjohn took only one of the several hours I lay awake. I could not stop thinking that, perhaps, as Mistress Byfield feared, I had travelled through that vile storm simply to find my death before the age of twenty and cheat the world of all that I could accomplish. If I had to muse on death, it should not be my own, and I turned my mind's eye to my grandmother's passing instead. The hopes I had at that time were the ones I endeavoured to recall to mind in that fortress at the scrag end of Great Elizabeth's realm.

Kilcolman Castle lay to the north of Cork. We passed through the north gate of the city and were soon on a road that had me thinking fondly of The Great North Road and all the life that teemed along it. 'A road', I said, nay a track, a scratching on the surface of the earth, but we at least had the splendour of a band of soldiers accompanying us. Master Spenser's life was too precious to Her Majesty for it to be cut short on the day after his return to Ireland and twenty men were given the responsibility of preserving it. I had never before travelled with a detachment of soldiers although I had admired sundry of Her Majesty's troops at various times in London. Some of those who accompanied us on that damp April morning were quite outlandish to my view. Their captain rode a fine horse and was encased in good English armour. We ourselves were mounted, of course, as were the dozen light cavalrymen, but eight foot soldiers had come down from the town of Buttivant to keep us company for at least part of the way. This band was composed entirely of Irishmen in the service of England. I was told that this was a most strategic way of managing our journey home and that we would have out-paced them by the time we reached Buttivant, but I was in no way reassured. These weathered men had a steel helmet and a new musket each but no shoes. To my mind, shoes were, amongst other items certainly, that which distinguished us from the savage, from the Irish in fact. Civilisation enriches a man and living in a house, as civilised people do, inevitably softens him a little. It certainly softens the soles of his feet. I had seen the worst kind of person run barefoot in my grandmother's village and I knew all the dishonour of which such people are capable. Looking at these creatures who spoke to me in no tongue but their own, I expected the worst and I confided this to my master on several occasions until he bid me sharply hold my tongue. I knew that he felt as I did about the significance of shoes and I was deeply surprised that he would entrust his life to a man whose toes he could see. We might just as well, I thought, lie down with the painted and be-feathered natives of America that Sir Walter had so entertainingly described to us. This band, this rabble, set to scout for us and defend us, had torn shirts and fouled breeches and each draped over his shoulders a shapeless woollen cloak. I was convinced that every word they spoke was treason against our persons and I determined after the first mile to set myself to learn their tongue as quickly as ever I could. I would catch them at their tricks and prove to my master how cunning a strategist I was. An old man and a youth of my own age looked after our baggage cart. As soon as my scheme was formulated, I fell back and engaged the man in conversation. I had recognised the North of England in his accent and I fancied that he would be as little fooled by treacherous schemes as I was. The youth was Irish and his ready smile put me on my guard immediately.

'I wish to speak to this man alone,' I said inclining my head in a way that should have made my meaning clear. I meant that the youth should ride further behind the cart so as not to overhear a word of what I intended to say. Any English servant would have obliged me at once.

'Ride further back, will you,' I said, irritated at having to explain myself twice.

Our eyes met across the piles of baggage and the smile translated itself into a smirk. He pressed his bare knees into his horse's side and took up a position so far behind us that he no longer appeared associated with us at all. Let him be ironic, I had gained my point, but, if he were a permanent member of Master Spenser's household, I should make it my business to see him smart whenever I could.

I turned my attention to the man. 'I have a mind to learn their language,' I said.

'Never saw no reason for that myself,' was his foolish reply.

'Who knows what they are plotting.' I nodded towards the foot soldiers.

The man laughed.

'Will you laugh with your throat cut?'

'No-one laughs with his throat cut. He's dead.'

'So you have never learnt their language?'

'Never set about learning it. I'm no scholar.'

I let out my breath in a sigh of disappointment. More than ever I was convinced that I should never see this castle of Kilcolman which had been confiscated from the brigandish Desmonds. I had stayed overnight in a castle, but perhaps I was destined never to take up residence in one. All I could do to prolong my life was to ride closely in the wake of the most heavily armed man in our company. I had rarely used a sword and could out-ride no-one. I wished I had my prayer book with me.

The man turned round in his saddle and called out to the distant youth. The words he used were Irish and I was immediately angry with him.

'You said you did not have their tongue.'

'I said I had never set out to learn it. It came upon me unawares, you might say.'

The youth was quickly with us and took an obvious delight in mouthing sentences I did not understand. How I should make them both smart. My master would be told of this mockery. At the Grammar School they would have felt the flat of my hand already.

'Calvagh will teach you all you wish to know, sir,' said the man suddenly penitent.

'Does he speak English?'

'That I do, sir.'

And I shall teach you to speak when you are spoken to, I thought.

He could not tell me all I wished to know. How could I ask him to give me the phrases which meant 'Let us drive the English into the sea,' or 'At which one are you going to throw your javelin?'? And nor could I simply ride away and leave him in possession of the field. I was obliged for an hour at least to be his pupil but I would be a very testy one.

The man made an excuse to do with I don't remember what and rode away. We two youths looked closely at each other again. Once more I refused to smile. We were of an age and both were well-formed. A credit to both our races, no doubt, with the important distinction that I was English and destined to consort with gentlemen and he was a lad who sat his horse well but who all too easily forgot his station. His face was long like mine but, where his was framed by dark, unruly curls, I had paid for the services of a barber and my lighter hair was in a state of neat governance.

'This will be your first word of Irish,' he said presuming to speak first.

'I believe I shall choose my own first word. Tell me the words for *the man*.'

'*An fear*.'

'*An fear*.'

And so our lesson continued for a full hour. I noted his courtesy as a teacher and he noted my quickness of study. It was not a tongue I had ever thought worth the learning, but the effort cost me little and I was sure I silenced the voice of mockery that had been laughing at his ear. At the end of the hour I rode away with thanks as brief as I could make them.

We passed through Buttivant where we took a meal at the castle to renew an acquaintance and shook off our handful of foot soldiers. I was glad to see them go, although I was convinced that they left us simply to hide in coverts and take aim at our hearts. I did not confide my fears to Master Spenser as he was too agitated with the thought that his own castle would shortly come into our view. He was correct in this as the castle of Kilcolman was visible a long time before we rode to safety through its gateway. I had been musing that the gentle undulations of the countryside were much like those I enjoyed when I rambled into the county of Northamptonshire so adjacent to my grandmother's home. The grass was of the same hue and there were no mountains or crags or bears to fright us. Behind the castle was set a range of dark, brooding hills against which the tower rose firmly in an act of defiance that caught the essence of our place in a land where hatred assailed us on all sides. We were that tower and the Irish themselves were the dark hills, brooding and festering in their unjust sense of an injustice done to them. We were the light and the strength and they were the darkness. I could have wept when I touched the stones of Kilcolman Castle for the first time. I felt so at one with Master Spenser's sheer Englishness that I did not then, or for a long time, think to investigate all the sources of his inspiration or those energies which made him the man, *an fear*, that he was.

CHAPTER TWO

I understood why the outlaws of the Desmond family had placed their stronghold in that spot some hundreds of years before when the land was even less inclined to order. It stood upon an eminence with low cliffs at the back and a lake in front. Master Spenser called it a lake but to me it was a Fen. I had seen the Fens and I knew all too well the awkwardness of reed beds to a boat and the plaguing by flies when a July sun has drawn up the water.

We approached by a narrow, straight road that skirted the northern shore of the lake. I could imagine the waves over-running it during winter months. The road led to a shore directly in front of the castle, a black strand pitted with the marks of cattle hooves.

A collection of healthy beasts grazed beneath the outer wall and made little attempt to step aside as our train passed through the gates. Obstinacy was in the very beasts of the field, I observed, but I would tame this errant spirit wherever I could.

In the castle yard beneath the great keep a party had assembled - scullions, housekeepers, men on official business that had kept for eighteen months, and two small children. In all the time that I had known him, Master Spenser had talked at length of his poetry, of Latin metres naturalised into English, but never once had he mentioned the son and daughter who jumped about recklessly beneath the feet of his horse. In some way I felt that they challenged my own position. Would not a man prefer to have his own son as secretary as soon as he had conned his letters well enough?

For the moment I put such fears aside and basked in the goodwill that included my own self as much as anyone. I was smiles to all, particularly as I meant to be lodged as fairly as I could. The castle was very old and bore clear signs of recent repair. It might be stalwart, but I expected that it would offer little in the way of comfort.

Imagine my delight, therefore, to discover that Master Spenser had contrived to insert a comfortable English gentleman's house within the very fabric of this forbidding pile. The outer walls of the keep had been reduced in thickness, windows of a good size inserted and plaster and panelling applied where none had ever been dreamt of before. Above the great hall, two new floors contained our private chambers with a degree of pleasance I could never have anticipated. There was a separate parlour a step across from the keep and the usual offices, kitchen, servants' quarters and stables stretched along the east and western walls. We even had the luxury of gardens, two indeed, but of modest size for they had to be accommodated with the walled ground, the *bawn* as they termed it, of the castle.

A man came forward and was acknowledged warmly.

'Welcome home, master.'

This must be the steward. I doffed my bonnet to him and jumped down.

'My factotum,' said Master Spenser. 'Lodge him near me.'

My mood was at once lighter and I joined in the embracing of the children, an act I usually avoid. The boy was to be dispossessed of his room in my favour it soon transpired. I expected him to regard me with dislike thereafter but he was happy to be lodged with the steward whom he had made his particular friend in his father's absence.

We dined that night in the great hall of the castle. I soon understood that Master Spenser used this room when he was the lord and the parlour when he was the gentleman. He was a poet in both and from one day to the next I could not tell where I should be obliged to spread my papers. Our meal would have satisfied a king and his court. There was music and the youth Calvagh sang a song to which I did not listen. I was too busy delighting in my position at the lord's right hand near the top of the table set along the wall. The meat was succulent and the gravy rich and I drank all the wine I could have wanted.

Our first week was given over to business, both concerning the Spenser lands and to Munster as a whole. The castle gate was regularly opened to visitors and all manner of secrets flowed through my pen as I wrote and wrote. A gift I have is to write at enormous speed with never a blot or the need to cross through. My penmanship became quite the wonder of the castle.

The poet re-appeared in due course. It was nearly May and the sun had shown an inclination to shine.

'I hear the voices of my Muse,' Master Spenser said to me. 'But is it the voice of river or hill, water nymph or faun?'

Such conversation was new to me and I merely smiled. We had been sitting at the highest window of the castle pointing out features of the landscape to the children. The game was for the boy or girl to say, 'Look the sun is shining there now,' and Master Spenser would name what they had seen. His knowledge was substantial and mine, of course, was nothing. I was glad of the prospect of a ride to some spot or other so that I might acquaint myself with the geography of my new home. I still harboured doubts that one day I might need to flee from it and I at least needed to know where the main roads or watercourses were. The girl, Katherine, seven years old and a favourite of the household, made the decision for us.

'I hear them calling from the river,' she said. 'Hark.'

And so to the Awbeg we went, the stream that washes the feet of the castle at Buttivant. There would be poetic composition and visiting and I should have exercise on a horse. I wondered whether I might be required to stand *in* the stream itself while my master, equally wet-shod, intoned his verses and I scribbled and shivered. It was not like that. He sat at a distance under a tree and pondered and I sharpened quills and poured his drink. It was an agreeably lazy way to spend my days and I was sure it could not last forever. The youth Calvagh rode with us as it gave him a direction when he exercised a trio of horses from the castle stables. This, I gathered, was his major skill and I did not resent him overly as he took pains to remain obscured once we were settled by the river.

By the end of the day I was surprised to see how thorough this visitation of the water Muses had been. The stock of paper I had carried with me was almost used up.

'The work has unfolded itself to me,' said Master Spenser as we prepared to depart. 'Generally I struggle more with the arrangement of my verses. You, Hobbinol, and Cuddy yonder are on the page fully-fleshed so early. My thanks to you.'

'Who are these people sir?'

He shuffled through those pages I was yet to reproduce in neat copy.

'*A bonny swain that Cuddy hight.* By him I mean the boy Calvagh. He asks Colin, myself, a shepherd, who has of late come home to recount *The passed fortunes, which to thee befell In thy late voyage.* By this I mean my year in London where I chanced to observe much that I shall sharply glance at in my poem. The conceit of it contents me greatly.'

'And the other person, sir?'

'Hobbinol, yourself.'

'Who is this *Hobbinol*? A wandering knight?' I spoke my thought out loud and much too soon. My master's laughter brought Cuddy from behind his tree. I glowered as much as ever I dared.

'You are to understand that we are all countryfolk in this poem. You have read Vergil. It was indeed your excellent translation of his *Eclogue* that brought you to my notice. We are shepherds in Arcady. Listen. "*Hobbinol: a jolly groom was he, as ever piped on an oaten reed.*"'

Let me not be a groom! I was disgusted. My name combined *Dobbin* and *clodpoll* and *hobby-horse,* utterly unworthy words. Master Spenser laughed again.

'You shall write me a fair copy as soon as we return home so that tonight I may polish and re-fashion these lines.'

He might use them in the privy for all I cared. *Hobbinol.* It was a name unworthy of my arse and I longed to tell him so but I smiled and was no fool. What made my smart the sharper was that he so loved his conceit he explained it to our saucy Irish companion. So this was what it was to be the plaything of the mighty. What foolishness had led me to think that if I chose to strut along those corridors where greatness strode I should not be made to confront my own lowly station.

Our journey home was a time of great distress for me as Master Spenser expanded upon his scheme for the poem and refused to address me by my own good name. I was mortified to a degree that no schoolmaster with his sarcasms and his cane had ever managed. How I hated *Colin* and *Hobbinol* and *Cuddy* and wished all the plague marks of a stinking London summer upon them.

When my master rode ahead to contend with all the thoughts of Arcady that were buzzing in his brain, the youth Calvagh drew close to me and made mouths, forming the name *Hobbinol* with great deliberation. His own wit proved too much for him for of a sudden a yell of laughter roared from his lips and set the horses a-fidget. My master turned around and laughed too, not bothering to ask the cause of the merriment which I was most eager to impart.

'Such a day we have had,' he said to us. 'Such a day. A hundred lines of verse, good fellowship and a bright sun. A man could ask for no more. Look there is our castle framed by old father Mole that mountain grey. How I do love it here in

Mulla's bosky vale.' Such were the fanciful names he had given to our surroundings and I determined that not one of them should ever pass my lips even though I was duty bound to write them down for him. We re-entered the castle to the sound of his own laughter, to that of our peasant companion and to that of the children who scampered to meet their father. I alone scowled, but inwardly.

'Sir, I shall begin my copying now,' I said and took the pages which had caused me such offence. I wrote them out in my fairest hand and hated them the more for it. *Hobbinol.* I was no man's *Hobbinol* or hobby-horse.

After our evening meal, taken in the comfort of the parlour, Master Spenser retired with his own thoughts and my neat copy of his verses. Once again my speed and clarity of writing impressed him. Rather than sit despondent, I decided to venture where hitherto I had felt it beneath me. The outdoor servants lodged in a low rough-cast building which I would dearly have liked to call a hovel although it was tidy and in no way tumble-down. I assumed that the youth Calvagh repaired here when his duties of the day were over. My rage against him had grown each time I wrote his name or mine in Master Spenser's poem of Colin come home. I would scold him, teach him a lesson. My plan was ill-formed and childish, but yet I proceeded with it.

The sound of conviviality drew me to a door that was shut against the coolness of the night. An instrument was being plucked and a man's voice sang plaintively. I stood for a while to listen. I am no musician myself but I have an ear for good music and I applauded the skill of the performers. This did not assuage my anger, however. Rather it sharpened my discontent that Irishmen should have not a care in the world while I stood in the darkness with an unruly youth's laughter still sharp in my memory. I seized the handle of the door and threw it open with all my force. What a collection of rapscallions was there exposed before me. By the light of a small fire, they lounged or squatted while Cuddy himself, his eyes closed and his head thrown back, entertained them. The music ceased at once and they stumbled to their feet. The old man who had ridden back from Cork with us gently nudged a jug with his foot lest it be knocked over. My master's stolen ale no doubt.

'Be you welcome, sir,' said the old man.

Welcome be damned! I would never squat down by a fire with the enemy and my look told them so.

'Shall I sing for you sir? We know some melodies in the English.'

Calvagh had bowed to me but the bow was not enough.

'You have no shoes,' I said. 'I could never listen to a minstrel without shoes.'

This was the observation of a fool, an angry fool. In attempting to reprimand the one, I had made myself ridiculous in the eyes of the many. I recollected myself.

'Your manner today was offensive,' I said. 'My master shall know if it.' Then I walked out and shut the door behind me. I stood still to gather my thoughts, taking shallow, frequent breaths. The door opened and shut again. He came and knelt before me. Knelt. No man had ever knelt before me not even in my silly, fanciful dreams where I had wealth and enormous power.

'Do not kneel,' I said. 'I find that offensive too. The horses have fouled the ground in this spot.'

Without further words I walked away from him. Such dignity as I had assumed for myself lay on the ground there with the horse dung. Perhaps I was not made for greatness after all if my conscience did not let me carry it off better than this.

CHAPTER THREE

There was the question of my bed. When Master Spenser's boy was despatched from his room to lodge with the steward, his bed remained behind until such time as a bed of the right size could be constructed for me. For three nights my legs extended as far as my shins beyond the end of the bed. I did not ask whether the child during this time was obliged to lie on the floor or even to snuggle with the steward himself. Their chamber was in the upper-most storey of the keep where the meanest rooms were, a fact which should have filled me with guilty feelings. I reasoned that if the boy's own father was contented with the arrangement then it was not my place to speak up.

One aspect of the boy's life that disturbed me as I thought it reflected on us all was that he received very little in the way of instruction. If it were not enough that his father christened the unfortunate mite Sylvanus, at least it was not Hobbinol, he paid little heed to the companionship the boy kept with Irish and outdoor servant alike. The boy's mother had, it appeared, died a year or two before and the life of the castle was noticeable for the lack of a guiding female hand.

In a sense I set out to provide this hand myself as I did not intend to slip into uncouth ways of speech or habit simply because I was banished from England. I put a suggestion to Master Spenser: in the mornings I could spend an hour or two instructing his son. My competence in Latin was acknowledged and, if primers were sent for, I did not doubt that I could make the ludicrously named child ready for any decent English school in due course. The plan was accepted and we set to. My first words to the boy were, 'If you are lazy or pert I shall thrash you,' but the threat was unnecessary. In pleasing me with learning his lessons, Sylvanus sought to please the father who largely ignored him. At least he knew his father; others of us have not been so blessed in that regard. I did not care to think how many afternoons Sylvanus must spend looking at the door of whichever room contained a father wholly occupied with quaintly named Muses oblivious to the filial distress his coolness caused. Whenever I could, I introduced the boy to his father and commended his learning. About the castle I was regarded as the boy's champion and I gained respect from those whose respect I valued not at all. It seemed to me to be worth noting in a book somewhere that our detailed schemes often have consequences we never envisaged. The boy partly adored me and it was very easy for me to estrange him from those rough fellows he had begun to call his friends.

My own rough fellow, the *bonny swain* as Master Spenser had named him, avoided my company for days after he had demeaned himself in the horse dung. When he was not flung from the castle he realised that I had kept my peace. The old man, Joshuah Parkin, approached me on one occasion but I waved him away without asking his business.

My afternoons were spent by the River Awbeg at Buttivant as the tale of Colin come home continued apace. The youth Calvagh had been told to ride with us on most occasions but he kept as far from us as he dared. My master did not notice this, being so taken with his verses. There is a wide path beside the river which is itself a goodly stream, not wide or deep but fast-flowing and clear. I enjoyed the melody of its gurglings as, from day to day, we changed the spot where the Muses would speak to us. Beside the path was a high bank, taller perhaps than the height of two men, and steep. Trees fringed the bank and had established themselves along the path itself so that we sat at best in dappled sunlight. It was never warm, but light flashed on the water and I was kept busy. I could fancy myself quite elsewhere, not on that island inhabited by too many of God's forsaken, but in some tranquil corner of the Arcady that Master Spenser always carried in his head. Our meals were taken in the castle of Buttivant and much was made of both of us. My life was what I felt it should be with my talents recognised, my belly filled and the servants in awe of me. I had a pair of new short boots, purchased at Master Spenser's cost in London, and none but the best of tableware and dainties would please me.

Some days, Arcady flew away like a cloud before the breeze and Master Spenser's head cleared remarkably. This happened when certain men arrived at Kilcolman with despatches and we repaired to a closet set in the thickness of the keep walls directly off the great hall and where not even the mice might overhear us. The men were rarely named and I became simply 'My secretary whom we may trust.' My age gave rise to comment but my master would have none of it. 'Older than his years,' he said although I confess I scarcely felt this. It was now I became the patriot and the politician, scribing letter after letter and becoming privy to secrets of policy that frightened me. After the second visit, Master Spenser took me back up to that eyrie where none might hear us.

'We must talk a little,' he said. 'Be Hobbinol no longer. The safety of Her Majesty's realm is in our hands although you might not realise it.'

I simply nodded as if I had understood the full import of what passed between him and the un-named gentlemen.

'You surely know, Edward,' he began, 'that the Irish do strongly hate and abhor all reformation and subjection to the English by reason that, having been once before subdued by them, they were thrust out of all their possessions.'

I remained silent not knowing whether to allow any justice in the hatred of the Irish. That they had lost all their possessions no doubt followed because they were unfit to hold them. He took my silence as deep thought which, indeed, it was not.

'So now they fear that if they were again brought under they should be likewise expelled out of all. This is the cause that they hate the English government which is represented by both our persons, yours no less than mine.'

'Dark words sir. But will not good laws and sharp penalties for their infringement amend all that is presently amiss?'

'This is the realm of Ireland, Edward. It is unlike all other realms. All men have their ears upright waiting when the watch-word shall come that they shall all arise generally into rebellion and cast away the English subjection.'

'How then may the country be reformed, sir?'

'Even by the sword. All these evils must first be cut away by a strong hand before any good can be planted.'

Such words I had not expected to hear as we dallied by the riverside. I looked beyond the window now and appreciated all that I saw in a new light. Enemies with javelins aimed at my heart certainly lurked behind every reed and under every stone. I wondered that Master Spenser kept his children with him at such a time but good manners held me from saying so.

'No more of this,' he said. 'You have been shown enough of the thoughts of princes. I had lived many more years than you before I began to think about such matters. How old are you now?'

'Nearly twenty, sir,' which was, quite possibly, untrue.

'An interesting age. Is it man or boy still? Come, let us cross to the parlour and drink some wine. The lack of colour in your face betrays you.'

In the days following this conversation, I viewed any excursion away from the castle with great trepidation. Master Spenser behaved otherwise. His delight in gazing upon 'Old Mole' or sitting beside the 'River Mulla's' side, as he re-named them all, was unabated. He seemed to be two men, the one quite willing to root out all Irishmen so that the other, the poet, could enjoy their countryside in peace. I found him a conundrum, with his hair and beard trimmed and yet his poet's dress a little disordered, the shirt more than willing to push its way through the fastenings of his doublet and the threads of his everyday breeches all tugged. The colour of his stockings on poetry days rarely accorded with any other main colour in his apparel. For myself, I had brought from London Master Byfield's parting gift of a leather jerkin which at first I avoided as being too drab or mean for my new office. Now I regarded the leather as my best defence against an assassin's knife and I wore the garment in all weathers.

'We must have you fitted for a new jerkin at Cork,' said Master Spenser. 'The cow that gave you your leather was a sickly beast I think. Besides, when you accompany me outside wearing it, I am put in mind of a common tradesman. I would not have my neighbours suppose I deal in dried peas.'

The prospect of a visit to the city of Cork pleased me and I wore my old jerkin all the more, if that were possible, so that my Master should be reminded of his promise. It was soon forgot, perhaps because the Queen's pension, granted in February last, was still not paid and letters had to be written to release it. It was I who penned the letters and whether it was the elegance of my hand or the plaintive, bleating words of Master Spenser that brought the money I never knew.

A dagger was worn each time we rode out, but, for me, the decoration of the hilt had mattered more than the sharpness of the blade. Now, with the word 'rebellion' taken to my heart, I ventured for the first time into the guard-room at the base of the keep and made one of the handful of soldiers Master Spenser kept always to hand oblige me with practice in the use of my dagger. No doubt he relished twisting my arm or tripping me to the floor, but I advanced in skill and did not care who saw me tumble. Only one time was it the youth Calvagh and he was careful to avert his eyes. At least I should not be mocked from that corner again.

I admitted that I was surprised when a visit was planned to the range of hills at our rear, the *Mountains* of Ballyhoura so-called. Even if we avoided the stretches of woodland, I still fancied that a band of cut-throats could lie concealed amongst the rocks and tussocks until we were too close to make good our escape. My master seemed reckless of such danger and told me that young Sylvanus would have no fear of riding to such a place. We took two soldiers with us, however, although their brutal presence frightened the Muses all day long and not a word was written. We admired the view back to the castle and beyond and sat about at our ease as Master Spenser besought the inspiration that evaded him.

'No soldiers next time,' he said which I thought most wilful as he had spoken it in front of the youth Calvagh. I determined not to mince my words about this subject when we were home again. I did not mind courting his displeasure if I could save his life. Joshuah Parkin had brought my master's dinner in a basket. He was a man of clean appearance and his clothing was always in good order, but I relieved him of the duty of actually serving the meal. My grandmother had always impressed upon me the necessity for clean hands and a clean knife at table and I wanted to make sure that my master had both of these for his meal. His beef was accordingly presented without grit and the bread had no grey thumb print of the kind which often prevented me from eating it at public tables in London. After dinner, Master Spenser slept, perhaps hoping that the fauns of old Mole would visit him in a dream. The soldiers sat near him resolutely awake, muskets cocked up and down the hill and casques firmly on their heads. I wandered about playing my game of *What is it I can see now?* I knew the direction of the castle of Buttivant and, some miles beyond that, the Blackwater River that could be followed to Sir Walter Raleigh's house at Youghal. My several escape routes were becoming clearer daily.

'Would you permit me to show you something sir?' The youth Calvagh had approached silently as I stood debating the virtues of swimming all the way down the Blackwater to Youghal. I was wondering when the tide would catch me and ease my weary arms. When he spoke, I sprang round at once with my dagger drawn.

'You fool!' I said. 'This is no land to whisper in a man's ear.'

'I mean you no harm, sir.'

'Nor I you.'

Were we both lying?

'There is a trick of the rocks here that I thought might amuse you.'

Might it not amuse *him* to tumble me down these rocks and then claim that I tripped and broke my neck?

'What is this trick?'

'A trumpet in the ground. An echo. Shall I show you?'

'Is it far?'

'Minutes only.'

Minutes were enough when a man's life was at stake.

'Does Joshuah Parkin know of this natural trumpet?'

'I have never shown it to him.'

I did not re-sheathe my dagger.

'There is no need for that,' he said. 'You can see I carry no weapon and I have removed my shoes.'

I had indeed noticed this and it was on the tip of my tongue to observe that by removing his shoes he had taken upon himself the Irishness against which I needed to be on my guard. Did he really pose a danger? The only clothing he wore was a flapping yellow tunic that left his long legs bare. The soldier in the guard-house had shown me how easily I could grasp the sleeves of such a garment and throw the wearer to the ground. The sleeves could also serve to throttle him. He was slimmer than I and perhaps too nimble although no-one would ever call me lumbering.

'How you English are given to thinking.'

'We are at times. I shall tell the soldiers where you intend to take me.'

'They must not come too.'

'So I am to be isolated?'

'No. It is a sight for your eyes alone. They are inclined to jeer. It is only a crack in the ground after all.'

A crack down which I might plunge while screaming unheard. Fool, I went with him.

We passed into a group of trees and I was at once alarmed.

'These are oak trees,' he said. '*Na crainn daracha*. They should not grow here.'

'I know they are oak trees. You are not the only boy who wandered the fields and picked at leaves. The spot is windy and quite above the plain, but you are wrong to say that they should not grow here. They will not grow high, that is all.'

'I thought all Englishmen came from London.'

'I have lived in London but I was not born there.'

'Where were you born?'

I let his question hang between us unanswered. 'In a modest cottage, the unacknowledged whelp of some careless-loined gentleman,' might have been my reply. He did not need to know that.

'Where is the trumpet you promised?' I asked.

He led me in amongst the trees where a scatter of rocks had almost bubbled from the ground. I would have passed the spot without casting a second glance. Stones bubbled the world over.

'Look,' he said and led me to the centre of the stones.

'They look like a boil,' I said. 'The circle is neat and there is a hole in the middle.'

'That is my trumpet.'

'He lay at length with his head over the hole and made a hooting sound by cupping his hands. The sound echoed deep within the earth and was most unsettling. He stood up and motioned for me to repeat his action. More words of alarm raced through my brain. With a blow he could sever my head and watch it disappear forever into whatever cave or well lay below.

'I shall stand over here,' he said guessing my thoughts.

I lay beside the hole and made my own hooting sound that I fancied was louder than his. He returned and made a chittering sound like a sparrow that has been embraced by a magpie. We both smiled at the echo. I showed that I could do this too.

'The hole is too narrow for a man,' I said. 'I should dearly love to know what is at the bottom.'

'Some say it is a window to that other place.'

'Hell? Have we been hooting at the Devil?'

'Not Hell. *Tír Na nÓg.* The land of the *Sidhe,* the *Other* folk. Do you notice that the oak trees have been planted in a circle?'

'They have *grown* in a circle.'

On an impulse I lay down over the hole again and shouted as resolutely as I could, 'My name is Edward Harry. I am an Englishman and I bid you all good morrow.'

'Anyone sitting by the window will have heard me,' I said as I sat up.

My words had impressed or frightened Calvagh. He could do nothing but imitate me for his pride could not allow an Englishman to be the sole flouter of the old mole at the bottom of the trumpet.

'My name is Calvagh Ó Gamhnain, kin to the Desmond, and I also wish you good morrow.'

We looked at each other. He had confided a great secret to me.

'Why did you tell me you were kin to the Desmond?' I asked. 'We killed him not ten years ago. You should not have mentioned his name.'

'I am bastard kin. It was a boast. I am not recognised in their houses or welcomed. I have more welcome amongst the English.'

'You still should not have told me. What am I to say to Master Spenser?'

'His other spies will have told him. I could be held hostage, with you as my jailer.'

'I would make you wear your shoes in which case,' I told him roughly.

'Perhaps I would obey you.'

As we walked away, he glanced back over his shoulder.

'There are many windows and doors to that other realm. There may even be doors in England. Sometimes we do not know of their windows and doors and they are secretly watching us. Our words were offered in friendly greeting, I think.'

I did not mock him if that was what he expected. My grandmother had often talked of Robin Goodfellow as we perched by the winter fireside and who was I to scoff at Robin's Irish cousins who lived in a trumpet? These notions seemed somehow treacherous and foolish and I marched ahead saying I needed to see if my master were awake. I needed also to decide whether I wished to be drawn into this pert young fellow's company. Bastard kin. Like with like. Was Destiny offering me a sharp rebuke as I reached out for glory and the company of my betters?

CHAPTER FOUR

'I knew that he was kin to the Desmond. How did *you* come to know?'

'We were talking about out families and he told me.'

'Have you told him much about your own family?'

'Very little.'

'Exactly. There may be a day when we shall need him as a hostage. But I am quite fond of the lad. Are you fond of him?'

'*Fond* is not the word I would use, sir.'

'But you told him about your family.'

'Very little, sir'

'Tell him nothing more. Better still, for the moment, do not consort with him. You have heard far more of Her Majesty's business than any young man in the land I think. Not a word of what you know must ever be let slip. There may come a time when I shall need you to discover what *he* knows. For the present he belongs to a different world.'

We still rode out to the river or grassy spots here and there as Master Spenser strove to complete his tale of Colin come home and the youth Calvagh exercised the castle horses as usual. When he saw that I did not respond to his beckoning or mouthed 'Come with me', he understood that he had entered the realm of the invisible, that land to which one only makes a *holla* down a natural chimney, perhaps. I regretted the other secrets that he might have shown me, but what were these when I had a small part to play in the safekeeping of Her Majesty's territories? I did not wish to know if he felt disappointment for what would this be but one step from showing mercy to the Spaniard when he was washed ashore after the failure of their vainglorious Armada. Their throats had been cut even as they stumbled to dry land and God had ordained it so.

Every morning the parlour became our schoolroom. I entered wearing my cloak, it was dark blue with no trimming and I longed to replace it, and banged on the table to show that Sylvanus should stand in silence until I myself was seated. Very early on in this little scheme, Katherine had hidden at the back of the room and I was happy to entertain her and gradually to allow her to participate in what we were about so long as she did not show more ability than her brother. The little boy, he was nine, stood like a post with his eyes unblinking until such time as I chose to say 'You may be seated.' He loved even this standing to order and he would have manfully struggled to con by heart a whole *Eclogue* that he did not understand if I prescribed it as his evening's task. We had handwriting, with my own work as the example to copy, such simple mathematics as I could remember and we set about the improving of his Latin declensions. The prayer book gave us our English reading matter and when we, all three, tired of the frequent sound of the rain and the repetition of our *mensa*s and *nauta*s, we drew pictures of knights in armour with stubs of charcoal on squares of wood I had the steward find for us. I should have liked to take the children out in a boat on Master Spenser's lake, but the all too common rain never produced a sheet of clear water for us to row upon. It simply rendered the quagmire oozier and more dangerous.

The tale of Colin come home now drew its inspiration in Kilcolman House for my master had reached the point at which Colin tells Hobbinol and Cuddy, at enormous length, of the great men and women he has seen at court. He did not need to be *patulae recubans sub tegmine fagi,* which is to say seated at his ease beneath the spreading shade of a beech tree, to turn his thoughts on these matters into pentameters. In the afternoons I made the fair copies and read aloud to my master who had grown to enjoy hearing his poetry through the medium of my voice.

The end of June approached and I gave no thought to the celebration of the birth date I had selected for myself. Colin's narrative was many hundreds of lines long and my master decided to show it to his friend Sir Walter Raleigh at Youghal. He had been invited there to dine on potato and there was enough of the poem completed for him to take it as a travelling companion. I had heard of this remarkable potato which Sir Walter brought back from the New World and cultivated at his house of Myrtle Grove. At first I thought it might be an exotic species of chicken, or the eggs of such a bird as I once heard a fellow describe potatoes as white and about the size of a farmyard egg. When I put this to Master Spenser, he laughed inordinately and said they grew on a small yellow tree and then laughed again. I was not to be taken to Youghal with him although I might be allowed to sample the potato on a later visit.

'One cannot simply arrive on Sir Walter's doorstep with the words "I should like to sample your potato,"' he told me seriously. 'Only six people in the whole of Ireland have tasted it as far as I know, although I expect the Irishmen who grow it for Sir Walter steal half the crop and sell it to their Spanish friends.'

My Master was not consistent. He would travel to Youghal by way of Cork in the company of half a dozen armed men. I was to go as far as Cork where I should be measured for the leather jerkin he had suddenly remembered. Joshuah Parkin and the youth Calvagh would ride with us so that they might see me back to Kilcolman in safety. I ventured to suggest that, either from Cork or Youghal, a gift might be purchased for Sylvanus because he had applied himself to his lessons so well.

'Of course you may purchase a gift for my son,' he said. 'There is no need to ask for permission,' which is not what I had meant at all.

I was to receive the jerkin, no mean expense, so I did not feel too grudging when I went to the chest in my room and took out some coins of small value. I had no idea what I might find for a child in the city of Cork but, as there were undoubtedly other children of Sylvanus's age in that city, there must also be shops which sold playthings for them.

We set off in the rain. The more the summer progressed, the more the air seemed awash with dampness that would set us up with rheumatism for the winter.

'How refreshed the landscape is,' said Master Spenser from the comfort of the thickest cloak in our party.

As I turned to wave goodbye to the children at their upper window, my collar funnelled a pint of rain into the back of my shirt. Only the thought of my new jerkin kept me from swearing.

The soldiers will be all rusted by the time we reach Cork I thought *and the rest of us will have been smitten by a fatal fever.*

Perhaps the youth Calvagh had the best idea. He embraced the rain or made light of it for he wore only his yellow belted tunic with no hat, cloak or shoes. Normally he took care to be shod in my Master's presence, but who would bother to turn back to look closely at him through the shroud of Irish rain that draped itself so dismally around us? We rushed to the fire in the castle at Buttivant and again at Mallow and by the time we were installed in our lodgings at Skiddy's Castle in Cork we felt we had been swimming in a second Noah's flood. My master would depart the next morning for his assignation with the potato and I was to be allowed two more nights in the city before I need set off for Kilcolman again.

I attended Master Spenser at his breakfast and wished him a safe journey and then set my face to my own adventure. I was given five shillings, a huge sum, and the name of two tailors who could measure me for my new jerkin. The gift was a mark of my master's satisfaction with my service and I was a happy young man, although it rained still and the change of shirt I brought with me had not escaped dampness.

I disliked the first tailor who kept repeating that he had measured the finest young gentlemen in London.

Then why are you here? I thought. I left his shop without a promise that I would return. As I stood in the wet street again and observed that I needed to pick my way here as carefully as I did in London, the youth Calvagh appeared at my side.

'You have a holiday too,' I said.

'But no money for a new jerkin.'

Now that we were within the city walls he had dressed himself more in the English fashion. He still had on his yellow tunic but beneath it was a pair of breeches so moth-eaten that I found it difficult not to smile. I had not noticed, before, how poor his shoes were. They would spoil as he waded through the various excrements of the streets.

'I am at my best so that I may accompany you,' he said.

He did not accompany me by my invitation and I wondered whether mockery were his real intent.

'I must visit my other tailor,' I said. ' I still have to be measured for my jerkin.'

My other tailor. The phrase sounded so important. I wanted to repeat it but I could think of no excuse. Together we walked back into The Queen's Majesty's Street and found the lane that formed part of the lower herringbone. Temptation flaunted itself immediately.

'Look,' said the youth Calvagh. 'Those are very fine clothes indeed.'

A shop which dealt in parti-coloured breeches, doublets with rich thread, ruffs, cloaks with lace collars, offered its wares very enticingly. They seemed to me like popinjays in a farmyard. My companion slid away as the proprietor of the shop came out to take my arm.

'Everything in my shop has been worn by the finest men in London.'

'You mean that you have taken this clothing from dead bodies?'

'From living bodies, sir. The owners of these clothes were most reluctant to part with them, but they had fallen on temporary hard times. Every item is of the newest fashion, the best quality and quite free of disease.'

His last comment almost brought me to my senses. All the same, I allowed him to lead me inside the shop. I have always assumed that one may tell a man's quality or at least his education merely by looking at him. I wondered what this man thought of me. I had on only a serving-man's jerkin, albeit one purchased in London, and I had stood outside his shop with a youth dressed like a zany. I would need to make my station absolutely clear.

'Fine scarlet breeches, sir? This cloak with quite three layers of exquisite lace?'

He was possibly laughing at me.

'I am Master Edmund Spenser's secretary,' I said in my strongest tone. 'He has given me money as a birthday gift that I might buy myself an article of apparel in which to accompany him on significant business. What is the very best that you can provide for five shillings including all fitting and alteration?'

I displayed the coins on the palm of my hand.

'The secretary to Master Spenser himself you say?'

'I do so say so, sir, and if you would care to accompany me to Skiddy's Castle you may confirm the truth of it.'

The sight of the coins and the confidence of my assertion made him obsequious after that. There was a particular suit of doublet and hose that he would have me buy and which tempted me dearly, but 'jerkin' Master Spenser had said and a jerkin I should have. I tried on a number and, as I pranced around the shop in them

I noticed half a face peeping around the wall and scrutinising me.

'Is that your man?' asked the shop-owner.

My reply was very loud. 'He is newly in my service. I may have to beat the exuberance out of him.' The face remained hidden after that.

In the end I chose the dark blue with black facings and yellow buttons. It was somewhat faded, but still a formidable jerkin and must have caused heartbreak in the young gallant who was forced to part with it.

'Can the pox linger in a garment?' I asked, having had this sudden thought. The shop-keeper feigned outrage.

'The very best of Cork society purchase their apparel from me sir. I could not bear to be responsible for an attack throughout the town of that wicked disease.

The shoulders were too tight and the waist too broad.

'You have an excellent shape, sir,' he said which I acknowledged to be the truth. I submitted to the insertion of sundry pins and tucks and was told that the jerkin would be ready on the morrow which was the day set for my departure.

'There are your five shillings,' I said. 'You may deliver it to Skiddy's Castle tomorrow before noon. My name is Master Edward Harry. I hope to be able to recommend you to Master Spenser.'

As if the Clerk to the Council of Munster would want it known that he paraded about in London's cast-offs, but it was an excellent sentence with which to exit the premises.

'So I am your newest servant?'

'No, you are my shadow.' But would he be my nemesis? Was he, for all his good humour, the smiler with the dagger beneath his cloak?

'You parted with five shillings.'

'Every penny of it.'

'I have never had five shillings in my life.'

Nor had I but I would never admit it to him. The small collection of coin in my chest at Kilcolman was still barely above the two shilling mark.

'This was a birthday gift?'

'No. Master Spenser does not know the date of my birthday. I celebrate it tomorrow and if I have money left after I buy a gift for the boy Sylvanus we shall drink to it.'

'Even if there is no money left after you buy the gift, I thank you for the drink. You will look splendid in your jerkin.'

'I assure you that is what I intend. If I do not look splendid, Master Spenser will not lightly forgive the wasted outlay of his five shillings.'

I had by now decided upon the gift for the boy. It would be useful and appropriate and might leave me change from my handful of coin.

'Do you know where in this city I might purchase a knife?' I asked.

Calvagh laughed. 'The Irish do not purchase knives. No more do they purchase muskets or cannon or pikes.'

'This is no weapon I mean to buy. Sylvanus shall have his own penknife so that he may trim his quills at our lessons. It is a gift I know he will value.'

I had with me an Elizabeth groat and two Edward pennies. The penknife cost me twopence halfpenny although I informed the shopkeeper that I was secretary to Master Spenser and I guessed he might make me a present of it.

'I had thought you might reduce the price,' I was moved to say, 'but I do believe you have raised it.'

Perhaps he daily met young men who claimed to be what they were not. It was a sturdy knife, however, and I knew what Sylvanus's reaction to it would be.

I was left with enough money for two cups of ale and a dish of faggots which we shared. The *inn* was no more than an opening onto the street but this made my purchases the easier and Calvagh was able to enjoy his food in peace.

'Did the innkeeper mark your generosity to your servant?' he could not prevent himself from asking as we sat together on the bench nearest the street.

'He did not mention you. You are a customer and they were sound Edward pennies.'

'Joshuah Parkin bought me ale once.'

'I expect he did. He seems your special friend.'

We wandered several times more about the city avoiding the rain where we could. I had very little money left so our entertainment was watching barrels rolled from a ship or a man beating his horse. We pricked our ears at the conversations that went on, but even the quarrels were lacklustre, diluted by the rain, always rain. When we returned to Skiddy's Castle we knew that we should have to part company, I to a respectful reception in the upper rooms and he to a cave somewhere below with a seat of straw. He was the only person I knew of my own age and his alertness to everything about him made me linger in his company more perhaps than I should. I could not really be seen to enter the castle yard in friendly conversation with him, which might make our farewell strained. This shared thought turned our steps every time we came within a street of the castle.

'I could give you an adventure for your birthday,' he eventually said as, tired with our tracing the herring bone, we lolled against a wall and contemplated parting.

'Where is this other natural trumpet?' I asked. 'They have not returned our greetings from last time.'

'There were other things I wished to show you but you would not speak to me.'

'My master's instructions. Let us say no more about it.'

'I shall tell you of my family.'

'Is this the adventure?'

'No, it is the introduction. I am, it is believed, kin to the Desmond, conceived unwillingly when my mother was unable to defend herself.'

I shuddered.

'You believe the Irish always conceive their children in this way?'

'No.'

I could not tell him, not yet, that my own entry into the world might also have been arranged thus, my mother, whoever she was, forced into unwilling congress with a gentlemanly oaf who never owned me as his child. Was my grandmother the parent of either of them or simply a crone in the village who was willing to nurture this unwanted scrap in return for the regular payments that were made throughout my childhood? I did not like to explore these thoughts and I resented him for having brought them to my mind after so long.

'Shall I leave you, sir?'

I took the sleeve of his tunic in my fingers. 'I have my own secrets,' I said. 'Continue with your story.'

'My mother has been dead many years. She had other sadnesses, other secrets, which you do not need to know. Her brother, my Uncle Hugh, has two sons but he gladly took me into his house. It is his name I bear, Ó Gamhnain. It means *A keeper of calves,* but he is a fisherman from the town of Kinsale. I am to make my way in the service of our English lords, but I often think of the small boat he keeps for me and the joy I have in sailing her. We could ride to Kinsale. That is the adventure. She is a fine little boat and the two of us will manage her easily. I will show you.'

Master Spenser would not approve of such an adventure, of this I was certain, and Cork would not be so stoutly walled if the surrounding countryside were full of friends. As always, suspicion wreathed itself about our talk, but my refusal was offered for a different reason.

'You did not see how ill I was when we sailed from England. On a small boat would I not fare much worse?'

'The weather will be fine tomorrow. There will be no rain and the wind will drop. It never teems two days in a row in Cork.'

'There is not a word of truth in that.'

'No, there is not, but I long to show you my boat. You cannot understand the delight as you skim like a sea-bird across the wave tops.'

'It is not safe for me and my master would not approve,' I said giving him my real reason at last. But I was persuaded. He told me that the countryside was somnolent, all men were at peace with each other and the Virgin Queen was beloved of all. Besides, the road to Kinsale was known to be a secure one and we should reach the town in only a few hours. This plan had been laid out to Joshuah Parkin earlier, I soon discovered, for he immediately agreed to explain away my absence until the following day. We were to ride to Kinsale on Master Spenser's horses that afternoon, to sleep at Uncle Hugh's house and to put to sea on the morning of my birthday. By the following evening we should be back at Skiddy's Castle with our brief disappearance barely noticed by any.

'I have only three halfpence in my pocket,' I said, 'and I must leave the penknife in my lodgings.'

These were late, feeble excuses which were easily swept aside. I could not believe that this stranger had so soon persuaded me to an act of disobedience that might cause me to lose my life. And if I were tortured, what then?

'Joshuah Parkin, have you heard of rebels on the road to Kinsale?' I asked.

'There is not a word of them in the city, sir. I would tell you if I suspected danger.'

Would he tell me? Englishmen had been bought by the Irish before now. He had allowed their language to come upon him and who was to say that their sentiments had not found root in his heart. But still I went.

We rode through the rain quickly and with little conversation. Calvagh, the better horseman by far, led and I followed. They might as easily have been damp English hills and meadows that we traversed, gentle in their shape and green. I could have enjoyed the ride if I had been that way before and knew any landmarks on our travel. As it was, I rode into the unknown, wet, and with a laughing Irish lad taunting my horsemanship over his shoulder.

'My Uncle Hugh's town of Kinsale,' he said at last. 'You shall spend such a birthday here.'

The town was at the foot of a hill and appeared prosperous if small. Our arrival aroused no notice and we were able to ride directly up to his uncle's door. Again I expected a hovel but the house was solid and I had just been told that the man had complete ownership of two fishing vessels which made him a figure of some credit in those parts.

The frontage of the house was littered with fisherman's business and my first thought was for the horses. They were my passport to the English Pale and they required good stabling. My master would not forgive me if they were lamed or stolen. I told this to Calvagh in a way that could not be brushed aside.

'I am the horse boy at Kilcolman,' he returned with irritation. 'I always put their comfort before my own.'

'I am glad to hear it, so perhaps you would like to point out your uncle's stables to me. They are hidden beneath these nets and pots it would appear.'

He flung the reins of his horse at me and marched into the house.

'There will be a single shot to the back of my head from an upper window,' I mused. 'Farewell world and all my ambition.'

Calvagh emerged with a man who was shorter than himself by several inches. His upper arms were bowed with muscle and his face leathered like any shoe.

'Uncle Hugh, this is my friend Edward Harry. He is English.'

I stepped forward in greeting as a woman in blue skirts and apron followed her husband out of the doorway.

'I am Edward Harry, sir, secretary to Master Edmund Spenser, Clerk to the Council of Munster and Her Royal Majesty's loyal servant.'

I do not know which was uttered first, the uncle's gasp or the aunt's scream. To assorted in-goings and out-goings of breath I was dragged into the house and heard the front door slam with a finality that suggested my hour was come. I did not wait until my eyes adjusted to the gloom before I felt for a wall against which I leant with my dagger drawn at the level of my breast.

'Am I your prisoner, sir? I must say this is no more than I expected.'

'You are not my prisoner, sir. You are the guest of my idiot nephew who should never have brought you here. What was he doing hauling such trouble down upon us.'

The front door opened and a voice asked quietly, 'Is all well uncle?'

All was *not* well for his uncle fetched him such a blow I thought his head would fly quite across the room.

'You are welcome, sir. You are welcome.'

He paced about shouting in Irish at his wife who was only feet from him but who was wailing uncontrollably and beyond all instruction.

'Get in here!'

'I cannot, Uncle Hugh, I am still holding the horses.'

'I shall attend to your horses, sir. They will be safe.'

He seized the reins and I fancied I saw a brown muzzle, my own mount Charger, come partly into the room. Calvagh was elbowed aside and told to find me a chair and drink. I put away my dagger and smiled at Uncle Hugh's wife. In the darkness of the room no doubt she did not see my smile and she was, in addition, still shaking her lifted apron as if to fan away all the difficulty that Calvagh and I had brought under her husband's roof.

'What is to be done?' I said.

Calvagh found me a stool by the hearth and set about his aunt whose clamouring and stamping made us fear for her reason. Shortly, Uncle Hugh returned and resumed his shouting, at me in English and at his nephew and wife in most belligerent Irish. I made to rise several times and was, I think, pushed down by all of them. Here was not the welcome home Calvagh had anticipated to me. I might have enjoyed the tableau had my own safety not been so much the subject of it. After many minutes, when exhaustion had slowed the combatants to a pace where information might be imparted and instructions understood and acted upon, we found ourselves all seated by the small peat fire.

'My nephew has done a most foolish thing.'

'I gathered you thought so sir.'

'He has placed your life in danger.'

'How so?'

'Certain men, and I name no names and I do not say where these men might be, would consider it their very good fortune to have you here.'

'Do you intend to tell these men?'

'I do not, sir. Our own lives are at risk too.'

'How so?'

'If you are harmed, I shall be held responsible and the English will hang me and no doubt burn Kinsale. If these men I spoke of learn that you have been here and that I have not told them, then I shall be regarded as a greater friend to the English than I am, as a spy perhaps, and they will cut my throat.'

'I meant no harm, uncle.' Calvagh began to weep noisily into his sleeve. 'I have killed my uncle and my friend.'

His aunt cuffed him viciously and Uncle Hugh stamped on the floor.

'You have also killed your cousins Fergus and Micheál and all the good men of Kinsale who will rise to avenge us. You are a widow-maker, boy.'

'He truly meant no harm,' I said putting my hand on his sleeve next to the sobbing head. 'He wanted to sail his boat with me, like a small boy on a pond. The fault is mine for not standing firm on what I knew to be the recklessness of the adventure. But think. Your nephew has visited you with an English friend. I am known to no-one here and I am hardly dressed in splendour. An English friend may surely come and go so near to the garrison at Cork.'

'It is to be hoped that is the case sir.'

Calvagh lifted his head. 'I am very sorry, Edward Harry. I never meant to kill you.'

'You will not kill me if our luck holds.'

His aunt spoke quietly to her husband.

'My wife has very little English, sir.'

'She had enough to scream when she heard my name.'

'We all understand the Devil's name in whatever language. My wife says we must keep our two sons away from the house and that you must leave early tomorrow. My sons are hot-heads as Calvagh should remember. They love him dearly, but they will not love any English friend of his. I told the neighbour who has care of your horses that Calvagh had arrived with a fellow servant from the garrison at Cork on horses borrowed without permission. He knows the boy never thinks before he acts and he will tell no-one.'

'Thank you uncle. So may I still show Edward my boat tomorrow?'

Uncle Hugh stormed across the room in silent rage while I sat and mused on being so easily thought a servant or Old Nick himself.

From the other side of the cottage Hugh Ó Gamhnain gave his wife orders that meant I was soon ushered to the table and presented with a half-loaf as my trencher. There was a re-heating of the stewpot hanging at one side of the hearth and, after our long ride and the turmoil at the end of it, I was glad, eventually, to have spoonfuls of mutton and the bread to engage my attention. Calvagh ate the food greedily, making me think of a pet dog that has been smacked and yet forgives all when his dish is filled before him. Seated, full, and thankful that my life was in no immediate danger of being taken from me, I looked at my surroundings. The doors at the front and back of the cottage were closed, as were the shutters on the windows so that my presence might not be broadcast to a world which did not relish Englishmen. The peat in the hearth gave off heat but little flame and Calvagh's aunt would have been hard pressed to prepare our meal in such darkness if two tapers had not been lit. We also needed the light brought to the table to help us put the food in our mouths. I had heard that most Irishmen lived with their animals, using a beast's warm flank as their winter pillow. By the light of the dying tapers, I was glad to see that this was not the case. The hearth was the heart of the room as it had been in my grandmother's cottage. Our furniture had been more smoothly fashioned but we had also had the large table and stools that enabled us, on cold winter nights, to take our meal with our heads half up the chimney. At the far side of the main room were jumbles of what I took to be fishing tackle, objects which had no clear shape by taper light. Uncle Hugh busied himself there as we ate. There was a door to a second room and a ladder to an upper floor. Uncle Hugh's proprietorship of the two fishing boats made him a man who would have been well thought of in my own village as he could afford to serve his guests meat. I stamped my foot lightly and recognised the feel of an earthen floor. I had grown used to stone and tile at Kilcolman but the deadening lack of a ring when I brought my heel down took me back to a dawn departure and the corpse of the old woman who brought me up. I had come so far and yet not so far, after all, if I was to die in the kind of dwelling I had expected to leave for ever.

With the tapers extinguished, we moved to the fire to talk as if my visit were of the usual kind. Thin rays of light permitted by cracks in the shutters told us that outside it was daylight still and I judged the hour to be about eight or nine of the clock. There was talk and silence and talk again and yawns but I never lost the feeling that it must be like this in his cell for a condemned man who awaits the rope or axe. He sits in the darkness fearing his last summons. There was one knock at the door when the man given charge of the horses came to announce that they were settled for the night. He asked to see Calvagh and the miscreant was duly pushed to the door where he spoke words that would have sounded contrite in any language. I heard the sound of a slap, a playful one this time, and the door was barred again, against all discovery we hoped.

So these were the people who so resented the Munster Plantation that thoughts of rebellion festered and my master was inclined to bring them to order with the sword. I was alert for any question which might be meant to trick me into revealing what must never be revealed.

'I thank you for the meal and for your good offices,' I said as soon as we were seated at the hearth, 'but you must understand that I shall answer not a single question about my master or his business.'

Uncle Hugh nodded.

'And *you* will say nothing,' I said to Calvagh with a sharpness that surprised them all. 'You are a groom and tonight I am a servant and we have only the conversation of a groom and a servant.'

'May we speak of the potato?'

'That is a fruit that grows on a yellow tree. My master told me,' I said. It could be no secret that Master Spenser was with Sir Walter Raleigh at Youghal.

Uncle Hugh laughed at my information. The potato was a strange tree indeed.

Then we talked of mutton and when apples ripened in England and of the mackerel and herring that were to be caught in the waters off Kinsale. Calvagh's boat made many an appearance in the conversation. It was in good trim, his uncle said, as Fergus and Micheál looked after it carefully against the day when he should make a proper visit home. I asked him to sing for us which he did quietly and touchingly, a melodic whisper so that no listener at the shutters would know of his presence. It was quite impossible for me to offer a good English tune in response which I longed to do. My voice is strong, though not lovely, and no action could have been more lunatic than for me to make the cottage resound with the tale of the North-country maid who *down to London had strayed*. Like her, I pined for the oak and the ash in my own country.

Fergus and Micheál were presently at sea fishing and would be no danger until dawn. Calvagh longed to see them and was scolded once again for his lack of sense. His aunt had forgiven him by now and stroked his curls as she carried on a mother's quiet conversation.

Of a sudden, Uncle Hugh said to me, 'While it is daylight you may piss in the back of the hearth. If you can wait until night you may stand at the back door.'

'Thank you I shall wait,' I said in some consternation. For me to piss while three people watched and compared, no doubt, an Englishman pissing with an Irishman engaged about the same business, was not to be contemplated.

'Very well,' said Uncle Hugh as if he had done no more than pass me an apple.

'We shall piss out of the door together, Edward, when the time comes,' said Calvagh.

'Very well,' said Uncle Hugh.

When I had an establishment of my own, I decided, I should not declare to my guests where they might or might not piss. And if Calvagh came to visit, he should be told that I did not admit this as a topic of conversation.

We retired early, an arrangement which suited everyone. Calvagh and I were to sleep upstairs in the bed of the master and mistress of the house themselves. Normally I would have refused such a thing but I could see the sense in the arrangement. To be upstairs was to be as far as possible from intrusion unless assassins dropped from the sky. Uncle Hugh told us that we were to place the chest in which he stored his clothes against the door and he would keep watch nearby.

'He has a sword, which is forbidden,' Calvagh whispered to me. 'You are not to know that he keeps such a weapon and he will not take it out until he has closed the door upon us.'

'Then if I am not to see it, you should not have told me about it.'

Upstairs the bedroom was very simple and there was no ceiling beneath the thatch. I had grown used to ceilings at Kilcolman and once again I was a little boy listening for the scurryings of birds and vermin in the straw. We were allowed a taper to undress by and were commanded to keep the shutters tightly closed. Calvagh told me that he wished to smell the sea as he slept and that he would open the shutters as soon as we placed the clothing chest against the door. His aunt took pillows and blankets from her store and it was clear that she intended to sleep beside her husband rather than in the bed of one of her sons. The landing at the top of the ladder would be unyielding and I both thanked and pitied them.

Calvagh and I had daggers, but Uncle Hugh presented us with a yard or two of fishing net each and a length of wood as hard as iron. This is what he had been arranging while we ate our mutton stew.

'If you are not able to use your dagger, then cast your net like this,' he said, 'and strike with the wood until the man is senseless. I tell you, Master Harry, I would rather meet with a Sheerie or a Pooka on the loneliest of roads than have to use a weapon against one of my neighbours to defend an Englishman.'

To Calvagh this was a game and he draped his net around my head. If he had done this to his uncle, as I fancy he at first intended to do, he would have received such a cudgelling as he would not have believed. I wondered whether I was the only one there who knew how much we resembled the gladiators of Rome. This thought led me to remember their phrase *Those who are about to die salute you*, which I much regretted.

I undressed first and felt ungrateful when I found the sheets coarse. Calvagh was busying himself with the silent opening of the shutters. When he came to slip his tunic over his head he observed me staring at him. I turned away in shame whereupon he picked up the taper and brought it close to my face.

'You will set fire to your uncle's bed,' I said.

'You were staring.'

'I wanted to see your tattoos,' I confessed.

He sat down beside me on the bed.

'We are not wild men who paint ourselves and eat our enemies,' he said, hurt.

'I am ashamed of my thought.'

'My skin is as clear as yours,' he said and stepped out of his breeches to prove this to me.

I covered my head with the sheet and he tapped it lightly with his piece of wood.

'You are punished now,' he said and entered the bed beside me. '*We* do not piss in the bed. I have heard that Englishmen do it all the time.' So my punishment was to continue.

'I have said I am ashamed of my thought.'

'Why do you not grow a beard? I thought your queen commanded all her servants to wear beards?'

She was *his* queen too but I would not insist on this point.

'My beard is lighter than my hair and the colour does not please me. It looks like a false beard in fact.'

He giggled.

'Am I punished enough now with that confession?'

'Yes.'

So I ventured a thought which unsettled me. 'Your people and mine would not approve of our lying here together.'

'I know that.'

'They would consider that we were sleeping with the enemy, like harlots.'

He was silent for a moment and I guessed some devilry was coming. 'If I am a harlot, will you give me a baby?'

'I shall whip your bare arse,' I said too loudly.

He sat up. 'Uncle,' he said timorously, but he got no further as I stopped his mouth and pulled him down. There was a stirring at the door and we held our breath.

'Let him sleep,' I said. 'You are a thoughtless baby. Will you never learn?'

We lay in silence again but youth and the prospect of sharing confidences led us to begin our talk anew.

'Your Uncle Hugh said that a Pooka was not a thing to meet on a lonely road. What is a Pooka?'

'Not a thing to meet on a lonely road.'

'I shall *make* you answer me properly.'

He made a scoffing sound at me. 'It is the most feared of all our...'

'Faeries,' I said. 'My grandmother left milk for the faeries. I shall not laugh at you.'

'I like your grandmother.'

Again I thought of that summer dawn and an old woman cold in her bed. I had placed the pennies on her eyelids, but there was no making me kiss the lips of a corpse. She had frightened me many a time with her stories of bugbears hiding in woods that were my frequent and solitary playground.

Calvagh turned on his elbow to face me. 'The Pooka is often a horse with a black coat and burning yellow eyes. It is only interested in causing mischief and you should not go out after nightfall if you mean to avoid it. Sometimes it is an ugly little fellow or an eagle. Only one man has ever ridden it and that was Brian Bóroimhe, the High King, who tamed its magic.'

'As I shall not sleep tonight will you tell me about other creatures I might fear to meet after nightfall. As long as talking about them will not bring them here amongst us.'

He was happy to oblige me and he told his stories well. I learnt the shapes of merrows and leprechauns and the grey men who are a fog and have no shape at all. They all intend us harm in their different ways and I understood why, when his other clothing lay in disorder on the floor, Calvagh kept a cross around his neck.

'Are there not changelings too?' I asked, glad to show that I knew of something he had forgotten.

'Do not ask me about changelings.'

He turned away in a manner I knew was not playful.

'Are *you* a changeling with your merry black curls and your horsemanship without stirrups?'

'Do not ask me.'

'What is there here I should not know? If I am ignorant of this creature how shall I defend myself against it?'

'If I tell you will you never speak of it again?'

'I promise.'

He turned back to me and spoke in subdued tones that I had never heard in his voice before.

'I was born one of a pair of twins. There was a sister my mother wished to call Maebh. She had copper hair from my mother whereas my blackness I assume is all I shall ever have from my father.'

'She was born with her hair?'

'Perhaps it is not the fashion in England. She was a special child.'

'Did she die?'

'She was taken.'

We both rested here, he from re-living the details of his tale and I because I did not wish to offend with a thoughtless question. I broke the silence first.

'*Taken?*'

'When *They* take a child, it is their custom to leave behind some monster of their own, some wizened, mis-shapen thing that its faerie mother cannot abide. The changing is done so quickly the human mother has no idea of the beauty of her own child. In this case they were late or careless or cruel. My mother had rejoiced in the beauty of my sister and then she found this crooked, ill-natured parcel in her arms. She killed it.'

'Your mother told you this?'

'Of the exchange?'

'That she killed your sister?'

'She killed a *changeling*, Edward. I should not have told you my story. What will you think of me now?'

'What I have always thought of you.'

He snorted and covered his head with the sheet. I knew of two women from my own village who helped mis-shapen babies to die. They were not condemned, but nor did they explain to their other offspring what they had been about with a pillow.

'Come from under the sheet,' I said. 'You have no need to hide from me. At least you knew your mother. I have not the least notion of my own parentage and the old dame I called my grandmother was the village wise woman and generally feared. It is fortunate, I suppose, that both she and I were not hanged for being what we were.'

This brought him out again as I expected it would.

'Yet you are so near a gentleman,' he said.

So *near*.

'Money was provided, I do not know from where, and I was sent to school.'

'Let me finish the tale,' he said, 'and then you will not judge my mother in this way. She would have kept the thing in her arms if a movement near the hearth had not caught her eye. She turned to see a little old woman with a human child in her arms, a faerie midwife with such a look of triumph on her face. The vision was gone in an instant. They can step in and out of our hearths, you know. My mother flung the changeling after her and it was struck dead. This was right. Edward.'

'I do not doubt it.'

We turned from each other again, divided by truth or custom. This was a most uneasy friendship we had embarked upon and I fell into a troubled sleep puzzling on it.

CHAPTER FIVE

Before dawn, Uncle Hugh hammered on our door fair to burst it down.

'Be ready,' he said. 'The fishing boats will soon be home.'

We dressed swiftly and I was gladdened by the thought that noon would see us in the safety of Cork city's walls. It was my birthday and I was to ride for my life.

'The rain has stopped,' said Calvagh from the window. 'I can smell a fair day, Edward, a playful breeze and bright sunshine.'

I should have known then what he planned.

'Thank you for the protection of your house, sir,' I said to Uncle Hugh as we came downstairs.

'You must eat your breakfast on the way. The fishing boats will have tied up in the harbour by dawn. Fergus and Micheál will only learn of Calvagh's visit when it is safely over. My wife and I go down to help them unload the fish so this must be our farewell.'

I took his proffered hand and he slapped my shoulder. Calvagh embraced his uncle and aunt tightly and our visit was ended.

'Your horses are in the keeping of Tomás Ó Conaill. Calvagh knows where to find them.'

We came out of the cottage to the grey light that is the direct harbinger of sunrise. I had been given the packet of food for safe keeping and Calvagh walked across the path to the sea, scenting the air.

'Come,' he said.

'You uncle and aunt have gone that way. Surely there are no stables by the waterside?'

'We shall collect the horses later. I have something to show you.'

He ran off and what could I do but follow him?

My suspicions were not stirred immediately. We followed the path downwards, standing still when we heard the sound of voices and rushing on when my companion thought it safe.

'We are almost at the harbour,' I said.

'Where else should I keep my boat?'

'No!'

'Will you call out to my uncle in your firm English voice? Or perhaps you can find the stable with your nose.'

'We have been offered safety,' I said. 'Will you kill us all again?'

'There she is. Have you ever seen such a boat? Fergus has trimmed and caulked her for me. She could sail to America.'

'We could sail to Cork and send for the horses.'

'I plan to show you what a sailor I am. Just a short voyage and then we shall return and ride away as Uncle Hugh intended. Have you ever had breakfast at sea?'

'Yes, when I sailed to Ireland. I puked it all over my breeches shortly afterwards.'

'You English are no true sailors.'

'We do not sail into the jaws of danger when two good horses are waiting to take us home.'

He dropped down into the boat and held out his hand for me to follow. I am no judge of boats, those that ferry play-goers across the Thames or those that took Sir Walter to America to retrieve a potato. A boat had brought me safely through the tempests of the Irish Sea and I knew they could be sturdy and worthy of our trust, but I did not like them particularly and I gave my hand to Calvagh with some reluctance.

He was keen to show me around the vessel before our voyage began. He did not know the English words for its many parts, no more did I, so it was 'This and this and this', as he pointed. I sat down at the back, the stern, at least I knew that, our packet of food in my lap.

'I would far rather ride than swim home,' I said.

'Oh can you swim?' he answered idly as he tried to explain what I should need to do with the rudder. 'I cannot.'

'You cannot swim!'

'Death is less of an agony when you sink like a stone.'

'I shall carry you to the shore then, when your foolishness makes us overturn,' I said angrily.

'How far could you carry me, do you think?'

'Until I was minded to drown you myself. Will you never speak or act with good sense?'

He took the pair of oars and rowed us east into the channel that grew wider as it snaked towards the sea. We kept close to the shore as one fishing boat after another sailed home with its haul.

'They will not see us,' said Calvagh confidently. 'Little boats with rod and line are beneath their notice.'

I hoped that, rowing against the tide, he would soon grow exhausted and allow us to drift in with the last of the fishing fleet. I had not allowed for his strength nor for his skill in telling me where to direct the boat so that the pull of the tide was least.

'It will soon turn,' he said. 'Once we have reached Sandy Cove, we can moor the boat and eat our parcel of fish-heads. After an hour you shall help me push the boat into the tide again and the sea will race with us beyond the first fist of land towards the Seven Heads which are my birthday gift.'

'A better gift would be the reins of my horse.'

He would have none of it and I knew that if I disobeyed his instructions I might capsize us and send him to the sea-bottom as he had foretold. I could not even jump ship and run back to Kinsale as dawn was still only a suggestion on the sea's rim and I fancied I should have to swim across the channel in any case. We ate our breakfast bobbing inshore at Sandy Cove. It was not fish heads, but mutton stew pressed into two half loaves. The sun flared above the horizon at last, a wonderful sight, I admitted, as an edge of blue danced across the water towards the land.

'Do you feel the breeze change with the tide? That is our sign.'

'My hour has come,' I said miserably. 'Drowned by a mooncalf on my birthday. Did you not say once that your name meant a keeper of calves? How true.'

My taunt was wasted for he had the oars again and was working us into the current.

'When we are out at sea,' he said, ' you will need to give very careful attention to the rudder for the breeze will be strong and it will take all my strength to manage the sail.'

Out at sea! *All his strength*! This was madness, not mooncalfery, and the further we went the less was my power to stop him. I stood up suddenly and we both shrieked as the little boat rocked deeply to one side. It was a very little boat indeed and each brisk wave had the power to send us to an un-marked grave.

'If it needs both of us to attend to the rudder *and* the sail, then you have never come out so far nor in such a breeze,' I said.

His laughter told me the truth of my words.

'For mercy's sake, take me back to land. I will give you anything,' I implored.

'If I stretch my arm I can hold the sail-rope as well as the rudder. Give it to me, Edward. Just look at the sky and the shore as we race by it. Was there ever such enjoyment?'

Both rudder and rope slid from his hand at that same moment and we fell together in the bottom of the boat. The waves splashed over us, first right and then left and I put my arms about his waist for I was sure we would founder. He fought free of my clasp and threw himself at the wild sail which battered the mast in its desire to be free and off in the wind.

'Do not watch for me. Take the rudder!' he screamed.

This was no easy task and I pressed all my body weight against the thrashing wood until it yielded once more to my control. When I turned back to him, was it joy I saw drawn on his face? He had the sail-rope and was teasing it like a yearling he had broken to his will. The boat skipped over the wave-tops once more but there was no skipping in my heart. The shore grew smaller and smaller and, for all I knew, Calvagh was now intent on reaching Spain. My life depended on his instruction and hatred for him surged within me.

'The breeze will lessen once we come into the shelter of the bay,' he said, and it did. The rudder was more compliant to my touch and he was able to move the sail with a single hand.

'You are not a mooncalf, you are an assassin,' I said bitterly. 'I curse the day you knelt in the horse shit and I did not beat you senseless.'

'If you do not hold your peace,' he said over his shoulder, 'I shall take my calf's horns and push them up your arse.'

'And when we stand inside Good Queen Bess's walls once more,' I told him, 'I shall trim your raven curls to make a halter that will hang you.'

'Then I am sure I shall die laughing at the sight of my two horns growing out of your breeches.'

There was no humour in our words. He had planned an adventure for my birthday, a voyage to the Seven Heads whose dark cliffs beckoned, and now we were almost wishing each other dead. I had cursed the enemy, then slept with him and cursed him again.

'Those are the Seven Heads of Kinsale,' Calvagh said. 'You see them well enough.'

'I do.'

'Then we should go home.'

'We should.'

'You seized hold of me so I should not drown.'

'I did and I should do so once more.'

'Save a mooncalf from the ocean?'

'The breeze has addled my brain.'

It was not good humour again, but we had withdrawn from hatred.

'We must cross the bay against the tide if we are to round the Old Head and find ourselves in the channel to Kinsale. I am not sure I can do it.'

'Can we not make a landfall here?'

'And be dashed against the cliffs?'

He had no plan, no plan at all, except to show me the cliffs that had lost all their savour and might dash us to fragments if we did not change direction. This was only my second voyage; how could I offer advice and yet he now looked to me for a word.

'Could we follow the tide, but far more slowly, and then wheel about as soon as it turns?' I asked.

'I could do that, I believe. Dawdle rather than fly, but flying was such heaven.'

'I forbid it!'

Every moment took us further from Kinsale and the quiet departure that his Uncle Hugh had planned.

'We should follow the coast as closely as we can,' I insisted. 'I can carry you one mile, but not a dozen.'

'The worst is past.'

'I do not expect so. Look a ship is on fire!'

At that moment I chanced to lift my head and saw a strange cloud out to sea. A burning vessel was all that came to mind although the cloud had a ruddy colour without the darkness of smoke.

'There might be people to be rescued,' Calvagh said and turned his boat's head towards the new sight.

'We have no room and it is almost on the horizon.'

But there was no telling him.

'The tide will take us there in the time we have and then we shall be directly in front of the channel,' was his argument. 'We have only to let the tide carry us home again.'

It was a strange cloud indeed, sometimes ruddy and at other times purple with flashes inside it if our eyes were to be believed.

'It is a Spanish gunpowder ship that is bound to explode,' I said. 'Leave well alone. They will welcome an English throat to slit.'

None of my fears had any power over him, no talk of a pirate vessel or the breath of a sea monster, and soon I was at my post by the rudder and he was shouting my orders. How had I let this happen and how had he gone from helplessness to command without my noticing or stopping it?

We drew nearer and nearer and the sight grew stranger. There was no fire, surely, and no masts or high poop that suggested a galleon. The coloured cloud or smoke had a clear edge and swirled slowly like a heavy whirlwind that was sinking to the earth. Beneath it we could just discern the sides of a vessel which was very low in the water and sinking. It was such a vessel as we had never seen, without sail or oar, a barge perhaps but fashioned for speed with its sleek sides and sharp prow. The wood of the ship was a deep chestnut, a depth of colour that a craftsman would have taken a lifetime to polish into it. Despite the lack of flame, broad scorch marks had blistered the planking and cut so deeply into it that water was seeping in. Who owned such a vessel and how had it been damaged? In the port of London I had seen ships from many countries but, when Calvagh looked to me for a suggestion, I could only shake my head.

'Stop your boat,' was all I could think of to say to him. The danger of an explosion was still uppermost in my mind and, being so low in the water ourselves, we were below the deck of the vessel. Who knew what perils lay behind its carved bulwarks?

'Let us leave the ship to its fate,' I said. 'I imagine it is Spanish and soon it will be gone.'

Calvagh sailed us close so that we were able to follow the ship as it turned slowly on its axis. We would make one circuit and be gone. Even he, with his playfulness and his curiosity, did not wish to remain close to the death of such a vessel. If we were too near when it finally slid beneath the waves, its size would draw our trifling pinnace with it. We gained on its movement and soon passed directly beneath the prow. The figurehead chilled us both. It was larger than a man and green, yet it was not a man. It had all the lineaments of a man with its cupped hands and its muscled breast but the eyes were narrowed and not friendly.

'What game are the Spanish playing now?' I said. 'Are they drawing their figureheads from some country of devils I have never heard of?'

'This cloud is settling upon us.' Calvagh was brushing at his skin. 'It is warm and...nudging at me.'

Neither of us had words for the way the coloured air nibbled and investigated us. It was growing difficult to see through it to the clear sky beyond. This was not a place for two boys, even those hungry for glory and adventure like ourselves.

'Sail away,' I said. 'Let us find the tide again.'

'No!'

For a moment I thought it was Calvagh who had spoken and he thought the voice was mine.

'Help me.'

We had by now sailed past the figurehead and were approaching that section of the deck which had sunk deepest. A figure lay half in the water with his long fingers stretched out to us.

'A man,' I said.

'Not a man,' my friend corrected me.

The figure was battle-injured, scorched, scarred and perhaps dying. We were an unexpected source of hope to him, two youths in an egg-shell.

'Help me.'

'Our boat is small.'

'I am light.'

'Do you not have a ship's boat?'

'It is lost. Help me.'

To judge by his attire, you would never have guessed that he intended to go to sea. He was all silk and satin of the finest kind that now hung sopped and ruined about his limbs. His doublet was slashed and slashed again with an iridescence of colours that even the salt sea water could not reduce and the tops of his hose at least, the rest being under water, were a miracle of embroidery. He even managed to retain his bonnet despite the imminence of drowning. No doubt, when he set out, it stood proud from his hand with its plume another foot higher. Now, somewhat comically, the wet sides dangled behind each of his ears like the flaps of an invalid's cap. He was pitiful and yet, strangely, not pitiable.

'Are you a Spaniard?'

'I am not. Take these as a gift.'

He held out two large stones. I would have called them emeralds but no emeralds could have filled the palm and gleamed as these stones did. Even if they were glass they were beautiful and would command a high price.

'The ship is breathing out its magic,' said the figure. 'There is danger for us all if we linger.'

'You are not human,' said Calvagh.

Neither of us had come within reach of the fingers to accept the stones.

'No I am not.'

'*Lios Alfar.*'

'As you say.'

If we left him there he would certainly drown. Whatever sea-fight he had survived, there would not be strength enough in his arms for him to swim ashore.

'We mean to let the tide carry us back into Kinsale,' I said. 'I do not understand who you are but if you mean us no harm you may travel with us.'

'He is not a man, Edward.'

'I cannot let him drown and if he does not sit still your little boat will overturn. If that happens I shall save only you, being the ablest swimmer. I do not fear to take him with us, Calvagh.'

I leant towards the chestnut vessel and pulled us as close to it as I could. The figure held the emerald stones to his lips for a moment and then placed them in my hand. I assisted him aboard and he sat down in our midst, cross-legged and caught up in his own thoughts, perhaps ones of gratitude or sorrow for ship-mates lost. He said not a word as Calvagh used an oar to push us away and then set the sail to take us home as soon as the tide was compliant. For a while we could not disengage from the doomed ship's spiralling and it was only after Calvagh pulled strongly on his oars for a quarter of an hour that we could breathe clear air and not feel our skins tickled.

The sun was high in the sky now and its unobscured rays were most welcome. It should not be long before we could begin the first part of our journey home. I decided to use the time to make the acquaintance of our survivor from the shipwreck.

'Do you care to tell us your name, sir?'

I dreaded to hear that he was a Miguel or a Fernando.

'You are Edward and Calvagh.'

'We know *our* names,' said Calvagh sharply.

I had thought, with his back to us, he was concerned only with managing the sail.

'Your name sir?'

'I do not choose to tell you.'

'Though we have saved you from certain drowning?'

His manners were of a piece with his clothes, outlandish in cut and far too costly for a man to wear on a sea voyage when, as everyone knows, the salt spray and the sharp air shrivel a good weave.

'I can show you a trick with the green stones.'

'You mean to take them back?'

'I mean to entertain you with a trick.'

Perhaps the shipwreck had overthrown his mind and he intended to cast the stones into the sea. Did he think they had brought him bad luck in the way that some mariners will not have a woman aboard?

'Take them,' I said. If he had become a lunatic, then he was safer when contented and still.

He took the stones in his flat palms and held them in front of him on the side of the boat away from the land. With fierce eyes he looked first at the stones and then out to the horizon. Gradually a line appeared on the surface of the sea, a shifting line that at first was indistinct and wavering and then became clear and straight and green. The bow of our little boat turned round to face along this line.

'This is my trick,' said our stranger.

He thought to catch me with his eyes while his hands were elsewhere but the soldier in the guard-room at Kilcolman had trained me in avoidance of this trick. Even as the stranger's hands reached for Calvagh's shoulders to hale him into the sea, my dagger slid into his back, not once but three times. My blows were quickly fatal and he was left with little time to look at us before he died.

'You would have killed my friend,' I said. 'Shall I slit your wizand before you die. Of all the devils in the world I hate an ungrateful man the most.'

He gave a squeal, a frightening pig-stuck sound, and then, with frothing and writhing he lay still.

'He was not a man,' said Calvagh. 'He was *Lios Alfar*. Look at him now.'

Some faces relax in death. Cares slip from eyes and lips and those who are left behind are warmed by the expression of peace. This was no human death. A mask of humanity that he had kept in place now slipped and the eyes and mouth were those we had seen on the figurehead of the sinking vessel. I could not bear the wide, arrogant, violet eyes and I did my best to close them. His blood, I noticed, was dark, crimson suffused with black, as a man's blood is when on the point of congealing.

We dropped him overboard and hurled the green stones after him. We then had time to sit and bemoan our situation for the sail and rudder functioned of their own accord. We were drawn wherever the green line led, to the rainbow's end, to the rim of the world, or perhaps to Hell. If our journey did have an end, we swore we would fight whomsoever we found there and die defending each other. Our boat swept out to sea, barely acknowledging the water. And then, with a shock that battered Calvagh's little craft to pieces, we passed from one world into another. At last I was made to keep my promise. I swam with my arm around my friend until our feet touched the sand of the island where an extraordinary adventure lay in wait for us.

CHAPTER SIX

We lay exhausted above the tide line for I do not know how long before either of us stirred or spoke. My face was so deeply pressed into the sand, I could have been biting it. I lacked the strength to care. At length I heard a throat clearing and hawking violently. I presumed it was Calvagh's throat although the sound was so rasping it could easily have come from the maw of a gigantic hound. Calvagh had certainly swallowed half an ocean as we swam ashore. I shouted at him that if he struggled in my grip he would drive us both to the sea's bottom. Despite all my good advice, he would keep his mouth open in great gasps that invited the sea to wash in. He had only himself to blame if his tongue now tasted like a piece of ancient stockfish. For my own part, I had maintained a sweetness of mouth by the expedient of keeping my lips closed. My limbs burned from the difficulty of keeping us both afloat when my movements had been constricted by the heavily-sodden doublet and breeches there was no time to discard. With my right arm tightly under Calvagh's armpit, and my left arm drawing us to the line of shore we had spotted, I had managed to defy the sea's malice for longer than I expected. I simply was not prepared to die, either at the hands of a malevolent near-man with violet eyes or sent to the ocean bottom by the greed of the waves.

I heard more hawking and an oath. It was certainly Calvagh and I wondered whether I might allow myself a proper slumber now. I had saved him twice, from the *Lios Alfar* and from the sea, and he could watch over me as I shifted limbs that felt as if they had been racked. Such tiredness, and such ruined clothes no doubt.

I was eventually stirred from my idle thoughts by Calvagh nudging my back with his foot. I half sat up and faced him.

'I have been thinking,' I said. 'Do the natives of this land eat roast beef? I was just now telling myself I would enjoy a trencher of roast beef.'

'You think a good many strange thoughts,' he said. 'I have brought you water.'

He held a cup made of grasses twisted into a tight spiral.

As I reached up to take the water, I suddenly had to let my hand drop. This was the first time I raised my head erect and the effort proved sickening. I had felt such discomfort before, after two bottles of canary wine and once at school when a low fellow struck me with a roof tile. I attempted to recollect myself by looking beyond Calvagh to the sand dunes which fringed our landing place. There was a strong need to remove the glare, the shimmer, the painful quality of the light that I found distressing.

'I cannot bear to look about me. It would seem I have struck my head,' I said. 'The air itself is dancing.'

'You mean we must endure it constantly?'

'I hope to grow used to it.'

'I think I shall sit here for the moment with my eyes shut.'

'Then I shall help you to your water like a blind English baby.'

This he proceeded to do and I was glad of his courtesy. The mouthfuls of water that had not seeped out of his grass cup were sweet ones and I could have drunk many more of them.

'I was afraid you would not like my cup.'

'You meant no insult.'

Pettishly, I chose not to tell him that I had made quite as many grass cups in my life as he. In that distant village where I shared my boyhood with the old woman, I was no English lordling, just a lad who grubbed his days away. Calvagh still hardly believed how alike we were and it did not suit me to undeceive him.

We sat side by side uncertain what to say or where to go. I kept my eyes half-closed, still feeling as I did when clouted by the roof tile. While Calvagh toyed with a handful of pebbles, I allowed my squinting gaze to wander down my breeches to my hose and my shoes. My breeches were not new, certainly, but the salt water had depleted them to a wretched state. I could feel them drying stiffly and uncomfortably. It would take a maid a week of rinsing and sweetening with herbs to make them fit again, even for a secretary of little significance. My uncomfortable collar, thankfully had soon parted company from my neck and was now a sodden scrap at the sea's bottom. My fine netherstocks bought for fivepence in Cheapside were beyond the redemption of any servant. They had snagged and torn as we made our way out of the sea. I looked like some indigent who begs for halfpence at the church door. I regarded with envy Calvagh's bare legs stretched out beside my own. The scratches would heal and none would think him less than he was, whereas I was definitely a young man who had seen better days and was now visibly humbled. I vowed to divest myself of my hose as soon as I could move my head about without wanting to puke. And lastly there were my boots, or, rather, my boot. I was now reduced to 'one shoe off and one shoe on' like 'my son John' in the children's rhyme. For a second time I looked across to Calvagh. His poor-boy's shoes, no more than shapeless leather bags tied with a thong, were firmly on both feet despite his thrashing in the water. I, on the contrary, had managed to kick off one of my sturdy London boots, the ones that confirmed my solid English steps when I set foot in Ireland.

'I cannot believe such ill-fortune!' I shouted. 'We have indeed tumbled into a privy.'

'What is it, Edward?'

'I have no boots. Or, rather, I have one boot which is as bad as no boots at all.'

I hoped my companion would not break some jest upon me, such as that I might hop when we set forth on our way. I knew I should disgrace myself by a display of pouting and even punching of him who could not help how unfairly I had been treated.

Calvagh pushed aside the tower of pebbles which he had been carefully building. He placed his hand on the sleeve of my stained doublet.

'We shall take turns with my left shoe every half hour. That way, neither of us shall rest unhappy.'

I was silent with mortification.

'Thank you,' I whispered at last. And then I burst into tears. I truly believe that the fear, despair even, which I felt as we struggled in the water had at last chosen to overcome me. I shook with the power of the sobs and could find no sensible words to release me from this sudden onset of misery. All I could manage was to gabble occasionally about my boots which made the scene yet more ridiculous.

At first, Calvagh seemed taken aback that I should be so girlish in my humour, but then he slipped his arm through mine and let the melancholy fit run its course.

'The tears make it even harder for me to see,' I said when I was at last able to utter a whole sentence.

'I think you still have your dagger,' he said, tired no doubt by the repeated mention of the tragedy of my footwear.

It was true that my weapon was still firmly at my belt. I thanked fortune that we were not defenceless, though I had been reduced to the state of an Irish beggar.

'I take comfort in the possession of sharp English steel,' I said, taking out the blade and examining its edge thoughtfully.

'Take more comfort because it is made of iron. They say that iron is feared in this country.'

I remembered the harm my dagger had caused to the *Lios Alfar* who sought to murder Calvagh. The sound of his scream still lived with me.

'This will be a good defence for us, I hope.'

'Indeed it will.'

I waved the dagger about my head in a figure of eight gesture. I meant nothing by it except to say, in a general way, 'I have my youthful strength, my wits and my friend. Come at me who will.' With each swish of the blade, however, I noticed that the shimmering in all the world around me became less. I renewed the action with great vigour and, when my head was quite clear, I stood over the bemused Calvagh and subjected him to the same medicine.

'Your brave English steel has some use at last,' he said wryly. 'You have cast a spell about us, I do believe.'

'We now have two choices…,' I began.

Calvagh turned towards me and flicked at the sand. 'I would agree with you there.'

'I have not named the choices.'

'To walk into the ocean and swim home to Cork or to take the lie of this new land.'

'Those were my very thoughts.'

He squeezed my shoulder. 'Could you swim so far with these arms?'

'No,' I replied. 'It is an empty question. I should manage to take us as far as the water was deep enough to drown us.'

'So we must explore.'

'Yes. We have but one choice after all.'

We tried to shake the sand from our clothing, but it had become a second skin and no amount of brushing or picking could clean us. I buttoned my doublet in a show of tidiness and ran my fingers through my hair. Calvagh re-tied his two shoes and slapped at his breeches. Together then, we climbed through the sand, the grass and the first bushes to see what country awaited us.

The sand quickly gave way to earth with softer grass and prickles and I was indeed obliged to hop on my one boot. Following the line of the stream which had provided us with such sweet water, we soon passed into the shade of trees and then, beyond them, to a crest of land which offered us a wide prospect. This was the kingdom of the *Lios Alfar*, the *Sidhe*, the *Other* folk, the *eldritch*, or what you will. I was in the country which was home to so many of the tales I had been told by the fireside and which excited and terrified me in equal measure. With my stubbed toes and my salt-stained clothing, I was not having the adventure among these creatures that I once dreamed of. The land, at least, did not cry out against us. There were neat fields and hedges, spinneys, eminences, birds flitting. It could have been the landscape of Huntingdonshire or Cork for its lack of true strangeness. The colours alone were different. Imagine grass with a greenness that almost burns, or the branch of a tree gently undulating like fingers lightly curled. It was both what we knew and yet far from what we knew. It seemed alive.

'They are after providing us with a road,' said Calvagh. 'Are we to go in that direction?'

Directly in front of us, a narrow road, dry and straight and with a surface of small, pretty stones led enticingly between flowery hedges. The blossoms, as we might have expected, were the deepest blue or pink I had ever set eyes on (neither of us recognised the flowers) and their perfume assailed us with its sweetness from a long way away.

'Things were paler at the seashore,' I said.

'And quieter.'

The drone of bees and flies in the hedgerow was so loud they might have been sealed in our ears. We looked about us, still reluctant to follow the road that was, really, our only option.

'I think they are mountains in the far distance,' I said. 'True mountains, not those little lumps you call mountains around Master Spenser's castle at Kilcolman.' I had chosen my words without thinking and I saw Calvagh blink at them.

'I'm thinking they are clouds,' he said.

'Mountains, I believe, with snow.'

'Silver clouds.'

'I am strongly of the opinion that they are many, many miles away and that these *mountains* are imposingly high. Please do not say they are high clouds because I know they are mountains. Perhaps they are the mountains of Heaven,' I surmised. 'A voice tells me we shall need to climb them one day.'

'Or walk on those clouds with angels.'

'Why do you vex me with your games?' I asked, knowing very well the answer to my question. I had been offensive and was too obstinate to withdraw the slight I had offered. 'Our lives may last no longer than today and yet you put me out of temper by saying things you do not believe.'

Calvagh smirked and kicked a pebble.

'I have a good mind to tan your arse with a bunch of nettles!' I shouted.

He expertly sent another pebble bouncing along the road. 'Our lives lasting no longer than today and he wants to tan my arse.'

I chose a pebble of my own to kick and watched it fly into the undergrowth, all kecks and ragged robins that glowed like pink candle flames.

'Damn your brightness!' I cried. With that, I took the steel dagger from my belt and marched among the pale keck umbels which flourished in such profusion by the roadside. With a swift slash of my blade I took off one of the creamy heads and watched aghast as the stalk turned black in an instant and shrivelled right down to its root. Thrashing about me, twisting this way and that, I cut a path back to my companion. We both stared in silence at the ruin I had made.

'I am a fool,' I said, 'and you bear it patiently.'

'It is good to know the power of your dagger. Perhaps such people as live here will wither and die if they cross you. These rages, Edward. Do they not unsettle your stomach?'

'I am all English bile,' I told him. 'Pray do not mind me.'

A cuckoo startled us with its mocking cry. At home I would have thought, *Summer is truly come at last,* and yet in this land of bright colours and blackened stalks, the sound was not at all reassuring. It seemed an observation on who I was and what I had just done.

'Let us imagine we are visiting a relative in a distant county,' I said. 'It is nothing more dangerous than that. We have walked beside fields that look familiar and not been frightened.' I wondered whether I might be safer here than in most parts of Ireland where an Englishman's breast is the target for every ruffian.

'A cuckoo is certainly not frightening unless it happens to be a yard high and angry.'

'The power of iron is called for before we move any further,' I announced. I unsheathed my dagger and told Calvagh to stand still in front of me whilst I waved the blade around every part of him.

'Do it twice over my privy parts,' he said with great seriousness. 'I arrived here a complete man and that is how I intend to leave.'

Although I inwardly smiled at him, I dealt my own manly appendages the same careful treatment. It was not my fancy, I am sure, that, as I swished my dagger this way and that, there was an indrawing of breath in the foliage around us, a susurration, as if it recoiled from what it hated most.

When the business with the iron was done, we decided each to take the largest stone he could find on the road's surface and to carry it as a weapon. They were mean weapons, truly, but they were all we had apart from my dagger which would only be of use in close combat. As boys, we had naturally shied stones at birds and cats and other boys, so any unfriendly creature would need to look to its eyes, a nonsense phrase of course, before it set about eating us.

We walked for a good hour, although slowly, because my having a single boot meant I had to choose carefully where to place my unshod foot. Calvagh was, I concluded, as uncontrollable as a puppy. He walked twice as far as I did, darting from side to side, thrusting into the hedgerow with a stick he had found and calling out the names of any plants or creatures he recognised. I refused the offer to take a turn in his shoes, although my bare left toes were stubbed and bloodied.

It was distinctly smoke. And, after further progress along the road, we were sure we could see chimney pots and, perhaps, the edge of a roof.

'I hope our relative is at home and he welcomes us,' I said.

'Roast meat and a clean bed.'

'As long as *we* are not the roast meat! I did not come here to have a spit thrust up my arse.' I turned the stone in my hand, looking for the sharpest edge in case I was obliged to throw it. The need was sooner than I thought. We were approaching the junction of our road with a second which was screened by a higher hedge and a number of trees. As we drew abreast, we were surprised to see another person, a man of about forty years, accompanied by a few head of plump, tawny cattle. We drew our arms back menacingly and measured the flight of our stones. The man waved his hand as a signal that he meant no harm and that it was unnecessary for us to stone him. He had on the worn shirt and breeches I might have seen in a farmyard anywhere. There were no tail or fangs and both Calvagh and I lowered our hands. The stranger said some words to us, with a tone of bitter humour I fancied. The words made no sense to me in English nor to Calvagh in Irish. And then it came to me that he had spoken the language of Her Majesty's and England's most bitter enemy, Spain. His swarthy, unattractive face confirmed it. When I lived in London, I had made it my business to acquire whatever phrases I could in French, Spanish and Italian. There were always idlers or drinking companions of a foreign cut who could teach me a few sentences. I distinctly understood the stranger to ask, 'New arrivals?' His question made those fields, which were to most people a matter of wonder and speculation, sound like a port into which travellers from every corner blew.

'Yes we are,' I replied in Spanish and surprised him.

Calvagh seized my arm. 'Do not tell him our names! We shall fall into his power if you do.'

I brushed away his concern. I had heard too many stories of the *Fair Folk* to make such a mistake so easily. '*Sailor?*' I asked, again in the man's own tongue.

'*Sí.*'

'*Here years?*'

'*Cinco meses.*'

I lacked the knowledge to ask a complex question, so our conversation necessarily went on in a childish way.

'*Here good?*'

'*Quizás.*'

'*Get away, us?*'

'*No.*'

'*Where we go?*'

'*Van a casa.*'

'*Die?*'

'*No die. Quizás.*'

I turned to Calvagh who had been listening to our exchange of fragments open-mouthed. 'He recommends that we continue to the house yonder and he imagines we shall not die of it.'

'Did he wash up like us?'

'He says he was a sailor and that there is no escape.'

'There is always escape. But he's probably happy walking up and down the lane with his cows. We'll escape, don't you worry.'

'Not escape. Danger.'

So the creature understood English too. I wanted to explain to him that we weren't like King Philip's sailors who were apparently satisfied with their new lot and happy to spend captivity in the company of Rosebud and Daisy. I took Calvagh by the arm and hurried him beyond earshot of the Spaniard. 'Do you believe we should approach this house? We have time to take to the fields and manage as best we can. I doubt whether the cowherd will raise an alarm.'

'Edward, you know we cannot live forever in the fields. That Spaniard was not thin like a prisoner. I didn't see bruises on him, or irons. He was in a better state than many Irish, excuse me. We must continue to the house and see what we are after finding there.'

'My mind too. Let us shake hands with this man, so that he thinks well of us, and proceed.'

The road soon passed amongst trees in rich leaf, oaks and chestnuts, and then, set amidst its gardens, we saw the house. I am reluctant to say again, 'Like a grand house at home, and yet not like it at all.' The main building was a tall and elegant square, brick-built, the bricks being a deep russet colour and small. It gave me the feeling as if a giant hand had grasped a castle keep and stretched it unbelievably skywards. There were many small turrets and towers, apparently added here and there at whim, and all the windows were wide and full of delicate tracery. Offices and lesser buildings clung to the lowest storey of the central tower like children at their parent's knee. I thought it a home rather than a castle and was put in mind of laughter rather than 'Keep away'. The slates of every part of the roofing glistened as if wet, although they were not, and they had a chequer board pattern of many colours that delighted the eye. At the corners of the roof, twisting, tapering chimney-stacks rose high and breathed out the smoke we had spotted from a mile away. There were neat orchards and gardens and, I trusted, stables and all the usual workshops a great house needs.

'We could hide in the woods and steal from the garden when we are hungry,' suggested Calvagh.

'For a week until they set their dogs on us,' I told him. 'The question is, at which door do we knock?'

A thunderous growling made our choice for us. As we gazed in wonder and indecision, a shaggy creature with four legs and a fanged mouth, had crept behind us. It was not a dog, not a bear, but a brown, raggedy thing that clearly brought cunning to its guarding duties. We endeavoured to face it down and saw an expression in its filmy yellow eyes, three of them, the third half-concealed by its forelock, which was most certainly not, ' Good boy. Sit.' We took to our heels in the direction of the nearest building which had an open door. Our speed was remarkable, mine even more so as I was wearing my one boot and the cobbles of the path chopped wedges from my bare foot. We darted into the building and Calvagh closed the door immediately. What with the creature's scraping and howling outside and my yelping at my wrecked foot, you could not say that we entered the house of Lord Trim 'l Nior unannounced.

We had entered a servants' hall, a spacious room notwithstanding, with a large table in the centre of its black stone floor. Calvagh turned the key (a bronze one) in the door and then joined me behind the table. We were not alone. An old man, a younger man and a woman my own age had been enjoying a meal when we hurled in in our unruly fashion. The two men called out, I thought, in Irish and the young woman perhaps in French. As the pounding and snarling at the door continued, the old man walked up to the door and shouted a couple of sentences loudly. The snarling gave way to whimpering as the creature moved away.

'I believe that was a spell,' Calvagh whispered to me. 'I have the words in my head now.'

'He spoke your language?'

'It was like a little poem. He said the word for blood they use in Ciarraí.'

The old man motioned for us to be seated which we were glad to do. No other words were spoken as two earthenware dishes were placed in front of us and a kind of pottage ladled from a cauldron hanging over the fire. I straightway thought there might be some foul creature shredded in the meal, but I could see no meat of any kind and so I followed my friend's example and set to. There was a wooden spoon for each of us, an end of what I would call village bread and a cup of ale to share. In my childhood I had oftentimes dined on fare no better than this during the harsh winter months and I gobbled it quickly. Once the meal was done, it was clear we were to give an account of ourselves. This would fall to Calvagh, but, if my guess about the French had been correct, I might at some time direct questions to the young woman. She was pretty, in a knowing way, and probably not to be trusted.

The old man made himself comfortable in his chair at the head of the table and folded his arms. He was the senior servant and his dress bespoke his significance. I could not see his breeches or shoes, but he had on a clean shirt with buttons and a pale green waistcoat trimmed in places with gold braid. From the lack of smears and splashes on him, I imagined he gave commands only and did not dip his own fingers into the usual household messes. His hair was trimmed and his face plump and shiny. I could easily imagine him on a high day or holiday lording it over a prosperous tavern like The Cock, a favourite of mine in Eastcheap. His companions were less well dressed, although still a cut above the menials Master Spenser employed. The man nodded to Calvagh who told a tale I could not follow. I expected it was the truth of our adventure minus the stabbing. Occasionally, Calvagh nodded towards me in a way I hoped made clear that I had connections with an Englishman of great dignity.

The imagination of Man is a remarkable thing. As Calvagh went on with his tale, I examined our new acquaintances and wrote their histories in my head. Like us, they had found their way to this enchanted strand by dreadful mischance, shipwreck, whirlwind, kidnap, who could tell? Now, they were the retainers of the lord of a great faerie house and ate simply, if wholesomely, in his servants' hall. I had quickly convinced myself that these were my fellow human beings as I glanced at the hair, teeth, fingers, eyes of all of them and could see no horns, fangs, extra digits or the cold strange eyes of the *Lios Alfar* whose murderous intent I was so hearty that I had thwarted. These people had a solid roundness, particularly of the ears, that I knew to be such a feature of my own kind. They scratched and fidgeted and I could look them squarely in the eye without fear of what I would find there.

'Dónal was a fisherman with his boat at An Daingean,' said Calvagh. 'He is not sorry he arrived here as his wife is dead and his sons are seeking glory against the English. He told me he has been in this house two years and asks if it is now fifteen hundred and seventy back in Ireland.'

'What was your reply?'

'I told him my friend had need of a boot.'

'My thanks.'

'He said he could not give us something like a boot until we had been presented to his master.'

'*Presented?*'

'That is what he said.'

'I still keep my blade, so let his master have a care.'

'Let you have a care, Edward Harry. We are friendless in a dangerous land. I believe we should bow our heads…'

'And not speak out of turn. At least let me wash my foot. No lord would want to see this blood and dirt in his chamber.'

Calvagh spoke to the old man who gave an order to the young woman. She poured some warm water into a pail and allowed me to splash my punished toes.

'*Merci.*'

'*Monsieur.*'

Word of our arrival below stairs had already travelled to the master as a door opened and a lackey entered. That he was a member of the other race I knew at once. The eyes, again, had an upward curve which drew the cheeks and lips into a natural sneer I found intolerable. His hair was spun into an auburn poll which reminded me of a player queen I had seen strutting her majesty in the theatre. His clothes were sumptuous and I envied them: a tight fitting doublet of green satin over a shirt of the softest white stuff and elegant breeches of a darker green. His hose were a pale lavender and his shoes dainty leather concoctions of the same colour. How disagreeable a visit to the servants' quarters must have been for him. He looked as if he could barely tolerate the air we exhaled around us. His expression as he took in us two newcomers was such as one might see on the face of a man who has been told he must lie abed with a leper. I may have no parentage, no crest or wealth, but, by God, I am no man's leper. I will not be sneered at as if I am all scabs and vermin. I thought nothing of the slight pointing of his ears; it was his eyes that said all.

'Look you, sirrah,' I cried to the amazement of all. 'Do not you cast those sneers in our direction. You are a servant and I am an Englishman!' Foolish, meaningless words, but I was in some heat.

The creature took a backward step as if a noisome vapour had blown from me towards him. He uttered a harsh sentence to the old man who bowed his head.

'Address yourself to me, popinjay,' I went on. '*I* shall answer for my words, not that old man.'

My tone would have been clear in any language. His hands flew up as if the noisome vapour had slapped him on both cheeks and tweaked his nose. With his inhuman eyes he glared at me and spat more words in his own tongue. They cannot have been a spell as I felt no change, but I have no doubt that they contained an unpleasant threat. Several times Calvagh shook my arm and whispered 'No', but I was quite beyond restraint. I had decided that more than likely I should die in this strange land and I certainly had no intention of slipping to my death weakly like a drowned kitten. I laughed at the messenger, I mocked his hair, I made a gobbling sound in imitation of his language.

'Edward, our friends will surely be punished for your temper.'

It was true that the younger man and the woman had moved close together as if expecting a disastrous outcome. I was surely no pleasant addition to their lives.

'You have twice given them my name,' I said quietly to Calvagh. His look of deep shame made my own shame at such waterish words all the more painful.

'Lead on, Master Satin and Lavender,' I called as tauntingly as one boot and a sea-soiled doublet would allow me. 'And if you look at me in that insolent manner once more, I shall kick your scraggy arse to the gates of Hell and back.'

'This is not the place for your arse, Edward.'

He gave a small gasp at having revealed my name for a second time.

'I fancy it is the place, my dear friend. Dame Fortune has brought us here where we never wanted to be, so let us kick *her* arse too and the arses of all those who work with her.'

I was laughing on my gallows. I was blowing kisses to a row of sweethearts who waited tearfully for me to swing. What possessed me I cannot say, but I know whose heart beat the most strongly as we went to meet the master of that hall.

We set off in train, the messenger leading, the old man, Dónal, a respectful distance behind and then the two pieces of flotsam, Calvagh and myself. We walked along a corridor with walls of plain brick and a stone floor and quickly came to a door fashioned from a rich cherry-coloured wood.

As he reached the door, our popinjay stopped and turned to face us. 'My master is not known for his patience. Be warned,' he said in English that was wrapped in an accent I can only call serpentine.

Oh yes, I was duly warned. *But let him be warned too* I thought. All the time as we walked, my fingers played with the edge of my dagger that I had slid up into my sleeve. Let him be warned. His kind had no liking for the bite of iron and the corpse now washing in the sea somewhere bore testament to the injury it could inflict.

CHAPTER SEVEN

To walk beyond the cherry door was to pass into a different world, the world of fable and wonder. We entered a second, wider corridor, its floor an intricate arrangement of burnished woodwork. The walls were panelled in a lighter wood, perhaps a species of walnut, to the height of my shoulder, and above this hung heavy, strongly-coloured tapestries I wished I had the time to examine. As it was, we were swept past these pictures of folk in strange dress and armour besporting themselves in wondrous gardens or fending off dire beasts. The air was warm and scented and I had to smile at the comfort it gave me. I should have liked to be the lord of such a corridor and such a second doorway as now met us. This second door frame was a feast of inlay. Panels in every colour a tree trunk has ever attained were cut in so many scrolls and fans and general fanciness as to make passing through a dizzying experience.

The door opened at a touch, or perhaps at a word, and even greater wonders appeared before us. Calvagh gasped loudly, but I held in my breath as a matter of policy. I do not know how best to describe this next room. The word 'hallway' is a puny thing, although that was its actual function. A gilded staircase flew in an insubstantial spiral almost the full height of the tower or keep in which we now found ourselves. I am no architect, but I do know that in any great house in England, Nonsuch or Richmond, such flying construction would be impossible. It made every staircase I had ever climbed seem an earthbound, boorish thing and no better than the rough ladder which led upstairs in Uncle Hugh's cottage. Dónal was left behind us near the stair's foot, dazed and immobile, the victim, I imagined, of some enchantment. It was a coward's way of keeping your servants in order, I thought, to mouth a spell rather than to quell them with the force of your authority. My fingers clenched more tightly around the dagger blade in my sleeve, nicking the skin and making the pads of my fingers sticky with blood. If enchantment were afoot, my several inches of iron ought to offer me some small defence. I took Calvagh's arm, thinking that, perhaps, what protected me might link to him as well.

The lavender popinjay stopped on the first turn of the staircase and cast a disdainful purplish eye on us two human lads. We were not in our Sunday best, it is true, but we were healthy and vigorous, fine-featured and alert, and, even in a shabby state, we were clearly his match. We bloomed and he preened, a distinction that heartened me. A slight movement of the lips betrayed his speaking another enchantment, to seal *my* lips, I'll be bound. An immediate widening of those cold eyes made clear that the magic had slid off us. I pinched Calvagh as if to say, 'Trust me.'

As we climbed the many stairs to the increasingly hoarse sound of the breathing of our guide, I reflected that, perhaps, it had been a spell to make us fly around the many turns of the staircase. The result of my interference was that we now had to toil somewhat, but the knowledge of my dagger's power was invaluable. At the tenth spiral, our guide stopped and spoke to us in his usual way. I fancy a major reason for the pause was that he needed to draw breath and I hoped my agreeable simper showed him I understood this.

'My Lord Trim 'l Nior is the greatest figure in the outer plains. You will treat him with respect and never be the first to speak. Lower your eyes to the floor unless he commands you otherwise.'

'I have been in the company of lords before now,' I said lightly.

Calvagh joined in: 'I was never yet seen kissing the ground before an Englishman and damn me if I do it for you!' Excellent man, although his words did not ring entirely true with me as I had seen him fawning before his English overlords in Master Spenser's castle of Kilcolman.

The profusion of windows I had marked as we approached the building held sheets of pure crystal or coloured and patterned glass, so we were showered with silver light or rainbows all the while we ascended. There were cages too, every now and then, suspended by the thinnest imaginable golden cord. Gilded cages, naturally, but with few bars, as if some other restraint prevented their occupants from flitting away. 'Flit' may not be the aptest word as these scraps of fur and feather were like no linnet or finch I knew. They were strange in the extreme and sat on or hung from their perches in a variety of awkward poses. Some cackled, some crooned, while others remained in dull silence. They were not pretty; they were interesting rather or, in some cases, utterly monstrous. Imagine a blue and orange cat with a single scaly wing, a set of ill-matched claws, a frilly top-knot and the whole thing a mere three inches high. There you have one of these caged specimens. They were all different and, on a greater scale, would have inhabited a child's worst nightmare. I put my face near the cage of a, what shall I say, of a mouse-robin-fly and was sure I heard it whisper, 'Go away. I'm busy.'

'My aunt would love one of those,' Calvagh announced boldly. 'Are they for sale?'

This at once set up such a squawking and cheeping that Master Lavender had need to wave his arm and, with a gesture, set them all a-slumber.

'I was just getting to enjoy what they had to say,' said Calvagh winking at me. 'Lead on my friend.'

'Jest while you can,' warned our guide.

'You can be sure we'll do that,' I told him.

Very soon we reached the top landing of the staircase and I looked down in admiration at the distance we had come. I felt as if I were suspended in the air, as near to flying as I am likely to experience. A gilded door awaited us and the demeanour of our guide changed markedly. He ran his hands over any creases in his doublet and wiped his lips. We were a little abashed ourselves, I have to admit, but fascinated too. I must confess the thought did cross my mind that he who awaited us might conform to my view of Satan with horns, a forked tail and a malevolent personality. There was no smell of sulphur, however, and I could not imagine that a devil would tolerate such intricacies of gilt or resist the temptation to treat the caged creatures as tit-bits. The doors opened and we were pushed into the presence. The popinjay remained outside.

The Lord Trim 'l Nior was very tall, at least a hand taller than myself, and I am no dwarf. So this was one of the lords of the *Sidhe*. He sat in a comfortable wooden chair on a small dais and in full sunlight. Here was no furtive creature of the darkness, frolicking in midnight woodlands and glimpsed only by the unwary traveller. I almost wanted to ask him how he did. The main colour about him was silver. There was a moonlit luminescence playing through every other colour in his garments. He had a loose white shirt of a texture which made even Her Majesty's finest lawns seem like sack cloth. His breeches were a shifting silvery blue and his hose pure silver of an intensity that shocked. Sitting loosely on his shoulders and trailing in gathers over the arms of his chair was a day robe of many pale colours and so delicate that it could almost have been a haze or a trick of the light. His fingers, I noticed, were beating a slow rhythm on the chair, whether with impatience or anticipation, who could tell? On his right hand he had a single ring with a vast stone of deep crimson. I have heard men talk in tales of objects worth a king's ransom. This was surely such an object. His hair, strangely, was a light brown, a human brown, indeed, and short with very little sign of dressing or care. How different from the womanish concoction of our guide. I have left his face until last. Such a powerful gaze and one so absolutely certain of its own authority. I would be foolish to attempt much of my pertness here, but pertness will always out. The eyes, as ever, were inhuman, incapable of tenderness or humour. Their colour, if you can believe me, was a dark burgundy-purple. If you have never had a being with such eyes raise his head and try to look into your very heart, you cannot begin to imagine how awful was this figure seated before and above me. As much as I was able, I refused to meet his gaze and I think I was helped in this by the closeness of my dagger. He would surely have transfixed both Calvagh and me if the iron had not been there to aid us. His lordship's teeth gleamed between the narrow lips, the iciest of half-smiles. Ah yes, the ears. Quite round and not at all goblin-like which I have to confess I found a little disappointing. That we were his to play with, was my immediate thought and my fingers remained clenched around the point of my dagger. I am an adept with the thrown blade so he had need to be on his guard as much as Calvagh or myself. Our guide bowed low and long, a bow that went entirely unacknowledged. I gave his lordship the briefest of nods, so did Calvagh, and then we waited. I saw the fingers of our guide play with the seam of his breeches as the moments lengthened. I would not be frightened by this lord's gaze and I would not stare at the floor like some schoolboy who has been caught scratching his name into a desk top. I tore my eyes away and looked about me, examining the furnishings with theatrical interest.

'Defiance is pointless.'

'But quite necessary,' I replied.

His voice was calm and sonorous and his English as elegant as any I might expect to hear in the greatest London houses. My own voice was firm and light. I only hoped that his next words were not, 'Take him to a place of execution.'

'You will tell me how you came to these shores. It was most certainly not at our invitation.'

'It was a mistake, sir!' shouted Calvagh.

'On *your* part it certainly was a mistake.'

'We were sailing out from Kinsale when we came across a sinking vessel.'

I wondered how much of the true story I could avoid telling. Very little, I fancied.

'And?'

'Someone was still aboard the vessel. One of *your* kind.'

'And?'

'We mercifully took him on board our craft intending to give him passage back to Kinsale. He had other intentions. He threw a pair of green stones into the sea and they directed our boat here. Then he tried to kill my friend.'

'And?'

'I stabbed him. And I would do it again in an instant.'

'Do you know who it was you killed?'

'How should I know or care? He refused to exchange his name for ours.'

'And so you stabbed him?'

'I stabbed him because he was a treacherous ingrate who wished to murder my friend.'

'Do you realise...?'

'No, do *you* realise! Sitting on your throne as if presenting the judgement of Solomon. We offered him help and he repaid us with treachery. We did not seek to make him captive. He had a seat in our boat and he was free to leave us when we reached land.'

'Do you think I care...?'

'Do you think *we* care? We are not your kind or your subjects or your friends. We have heard countless stories of your people's cruelty and childish ways, my Lord Trim. So I spit at your world.'

Where had I found these words? They were not the way to ensure our lives lasted longer than the next moment.

'Why do you think I have allowed you the power of speech for so long?'

'Because I am holding an object of iron and you cannot stop me.'

These words unsettled him. I took a firmer grip of Calvagh and awaited the worst that was bound to happen.

'We may have a use for a creature like you.'

Use? Creature? Had he not enraged me enough?

'Because, of course, you will never leave.'

'So you are pleased to say.'

Attempting a mockery of an easy smile, he rose from his chair. I knew he did this the better to aim some bolt of power at my head or heart and I was ready with a shot of my own. I slid the dagger hilt into my palm and hurled it breast-ward with all my might. Immediately I did so, the protection of iron left us and both Calvagh and I were enmeshed in heavy and invisible bonds that dragged us to the floor. We could feel, but not see, them looping around us in endless constricting tangles. The dagger flew swiftly at first and then encountered a kind of shimmer which absorbed and smothered its onward flight. It struggled to strike its target and then dropped to the floor like an injured bird. There, it broke into many pieces, its power gone. The thwarting of that power had required great effort on the part of my Lord Trim who fell back into his chair with beads of perspiration across his brow. No doubt torture and death would follow, but I, for one, would die happy knowing I had left him so discomposed. I regretted that Calvagh must suffer for my temper when he had mostly curbed his tongue and might well have been permitted to spend his days in the servants' kitchen chatting in his own tongue to Dónal.

'A skilful aim,' said his lordship after he had gathered himself. He twitched at his robe and I distinctly heard the sound of his ring as his fingers drummed on the arm of his chair. 'If there were others present to witness your insolence, I would, of course, have you despatched.'

'If there had…,' I began, but the power of magic muzzled me. He could flaunt his triumph without fear of my reply.

'I do not want you in my home, but there are others who may find your determination, your lack of control, a help.'

My hearing was unaffected by our bonds and I wanted to shout that I would help none like him and that he had better kill me now. The nature of the power oppressing us, regrettably, meant that even the silent defiance writ plainly on my face would soon be denied me. A heavy slumber overwhelmed us both and when we awoke we were in a very different place.

CHAPTER EIGHT

Perhaps surprisingly, given the wilfulness of my tongue, I had never been in a prison before and this one, though cold and dark, was not noisome. I was glad to note that, unlike Mankind, who delight in subjecting those they hold captive to every filthy experience imaginable, the *Folk* of the *Sidhe* took imprisonment simply for what it was – the denial of freedom. In the dimmest of lights, I could see a platter of simple but acceptable food and a jug which contained clean water. We had been laid side by side on thin mattresses which were neither damp nor verminous.

After I had lain awake for perhaps a quarter of an hour, I said, 'I am so sorry, Calvagh.'

'Why are you so sorry, Edward?'

'My uncurbed English tongue has brought us here when a humble "Please, sir, may we go home?" might have worked much better.'

'I thought you were *go hiontach*, wonderful. I wish I had such words to throw at him. If ever a man needed his arse tanning with a bunch of nettles, it was him.'

'So you do not blame me that you are in prison?'

'What is prison between friends?'

'Still prison.'

'Sure, you have me there.'

'We have food and drink, so shall we eat to maintain our strength? I do not suppose you have an iron blade about your person?'

'No.'

'I feared not.'

There was no window and so no light from outside made its way into our cell. Such faint illumination as there was must have had its origin in a source we could not see. We could not tell if it were day or night and in the near darkness we lost even our sense of the pace at which the minutes passed. Food and water were served, we spoke briefly and did our offices as unobtrusively as we could in the bucket in the corner, and that was all we knew for a long time. Our conversation simply repeated that our spirits were not abashed and that if we died there we would die with curses on our lips.

At last we were remembered, or their arrangements for us were settled. The door of the cell opened and Dónal called us out. He addressed us in Irish which Calvagh immediately translated.

'You are to be sent away,' the old man said in a voice that did not invite question. When Calvagh began a question, all the same, it was brushed aside with an abrupt gesture.

We emerged into the daylight reasonably clean, if untidy, and wondering what plan lay in store. My fleeting thought, and heaven knows what prompted it, was that we were to be used as a kind of gladiator for some lord's amusement. What if we were told to take up swords against each other? As I had never heard tell of such bloody practices among these folk, I did not share my disturbing thought with Calvagh. His face was pensive as if he harboured disturbing imaginings of his own. Lord Trim was not there to witness our departure, nor was his servant with my lady-in-waiting's hair. There was, instead, a trio of mounted soldiers, grim-looking individuals, as soldiers ever are. They wore quilted tabards as protection for their bodies, each square of the quilting decorated with a small white flower on a field of green. I surmised that this was the blazon of some great house as one of the trio carried a pennant bearing the same device. The effect was strangely beautiful, as the artefacts of war perversely can be. Two of the soldiers were bowmen with long bows slung at their backs. Their helmets were leather, topped with a green and white spray that might have been cut from a larger version of one of the odd creatures we had seen in the cages on the staircase.

'You are to ride,' Dónal told us. I understood him without the need for Calvagh's translation. He indicated a strapping chestnut stallion that was saddled and riderless.

The matter of my bootless left foot had not figured in our conversation with Lord Trim. I expect that he had never discussed an underling's boots in the whole of his life. Not that I was, or would ever be, his underling. The question had been dealt with, however. Dónal collected a pair of boots and handed them to me as I stood looking at the horse and imagining the damage its brazen stirrup would wreak on my already much abused foot. The boots were far from new, but they were without holes and they fitted well. Someone, Dónal himself?, had taken note of the size of my feet and my toes felt immediately at ease in their new home.

Calvagh smiled at me. 'Once again you can feel that you are grander than a mere Irish boy.'

Was I so transparent?

It was with a pang that I removed my one remaining English boot and handed it to Dónal. A further tie with England, and Ireland, was broken. Rather foolishly, I bade the old man take good care of the boot as I should like to wear it again on the way home. Calvagh translated and Dónal said nothing.

I sat at the front of our horse with the reins and Calvagh climbed up behind me and put his arms around my waist. With one of the soldiers beside us and two behind, we trotted out of my Lord Trim's stable yard, astonished that such a conveyance should have been provided for us. It remained to be seen whether our escorts permitted us to chatter for there was bound to be much that would call our attention and need discussion. As Dónal had helped us to mount the horse, he muttered a few words. When Calvagh followed me up behind, he pressed his face into my shoulder and whispered, 'It was a blessing. "*May friends wait to greet us on the road ahead. And our enemies stay at home drunk!*"'

Strengthened by this blessing, we went on our way. Dónal was a good man, I firmly believe, and probably as happy there as he would have been gutting fish with arthritic fingers at home. If he really did believe the year was 1570, then his life had been prolonged beyond its normal span. As we passed into the open countryside, following this train of thought, I could not help but wonder what year we would find if we ever reached our homes again. 1670? 1770? What a notion! I kicked our horse to make him stir himself.

I thought it a fair assumption that the sun in the land of faerie was the very same sun as I had known every day of my life and that it kept the same hours in the sky. It was therefore about ten of the clock when we rode away from the mansion of my Lord Trim. Our captors had only a mild sense of urgency and both Calvagh and I took the opportunity to look about us and draw our conclusions. My attention was very little given to the governance of my horse as the beast was either so well trained or under some enchantment that it followed its leader closely whether I gave it instruction or no.

At first, when Calvagh noticed a detail he wished to share with me, he would jolt his face into my shoulder and mutter his words. If I had not, myself, already noticed the creature or building to which he drew my attention, I would direct my eyes towards it in a casual manner. Oft-times it was I who spotted the wonder first and I would squeeze the words furtively out of the side of my mouth. By the time the midsummer sun was at its zenith and we had travelled perhaps twenty miles, it became clear that we were free to converse as we wished so long as one of us did not kick our mount in the ribs and shout, 'Giddy up to the hills boy!' or suchlike. We had no knowledge of where an escape might take us, so, for the time being, we were content to jog along and chatter.

One thought had been exercising my mind off and on ever since I lifted Calvagh ashore in this strange land. What did its inhabitants call it? Now I seized my opportunity. 'Will you answer me a question?' I asked the leading rider of our party. He did not acknowledge my question with even the barest shrug.

'I do not ask where we are going or why, or in whose name you hold us captive. That is the lord whose livery you wear, I suppose. It is a simpler question and surely no secret. What do *you* call this country of yours? I am reluctant to play the child and call it Faerie Land although I understand such it is. You must have your own name and, as a point of fact, I would dearly like to know it.'

There followed a short conversation in the faerie tongue between the rider I had addressed and his two fellows, accomplices rather. Shortly, he turned to me and spoke some words, also in his own language, which my own unpractised ear could not seize. Their language, I should add here, is greatly mellifluous with tones and trills that make you think of articulate birdsong. I imagined they had their past perfects and declensions as the many human nations do, but how could these ever be distinguished in such tunefulness?

I smiled and cried, 'Too fast, too fast. These are new words to me and difficult for my ear to catch.'

He patiently repeated the words more slowly, but still I found them a great challenge. If Dónal, a mere fisherman with the benefit of little or no schooling, could master enough of these sounds to converse with his master's lackey, then pride said that it was a challenge I must overcome too.

'I know it! I know it!' shouted Calvagh. 'It is Hy Brazil. *Hy Brazil*. I have heard people say the name.'

'It is not *Hy Brazil* or anything like it,' said our reluctant teacher, 'But if that is the best you can say, then say it and trouble me no further with your thick tongue and donkey's ears.'

This called for a riposte and, naturally, I provided one. 'What are you, therefore?' I demanded. 'Are you *Hys* or *Brazils*? Which of the two?'

Our captors roared with laughter at my tetchy words which had not spoilt the slight mood of bonhommie between us.

'Are you Faeries, then, or Sidhe? Pookahs or Pixies?'

They snorted.

'These are *your* names for the lying tales you tell about us. Our own name for ourselves is…' Again there came a trilling with the occasional consonant tossed into the mix.

Calvagh put me in a dump by being able to produce a passable imitation of their words, but my own mouth was still obstinately incompetent.

'It sounds a little like *Elven*, Edward,' said Calvagh as he felt my body tense. 'They live in the *Elvenfold*.'

'Let us be the *Elven*, then,' said the rider I had questioned first. 'More about us do not presume to ask. It is not your place to know and we have been sworn to tell you nothing.'

The half jolly mood was gone and we trotted on. From time to time, Calvagh would practise the warbling name in my ear and vex me unnecessarily. Unbeknown to any, I also practised the words silently in my head, a difficult task, but one I felt bound to undertake. The Elven had an easy command of English and Irish, and probably of most of the major tongues of Europe besides. They had the advantage of us there. If I were to match them at their game, I would need to understand what they said to each other in unguarded moments in their own tongue. I doubted that Calvagh was capable of such politic thought and I planned to suggest it to him when next we were alone.

The other question that rose often to my lips, schoolboy-like, and needed to be fought down each time it threatened to turn itself into speech, concerned their ears. It was a vain, prattling question and yet it would not go away. I was alert each time a helmet was removed and, before the end of the first day of travel, I could have drawn excellent pictures of the ears of our three Elven guards. The one who rode in front and snapped orders had round ears and eyes that seemed, at times, as pale as lilac. Round ears might be a sign that one came from a better family, I conjectured, remembering the circular nature of Lord Trim's ears. The other Elven, he with the pennant and the second archer, had identical violet eyes and very dissimilar ears – one set sharply pointed and the other set almost square. Oh, how I burned to ask what their shapes meant. All three pairs of eyes were far less of a mystery. They shared the supercilious lift I disliked so much. Elven babies must be born with a sneer, I suspected, and they spent the rest of their lives perfecting it. Their lives. There was another troubling question. I yearned also to know how long they lived, whether a great person like my Lord Trim had witnessed the fate of Saxon Harold five hundred years before, or whether he had been present at the very Creation of Man. A blasphemous question that would be and I shocked myself in forming it. Calvagh must have wondered at these occasional jerkings of my body as such notions convulsed it.

And so, for a day and a half, we journeyed through the outer territories of Hy Brazil, the Faerie Land. Who would have believed it? In the broadest daylight, unblindfolded and under no prohibitions wrought by spells, we jogged along, never guessing the dark times that were soon to come upon us.

Rather than describe our journey mile by mile and wonder by wonder, let me give a general account of the country we passed through. Imagine a great semi-circle of land extending from the feet of wild mountains, the very mountains I had identified and which Calvagh, in his boyish way, persisted in seeing as clouds. This land mass is not continuous, for wide rivers divide it into three strips. An eagle soaring would look down on it as upon a half-target: a half ring of land and then inside that a half ring of water; next, a second half-ring of land, more water and then a great central island which contained the capital of the kingdom, the only city of real note. These half circles of land were by no means narrow or flat. They were at least thirty leagues wide and had every kind of hill, valley, fen and forest you find in the counties of England or Ireland. Our journey was taking us athwart the Outer Circle, as it was called, since our destination was the great Elven metropolis, for reasons undisclosed. Calvagh and I had landed on the eastern shore of that land and were being made to travel sharply north west to achieve our journey's end. There were fields of grain and orchards, the land being obviously fertile. Windmills turned on hilltops and carters moved goods about the roads. 'Hampshire or Suffolk,' you might have said to yourself until you saw that the carter had a blue face and cloven feet or that the sheep in a field were beset by a vexatious, snapping creature with quills and leathern wings. We passed no towns as such as Elven society is not ordered in that way. There are aggregations of buildings around the manors of local lords and there are small villages too, but the markets appear to be temporary events in fields which leave no permanent trace behind them. The manor is the focus of Elven society and a lord's influence may extend for a few fields or for the equivalent of several small shires. There is great contention between these local dignitaries who rule their little realms with all the unfairness and spite I have seen in the high and mighty everywhere. Master Edmund Spenser, a poet and scholar, was not above reducing his household and his children to a weeping state when meagrims overtook him. At such times I fled to his library and pretended to put his papers in order. The work in the fields of Hy Brazil is done by Humankind, by a peasant class of the Elven and those whom I can only describe as monsters. It was not unusual to see a man engaged in some rural task helped by a wizened, dwarfish, lug-eared, hobgoblin creature. Oddities fluttered or scampered across our path at intervals and I noticed the grimaces with which they were greeted by our fellow horsemen each time.

Once we passed a pair of gnarled figures leaning agreeably on a field gate and watching the world go slowly by. Our little cavalcade must have brought some interest to their day because it was not a busy road. One of the pair chewed a straw with difficulty through his fangs. He had a pig's snout and a single eye, as far as I could tell. His fingers were delicately formed, however, and he used them to make a small gesture of acknowledgement as if to say, 'How do?' His companion was but three feet tall and peered between the bars of the gate rather than over them. He wore clothes, but not necessarily ones made of cloth. His short limbs were wrapped in pieces of green and brown that might have been dock leaves or scraps of leather. He had a face that was part shrew and part nightmare but the general expression was not unfriendly. His arms ended in paws rather than hands and he clapped with animation as we drew close to him. Calvagh and I nodded as, strangely, we were in no way repelled. It might have been gaffer and his boy who had been cutting hay in the upper field for all the unease we felt. Both creatures grunted at us and chattered. The larger called, 'People lovely,' a phrase open to several meanings.

'Does he want us for his dinner?' asked Calvagh.

The peacefulness of the encounter was gone in an instant when one of the horsemen charged at the gate brandishing a stout whip I did not know he carried.

Screeching, the two bystanders fled, but not before the larger had time to drop his breeches and reveal a bristled rump from which he expelled a copious spray of dung.

'You were foolish to encourage them,' the rider said grimly. 'That sort cannot be trusted.'

And you believe that I am dupe enough to trust you? was my thought.

When we could, we avoided manor and village alike, save for the night-time when we lodged in houses of grand proportions and took on provisions for the morrow. Whoever had taken such an interest in us could clearly call on the hospitality of many significant members of the Elven kind. Was it the Faerie King or Queen themselves, I wondered, shocked at the importance I and my Irish friend had unwittingly assumed. In each of these great houses I always made a point of asking for, and was given, two buckets of hot water for us to wash in. The hot water provided some ease for limbs stiff from a whole day's riding which I was not used to. The water was presented with a look of condescension which, even in my weary state, ruffled my spirit. No servant was allowed to converse with us during our nightly stops and we slept out of earshot of our captors. Our sleeping room each night was no prison cell, thank God, nor was it a guest-chamber which soon made me revise my thought about our having been summoned by the faerie monarch. We were generally locked down in a store room with few or tiny windows through which I could not have pushed my leg, let alone my body. We slept on the floor, on comfortable pallets, thankfully, constrained by light bands of magic that stung if we moved too near the door or the shafts of moonlight falling through the occasional window. Our food was stew or broth, a good supply of it and a little sharp to the taste as if flavoured with strong herbs. Calvagh claimed to recognise a fowl of some kind in each of the dishes served up to us. The way our captors treated the zany creatures who leant on the gate made me wonder whether they were considered so 'not us' that they ended up in the pot as the stews and broths we badly needed at the end of each day. Hunger and my determination to remain strong compelled me to put aside the notion that I might be drinking a gravy made from the boiled remains of a pixie-hog or its brethren.

We arrived at the bank of the river dividing the outer from the second circle of land in the early afternoon of the fourth day. The flood was wide and fast flowing. Not even the strongest horses could have swum across it. If I had expected all the rivers in Hy Brazil to flow clear and sparkling, then this great stream showed me my error. It had brought down brown and red silts from the mountains where its head-waters were. The colour shifted from muddy to ruddy in an instant. Branches swirled in it and from time to time a long sleek back or a pair of eyes protruded a foot above the surface.

There must be bridges across, I thought. *Or perhaps the waters divide promptly at five in the afternoon.*

'A sail,' said Calvagh at last.

'No, to be sure, it is a cloud,' I replied.

'If you fall into these waters, do not expect us to save you,' one of the archers informed us. 'The river folk will draw you under before I can cock an arrow. They enjoy the drowning and then the feasting after. You would reappear gasping for air an arrow's length away and soon they would draw you under again to continue their play. I have seen it.'

'My friend Edward is a great swimmer. He carried me for miles,' said Calvagh proudly.

My name spoken for a third time in their hearing and he had not noticed what he did. I had yet to make this mistake with his name.

The Elven archer ignored him.

As the boat drew near us, I saw that what we had deemed a sail was no more than a banner, the small white plant on a green field set in the midst of a linen square fringed with more green. The boat lacked oars or even a complement of sailors. A single figure stood in the prow, sternly regarding our captors as the boat nudged the bank. I realised how deep the water must be if he could draw in so close. And how dangerous it would be to slip.

The fabric of the boat had that deep, burnished quality they always bring out in their woodwork. It seemed to be more a thing of pleasure than a thing of use. The prow and stern were shaped into a point and there was a shallow railing around the whole vessel raised perhaps a yard above the deck. A small cabin sat at the rear and a chair was placed for the boatmaster in the sharp angle of the prow. It was not a boat for cargoes, more a gesture of display. I was quite happy to travel on it, although I wondered whether I was expected to leap aboard and take my chance against falling amongst the deadly water sprites. My fears subsided when the boatmaster tapped the railing and a gangplank neatly unrolled itself and dug firmly into the turf of the bank.

'Just ride on,' I was told. 'The horses have done this often enough.'

They proved as intelligent and obedient as he had said. Our beast strolled aboard without a care and was content to stand with a nosebag in the middle of the deck for the whole of the voyage. Only the senior archer followed us onto the boat; the remaining two rode away, no doubt looking for other Humankind to bring into servitude.

Calvagh and I were directed towards the cabin as if we were miscreant schoolboys being sent to our beds. At first, the door was left open and we could see how the boatmaster set about directing his vessel home. He took a pair of the green stones from a fold in his breeches and held them to his mouth. Having whispered some incantation, he tossed them overboard. There was a hiss and a flash of light as if something important had happened. The boat then turned about in order to retrace its journey of earlier that day.

'The green stones,' Calvagh whispered.

'I truly believe we should not admit to knowledge of the green stones. I have no wish to re-tell the story of how I stabbed the owner of that other pair. The secret of their power may help us to return home one day.'

As we stood there plotting, the soldier turned towards us and flicked his fingers. At once, the cabin door slammed shut. Naturally, there was not a chink in the cabin's woodwork through which we might peer. A thing of Elven fashioning would never have a cranny or blemish, but it did have a pale illumination which began as soon as the door closed.

'I trust we are imprisoned again,' I said. The firmly shut door proved me correct. 'There are, at least, chairs and some kind of,' I nibbled a corner, 'sweetmeat. Let us partake, you and I.'

As we sat on cushioned seats eating with some enjoyment, we had no knowledge at all of where the boat was heading.

'Do you think they mean to bury us at sea?'

'If they planned our deaths it would be simpler to toss us into the river and give the water creatures a meal. I believe we have become of some importance to them and I desperately wish I knew what it was.'

Curiosity certainly now outweighed any fear of immediate execution I might have had. And I gave no thought to the shimmer which troubled me so much when we stepped ashore

Since that voyage, I have become quite conversant with the geography of Hy Brazil and so I should explain that we were travelling to join a great central waterway which runs from the island with the capital city out to the open ocean. As it does this, it cuts across the two rivers which flow between the island and the inner circle of land and between the inner circle and the outer. Our captors had no wish for us to be descried and puzzled about by witnesses on other boats or on the riverbanks. We were contraband, forbidden fruit, as we talked and munched on the sweetmeats until our palates were cloyed with them. I had once heard a story, and Calvagh too, as it transpired, of a girl who feasted on succulent faerie delicacies and entirely lost the taste for human food. She wasted away into death. I had eaten many a mouthful by the time this popped into my mind and by then it was far too late to be retrieved. Having eaten our fill, we dozed and, as we drifted into an easy sleep, the light dimmed and we were presumably left in total darkness.

CHAPTER NINE

If the prow of our boat bumped against its jetty, we did not notice. We were only awoken when we felt urgent hands shake us. It was night and we were given great, dark cloaks in which to wrap ourselves. The night was not at all cold, so I could only guess that we were once again to hide ourselves from general view. We hurried up a ladder and onto a spacious quayside. Two Elven in dark green quilted cote-armures with the white sprig at their breasts seized us and led us on the next part of our journey. Let no-one think that their warriors are flimsy creatures, light as a dandelion clock. They are generally an inch or two taller than your average citizen of London or Cork and, when they push you in a direction, you move that way. They would not let us talk to each other or utter words of any kind, I suppose because to hear good English spoken would arouse interest in us. To judge from the number of Humankind who worked in the fields of the Outer Circle, I was almost surprised not to see a crowd of Thames watermen surround our craft seeking a fare. I tried my best to see where we were and where we were going, as did Calvagh. If we slowed down too long to stare, a blow to the back of our heads made us gain speed again. The air was full of unfriendliness and I wondered if the death I had inflicted was now to be visited upon me. It fleetingly occurred to me that I could spoil their plans by throwing off the cloak and screaming, but that would certainly have led to an instant stab wound and there was also Calvagh to consider. He had to be party to such a plan; I could not on a whim of my own snuff out his life. And so I allowed myself to be bundled along.

As far as I could tell, and later we compared details of what we had seen, the port area was large and built of a cream-coloured stone which was probably marble to judge from the veins I could see in it. There were none of the smells and the indescribable deposits in which one dared not tread that I knew from my walks by London's river. Ordure and detritus were banished even from the most everyday of Elven activities. I admired them for this and wondered what a soiled ragamuffin they found me with my stained shirt and doublet discoloured with a week's smears. I remembered a tavern acquaintance, an untidy Frenchman, who once described an amusing visit he made to a cousin locked up in a convent somewhere outside Paris. My sudden picture of all the Elvenkind as a gaggle of spotless nuns brought a chuckle which surprised my guard.

There were tall buildings with double doors high up, warehouses no doubt, and other, much larger, boats which suggested trade. Were there unseen faerie realms in other regions of the world shipping pepper and lemons to these Elven in the same way as merchants in the Spice Islands and Muscat sent their wares up the Thames? Clearly there was orderly commercial business going on as groups of Elven men stood about in earnest discussion or walked purposefully on errands. Day and night, the port was a-bustle we learnt. I heard music and laughter of a subdued kind and I smelt hot food.

'Pasties,' said Calvagh and was smacked for the word.

I had a very strong sense of being in an important city. We entered thoroughfares, they were much grander than mere streets, surfaced with slabs of good stone. There were no runnels full of the inhabitants' cess being picked at by rats; it might have been the vestibule of a mansion rather than a public place where all and sundry were free to wander. The buildings were still of the cream-coloured marble. The materials and the work were of the highest quality as was revealed by the light of the glowing stones set both in the walls and in the ground. I could not help but feel that we drew more attention to ourselves by the mystery of our dark cloaks when the night-time streets were so full of light. If we had simply gone about our trade confidently and with none of the darting from shadow to shadow, not a head would have turned. A few did turn which led to a sharp word or yet another punch in the back. The glowing stones intrigued me amidst all the blows. I could smell no burning, certainly no stink of pitch, so it could not be flames producing the light. As ever, I took magic to be the explanation. When in doubt, assume a conjuring trick; that seemed to be the order of things in this all-too-different world. It was like walking about London on an overcast day and any footpad, if such existed here, would have been very hard pressed to find a corner from which he might fall upon the unwary. I felt safe despite the buffets.

We were beaten and hauled in this rough way along many thoroughfares, through a whole quarter of the city, I imagined, until eventually we reached a doorway in a very high wall in a street narrower and darker than most. 'Some great lord's secret rear entrance,' I mumbled – a tavern jest, but I could not help it.

'Very soon we shall be up to no good,' I said more audibly to Calvagh as we waited for the door to open.

'Get in!'

There followed more manhandling until we stood in an upper room of a great town-house. I felt a like a spy and was half-thrilled at the idea until I recollected that I might be told to divulge secrets of the two cities in which I had lived. Who knew to what use an unfriendly mind might put such information?

It was a small room and impeccably finished. There was the panelling with its inches-deep shine and we stood at the edge of a tapestry laid upon a tiled floor. The tiles were for servants or Humankind, whereas the feet that walked upon the tapestry were of a superior order. I counted a dozen soldiers, three each to Calvagh and myself to stop us running wild, and six ranged behind the exceptionally tall figure seated at a table that was almost the width of the room. There was nothing on the table; it was simply vast and splendid and I determined not to be intimidated by a construction of wood if that was what was intended. Did they believe we came from a world quite without furniture and that we were all shrivelled nobodies who were overcome with awe at the littlest thing? Conversation went on around us in the Elven tongue for some minutes before a soul looked with any interest in our direction. There were halberds crossed in front of us and invisible bands restraining our arms behind us, so we could not have harmed a fly. I imagined the conversation related to our history and the uses to which we might be put. I was expecting the tall figure to start if he were told about the murder I had committed, but I saw no such reaction. This did not mean he had not been told and I never knew exactly who was party to this particular piece of information. I strained to follow what was said to see if the occasional word became clear. If I had just a handful of words, I felt I could begin to see the shape of their language. Its musical quality was such a hindrance because I found myself listening to a tune and not to sounds which I could later try to imitate.

'I am the Lord Húon 'l Dainn. I tell you my name because you are now my men.'

'Do you mean we are to be paid?' I asked.

'You belong to me. You are my slaves in fact.'

'Stick your slavery up your arse!' Calvagh shouted immediately. He followed this with some oaths in Irish.

Lord Húon blinked. 'That is the last time you will speak to me in that way. With no effort at all I could tear out your tongue.'

When Calvagh attempted to explain what he felt about such a notion, magic gagged him. My lips had, as yet, no muzzle and I spoke quickly to make my feelings clear before I was silenced too. 'My Lord Húon, you have powers that I do not. But know that I have jerked good English steel through the dark heart of one of your kind already and I am prepared to do so again.' Could I never keep a secret? 'If you wish us to be part of some strategy you plan, you would be unwise to treat us as slaves or offer to maim us.'

My Lord Ding Dong Bell did not reply. He waved his hand and I froze, expecting to be struck down where I stood, but it was a command for us to be removed from his sight. How tired I was growing of being herded like a heifer in a pen. Another night was spent in a locked room, although now we had graduated to beds and our food was placed on a table. What was even better was that we had a separate privy with a door we could close. The arrangements in the privy were a source of consternation to us at first.

'I wish to empty my bowels and I do not know where to do it,' said Calvagh. 'Help me quickly, Edward, before I disgrace myself.'

I accompanied him into the room and looked urgently about me. There was a large basin attached to the wall and a capacious earthenware jug sat on the floor with a wooden ring on it. 'That is surely a chamber pot,' I said pointing. 'Sit upon that and do your business. No, wait until I have left the chamber!' He was already untying the thong that held up his breeches and I had only half closed the door when the first explosions started.

When he re-appeared, his face was a picture of delight. 'There was a basket of the softest leaves for me to wipe myself,' he said. 'And when I turned the white stone, a stream flowed in and took it all away. Why have you English never thought of such a thing? I am so glad I did not take my ease in the basin for I have discovered that it is for washing. The taps on the wall deliver hot and cold water into the basin and when you are refreshed you dry yourself on the softest cloths possible. There is perfume in the water too. Lilies.'

His bathing of himself explained why he had reappeared quite naked. My immediate fear was that he had explosively soiled every item of clothing he possessed and that we were both in for a distasteful time.

'You are glowing,' I said. 'We must never ask to splash about in buckets again. It is surely what their real slaves do.'

'I think there are barrels of water hidden in the walls and a servant fills them up every day. We are significant people and we are expected to keep ourselves clean.'

'He called us slaves,' I said.

'Clean slaves.'

I then went into the privy myself and used all its taps and waters. Afterwards, I chose not to disport myself naked and tied one of the drying cloths around my waist like a petticoat.

'Secret English parts,' said Calvagh knowingly and made me laugh.

'How I should love to sleep in a room with a window,' I said as I lay on my bed and enjoyed my new clean state. 'Who are they to treat us as criminals?'

'We Irish are ever used to it,' said Calvagh looking at me shyly to see how I took the jibe.

'You are no criminal,' I told him and we moved on to another topic.

I was the first to examine our fare. 'There are currants and other dried fruit, some meat that smells spiced, white bread, hard and soft cheeses and ale. This could be a fine inn if it weren't for the locked door.'

We ate our fill and then sat on our beds facing each other to think of a course of action.

'In a room with a window, I would scarcely notice the window at all,' I said. 'Now that I have no window, I feel its loss very deeply, as much as the loss of my boot.'

'You feel things very deeply, Edward. And one day I fear it may be the ruin of you.'

'I endanger your life too by my outbursts. I cannot bear to be dismissed in that insolent Elven manner.'

'You should be an Irishman for a day.'

'You have played that tune before, my friend. It jangles.'

I knew there was some justice in what he said, but I could not see that our wrangling about the state of Ireland would help our present situation. I shook his hand and said, 'When we are not confined to a room without windows, I promise to listen to all you have to say on that subject.'

To cover an awkwardness which now fell over us, we searched for the source of illumination in our chamber and found none.

'Magic light be gone,' said Calvagh and we were instantly in darkness.

'Morning light be here,' I said and the room was brightly lit again.

The door now opened and a hand appeared. It threw in two sets of clothing and was gone with no more than a, 'Be ready in the morning.'

'I presume there was a body attached to the hand and that the voice issued from a mouth,' I said jestingly. We amused ourselves by imagining the servants within the house being simply parts of bodies, hands to make the beds, floating lips to reprimand the chambermaids and feet to kick the dogs which misbehaved. I went over to investigate the new apparel which lay by the door where it had fallen. My doublet was stained and had begun to give me an itch and my breeches would have been refused by any self-respecting below stairs servant. Yet they were *my* clothes and I had a sudden feeling that if I wore these new attires I should lose a part of myself and truly belong to another man. And not even a man, at that. Calvagh harboured no such feelings. He was used to cast-offs and to having the breeze howling through many a hole in whatever clothingin which he had contrived to wrap himself. Here was a present from Heaven as far as he was concerned. The two sets of identical clothing comprised a soft grey shirt and brown jacket, woollen breeches of hazel colour, stockings, undergarments even, and soft shoes. They were a craftsman's best work and Calvagh fondled and sniffed them with great delight. He lost no time in donning his new outfit which suited him well. This prompted me to set aside my petticoat and to join him. I looked long and hard at the shoes. They were sturdy despite the softness of the upper leather. A man who wore them along the Strand need not feel any shame but I decided I could make a better escape, when the chance came, in a pair of boots. So it was Dónal's boots I put on to complete my outfit. Calvagh had never dreamed of possessing such footwear as his new shoes and he slung his old pair into a far corner. I folded my doublet sadly and laid it beside the bed. If only I could think of a way of keeping it with me for those times when I wished to remember that I was Edward Harry, late out of England, and amanuensis to the excellent poet and Secretary to the Council of Munster Master Edmund Spenser.

In the morning, or what I supposed was the morning, we were awoken by a hand pushing a tray of food just inside the door. A voice instructed us to, 'Be ready soon.'

As our new clothes were of a decent kind, I imagined that we would not be sent out to dig and haul. Calvagh's opinion was that we were meant for sailors, a prospect that carried with it the chance of jumping ship. How different was the reality, and a pleasure indeed.

We were 'ready soon' as bidden and sat on our beds waiting to be summoned. A captain of the guard, another longshanks of a fellow in the quilted green and white and with his top-knotted helmet, threw open our door and tossed us each a small leathern bag that jingled. We just had time to open our bags and inspect the contents as the soldier stood to one side of the door and directed us out. We both had twenty coins the size of a groat and minted with extraordinary fineness from a metal I had never seen. It was a deep gold tinctured with red, a swirling alloy that pleased the eye.

'Faerie gold,' said Calvagh. 'Will it turn to ashes?'

'They have taken great pains with the minting,' I said, 'which I would not expect if it is doomed to scatter as dust. The design is not the same on every coin. I have a bird, a ship and a tree.'

'And I have a queen with a crown.'

We conducted our discussion as we were jostled along three corridors and down a number of flights of stairs. The coins were such things of beauty, I played with several in my hand rather than replace them in the purse. They were not at all worn and there was no trace of the clipped edges that scoundrels are used to inflict on Her Majesty Queen Elizabeth's good money. 'Faerie gold,' Calvagh had said, but I hardly believed that when we passed into the bright light of day I should be left with a handful of something utterly valueless. One point I did make, as much for the soldier's benefit as for Calvagh's, was that my Lord Húon appeared to have had a tremendous change of heart. Last night we were slaves whom nobody was meant to see. This morning we were his well-dressed guests with greater surprises to come.

We passed through the back door of the mansion again and found five robust Elven awaiting us. I could sense an unease amongst our escort as if nothing of this kind had happened before. They were to accompany us to market where we were free to make what purchases we chose. I was stunned into silence by this news, but Calvagh slapped his leg and cried out, 'Indeed I will.' This was, it would seem, a sign of goodwill, yet Lord Húon's retainers knew how badly things would go for them if we absconded. As we had no weapon and no idea of the geography of the city, there was slight chance of that. They whispered together and their eyes darted everywhere.

'You are honoured,' the senior amongst them told us.

'We are dishonoured by being kept prisoner,' I replied. 'Let your master be told that.' I flattered myself that my audacious words of the previous night were partly responsible for this new more mannerly treatment.

'What is the metal?' Calvagh enquired. 'I have never seen any other like it.'

'Methinks you have seen very few coins of any kind in your miserable life,' said one of the Eleven whom I instantly detested. Another added, 'It is orchalc. Neither gold nor silver, and better than both. The coins minted by our Lord Húon 'l Dainn are held to be the finest.'

'And you have twenty of them each,' added another in a tone of unmistakable bitterness.

Revived by this evidence of jealousy, Calvagh shook his purse of coins vigorously. 'What will this buy me?'

'Too much.'

'Can we buy refreshment for all of us?' asked Calvagh, ever the diplomat.

'You can.'

'Then you must lead us to the best Ordinary or place of entertainment,' I added. 'We shall both contribute to your food and drink.'

'We have been told to carry your purchases,' said a fourth voice, again with its undertone of resentment. It was to be a shopping expedition as if my Lord's two daughters, Calvania and Edwardia, were to pick out ribbons and buckles and then have them brought home by a minion of no account. Inwardly I jeered and looked forward to my day as much as I had when I stepped out for the first time in London town.

Who can adequately tell the wonders of that morning? Directed by our entourage, we passed very quickly into the widest throroughfares which were thronged with the Elvenkind. Almost at once, I noticed the division of 'people' into three kinds. There were the tall, superior ones, the My Lords and Ladies. Dressed in gorgeous robes, they swept along the streets confident that the entire world bowed before them. With a flick of a loose sleeve, they commanded their servants to attend on them or creatures who presumed to obstruct their path to move aside. I had never seen such colours, such cherry and apple dyes. The lightness of the fabric meant that their garments lingered in the air behind them like a memory of their passing. Their hair was long and elaborately dressed in both men and women, but, again, their eyes. The expressions on every face contained no softness, only that icy 'I look down from my tower upon you all' sneer. It was an expression that needed its lips bloodied as far as I was concerned. Their eyes were violet or green or grey and blazed with the sharpness of gems. As their arms swept high in their arrogance, I noticed fingers that were soft and white and furnished with nails an inch long. Again, this was true of both men and women, none of whom had ever adjusted a sleeve or turned the page of a book for themselves. In its sheer self-importance, it was as near as I ever expected to be to the court of the Sophy or some other Eastern potentate of near infinite power. I wondered, also, whether the presence of so many figures capable of wielding so much magical power if they chose would fill my head with that distracting shimmer but this was not the case. Perhaps my crossness had shut the door on its influence for ever.

As these Elven aristocrats strutted through their day, it was what followed in their wake that distressed me. Their servants were sometimes ordinary examples of their own kind, sometimes grotesques, but all too often, they were of *my* kind. Frequently, they were pulled by an orchalc chain, a filigree, glinting thread that offered no real control simply an assertion of absolute power. I had no need to point out to Calvagh the ignominy of men, women and pretty children in such shameful attendance like dogs on a leash. As we were directed through the crowds, I tried sundry times to catch the eye of my fellow Humankind enslaved in this way, to tell them the outrage I felt on their behalf. Their eyes never deviated once from the back of each gorgeous butterfly they followed, as if to show any lack of devotion was to bring a severe punishment, which it probably did. The human attendants were comfortably, if dowdily, dressed so as not to detract from the splendour of their master or mistress. I at once noted that their fawns and greys and browns were the same muted shades in which Calvagh and I were dressed. I vowed then and there that, if any attempt were made to slip an orchalc chain around *my* neck, I would strangle the perpetrator with it or die in the attempt. And if they tried such a trick on Calvagh too, I knew they would dearly buy it. My mood blew from wonder to rage and back again many times as we made our progress. Just as I was wishing to make an Elven lordling swallow his chain link by slow link, so I suddenly found myself gasping at the novelty of the third kind of creature we encountered, both enchained and free. These were what you might call the true faeries of our childhood tales. None was similar to another, as if they chose their own shapes, and none was such as you would smile to meet on a lonely midnight. There were stunted goblins with faces as ancient and ridged as the hills. If enslaved, they skipped and capered behind their owners, lunging and snapping at any other captive creatures they happened to pass. I was reminded of dogs and their bad-tempered skirmishes with each other. There were flying creatures, manikins held aloft by moths' wings, bristling, bouncing oddities that defied all description and even, as Calvagh pointed out with a smile, a pair of leprechauns who did not trot at the end of a chain but were free to attend to their own concerns. He managed to exchange a few words with them in the Irish tongue. This made one chuckle and the other shake his fist, so I wondered what he had said to them – '*Your* outfit is a prettier green than *his*,' perhaps.

And so we came to market, and what a market it turned out to be. Now, a London market will be all bustle and argument and, above all, it will smell. Who has not sniffed warily and gagged at much of what is offered for sale on the stalls of Leadenhall or Gracechurch Street? This goblin market, for many of the stallholders seemed to be of that misbegotten race, exploded with every exotic tang your nose could ever want. It was a market for the ordinary folk as I hardly spotted three of those more refined Elvenkind. Their flowing dress would have snagged and tattered in the press that went on between the rows of stalls. It was also market day for the robust, for the powerful shoulder and the strenuous spirit. Haggling and quarrelling were all about our ears and, strangely, both Calvagh and I felt our spirits lift at the sound of it. And the smells. There was no shit or sweat, nothing putrid or unmentionable. There was only spice and perfume, sweet leather or pastry. As we walked amongst the lines of stalls, our guards were always beside us, but we were free to patronise whichever trader we wished. It soon became clear that a goblin stall beset by a gaggle of eldritch creatures was not for us. Once, we pushed to the front of such a crew and found a table-top strewn with the devilled corpses of shrews and assorted miniature rodents. The delight with which such vermin were bought and crunched made us beat the hastiest of retreats. We would have more joy at those stalls where both seller and purchaser were human. I managed to whisper to Calvagh that I thought we should separately purchase a dagger, although it would almost certainly not be made of steel. We decided to buy some personal pieces of frippery, a belt or a cheap ring, and then to seek a dagger almost as an afterthought or an accompaniment to our new belt. Our purses of coins turned out to be a most generous gift and we could, had we so wanted, have spent as much as Master Spenser paid me in a six month. Calvagh bought ribbons and brooches for his married sisters and that only took one of his orchalc pieces. Heaven knows when he expected to bestow the gifts. I was more practical and, for two orchalc pieces, bought a large, sturdy satchel as I felt such a bag would be useful if ever we were to run away. I put my own purchases into the satchel, but Calvagh preferred to taunt our attendants by asking them to carry his gewgaws.

'Your friend has bought a bag,' they said. 'Use that.' And so he did.

We felt we could not patronise a faerie market without spending money at a leprechaun's stall. Several of the little men stood behind stalls grouped together in a corner. They had very little we wished to purchase, footwear for feet less than half the size of our own comprising most of their stock, but there was a small pile of shiny stones on fine leather cords that we thought worthy of investigation.

'And what are those?' I asked.

'What they look like.'

'What do they look like?'

'Sure, the man doesn't have his eyes open!'

'The man has money, if you have a civil tongue,' I replied. I jangled the bag with its remaining coins which was foolish because it suggested I was master of wealth they could cheat from me.

'Does good luck come with these stones?' Cavagh asked.

'That it might.'

'With none of your tricks!'

'Who's to tell?'

I had listened to enough of his impertinence by now and I swept the hat from his head and tossed it onto the next stall.

'We offered good custom and good coin,' I told him sharply, not caring how much of an affront I had just offered. Our attendants laughed at the little man's discomfiture which made my action the more insulting to him. With what I took to be a slighting comment on the quality or design of the shoes on offer, the soldiers wandered on a little way.

In some annoyance, Calvagh said, 'Edward, you must not do these things.'

Why he needed to placate a tradesman who had trifled with us, I do not know. He retrieved the hat and gave it to the leprechaun who snatched it without a word of thanks. Calvagh then offered a whole orchalc piece for two of the 'lucky' stones and invited me to choose which I preferred.

'My friend is a man of some importance in London,' said Calvagh in a tone which I found toadying and would dearly have liked to tell him so. We had no need to bow to homunculi whose foreheads only reached our midriffs.

'That's for you to say and me not to believe,' said the little man biting the coin he had just been given. 'And when will he see London again? Some people I know could tell him.'

Our attendants at that moment had happened to step back to see why we lingered. They overheard these last words and, although Calvagh and I burned to know more, we were snatched away without our purchases which we had not yet chosen. Minutes later the leprechaun caught up with us and pressed a stone into each of our hands.

'I'm not a trickster,' he gasped. 'Goods for money.'

'Be gone,' said a soldier, and he was.

We still did not have a dagger of any metal and we were afraid that we were in danger of being taken straight back to Lord Húon's house.

'How much food and drink will we get for these?' Calvagh asked in his quick-thinking way. He tossed four coins into the air, bounced them off the back of his hand and neatly caught them again.

'Plenty,' said one of the soldiers.

'Plenty for all of us?'

'I expect so.'

'We should like to visit one more stall and then will you please show us where we can have good refreshment?' He had spotted the very stall and made towards it with our guards following obediently in his wake.

Two Humankind kept the stall and I cannot imagine that their sly looks made them welcome guests in the land of faerie. I knew I should be glad of this, because they were troublemakers born and bred, I am sure, but I did not like them. Our attendant soldiers fell to a discussion amongst themselves which kept them fully occupied. It involved pointing in several directions and led to a heated exchange of opinion which I presumed was regarding where we should go for our food and drink. This was a golden opportunity and we did not let it slip.

'We need a weapon each,' Calvagh told the two rogues as I felt confident in regarding them. He spoke in English and they replied with accents I would have placed somewhere to the East of London.

'Two sharp blades,' I said.

'These are all the best bronze, sir.' The chief rascal swept his hand across their wares. 'Dwarf-fashioned in the mountains. We have exclusive contracts with the finest craftsmen.'

'Do you have anything – finer, sharper?' I asked looking the stallholders directly in the eye. I am adept at holding any man's gaze and they were the first to turn away. They had read my thought and they regarded each other in the way that men do who are about to commit a felony.

'If sir would care to meet us later.'

'We have no time at all,' I said briskly.

'But we do have money,' Calvagh added.

'Gentlemen, I regret…'

'We have a great deal of money,' I said vigorously shaking the handful of coins I still possessed.

Faster than I could have expected, the huckster slid two small iron blades beneath his two most expensive bronze daggers. Before he was transported thither, he must have made his living by every kind of sleight of hand.

'We shall take those two large blades,' I said. 'The work seems most fine.'

'They command a high price, master,' said the rougher of the two men as our hands eagerly extended to pick up an iron and a bronze blade each.

'Four coins a pair,' said Calvagh at the same moment as I said, 'Five.'

'Seven a pair,' said the seller and seven he received. The money was in his hand and the blades were in my satchel within a winking. It was a small blow against our captors and yet it gave us great satisfaction. Despite my mis-liking for both the men who kept the stall, I was pleased to know that there was an undercurrent of rebellion that the great Elven lords had no knowledge or control of. I also wondered who had made the iron daggers. Were there blacksmiths here who could handle iron as well as any human or had they been brought to Hy Brazil by incomers like ourselves? We returned to the group of soldiers with the confidence that, if we so pleased, we could now cause them great harm.

'And now for the best food and drink,' Calvagh announced at once. I could not have managed his tone of good fellowship and I was glad of his skill. 'We must ask your advice,' he also said, which took me by surprise. What now?

'Show them our new bronze daggers, Edward.'

What madness was here? I stood stock-still and said and did nothing.

'Edward, the daggers.'

Seeing my reluctance and confusion, he needed to give them some words of explanation. 'We were sure *your* master,' (He did not say *our* master) 'would want us to have a blade to protect ourselves.'

'There are unsavoury men and other dangerous creatures here,' I said, beginning to sense my friend's plan.

'Will you kindly ask your master if we may keep the daggers? We could give them to you for safe keeping.'

All the Elven soldiers looked confused, partly, I believe, because they felt foolish at not spotting our purchase of the daggers in the first place. What would their master think of *them*? Awkwardly, one amongst them took it upon himself to accept responsibility for the daggers which he slipped into his belt.

'We shall understand if your Lord feels we should not have spent his kind gift of money in this way.'

I doffed my cap to the politician Calvagh had turned out to be. Whilst our attendants regarded the bronze daggers as if they dripped poison, the two iron blades which were certain death to their kind nestled in my satchel alongside all our more innocent purchases.

'What of our food?' I asked, anxious to turn everyone's thoughts in a new direction. The Elven group brightened and said they had decided where Calvagh and I might buy them the best refreshment in the city. They led us through the line of goblin stalls and past those selling fruits and vegetables. We had not previously walked in this part of the market. It was interesting to see that amongst the usual seasonal produce, more succulent and brighter in hue than we were used to, there were stalls displaying some of the oddest harvesting I could have imagined. Who would buy and eat a pound of dandelion polls or yew berries? We shared our surprise at these 'foods', if foods they were.

'Mountain dwellers,' said one of our soldiers. 'Vermin. Those are bees' wings and that stall has cakes made from bird droppings.' Our faces must have been a picture and he roared with laughter. 'I would no more eat bird shit than you,' he said. 'We are going to my favourite inn. Hoppity creatures are not allowed there and your kind must have an Elven escort.'

He did not sense, or care, that he had insulted us and that my face had darkened. We left the market and walked past a number of shops, still selling food of usual and unusual kinds, until we came to a street of many inns, or what passes in Hy Brazil for an inn. There was even an inn sign with a picture of a cobweb hanging over the door of the chosen building. The writing above it, their script is lovely, I presumed declared the name of the inn in the Elven tongue. I asked if this were the case and if it spelled out the word 'cobweb'. 'Trap,' and 'Snare,' answered two of them at once. This was an ill-omened word with which to enter a building in a strange land, but enter we did. Just inside the porch was another sign chalked elegantly on a board leaning against the wall.

Abandon hope all ye who enter here, I suggested.

'If you must know,' said one of the soldiers who was proving more talkative than the rest, 'It says, *No admittance to any creature shorter than waist height, particularly goblins, and all humans must be accompanied by a responsible Elf.*'

'I fart at it,' was all I could think of to say.

The main inn room was large and furnished with high-backed, comfortable chairs arranged around capacious tables. I was still smarting from the offence of the notice by the door when another worry assailed me. Did they expect us to stand like servants while they sat in comfort to feast themselves at our expense? The announcement might have said, 'All humans must be tethered on their Master's leash,' for all the joviality I now felt. If anyone crossed me in the next hour, I was sure I should reach for my iron blade and set about the whole room. As our guards drifted to the largest empty table, I quickly seated myself to make the point that I would be lackey to none of them. Whoever told me to, 'Get up!' would find that they were his last words. Fortunately for us all, the soldiers appeared unconcerned with what I had done and sat down themselves before calling for a serving man.

Calvagh took out four orchalc pieces and placed them on the table in front of him. 'Boys, we are in your hands,' he said.

A bill of fare was placed before us and discussions followed as to the choice of victual and drink.

'I would rather not have bees' wings,' I announced in an attempt to dispel my sour humour.

'Meat and beer for me,' said Calvagh, 'and plenty of both if you don't mind.'

So a helping of spicy stew and a glass of golden ale it was for each of us. I tried not to show that I had never eaten off such a fine plate before and, as for that odd food-spearer, a fork, could they not see that I used one nearly every day? The glassware had cobweb patterns contained within it and hardly made a barrier between your lips and the drink. I was worried that Calvagh, as he launched himself at his meal, would bite a section out of his spoon or glass but neither of us disgraced himself. One of the soldiers even slapped us both on the back in an obviously friendly gesture. We grinned in reply. Our landlord was an Elven creature of a coarser cut than our companions and his serving men and maids were mostly handsomer examples of the goblin sort, or possibly dwarves. They could be servants but not patrons, clearly. Two of the serving men were indeed men and I tried not to stare at these, wondering how they managed in such a situation. My question at heart was, 'Are they *owned* and are they *English*?' I had no chance to throw a single word at them in my mother tongue, perhaps by the design of the innkeeper. There was also entertainment taking place in a corner of the room for all who cared to listen. An eldritch piper, an almost human or almost Elven figure dressed in tatters, played melancholy and jolly airs alternately. When he was jolly, a female imp pranced about like a zany and, when he was melancholy, a human youth of our own age sang songs in Irish each time. Calvagh tried to hide his tears by leaning over his food and giving all his attention to his stew.

'He is singing of leaving his sweetheart with her bonny cheeks and her wild black hair,' Calvagh told me and, before I or our attendants could stop him, he had made his way over to the singer and dropped two coins into the hat on the floor. The piper stopped his playing, although the youth continued to sing, and would have seized the coins if Calvagh had not clenched his fist and made clear that this would be a foolish course of action. No doubt he took the money as soon as we had left.

When Calvagh returned to his chair, he was in a pensive mood that I could not lighten. I tapped his shoulder and poured him more ale from the jug. Our soldiers were simply relieved that he had returned to us and not darted through the doorway in search of freedom. Two had jumped to their feet and watched his actions closely. Calvagh set about his meal again and eventually said, 'I do not like to see a man become a performing monkey for that creature with the pipe. He does not even play well.'

When the meal was done, the host offered us all a dish of smoking weed and a contrivance to smoke it in, but our leader said it was time for us to return to the Lord Húon's house. We were not averse to this as the youth's voice was growing ragged and his tunes more melancholy still.

As we walked back to our place of confinement, Calvagh wondered where such numbers of Humankind as we had seen could have come from. 'Many must be thought drowned,' he surmised.

'Perhaps they are dead,' I said. 'Perhaps *we* are corpses too. In which case, all thoughts of returning home to Cork or London are without purpose. Imagine the faces of those who know us if they believe us sleeping in our graves and we reappear upon their doorstep. Could this be Hell, therefore? It is certainly not what I expected Heaven to be.'

Our return was by another route and was intended to take in the greatest sights of the city. It was the soldiers' response to their free meal. We saw a large square with fountains and many more of the splendid citizens of the place. By accident, we happened to obstruct the path of an Elven lord and lady and what a to-do there was. It was beyond their custom to step aside for our greater number and they pointed to Calvagh and myself in horror and made belittling sounds that we perfectly understood. At the mention of Lord Húon's name, their demeanour changed. With the most perfunctory of bows, to our attendants not to us, they moved off in another direction as if they had never intended to occupy the same space as ourselves. I was sorely tempted to shout some village rudery after them.

We saw gardens, statues, and one side of the great wall which surrounded the royal palace. When there appeared a squadron of heavily armed guardsmen in tunics of deep blue quilting and with breastplates of dazzling silver, we were swept away. We were a secret and yet not a secret, and, once again, my mind turned to the plans Lord Húon had made for us. I wondered whether they would be plans that appealed. I doubted it. I needed to convey to Calvagh that I thought we should not discuss, or even name, the iron weapons I now carried. Who knew what ears listened to our talk in our bedchamber, or cell, rather?

'Our purchases should remain in my satchel,' I said.

'But, Edward, I wish to take out my belt and wear it. I have never had such a belt.'

'I mean our special purchases.' I laid emphasis on the word 'special' and was glad to see recognition in his eyes.

'They are not to be named,' I said hurriedly. 'Walls have ears.'

He nodded.

'But we may speak about the ribbons and lucky stones as much as we choose.' And this is what we did. Any spy with his ear to a chink in our wall would have wondered at our girlish chatter and our squeals as we feigned so much delight at what the bags of coins had gained us. Lord Húon's brainless daughter could never have fussed so over ribbons and brooches as we did seated on our beds, the tears of laughter splashing off us as we thought how clever we were being.

Calvagh slept that night with the ribbons on his pillow, I noticed. That he missed his sisters I was not surprised. I missed Master Spenser's two children, although I did not expect to be missed in turn. I had a pretty belt for the boy Sylvanus and red ribbons for the young maid Katherine in case I met them again and they were still children. If time could move at a strange pace between the faerie world and ours, they could be long dead by the time we managed to return. I slept with the satchel beside me, although I knew no Elven hand could directly withdraw the iron daggers if they were discovered. We inspected the walls and doors before we slept, but who knew what spying could be done by magic?

'I do so love it here,' were my last bitter words before I turned to sleep. Let whoever cared to listen make of that sentence what he could and conjecture my true sentiments and the plans I had in store.

Calvagh sang a few phrases of an air we had heard in the inn, but it broke his heart and so he pulled the coverlet over his head and in turn looked for sleep.

Morning brought us ham and bread on green plates shaped like leaves and the return of our bronze daggers. When we were dressed and the tangles in our hair removed by a vigorous application of the large bronze comb which had been left in our bathing room, we were to be taken before Lord Húon again.

'To see if he has softened our displeasure, no doubt,' I said.

'Does he want us to be his monkeys?' asked Calvagh. 'For his own sake, I hope not.'

We took our time in consuming our meal, dressing ourselves and making our toilet and it was heartening to have a servant open the door twice before we were ready for our audience.

Lord Húon received us in a different chamber. The room was larger, but he was still enthroned and we were once again made to stand on the exposed floor beyond the limit of the thick tapestry. We shuffled as near to the tapestry's edge as we could and then looked at my Lord's servants in our sauciest manner as if to say, 'And you will do what?'

Lord Húon himself lounged on his great chair, his arms and legs disposed at angles to show the ease I am sure he did not feel. I had as yet no craft in reading the nuances of these Elven faces, yet I could have sworn we tested his patience and the smile he gave us was achieved with much effort.

'You have your daggers returned.'

'Your lordship has been most gracious.' I made a bow which I knew I managed well. Calvagh attempted to copy me and did it poorly.

'If you had asked, I would have permitted you daggers.'

'We did not dare presume.'

Such a game this was, he feigning graciousness and we feigning gratitude, and, all the time, certainly, such ill-will swirling between us.

'Many of your kind fall into our land of *Hy Brazil* as you call it.'

'So I have noticed, sir.'

A finger sharply prodded me in my side to remind me I was not expected to interrupt my lord's narrative.

'Each finds his appropriate station, some to serve in the houses of the mighty, some as soldiers...' He waved his hand dismissively as if those who found their place in other more menial occupations were not worth the effort of naming.

And you would have them all your dancing monkeys, thought I. *But not us. Not us by any means.* I fixed my smile and waited for him to continue.

'You two are quite different. You are both young and strong. But it is more than that. You have spirit, some would say defiance, and you are resourceful. I offer you the chance to be of considerable use to me. To be very important, in fact.'

He stopped and silence fell. It was not clear to us whether he would soon pick up his thread again or whether we should express a suitable degree of appreciation for having been singled out in this way.

'I need your decision now,' he said.

I looked at Calvagh. If we refused this invitation, life could become most uncomfortable for us; if we agreed, we should be in Lord Húon's favour and our chance of returning home might be greater. We nodded to each other and then to Lord Húon.

'Good,' he said. 'It would have been such a waste to have you killed.'

So there was our alternative. We tried not to shiver as we were led to yet another chamber where a further interview was to be held in camera with none of the other servants present. I came to think of this as the conspiracy chamber for it was protected by powerful enchantments and the air in it shimmered unsettlingly. We were allowed to sit at a large round table and left to ourselves for a good quarter of an hour. I pressed my fingers to my lips as Calvagh opened his mouth to speak. I felt that we were embarking on a dangerous game and the less anyone knew of our innermost thoughts the better for us. Had we not narrowly escaped being murdered for telling my lord nay? The silence quickly became intolerable and we were not a pair easily given to silence, so some words at least were necessary. We passed empty comments on the grain of the table, the comfort of the chairs and how a certain firmness in a cushion was best suited to the backside. I did not add that I sensed the magic floating in the air, the shimmering and tingling that lifted the hairs on my arms. Calvagh's eyes darted here and there and I knew he experienced the same, but he also held his peace. When we were suitably cowed, as they believed, by being left alone, there entered Lord Húon and a younger man whom he introduced as his son, the Lord Ailill. We had jumped to our feet and were told by the most arrogant flick of the fingers that we might be seated again. Lord Ailill had a dark face, by which I mean that the character I was sure I read there was dark. His skin was as pale as his father's and his hair was golden. You would have called him beautiful if you did not sense the high degree of hardness there. Our eyes met and he was not at all pleased that I was able to stare down his high opinion of himself. I should have lowered my eyes in a show of humility, but, such was my inborn rebelliousness, I found it very hard to bend. Thus I made a dangerous enemy without a word being spoken, ninny that I was.

'My father, may I speak?' The young Elven lord needed to show me that the enterprise about to be unfolded to us was predominantly his. 'There are factions amongst the Elven lords,' he began. 'My father, the great Lord Húon 'l Dainn, is the leader of one such assembly.' He looked to his father to see how much he might be permitted to say.

'Tell them all you wish,' said Lord Húon. 'They are our men now and they understand the penalty for disloyalty.'

'There is certain to be conflict in the time ahead between certain factions who hold unacceptable beliefs and my father and his friends who hold correct beliefs. My place is to help him when the time requires it. You have noticed many of your kind in our city. People like my father have encouraged this. The Elven lord you killed was, we hope, one who worked against us and that is why you have not been punished. Humans are not permitted acts of defiance of any kind against the Elven.' I nodded sagely at this point. 'Over many centuries, it has become almost a game for the Elvenkind in our highest and lowest forms to visit your world and leave childish tales behind us. Now my father and myself, and others like us, believe it is time to engage in more formal contact.' My eyes widened. 'There are many who would die rather than have this happen. You have a Queen in England and so do we. What if, one day, they were able to exchange embassies? You yourself could not be an ambassador.' He laughed at the absurdity of the notion. 'But you could attend on one.' I bowed in acknowledgement of the mixture of flattery and insult. 'If we were to remove the magic that cloaks our land from human intrusion, we should stir up a civil war at once. Who would want that? Brother against brother, countless dead and so on. Our aim is to become the faction of power and so to avoid civil disorder. My father has done me the honour of entrusting management of his plans to me. You will swear allegiance to us both and then accompany me on a journey I am obliged to make. I shall not ask whether you have questions because you have no right to questions. The choice again is yours: swear allegiance or die.'

The oath when we took it was a deadly serious matter. Calvagh and I were required to kneel with our palms together as if in prayer. Father and son then placed their own hands around the outside of ours and spoke an incantation that caused our skin to burn, as I shall explain shortly. For two beings who claimed to seek greater truck with the world of men, both Lord Húon and Lord Ailill touched our flesh with a reluctance that bordered on disgust. I, in turn, felt the touch of their skin as something marmoreal yet with a faint pulse. My doubt that this might be the land of the dead came back to me.

To make the oath as binding as an oath can be, it was required that Calvagh and I repeat certain phrases in the Elven tongue. We had to speak them exactly. A mumbling inexactitude would not do and so some rehearsal was necessary before we were perfect and the oath could be solemnised. It came as a pleasant surprise to both of us that our lips were soon able to trill and coo the Elven words so well, a skill that was to prove invaluable later in our adventure. And we had been taught this by great Elven lords themselves. A delicious irony.

When we spoke our oaths, with the two pairs of Elven hands clasped around ours, there was a moment of intense pain on the back of our right hands. Calvagh tried to snatch his hand away and was restrained but I made sure I did not flinch. When the Elven hands were removed, I saw that a design had sealed itself to my skin, the small white flower that was the emblem of the House 'l Nainn.

Lord Húon was pleased with what had happened and I thought I saw a grain of admiration that I remained unmoved throughout the ceremony. He motioned for us to stand and said, 'You are now fiefmen of my House. That sign on your hand makes you equal with my own finest warriors. No human in my long lifetime has been elevated this far. You will discard these peasant clothes. No-one with my blazon on his hand can be seen dressed in that way. Go through that door and you will be given the livery of the House 'l Nainn. Remember that it is an honour to wear it and those who dishonour it never repeat the crime.'

Our new garments were far far finer than those we had been wearing for the past two days. These had been fine enough in comparison with Calvagh's ill-tailored homespun and my London woollens, but we now had quilted tunics of a delicate apple-green which offered a light yet effective body armour. The white flower was embroidered on each shoulder. Our shirts were of a grey cambric soft enough for the bodies of angels. Our breeches were dark green and loose and our hose pale grey. The short boots were so light and comfortable we were hardly aware that we were shod. Calvagh remarked that it was most certainly worth coming to this shadowland if we were to be dressed so well.

'Let us see if that is still your opinion in a week's time,' I said.

We were allowed to keep our daggers, but there was no longer any need to slip them behind our belts. We were given green scabbards to hold them and splendid they looked. Having tried on all the clothing for the fit, we were made to undress again. The quartermaster or steward, an unbranded Elf and therefore subordinate to us, I suppose, led us naked to a room where hot baths of scented water awaited us. We had progressed from buckets to basins to baths. What could await us next – an ascension into Heaven? Although it was my habit to keep my body scrupulously clean, I had experienced a bath-tub a mere twice before in my life. Calvagh, for his part, had only ever lain down in a stream when he was hot or muddy. As if we had invented this custom, however, we stepped into the baths and sat down. I must admit, the experience was not unpleasant although I always felt that I could wash every part of my body adequately from a pump or bucket. There was a fragrant foam on the surface of the bathwater that Calvagh blew into the air playfully. I washed myself obediently with the cloth I was given and even permitted an aromatic oil to be poured onto my hair.

'This is the ancient Roman style,' I remarked to Calvagh just before my bath servant surprised me by pushing my head beneath the water to rinse out the oil. He also wished to make himself busy about my person with the bath cloth but I would have none of it. Nor would I allow him to dry me with the warm cloths when I stepped out of the water. Calvagh submitted to this which I thought undignified of him. On one point we both stood firm. When mirrors and razors were brought out, we dismissed them at once. All the Elven we had seen were smooth of face as if no hair could grow there. Neither Calvagh nor I had shaved since we left Cork and the stubble-fields on our chins showed this. It was a small sign of our humanity that we had beards coming and we were determined to let them flourish. When the bath servant attempted to make us do otherwise, I raised my voice in a number of European tongues and waved my right hand in his face so that he should see the flower burnt there and be done with his remonstrations. We did submit to his combing as the water had brought back every tangle in our hair.

'Were there ever two more beautiful young men in the whole of England or Ireland?' Calvagh asked me.

I doubted it.

That evening, Lord Húon showed that he had no fear of spies amongst his own household or that he could deal with them before they reached anyone else with their tittle-tattle. We were invited to dine with him and his son. Servants were present to lay out the many dishes, sweet and savoury, on a side table and to serve us our selection on two brilliantly white plates. Lord Húon chose five dishes for his savoury plate and Calvagh and I made exactly the same choices. This appeared to bother the lord as if it suggested that we were all dining from the same plate. Then we four conspirators were left alone. I imagined the meal would be an ordeal for Calvagh because he could never have dined with anyone of significance and at such a lavish table. I had broken bread with Master Spenser and Sir Walter Raleigh, so I felt at my ease. One of the birds was a swan, as I observed to Calvagh by way of pointing out to the two lords that fine food was not a stranger to me. The fruit sauce in which the earthly remains of the bird swam was beyond Heaven. I needed to exercise great restraint in not consuming it in two or three mouthfuls. I recognised the pink slices of beef and the flatfish in its pool of butter and herbs. The beans and peas were also no strangers, but I gave away my uncertainty at the sight of the round, waxy objects which sat side by side on my plate. It was a vast savoury plate, you will have gathered.

'They are potatoes,' Lord Húon informed us.

'Of course. Sir Walter Raleigh has introduced them to us from the New World.'

'New to *you*.'

I found the potatoes very tasty and could have eaten more. Calvagh's wrinkled lip showed he was not of my mind. Our drink was wine which Calvagh and I merely sipped, the better to keep our heads clear.

During the eating of the meal, the conversation was slight and when the servants, two domestic Elven, returned to re-charge our plates and glasses, we were entirely silent. At the end of the meal, the real talk began. Lord Ailill led it.

'Tomorrow morning before sunrise we shall leave for my father's estate in the foothills of the western mountains. You have a special task which does not need to be revealed until we arrive there. You will travel with my personal bodyguard and you will not speak to any of the others who accompany us, Elven or Humankind.'

Most of what he had to say consisted of *You will not*s to which Calvagh gave every sign of listening eagerly. I did not.

'May I make so bold…,' I began. A fierce look from the son was meant to silence me, but the father gestured at me to continue. He at least made a show of regarding us as worthy of a moment of his time. I could not imagine Lord Ailill thinking of sending us to market with our purses full of coins.

'May I make so bold as to ask whether your lordships will require us to fight and perhaps kill our own kind?' I asked.

'You will do whatever…,' began Lord Ailill loudly.

'I think it most unlikely,' interrupted his father in his smoothest tone. 'But as my son, Lord Ailill, was about to remind you, you are *our* men now. Your preferences are of no account.'

Lord Húon was an odd mixture. He would flatten and flatter in equal measure whereas Lord Ailill was a flattener and nothing else.

The evening ended with another gesture on Lord Húon's part which he was not obliged to make. He led us to a rooftop terrace from which we were able to view most of his fair city beneath the light of a nearly full moon. A gentle breeze cooled us and it was, I freely admit, one of the pleasantest spots in which I have ever stood. Lord Húon was genuinely proud of his capital city and he pointed out its landmarks in a manner which was almost familiar. Perhaps he was preparing for the day when her Gracious Majesty Queen Elizabeth's ambassador should stand in that spot and bear witness to the glories of Faerie Land. Lord Ailill lounged against a parapet well clear of us. It was not part of his evening's entertainment to point out the Royal Palace or the Eternal Library to people he had recently branded. We could see distant on all sides of us the ring of lights which marked the edge of the island on which the city was built. Every object was defined by light: the great thoroughfares that intersected at right angles in a way never thought of in higgledy-piggledy London; the Library that rose in pillared tiers in the blaze of the moon. But that was a lesser glory in comparison with the Royal Palace. Every part of the Palace soared in a way that astonished and excited me. Where was Nonsuch Palace now, a stunted barn in comparison. We build in fine brick, but the Faerie Queen's Palace was built seemingly of a stone whose colour you could not truthfully determine. In the moonlight it shifted between pearl and golden, so I thought perhaps their buildings had the power to change colour according to their owner's mood. Should I therefore look for somewhere dark in which Lord Ailill was used to scowl to his heart's content?

I asked whether the Queen were in residence and hinted that I had some knowledge of Whitehall and Greenwich and the activities of Her Majesty Queen Elizabeth's court there. But I had overstepped etiquette as was immediately made clear to me. I could be told whatever Lord Húon wished to tell me, but on no account was I to ask for detail. He could not suppose that I intended to make mischief with such information by assassinating his Queen! So I was left to gaze at the palace and share my thoughts with Calvagh alone. It was such a confection of towers scattered with a randomness of design I found hugely appealing. It was a true none-such, a nonpareil, blossoming like a moon-kissed alabaster flower from the darkness of the vast pleasure garden and woodland which surrounded it. Within less than half an hour, our company had proved irksome and servants were summoned to escort us to our cell. We had much to discuss, although we skipped on tiptoe around our true thoughts and intentions.

My satchel had lain beside my pillow all the time we were at dinner and, without conveying any sense of urgency, I looked inside.

'I have your TWO RIBBONS, if you remember,' I said to Calvagh.

'I made a point of giving them to you for safe keeping,' he replied with an ease which would have deceived anyone. Lord Húon's human servants could help themselves to our daggers whenever they pleased and we were not to know whether they had been discovered and left there so that we might believe ourselves immensely clever. There was a serious danger that they had indeed been noted and that we were being closely observed to see what use we tried to make of them. Such an idea was impossible to convey to Calvagh through hints and tricks, so I turned to my other preoccupation instead.

'Did you notice,' I asked, 'that Lord Húon and his son only had half-pointed ears?'

'I did not,' replied Calvagh and the topic died there.

'I have also noted,' I said, 'that there is no further point in our being careful with the speaking of our names. We are branded men now and, even if we called ourselves Edward and Calvagh at the tops of our voices thirty times an hour, we could not be more so.'

We then lay down to sleep, lulled for the first time by bellies full of feasting and the experience of being fully immersed in hot water. I did not necessarily want a bath every week of my life, but I felt most comfortable and I began to drift into a very easy sleep. The last thoughts I had any memory of holding on to concerned our iron daggers still. Would it be possible, I wondered, for the Elven to seize and use them if they were wrapped in a blanket of magic of a sufficient thickness? I felt myself agitated by this problem but sleep soon distanced me from any answer.

CHAPTER TEN

Our company did, indeed, set off before dawn. Calvagh and I were given mounts of our own, two chestnut geldings with rich leather accoutrements. We felt high and mighty as we rode behind Lord Ailill and his hand-picked bodyguard, his elite archers and swordsmen, six of them.

'Remember what havoc a loaded pistol could wreak here,' I managed to whisper to Calvagh. 'An iron barrel and an iron bullet for my lord's heart.'

'I shall add them to my baggage, next visit,' he said.

Behind us rode ten lesser soldiers, part of a private army, in breastplates and cuirasses of bronze and leather helmets with gilding that made them look very impressive once the sun rose and reflected off them. Our journey was meant to be of short duration so there was no baggage wagon. We would arrive the following evening, having slept at one of Lord Húon's many manors along the way. Attached to the backs of our saddles, Calvagh and I had a small roll of shirts, hose and undergarments which were pressed into our hands by a servant as we prepared to leave. So we were to expect to spend some length of time at our destination. I had my satchel and we shared out our remaining orchalc pieces, seven each with a scattering of silver and gold small change. We had an iron dagger each and I confess that I felt as significant in the world as I did when Master Spenser chose me as his secretary and conveyed me with him to Munster. Our pace was urgent, but not so hasty as to suggest that we were on an errand of suspicious import. The few Elven in the streets or at the north gate of the city at such an hour hardly bothered to look at us as we rode by. Lord Húon, it would seem, was often in the habit of sending his son to inspect his outlying manors. The round towers of the northern gateway were tall and slightly concave and managed to suggest both elegance and strength. I wondered how the stonework remained so white. If you have the use of magic at your fingertips, you need not bother to light smoky coal fires, I imagined. My first sight of the smoke stains on the buildings of London was a considerable shock to me, I have to confess. There was none of that here. Beyond the gateway was a flying bridge, a construction of silver wood that looked as if a single piece of heavy traffic would sink it into the waters below. The designer of the bridge must have wanted to see how little wood he could use, for it was almost a sketch for a bridge, an extraordinary fabrication that I was sure would be too flimsy for our combined weight. We rode across nonetheless and it proved sturdy enough. It arced from the gateway in the city wall to a small corresponding gateway on the other bank of the river which flowed around the island city. It was longer than London Bridge and, as we left it behind us, I could not help looking up to see whether the heads of traitors sat on spikes there. A nonsense thought. The Elven would never be guilty of such coarse taste, no matter how effective the lesson might be.

The route of our journey meant that we would eventually have travelled the lower territories of Hy Brazil in a diagonal from south-east to north-west. At the foot of the mountains was an extensive plain with orchards, villages, manors, undemanding hills, much of what we had seen before. In places of habitation, we almost sauntered, but, when we rode amongst trees or fields, our pace was far more pressing.

'Something is afoot that none here is meant to suspect,' I remarked to Calvagh.

'And we are part of it.'

If the company dawdled, Lord Ailill himself rode back and harried us. We simply bowed as he rode past and set our faces to look as if his every desire was our own. We heard him raise his voice from time to time and there was once the distinct sound of a slap. Each of us carried his own provisions and ate them quickly during our noon-time stop. I spotted smoke and rooftops and fields being worked, but we kept as far as possible from them and my concerns deepened.

Late in the afternoon, when Calvagh and I had exhausted what you might call 'safe' conversation, an unsettling incident occurred. Shouting broke out amongst the soldiers behind us and this was followed by squeals which could only have resulted from the inflicting of pain. Without thinking for a moment, Calvagh and I turned and cantered to the back of our party, more to witness than to help. It was not our right to leave our allotted place in the entourage and certainly not to throw ourselves amidst the ordinary soldiery. This was later made very clear to us by Lord Ailill. We found that a motley assemblage of oddities, flying creatures, gnomes and manikins, had taken exception to our passage and had begun to pelt our rear guard with twigs, burrs and dung pellets. They were no threat and might easily have been ignored. Some of the soldiers decided otherwise and, when the first had cut one of their assailants in half with his blade, the rest were drawn into the game. It took only a few deaths to scatter the raggle-taggles into the hedgerows beside the road where they tried to squeeze to safety between the lowest branches. The excitement of a game with easy victims meant that those escaping were pursued right up to the hedge-line where further murder was committed. My bronze dagger would not have thwarted the soldiers' work and I had no intention of using my iron blade, but I believed I could rescue a few of those trying to escape. I rode quickly by and, seizing an arm, used it to throw the body attached to it over the hedgerow and into the security of the field beyond. That I meant rescue rather than decapitation was quickly understood by the remainder of those who had scrabbled into the undergrowth to save their lives. I had only to lean from my horse and swing my arm along to find that half a dozen desperate creatures now clung to it. I have a powerful throwing arm and one firm fling was sufficient to send my passengers into the air and away from death's reach. I managed to do this perhaps four times before the arrival of Lord Ailill brought us all to a standstill. His appearance was timely because I had made myself unpopular with the soldiers and they wished to show me what they thought of my interference. Lord Ailill rode about amongst the pieces of our 'enemies', if you could call them that. His horse stepped delicately over torsos which had bled in an assortment of vivid colours. The smell was unpleasant and I longed to be dismissed from the scene.

'They were vermin,' announced my Lord, 'but to attack them in this way was unworthy.' He then turned on me, glowering. 'If you leave your place again, I shall have you whipped.' So we were all in disgrace. After some moments' thought, Lord Ailill decided that we could not leave the evidence of the eldritch massacre to incriminate us. He told five of his men to collect the pieces and throw them into the roadside ditch with whatever covering they could find. For an instant, I truly thought a soldier might refuse, but all set about their task with a sullenness that his lordship could not fail to notice. They fashioned brooms from branches snapped from a nearby tree and swept and kicked the little heads and limbs into their unmarked grave. When Lord Ailill cantered back to the head of our troupe, I followed quickly after for my safety's sake. I was aware, as not even Calvagh was, that a small blue creature, perhaps three inches long, still cowered inside my tunic. It had crept there chittering at the height of the battle. I did not intend to leave it next to my chest for long and I could not slip it into my satchel for fear that the closeness of our two iron daggers would shrivel it. As we rode on, I pointed to my shirt so that Calvagh might see my difficulty. He at once made a great fuss of letting slip his bundle of clothing and, as he snatched at it, I was able to throw the blue whatnot as far to the side as I could. I did not know whether it would fly or bounce, or even stab me with a venomed sting as I tried to set it loose. Its blueness was the only detail I could be sure of. It might have been a great bluebottle or the most exquisite blue angel, but it was free again. It, he, she, flew up into the sunlight and then dived behind a hawthorn and out of our sight.

'I saw your work,' I observed to Calvagh as we settled into a riding rhythm again. As I darted about in my act of mercy, he had ridden amongst the soldiers crying, 'Here and here!' creating confusion and drawing them away from the little dung-hurlers.

'It was not a brave action to kill them,' was all he said.

Our night time was spent in the great hall of one Lord Húon's manors, as I said. The entire company, apart from Lord Ailill, who was entertained privately, ate and slept amongst the long oak tables. I hoped our branding would protect us, but I caught unfriendly looks and heard the words 'Creature lovers' muttered in our direction as words of insult. The soldiers numbered Englishmen and I was ashamed that they had been amongst the most eager with their swords. When some of Lord Ailill's bodyguard stepped outside to relieve themselves, Calvagh and I followed and chose bushes quite near them for our offices as we had no desire to be caught and injured when at such a disadvantage. This country manor had none of the luxuries of the city and we both felt more comfortable because of it. A night's sleep with your head cradled between your elbows on a table top has something manly about it, I am sure.

The next morning, while the Elven soldiers poured buckets of warm water over each other and took time to comb their hair, the troops drawn from Humankind simply lounged and scratched. It was Calvagh's idea that we should make clear we were now of some significance by asking for buckets of warm water ourselves. This led to some derision from Elven and human alike, but we persisted with our point. I still found that the Elven features disturbed me with their natural superciliousness, but at least they could not settle into the oafish sullenness of their human companions. As we stood about, the Elven soldiers and Calvagh and myself, dripping with the water and rubbing the drying cloths vigorously over our bodies, I satisfied my curiosity as to whether the Elven men could grow hair on any region. Their chins were quite smooth, and, I now saw, their chests were too. Around the fulcrum of their loins they grew what might best be called silken tufts.

Calvagh followed the line of my eye and said, 'I too wondered whether they were made like all other men. Our priest tells that the angels have no private parts and now I know that these Elven are not angels.'

Our setting off took place under an immense cloud. It was to be expected that Lord Ailill would strut and shout whatever he was doing, but this was different. The shouting contained a tone of real anger and both Calvagh and I shrank into corners whenever he came near us. We longed to hear what had so upset him and strained our ears for any give-away words in English or Irish. Our curiosity took us where we had been expressly forbidden to go, amongst the company of common human soldiers. We did not so much talk to them as kick the dirt and re-arrange our horses' gear with our ears flapping like sheets on a washing line. Eventually our loitering was rewarded and we learnt of an attack by 'Them' or, more exactly, 'Them little ugly things' on a manor a few miles distant. Such attacks were becoming regular, it appeared, and this last one of all had been accompanied by some dreadful humiliation or insult that had Lord Ailill gnawing at his lip. Any action which discomfited my young lord into a seizure was welcome to us and we hoped to expand our information during the course of the morning. When the party was ready to depart, we made sure that we were in our rightful places and that none of the storm of anger could be directed towards us. I decided to wait until the rhythm of our journey became regular and then to whisper my speculations to Calvagh. He winked at me as we mounted our horses and was obviously of the same mind. As it transpired, we had little time to wait until the information we sought smacked us roughly in the mouth. Lord Ailill was quite beside himself and found fault with every one of his company. He rode furiously up and down our cavalcade shouting and slapping and then he stopped beside the two of us. I imagined that we were to be punished for consorting with the low soldiery and I was most disconcerted when my lord simply kept pace with me and stared into my face. Was I so different and ugly, I wondered? Or was I so devilish handsome that he could not help but regard me with rapture? This had happened to me twice in the London playhouse but I could not repeat now what I said then.

'You pair of bearded wonders,' he said scoffingly. 'What would they have done to you?'

'My lord?' It was a brief and, I hoped, a safe answer.

'There have been attacks on some of the northern manors.'

I nodded and said nothing as I did not wish to appear too curious.

'But this latest insult. This INSULT! What pleasure they would have taken with you and your Irish keepsake.'

'My lord?' I said quickly as I had noticed a movement in Calvagh's lips and his hand. If he told Lord Ailill what we thought of him or, even worse, knocked him off his horse, it would be the end of us.

'They cut off the hair of all the men and women, the Elven men and women, they molested, and made a great cloak of it. This cloak was left on our doorstep during the night to show their power, their contempt and whatever else.'

He then leant forward and tugged at my beard and I praised myself that I simply sat there while he did it and neither backed away nor fended him off. 'What joy they would have had with a beard like yours. They might have spun themselves a pair of stockings from it!' So pleased with his own churlish wit was he, that it lightened his mood and he rode off laughing distractedly. I forced a smile, although behind my apparent good humour was the wish that one day I might fashion a rope from my beard and Calvagh's and hang Lord Ailill from it.

'So now we know,' I said to Calvagh after our party had settled down again. 'A cloak made from topknots and left on the doorstep by dawnlight. Some would call it a Faerie story.' Oh how we longed to chuckle out loud at the picture of newly bald Elvenkind concealing their shorn pates with any rag or kerchief they could find.

As we rode through the morning, the land rose noticeably and outcrops of rock grew more frequent. The terrain was less soft and the eyes of the soldiers grew sharper, although I could not believe that great danger hid behind such low mounds of stone.

'Be sure to keep one hand on your hair and the other on your beard,' I murmured across to my companion.

'My hand is lower down,' he replied quickly. 'The little ugly ones pay much more for that sort of hair.' We both nearly choked.

To be truthful, I barely felt that we were in danger. A cloak left on a doorstep is like an insult shouted in the dark, a petty and ineffectual thing that hurts no-one. The assault of the previous day could hardly be called an attack, and it ended harshly for the perpetrators. Who would dare confront Lord Ailill when his father's properties seemed to decorate the entire countryside. On two occasions, nonetheless, as we rode through declivities with blind turnings, Lord Ailill rode amongst us and told us to have our weapons to hand.

'There are secrets to find out here,' I thought to myself, 'and find them out I shall.' I had already learnt that any creature of faerie that stood below a man's breast, that had an unpleasant face or that crawled or squeaked was of little account. Was this to be the traffic between our two worlds if Lord Húon had his way? Were the roads into London to be packed with every snarling, hopping, dung-hurling horror that the land of faerie could expel in our direction?

There were stands of trees about our path and, generally, we avoided them, but I found my eye increasingly drawn to an extensive woodland to the west. Black smoke rose above it which was most unexpected. My mind was full of questions. A house on fire? A wonder of Nature, perhaps even a volcano? As we turned into a side path that led amongst the trees, I licked my lips and nodded to Calvagh. This was the end of our journey, no doubt. The truth of what was causing the pall of smoke I could never have guessed and my mouth fell open as quickly as Calvagh's when the mystery came into view.

This was no country mansion set amongst carefully tended flower gardens and orchards. There was certainly a large house, but the delicate stonework of its gables was smeared with the dark shadow of soot. There was a sharp stink in the air that offended my tongue and made me want to spit and also to rub the water from my eyes. The hillside behind the house had been gouged away and I saw the entrances to numerous tunnels. Black heaps of coal rose up everywhere in mockery of the arbours they had doubtless replaced. Everywhere was flame and clatter. A deeply sullied stream ran away down the hillside to poison the large watercourse at its foot. What vision of Hell was this? It would have delighted any of the preachers whose sermons I regularly slept through. Of all the sights I expected to see in Hy Brazil, this was never one of them. Although I had heard of such filthy commercial activities in the Weald of Kent, this was all beyond Calvagh's knowledge. He looked at me in utter puzzlement.

'I have almost as little understanding as you, my friend,' I said. 'These tunnels, I would think, are the entrances to mines and that is coal to heat whatever they extract from the mines. Mayhap this is where our bronze daggers are forged or the orchalc pieces minted. Metals do not sprout from the earth fully-fashioned, as it were.'

'My nose is heartily offended,' he said. 'And I am used to stink. Surely no Elvenkind would put up with this?'

'I see no Elven,' I said. 'These are Humankind, every one, if I am not mistaken. Are we to be slaves in Lord Húon's mine!' The question blazed up as fiercely as any of the flames around me. I kicked my horse roughly and rode to accost Lord Ailill. 'What do you mean by this?' I shouted. 'Have you dressed us up in your damned clothing so that we might scrabble underground?'

In my rage, I fumbled with the buckles of my satchel. If I could get my dagger in his heart then he would surely pay for deceiving us. As I struggled to take out the daggers and throw both of them if I could, I was surrounded by Lord Ailill's bodyguard who took firm hold of my arms.

'Bring both of them with you,' said his lordship and rode off towards the house. They were obliged to knock me from my saddle in order to curb the paroxysms of fury with which I was now possessed.

'Do you not see those filthy men who are naked to the waist and who drip black sweat?' I called to Calvagh as I kicked and bucked. He too was pinioned. 'They are you and I and the work will soon kill them!'

It proved more sensible for the bodyguard to strike me unconscious than to spend their energies containing the beast I had now become. The first blow brought me to my knees and then the attack came and there were more urgent concerns.

My ears rang and my vision danced so I had no clear idea of the events that followed. Once or twice I felt hands beneath my shoulders which may have been Calvagh attempting to draw me clear. There was, I believe, a shower of tiny arrows which landed near me and struck several of the bodyguard at least.

'Pretty little arrows,' I mumbled foolishly and fell on my face in a puddle as I tried to touch one. I have since learned that there is no equal or antidote to the poison in which they are drenched.

It is difficult to describe a battle when you are lying with your face in a puddle. There was a great deal of running and yelling, which is usual in conflict. There was also gnashing and snarling which I imagined were sounds in my own head. The light of the burning house was reflected in the surface of my puddle.

'My own dear puddle,' I believe I said several times. Then blood was sprayed on it and I liked it less. A foot stepped heavily on my head and I took in a good deal of the puddle through my mouth and nose.

'I shall die quite soon,' I thought. 'I wish I knew at whose hands. If it is the miners', perhaps they know London and I shall be spared.'

Then the earth shook and shook again. 'An explonshun,' I said, finding the word unexpectedly difficult, but I liked its new sound.

It was an explonshun that came nearer in thunderous crashes.

'God's footsteps?' I wondered.

At once the answer appeared reflected in my puddle. I looked disbelievingly at it and raised my dull head to get a better view. The sky as far as I could see on either side was obscured by a vast bush that was not a bush. A creature, or a collection of creatures, or a forest yielding a club, many clubs, had come to rest right beside me. One of its two, three, four, five feet stood adjacent to my back. It could easily have stepped two inches to the side and made me as liquid as my puddle. This bush, or city of green, flailed its arms in all directions. Such a verdant green I had never set eyes on before. I found myself wanting to touch the greenness and hold it to my face. It was a greenness from God's creation of the world and I thought, 'I shall weep for greenness, now.' There were heads and tongues and teeth in the greenness and so many arms, each with its weapon of choice. A great foot stepped over me and then another and still I was not made liquid.

'Attack it with fire!' someone shrieked. 'Look to the fire!'

'Edward!' Was that Calvagh calling?

And, louder than any other voice, Lord Ailill, 'Look to the iron! Save the iron!' The *iron?* I hardly had time to phrase this question when my left arm was jerked up and backwards and I found myself in a crumpled sitting position. Rescue? Alas, no. My arm was tugged up the slope away from the house and I with it. I wonder, now, how my arm and myself did not part company. I bounced over stones and bodies as whatever had seized me made away from the battle. I looked with bleary eyes at the scene, at the life I was seeing for the last time. Men and Elven were beset by every kind of faerie 'other' while the house blazed gloriously, throwing into silhouette each separate battle to the death.

'Edward!' a desperate, yearning voice.

I wanted so much to ask for help and for someone to tell me why my arm hurt the way it did.

'Edward!'

'Save the iron, not yourselves!'

And then I was thrown up high like a titbit into a spaniel's mouth. The cavernous maw of the greenness swallowed me and there were shapes and branches and fingers whichever way I tried to turn.

'Such green,' I wanted to say, but little fingers were tweaking me and poking at my lips and soon I longed simply for oblivion. A fierce smack to the side of my head ensured I found it.

I was now certainly one of the damned. When I opened my eyes, I saw, not two yards in front of me, a pair of creatures fighting over the tripes of a third. Each pulled on an end and, as neither would give in, it seemed that the contest could never be won. The length of tripe simply grew longer. I looked down at my stomach to see that no part of my own innards had gone missing. I was still protected by the quilted tunic, I was immeasurably glad to know, but, once again, half of my footwear had gone missing. A ball of spines or fur was slyly approaching my naked toes and I used my voice and my other, booted, foot to send it packing with an indignant squeal. My satchel was still with me because the strap lay baldrick-wise across my chest and could not easily be removed. I was not weaponless, therefore. The strange angle with which my left arm rested by my side, however, told me that all was not well there. I shifted my position and nigh fainted from the pain in my shoulder. I remembered the tale of Jonah and my stomach sickened at the memory. Was I now inside the gut of a gigantic tree-being, condemned, until I died of starvation, to spend my days with horrors who were similarly trapped? At each stage of my adventure in Hy Brazil, my temper had brought me lower and now here I was waiting to be digested. The spiny, furry creature thought I had not seen it return. It managed a single nip of my big toe before the heel of my boot stunned it.

I gathered my knees up to my chest and retched at the pain this caused to my left arm. There were always the iron daggers. Using my good right arm, I struggled ineffectually with the buckles of my satchel. If my fate were to be bitten and chewed, then many of the spiny, furry kind would die at my blade's end. Perhaps I would be able to placate them with Calvagh's ribbons and brooches. My prospects were decidedly unhappy. Most of all, I missed my friend and his unfailing patience with my testy English manners. He rarely bridled at my arrogance and temper and I had not deserved him. I hoped, briefly, that the tree had swallowed him too so that we might continue our adventure together. Then I reminded myself what a selfish thought this was and that he was fierce enough to have emerged from the battle unscathed.

'Calvagh!' I called as a face appeared through the leafy walls surrounding me. I was not deceived for more than an instant. These were not the small ears or dark curls of my friend; the hair was brown and tangled with twig ends and burrs, the beard was straggly, the nose large and the smell overpowering.

'A cannibal!' I thought at once. 'Goodbye, dear tripes.'

His first act was to remove the spiny, furry creature which still harboured desires concerning the eating of my toes. It had recovered its equilibrium and crawled near to me again. With a fluent swing of his foot, he kicked it across the small clearing, through the leaves and out of sight. The squeal it made ended suddenly in the unmistakable sound of jaws snapping shut and I at once felt sorry for it.

I did not know how to respond to this wild man, this creature who approached me squatting on his haunches and who proceeded to sniff the air around me. I was affronted as he wrinkled his nose. I had doused myself generously from my bucket only that morning and there was still the scent of oil in my hair. Nor had I soiled myself despite all the fears I experienced during the battle, but, God knows, I had every reason to be a piss-rag. He, on the other hand, I imagined lived in a lair deep in his own filth, if I were to judge from the odour that clung fiercely to him. His ears were neither pointed nor tufted and his fingers and toes, if short and stubbed, were created after the same pattern as my own. Around his waist he had a kind of loin cloth arrangement of ivy and other leaves that remained fastened no matter how he moved. This was his only clothing, but I judge a man more by his eyes than his breeches. As he began to feel the texture of each item of my clothing, I did my best to look him in the face. Although this unsettled him, I persevered until I was certain of the impression I had received.

There was a mildness and a curiosity about his eyes that led me to think that he was unlikely to want to bite off pieces of my flesh for his dinner. I attempted to smile which is difficult when one of your arms has been near twisted off. A thousand questions sprang to mind, but I was yet to discover whether his head contained the sparks of intellect.

'Do you have a name?' I asked in the softest voice I could manage. 'My name is Edward. Am I safe and how may I get home?'

His eyes widened more with each question and I quickly found that he was ignorant of any of the words I used, even the shortest and most simple. I next tried to convey by gestures that I meant him no harm, that I was sure he meant me no harm and that he would be the most excellent fellow in the world if he were to lead me back to my earlier companions. I am no actor and I have no repertoire of gesture. I pointed to my heart and then to his and used my fingers to imitate the movement of a man walking along the ground. This delighted him and so I repeated the mime of walking, making sure that my fingers walked away from me in the direction of the branches between which he had entered. He nodded vigorously and used his fingers to make walking movements of his own.

'My gaoler is a simpleton.' I thought. 'Hey-ho. Am I to spend all day in this idiocy?'

The pain in my left shoulder had not abated one jot and when he touched it I cried out in some anguish. This distressed him and he stroked my arm in a gesture of sympathy which further intensified my discomfort. I moved away from him and was pulled back by a grip that was immensely strong and was used to having its own way. He took my chin between his fingers and pointed it away from my ruined shoulder. Then, with a speed and a dexterity which took me absolutely by surprise, he manipulated my shoulder back into its rightful place. The pain was so sharp, I thought at first he had broke my neck. I am sure my cry could be heard for half a mile. He now patted me on the shoulder as if to suggest that I had been a brave boy. Tears were certainly rolling down the brave boy's cheeks and I closed my eyes and collapsed into a feeble heap. I considered the wild man a simpleton no longer, although his lack of language still perplexed me. And if he were truly a man like myself, what was his place amongst such a goblin breed who held my life in their hands? I stiffened my spine and lifted myself unsteadily onto my feet. I could not bear more of the finger walking games, nor the attempt to communicate through face-pulling alone. I would march out of there and see who dared to try and stop me. I went directly to the place where my new companion had first appeared and swept the branches aside. You must understand that I had previously been in the kind of space you find beneath the lowest branches of a tree when they reach down to the ground and form a kind of bell. I now stepped out into a theatre, a broad woodland lawn thronged with creatures waiting for me to make my entrance. The wild man presented me to my audience and then squatted placidly beside me as the glade was filled with every kind of noise imaginable. There were words and chirrupings, chatterings and raspings that rose and rose and gave no sign of abating until I placed my hands over my ears. This action reduced the sound to a hum, but still they and I waited for some clear event to happen. Was I to deliver an oration? Were they to share my body out as their repast? Time passed and the expectation lingered. I turned to the wild man and pointed helplessly at the hundreds of faerie who were staring fixedly at me. He returned me an agreeable smile and beckoned to a group of creatures who were jumping up and down with particular animation. Many of them bore an unhappy resemblance to the spiny, furry being which had fallen in love with my toes. Was he, therefore, inviting them to have the first bite? They sprang and scurried towards me and attached themselves to both of my arms.

'They are about to tear off my arms,' I thought. 'My entrails are bound to be next.'

As I did not like to have strings of distorted beings clinging to my shirt sleeves (who does?) I swung my arms roughly upwards and the creatures, manikins, diminutive boggarts and suchlike let go all at the same time. They described a neat arc through the air before landing as a tidy group all facing in my direction. This performance would appear to be what all those present had been waiting for. The little knot of participants jumped up and down as if eager to repeat the sport, but the wild man rose to his feet and made clear that I was to be troubled no further. Carefully taking my recently injured arm, he led me across the glade to yet another clearing where quite another audience awaited. As we passed through the next leafy door, I suddenly realised what had just happened. These were the creatures I saved from murder and I had been invited to demonstrate how exactly I achieved it. Little wonder, then, that they showed such delight in being tossed through the air. I was chuckling, almost, when I came face to face with an altogether more exalted assembly of beings.

I stood at the edge of a second extensive glade. Trees of every kind formed its walls, trees that would never willingly grow side by side – yew, holly, alder, beech, oak, sycamore, pine, every one shaped into a neat poll and of the same stature, about five times my own height. All were in their summer glow, the leaves as full of sap and life as they could manage. Between the trunks of the trees grew brambles, gorse, broom, blackthorn and whitethorn, again a sampling of every kind of bush or shorter tree.

A skilled gardener works here, was my first thought.

The glade, at first, held only the wild man and myself. He would not let me step beyond the threshold, restraining me with a strong arm around my waist. I found this too familiar, but there was nothing I could do to escape his embrace. His breath and body smell also made standing there unpleasant. I turned my face to one side and breathed in little gasps. In the centre of the glade were two small mounds, each capped with a flat slab of polished stone, a kind of granite I would imagine.

As we stood there gazing at nothing at all, my wild friend squeezing my waist like a lover and I, for my part, making little snorting noises, the grass was suddenly overrun by, what shall I say, a flood of greenness. Beings of many kinds, on the ground, in the air, of knee-height, head-height, surged in until the grass was entirely carpeted with them. Now seated on the two stones were two of the Elven kind, a male and female. The wild man pressed me to my knees as all the other creatures there bowed and knelt, uttering a deep collective sigh. The two seated beings, Lord and Lady, King and Queen, I did not yet know which, looked with satisfaction at their prostrate retinue before fixing their eyes on me. Their hair was long, to the shoulder in his case and to the waist in hers, and of a russety, tawny, chestnut colour that shifted disconcertingly. Their skin was very pale, by way of contrast. They shared the same Elven slant of eye and ear, but their expression was possibly softer than I had yet found amongst their kind. Softness, I have noted to my cost, is not a quality cherished amongst the mighty. The tall figures were draped in, again I struggle for the words, garments that had a ragged appearance to them as if composed of strips of several lengths. His was every shade of brown, from chestnut conker to mud, and she was clothed in greens that reminded me of yew, apple, sage. They were faces in gardens, almost, and I had difficulty in keeping my vision of them exact.

At a glance from the seated male, the wild man took my hand, once more with a grip I could not resist, and we walked towards these two important beings. The ground was so covered with pixies and flibbertigibbets (the taller figures standing well to the sides) I was sure I would end the lives of several with my every step. Fortunately, they moved aside as we placed our feet before us and then fell back into place once we had moved on. It was an awkward progress and I was not helped by my companion choosing our speed. As we approached the two mounds, the firm hand was on my shoulder once more and down I fell. I was held there for what I thought an unforgivable time. The point of their importance had been made and there was no need to keep us abject for so long. Possibly after a sign which I did not notice, the wild man lifted his head and allowed me to raise mine.

The seated Lord's first sentence was in an Elven tongue and meant not for my ears but for those of his court. There was a general murmur of acceptance or approval as if he had told them news they all wished to hear. He then addressed his next remark directly to me in an accent which suggested that he did not generally converse in English.

'You are welcome.'

I bowed and decided to remain silent. A severe breach of etiquette would not be wise when I was awash in a sea of his followers.

'It was necessary for us to take you captive.'

'Why me?' I needed an answer to this question, etiquette or no. As soon as I spoke, five hundred heads were raised and all looked in my direction.

'Ah, why indeed? You have been told that there is…' He turned to the female.

'Division.'

'Division in…'

'In Hy Brazil,' I offered.

'*Hy Brazil* if you wish to call it. Our own name is…' He spoke the melodious name which had once been impossible for me. I now surprised myself and them all by being able to repeat it competently after him.

Again, five hundred bowed heads rose and many more than a thousand eyes regarded me with surprise. I smiled generally and trusted that none there could read my secret thoughts. These thoughts were twofold, that I must find my friend

Calvagh again and then together we would effect our escape, to Cork, to London, to a sandbank in the Wash, I did not at present care where.

'You have shown yourself our friend.' The Lord's voice was sonorous and yet with a woodland breathiness suffusing it as if the sounds he made passed through a mass of leaves before they reached me. I was their 'friend', now, was I? And how well disposed to me were they?

I was aware of a kind of heat, a palpable interest, directed towards me from the hundreds of eldritch creatures. They might be waiting for me to anger their Lord, or simply to say the one word *No* before shredding me for their supper. I am no strategist, nor yet a blockhead, and I was for the moment happy to stand and listen.

The Lady now spoke. If her consort's voice was leaves and branches, hers was much softer, water dripping onto moss, perhaps. 'You must rest and afterwards see a little of our way of life. Then you will come to understand why we value it and will not readily give it up.'

I have often noticed that, where men give orders, women give reasons, and so I directed a more genuine smile towards the Lady. I was prepared to sacrifice a little time sightseeing before I made my escape.

'The man will be your companion,' added the Lord. He meant 'gaoler', of course. He spoke the word 'man' as if it referred to some lower order of being, which for him, no doubt, it did. I noted the belittling tone and resented it. So he thought it appropriate for a Wodwo, a wild man of the forest, to have care of poor Hobbinol. Damn his superiority!

'My name is Edward Harry!' I declared with the full power of my lungs. I would not be reduced to such an anonymous presence. Let them know who I was and that I had a powerful sense of my own worth. The Lord raised an eyebrow at the sheer volume of my voice and I flattered myself that leaves fell as my name echoed about the grove.

'Edward Harry, you are our welcome guest.'

The audience had ended. There was a green turbulence about me, a sense of light draining away, and the wild man and I were left alone. The Lord and Lady had gone and every single fluttering, snarling thing had gone with them. I felt so giddy with the suddenness of it, I was not sure which of the two spoke the last words.

The 'man' clapped his hands and gave me an idiot's leer. I looked him hard in the face and held him there, pinned, until he put his paws up and hid behind them. I had a strong belief that there was intelligence beyond the cloudiness of the simpleton.

'You would entertain any audience in London with your zany grins and your cavorting up and down,' I said. 'I am not deceived, however. Take your hands away from your face!' Although he was much stronger than I, he offered no resistance when I knocked his hands down. 'Look at me!' He refused to do so. 'You are no ape, although you are these creatures' pet. You must surely have a history, a parentage. I shall now go with you because I choose to do so. And I shall leave this place when I choose.' (This was certainly an extravagant boast.) 'I shall set about making you exchange words with me. No matter what the cost to both of us.' I then softened my voice and took him by the arm. 'Come, let us be away. You have much to show me.' My gentler words revived him and he gave me a horrid grimace that revealed most of his teeth. I expected I should have many, many hours in which to fathom him.

CHAPTER ELEVEN

My wild man was unkempt, maladorous and without speech, but he was no savage. I decided to name him 'Salvage' as a gentler version of the word. He led me for a long time through glades and along paths until we must have been two or three miles from where I had met the Lord and Lady. The woods were full of high summer and gave no sign of being other than Dancey's Spinney which I had wandered in as a boy. Birdsong fluted about us and sunlight blazed down when the leaf cover was at its thinnest. There was not a spiny, scratchy, scrawny, misbegotten, fanged presence to be seen. More than likely they had been warned to keep their distance for fear of unsettling me. My companion walked at my pace which was a slow one partly because I was determined to assert myself and partly because I thought I might learn the geography of my prison. There was, sadly, no chance of this as our path was not a direct one and the best I could gather from my intermittent glimpses of the sun was that we were moving north. Once in a while, Salvage would pick me a flower, I recognised figwort and an iris but few of the rest, or stoop to gather me an interesting twig or pebble. My instinct, as my hands filled with the burden of them, was to pitch them at his back as I conceived this was part of some game he played at my expense. I forbore to toss them away, however, because he took such trouble in finding them for me. I accepted each new token with increasingly weaker signs of gratitude and urged myself to be patient as I was in the company of a persistent child.

The air was so sweet and mild that my irritation was never really strong and I tried to enjoy my walk as if it were an afternoon stroll and I should soon be home. At last we began to climb and I heard the sound of water. We emerged from the trees onto a green slope fringed with tall grasses whiskered like barley. There was a narrow cleft in the centre down which a spring danced. It was a beautiful spot, perfect for an hour or two of drowsing. Master Spenser would have gained much inspiration from such a place and no doubt would have conjured up many a dryad and nymph to fill it. Little did he suspect that I was now in a country where such beings were real and drew breath. The creatures he put down on paper only existed in the realms of his imagination. All the same, I did not look forward to spending my captivity here. Was I to walk around the perimeter counting grass heads because I had no-one to converse with and no way of engaging my mind? Our accommodation was, I gladly discovered, not the bare grass, soft to the tread though it undoubtedly was. At the top of the slope grew a solid line of brambles and behind them blackthorn and holly. My guide led me upwards and I discovered that the fronds of the brambles formed a doorway to what I suppose I must call a bower. We entered at a stoop and found a room perhaps fifteen foot square. The walls were the trunks of the blackthorn and holly with stems of other plants filling up the spaces in between. There was no real sense of being inside a constructed dwelling, yet I had a strong feeling that the branches above us had somehow been persuaded to make the tightly woven ceiling which was more waterproof than should have been possible. It was a dry and warm room although the light was dim. Salvage gestured with a sweep of his arm to the walls and ceiling. Yes, I had noticed how trim they were, as effective in their own way as bricks and plaster. There were even live blossoms growing in some parts of the wall which was an attractive novelty. In one corner lay a pallet, a springy bed of twigs covered with hay and soft leaves and a folded woven coverlet. There was a chair, a table with food and some platters and bowls. The room, to my companion, lacked nothing. His pointing and little expressions of delight told me this. There was a monastic simplicity about it but I did not doubt that I should remain dry and sleep soundly there. I am a boy who grew up in the country and a grass floor and a twig mattress hold no terrors for me as they might for someone who has known only walls bound with mortar and the luxuries of the city. The food was abundant and I was sure I should enjoy it so long as on closer inspection I did not find dishes of grasshoppers and snails.

Remembering that I was still holding the assemblage of stones, twigs, flowers, I dropped them in a scatter on the floor. Salvage slapped me on the shoulder and sank to his knees, roughly pulling me down beside him.

'What tiresome childish game is this?' I asked recalling the finger-walking which had so peeved me. My tone of voice led to another slap. He proceeded to arrange our gatherings across the floor in what turned out to be a long line near two yards from beginning to end. Each twig, each plant, was pointed at wordlessly and I was made to stare at it and make an observation.

'White stones from the side of that little runnel,' I said dutifully. 'Stinking figwort where the ground was damp and I left a footprint.' He was happy that I had a comment for each prized item, although I could swear that he did not understand my English words. I tested this notion by speaking nonsense when I touched the head of wild strawberries and another stinker he had picked, a stem of the roast-beef plant which had led to my grandmother leathering me once for bringing it into the cottage. This was to be my punishment, my own Elven Hell, to spend every day making an inventory of whatever scraps he picked up in his wanderings and for him not to understand a word of what I was saying. After a short while of this I should be uttering gibberish all the time whether I meant to or no. At last there was an end of the game and, clearly disappointed by my tight jaw and my lack of enthusiasm, Salvage jerked me to my feet and led me outside.

There can be too much of this slapping and prodding I thought to myself. *Much as I have no hatred of this fellow, I still possess a good blade and I am prepared to use it.*

He was anxious to show me his own dwelling which stood, or rather grew, beside my own. It too had its portico of brambles but, if mine was a spacious chamber, his was a kennel. There was no bed, no table and not a utensil to be seen.

'You cannot be asking me to admire your home,' I observed. 'Do you point it out in case I have need of rescue in the night? Are there wolves or bears in these woods?'

He appeared to understand neither my words nor my growing vexation. I was dragged into the sunlight once again and made to look, from afar, at the four corners of our glade with its little waterfall and copious grass. Was I being told that here I must remain until my captors decided otherwise? Such was probably the case. I was now beginning to feel I needed a respite from his attentions and his muteness. Hunger was starting to gnaw and I had need of my own company and my own thoughts. I had also, in the last few minutes, felt a great need to pass water. I did not intend to be like a bird that soils its own nest and leave my dung and urine deposited about the floor of my dwelling. But where to ease myself? More than ever I wished to cudgel him for his acting the silent fool. What could I do but perform in dumb show the voiding before and behind which would surely have told any man what I was about? He stared at my sundry mimes and did little else but rock with what I took to be silent laughter.

'Shall I piss my breeches before you decide to understand me?' I cried. There was nothing for it then but to march to the woodland edge and relieve myself in a great splashing arc. Salvage looked mortified in the extreme as if an adored child had just disgraced him in the company of his superiors. His mouth fell open and his eyes bulged, I swear it. Yes, he who was clad in a fanciful costume of leaves, who smelt and who did not speak. He was ashamed of me. When I had put my little warrior away, the salvage creature seized me in his roughest grasp yet and hauled me amongst the trees. There he showed me a large square of earth surrounded by a tall thicket which must have been planted for the purpose. This was my privy as his pointing and glaring and ridiculous squatting told me. Here I could excavate a pit using the wooden shovel which I felt he wanted to batter me with. There was a patch of mallows nearby which would provide me with soft leaves for the wiping and, all in all, it was the least noisome privy I had ever entered.

'You were fortunate I did not piss in your doorway,' I said. 'Do you realise your power to annoy?'

Then I was dragged off again, down to the flat stones at the foot of the waterfall. Here I might bathe myself, it was clear.

'You are a strange one to make such a fuss over washing,' I said. 'I have always prided myself on calling for hot water daily.'

As he seemed content, then, to sit and gawp at the water splashing down into the pool, I walked back to my lodging. I tried the bed which easily shaped itself to the contours of my body and proved most comfortable. The coverlet was light and perhaps a mixture of lamb's wool and down, I could not be certain. When, as an experiment, I laid it over me, I at once felt warm and at ease, the effect, presumably, of some enchantment woven into it. I would sleep soundly there, of that there was little doubt.

Next, my furniture. The chair was not a construction of turned wood and carpentry. It possessed an irregular shape, being no more than several twisting slices of tree trunk somehow intertwined to make a base, a seat and a back. It flowed from bottom to top, the knots and bark making it interesting to the eye but no less comfortable than the best of Master Spenser's costly London chairs. There was ample space for my behind, a shapely young man's rump if I might boast, and, although I expected the chair back to be full of sharp ridges, I found this not to be the case. My table was a flat slab of polished slate resting on a piece of tree trunk, sturdy and adequate for its purpose. None of my pieces of wooden tableware was circular or of a uniform depth or width. Every item, I sensed, was found rather than worked, or, rather, any working simply brought out a shape which Nature had already suggested. There were dishes of wild strawberries and other black berries which I hoped were no relative of the nightshade. I had nut bread, blocks of a pale cheese and strips of dried meat which I did not recognise and had no intention of putting in my mouth. They might be cut from the haunches of the last human prisoner there for all I knew. The idea might even be that my body in turn would provide victualling for whichever prisoners came after me. Such are the morbid thoughts one has in captivity, let me warn you. My drink, a juice extracted from berries, was contained within a foot-high block of hollowed branch. It served its purpose. The juice was a dark red and my initial fear was that I had been given a pitcher of blood to slake my thirst. It was not until I had swirled my finger in it and closely inspected the drops on my fingertip that I was prepared to let any pass my lips.

I sat on my chair, stretched my legs and ate my fill. A satisfying meal has always softened my temper and soon I was more at peace with the world than for some long time. I had no book and, worse, no friend, but I had my living walls of leaves and flowers to gaze at and my own thoughts to set in order. Presently, I cast my eyes on the line of gatherings which Salvage had placed so carefully on my grassy carpet. While occupied with my meal, I had not thought of the scent, or lack of it, of most of the plants in my cabin walls. Traces of stink made their way to me and I wondered with a smile whether a creature as grubby as Salvage ever realised how malodorous most of his trophies were. Why, in God's name, had he been drawn unfailingly to such unsavoury choices? As no more than a pastime, I began to remember where he had picked each flower or stone: 'White pebbles from beside the little stream where the path broadened; Strawberries growing near the two fallen trees.' Then, of a sudden, I knew what he had really been about. Who was now the salvage man, if not I? Once again I had pouted and been my little lord in a temper when my rough companion tried to give me important information. He had placed the objects on the floor with insistent precision because they formed a map of the way to the clearing where I had met the Lord and Lady. If I learned the sequence, then I had my route back there. And if they stank, I should have a greater chance of remembering where we picked them. Perhaps he had been told to lead me by meandering paths so that I should be quite lost, but his simple gifts had made sure that important knowledge was available to me. I carefully removed the items to the rear wall of my lodging so that I should not disturb them in a moment of heedlessness and lose the information they held. I would also sleep more pleasantly if they were as far from my bed as possible. No-one likes to sleep in a miasma. I walked up and down reciting and memorising until a crack, as of two stones being struck against each other, made me start. There in the doorway stood Salvage himself awaiting an invitation to enter like a wicked spirit who must be asked across a threshold. The stones were a door-knocker he had improvised.

'Enter,' I called. 'And look what I have been doing.'

I pointed to the line of objects we had carried with us and hurried through a recitation of each spot where we had gathered them. My English was almost certainly a mystery to him, but my sense was clear. He breathed out heavily as if to say, 'At long last, child.'

I shook his hand and slapped him on the shoulder. 'What depths there are to you, my friend,' I said. I offered him my chair and refreshment, both of which he refused. He did, however, by gestures suggest that I take a wooden bucket to the stream so that I should have water for an indoor toilet in the morning. I had wondered about the use to which I should put this container with its twisted flanges which served as handles. It was the base of a thick and ancient branch, hollowed with age, I guessed, and I blushed to recall that I had intended to use it as a jakes. The cloths which lay beside it now declared themselves as the ones with which I might dry myself.

'You are very concerned with the cleanliness of Edward Harry,' I said as we walked companionably down to the stream's edge. 'I note that you have not brought a bucket of your own. I wonder what the Lord and his Lady think when you are near them. Upwind is best.'

From time to time throughout the period I spent in Salvage's company, my mind ran over the possibilities of what and why he appeared as he did. He had no difficulty in hearing what I said to him although he steadfastly refused to respond with sound of any kind, not even a hiss. What could lead a man to make the double vows of silence and dirt? And what could have brought him to this island in the first place? I recalled Calvagh's story of his twin-sister stolen as a baby by the faeries and I wondered whether my salvage friend were victim of such an act of piracy. Perhaps, if left in the home where he was born, he would have been elegantly groomed and successful, a dignitary with titles and lands. His Wodwo's garment did not distress him, it appeared, and he yearned for none of the diversions of a chatterbox friend and books which I so sorely missed.

When the sun sank behind the trees, my room was filled with shadow and then, wonderfully, the stone table-top began to glow just enough so that I was not left in pitch darkness. It would have been all too easy to forget how many paces it took to cross the room and where the doorway was and where the bramble bushes. I had sufficient light not to scratch myself and to arrange my bed as I liked it. For the moment, I felt comfortable and secure and I had no difficulty in falling asleep.

In the morning, as I turned to look with lazy, half-opened eyes at my small domain, I felt an instant pang of betrayal. My suit of clothes had gone and, worse still, so had my boots. I had had the forethought to make a pillow of my satchel with its strap around my wrist so the iron knife remained in my possession. Nothing makes a man feel more of a prisoner than to lose his clothing. This was how they had tricked me, with food and a handful of woodland trash. No wonder it stank! How I ranted then, crying out that I had been all too easily gulled. How I mammocked my bed, kicking twigs and the hay mattress to every corner of my cell. I overturned the chair and thrust it half way through the wall. I scattered the dishes and stamped on the food until my bare feet were sticky with it. Tired and weeping with rage, I now sank to the floor, my skin smarting from the many scratches I had brought on myself. I wrapped my arms around my knees and became a parcel of utter distress. I wailed like some child who has lost his puppy. What a piece of work I looked and thus I stayed for a long time until the sun was high and made the room much lighter and the devastation more evident. It was then I spied what had quite escaped my notice earlier. Lying near the wreckage of my bed were several pieces of green cloth very like the colour of grass and therefore barely discernible. 'Sheets or blankets,' I thought and crawled over to investigate them. They proved to be two garments, a pair of loose breeches or slops and a shirt. Both were finely spun from a thread I did not recognise. Their colour reminded me of nettles and I knew it was possible to extract a thread from these plants.

'Oh, Edward Harry,' I sighed. 'They have left you their livery so that you might look like Robin Hood of the gay green wood. And you have once again been a brat of five years old.'

I decided to wash and put on my new clothes. In my rage I had wanted to kick the oddly-shaped bucket but, even in my fit, I realised that I could break my toes, so I still had water with which to refresh myself. The water made my scratches smart the more which I took as a just punishment. I dried myself and put on the garments. They were gentle on the skin even if their origin was a bed of nettles. When I looked about me I could see no shoes which occasioned some annoyance, but no more of the kicking and cursing. I pulled my chair out of the wall and collected the bowls and platters. The food was beyond rescue as was the bed which looked as if an autumn storm had blown through it. Now I bethought me that it was odd that my salvage keeper had not come running at the sound of so much disorder in my lodging. When Master Spenser's son Sylvanus was tearful, often for no reason that I understood, my habit was to walk away from him and give the lachrymose mood time to pass. Salvage had no doubt done this to me. He would know that some creature had come in the night, perhaps even himself although I doubted it, to steal the garments which bore Lord Ailill's crest and that the loss might disquiet me. I could grow to like being Robin Hood but could never tolerate the loss of my boots. Why must I always be fighting in this place to avoid going barefoot? The soles of my feet were as tender as any gentleman's and if I were expected to traverse the woodland paths, I should find myself lame.

I walked through my bramble doorway and, as I expected, found Salvage waiting for me. He lay at his ease, idly plaiting a few straws and looking with great composure at the scene before him. I chose to forget that he must have heard all my recent nonsense. 'My bed is a bed no more,' I said. 'My food is trampled to a paste and I have need of a belt and boots.' I waved my foot at him so that he should take serious notice of it. 'That is a gentleman's foot. It is tender and not used to treading on flints and thorns. I am not like you. If your master and mistress intend me to be of use to them, then I must be able to walk out of this grassy place. Without sturdy boots, that will be impossible. Do you understand me?'

Although he gave no indication that my words had been other than a dog's barking to him, I understood very well that subtlety of thought hid behind the vacancy of his gaze. He took an apple that had lain beside him and tossed it in my direction. This was to be my frugal breakfast. I laughed as I caught it and remembered how once I confined Sylvanus to his chamber with only a dry crust and a carrot because he used an oath against me. At least the boy had never tugged his bed to pieces or thrown his furniture at the walls. I consumed my apple slowly, savouring each small mouthful and leaving very little of the core behind. I had water and I had humble pie, so to speak. This apple had wintered in a store-room and gathered much sweetness to it. It was possibly the most delicious pippin I have ever eaten despite its unremarkable size and its wrinkled skin.

'At least they did not leave me a heap of foliage in which to dress myself,' I said eventually. 'It is a matter of wonder to me that you are able to make a decent garment of your leaves and creepers. No immodest part of you is on show to offend the eye, and nothing falls away when you move. I would truly hate myself if I were enfolded in bindweed.'

Once again, his cloudy eyes showed no reaction to my words or their tone, ungracious as they deliberately were.

Salvage eventually took to his feet and motioned me to follow him. There was a spot beside the little stream that gathered the afternoon sun and sheltered any sitter from the breeze. Here I was motioned to sit like the bad schoolboy on his stool in the corner. Salvage was off on an errand and I was to make do with sunshine and water until his return. By no means was I permitted to return to my lodging. I lay back on the warm grass, my arms folded across my breast and my eyes closed. I had never in my life delighted in receiving admonitions and, like the bad schoolboy, I would be up and about once my instructor's back was turned. I dozed for a good half hour before opening my eyes. Salvage was still beside me, watching me intently. I nonchalantly leant down and splashed some water at him.

'You will need to stay there all afternoon to catch me,' I said.

He tapped his nose in an, 'I am cleverer than you,' gesture and was gone. I stood to watch him step into the woodland. 'A belt and boots!' I called.

Thoughts are like stinks. They assail you suddenly and once you notice them you can never be rid of them. My suspicion was that my chamber was to be put to rights and that I was not meant to see this take place. My satchel was still there, however, with my orchalc coins and my iron blade. Fear of what might happen to my only true weapon came at me like a tugging of my beard. Noddlehead! I ran up to the bramble doorway and stopped dead. There was a chattering and a scratching taking place inside which alarmed me. The noises stopped as soon as I appeared and my shadow pointed like a dark finger into the room.

'This is *my* chamber!' I announced as I marched in. The room was empty, but the bed of twigs was half assembled and the trampled food was gone. I spotted my satchel at once. It lay to one side of the bed with the straps still buckled. My knife and coins were safe.

'I mean you no harm,' I said. 'Indeed, I thank you for your trouble.' Silence reigned. Looking about me, I saw no skulking faerie or boggart. They could slide through the narrowest space in a twig wall I imagined. Having nothing further to say, I took my satchel and left them to their business if they were minded to return.

I spent the rest of the day beside the water, singing songs to myself and idling like a lazy dog in the garden. There was an evening coolness in the air before Salvage returned. He dropped a long green cord and a pair of brown shoes onto the stone beside me. His pointing towards our dwellings brought out the passion in me again.

'Yes, I have been a wicked boy,' I snapped, hearing the voice of Sylvanus in my own. He had thrown a dish at the cat and smashed it, the dish that is. 'I have retrieved my satchel.' I shook it so that he might hear the contents jingle and be curious as to what they were.

My shoes were leather but odd in the sense that they had no heel and no shape. More than anything they reminded me of Calvagh's peasant footwear, a leathern bag with a drawstring, but I was not too proud to put them on. The soles were substantial and would, I knew, protect me from any roughness underfoot. Nonetheless, I could not hold back a small indication of my disappointment. 'These are from no master leprechaun's workshop. I can tell at a glance,' I said. 'However, they are solid shoes. Please thank the giver.'

I felt that I still languished in disgrace as he led me uphill. His back and shoulders were very eloquent in their disapproval. I am by nature an ironist, a trait made worse by the ill moods of others. Master Spenser had cautioned me about it when I answered him pertly and I now set about mocking the salvage man who had taken the trouble to fetch me what I requested. Gratitude struggled sometimes to find a corner in my awkward heart.

'I believe the servants have gone home,' I said. 'Shall we see if they have swept behind the door and made the beds? This brought forth no response. All was as before except that the stones, flowers and twigs we gathered in our journey thither had been removed. I would never know whether this was to deprive me of their information, a needless action, in any case, since the details were now quite set in my mind. I had rehearsed them perhaps a score of times during the afternoon. There was food in abundance, a ewer of juice and my wooden pail was also brimful with the addition of a few sweet flower heads. How they managed to fill it I could not imagine as I had only left the waterside once to ease myself and make my first experiment with an Elven mallow leaf. I can, by the by, recommend such leaves as a salve to a sore fundament. They have the touch of velvet.

A peace offering to Master Salvage was in order, I felt. I had no suitable gift for him, but what indeed would be suitable, a new loincloth of the choicest creepers perhaps, chosen and arranged by my own fair hand? He could, however, be my guest at dinner. This would be a dinner taken out of doors as his perfume was ranker than ever following his recent walk. I carried my chair and most of the plates of food out to the grassy space in front of our doorways. There was but one cup which he should have whilst I quaffed from the lip of the jug. I clacked the two stones together by way of announcing that I wished to see him. When he appeared, I motioned to my chair, which he refused to sit on, but he did accept the cup of berry juice. *It is easily washed* I thought ungenerously. The idea of our sharing a meal together seemed to please him and he ate well. If only we had had conversation. There was so much I needed to know and so little chance of finding it out. I would have been grateful even for a remark on the colour of my shoes or the design of my belt, but it was not to be. So we ate in companionable silence. Salvage chewed silently and did not drool, I was glad to note. With his bunches of leaves and his ripe tang, I would not have been surprised to hear him gobble like a farmyard beast in a trough. He lifted his food quite daintily to his lips, but oh, if he could have moved them in speech. Calvagh, present, would have entertained me with his liveliness, his saucy barbs and his respectful affection underlying both of these. It fell to me to provide the conversation for two which I did in a stream of magpie chatter. I asked myself questions and answered them in some detail. Were these slices of apple dipped in honey? Yes, Master Harry, they were. Should I put the flower heads, borage and marigold amongst them, in my mouth? Yes to that question too. Eventually, exhausted by my dialogue, I also sank into silence. The food was simple, but piquant, but I still eschewed all the meat dishes. I preferred to see the creatures on which I dined in their pastures before the butcher laid hands on them. Looking down at the platters of grilled and chopped flesh, I could all too easily imagine them the limb or haunch of one of the many frights that lurked in the undergrowth of this country. We sat together until the sky reddened and shadows gathered. The air cooled just enough to make a man sleep easily and there were no summer flies. I recalled the hot nights under the thatch of my grandmother's cottage and the crawling creatures which dropped onto my face from time to time. Long-legged spinners and their kind were banished hence and I need not fear mice or other vermin lurking in my twig mattress. It could have been an ordinary night in an ordinary home except that I lay down to rest in a country beyond man's knowing and was watched in my sleep by who knows how many eldritch eyes.

CHAPTER TWELVE

The next three days followed exactly the same pattern, a pattern which soon palled, like a diet of porridge or turnips. Whilst I slept, fresh food was left on my table and a clean set of Lincoln green apparel was placed beside my bed. As I never touched the meat, there was increasingly less of it each day. I yearned for roast beef or mutton, as I explained to Salvage, but none ever appeared. I lingered over my meals and washed my body several times a day both in my bucket and in the stream and yet there seemed forty hours of daylight which I could not fill. It was no consolation that I was cleaner than ever before in my life. 'If their intention is to show me the delights of their simple life,' I said to myself, 'they have not reckoned that their lesson may drive me to madness. There is nothing of the monk about me and I cannot bear silence for long.'

Sometimes Salvage shared a meal with me and then he would be gone for hours, foraging in the groves, reporting my behaviour to his masters, I knew not what. On the fifth day of my isolation in that grassy prison, that comfortable oubliette, a remarkable thing happened. I should add that I had itemised every sound in that place as a mental exercise to occupy my time. I knew the splashing of the little waterfall, the heavy whisper of the trees, the snap of a twig in the woods when I was being spied upon. And then, loud and vexatious, there was a buzzing next to my ear. I at once imagined a hornet with a deadly sting for which I had no salve and I jumped to my feet windmilling my arms to send the insect on its way. Flying creatures, of course, have the extraordinary ability always to be just beyond the reach of any weapon we use against them. We can swat and flail and they remain unswatted and unflailed. My new annoyer took up residence in the air perhaps ten feet in front of my face. It described circles and figures of eight which I took to be a kind of taunting. It was large bodied and blue, I noticed, and then I smiled and extended the palm of my hand. After only a few moments of consideration, it settled there and looked up at me. I will not say it smiled as its face was, in truth, too small for me to distinguish expressions and I am not certain, in any case, that diminutive flying fur balls are capable of such niceties. It was the blue creature I had rescued from a massacre come to thank me, I did not doubt. Well, we could not exchange news like old friends, but we sat together,

I on the grass and the blue creature on the seat of my chair which I brought out for that purpose. So desperate was I for company, that I talked to it and it replied with a shrill buzzing of its wings. At first, I leaned my ear towards it in the hope that I should hear tiny words, but there were none. Still, its assortment of high and low buzzing enabled me to pretend that it understood my remarks and was offering a considered response to them. I imagined how my London acquaintances would chortle to see me now. I was like some poor soul forgotten in his cell in a lonely castle. He makes a friend of a mouse or beetle, feeds it, cherishes it and is broken-hearted when his callous warder crushes it with his oafish tread. I had not been so comfortable for an age and I wondered whether my reason were not already half-addled. When I fed my small blue visitor scraps of apple, little paws, hands even, emerged from his fur. He also enjoyed the meat which I would willingly have parcelled up and made a gift for him.

'You must have followed my adventure at some risk to yourself,' I said. 'We found ourselves in the midst of a battle. A walking tree figured in the story also.'

There was some animated buzzing here which I took to mean, 'Yes, I saw it all. And wasn't I brave?'

'Your courage does you credit,' I continued. 'But what of my friend Calvagh? He did quite as much to save your kind as I. He rode up and down and everywhere in order to confuse the riders. I would give all I have to know my friend is well or that his captivity is no worse than mine.'

The buzzing became of a sudden very loud and deeper. A change of key, you might have said. As I began to translate it in a way that suited me, I realised it was the frantic recognition of Salvage's return. When my human companion emerged from the woodland, my blue friend popped from sight like a bubble. He was frightened of Salvage, that was evident, and I decided at once not to mention the visit. I swept the pieces of broken food onto the greensward and took my chair and plates indoors.

Salvage had a gift for me. I hoped that his concentrating on it meant he had not caught sight of my visitor. The gift was a stone knife, lying on a green cloth and presented to me with great ceremony. As I extended my hand to receive the weapon, it was snatched away with a snort which was as near to speaking as he ever came with me. I also snorted, as if to say, 'I have no patience with foolish games of "I give you and I give you not."' As we sat together outside my lodging,

Salvage laid the knife and its cloth very carefully on the ground as if it were a treasure. It had come from their Lord himself, for all I knew. He made sure that the cloth was perfectly flat and then tapped his finger several times on the point of the blade.

'I know which end is which,' I said. 'The handle end is possessed of a solid wooden *handle*.'

There was a second snort as I went to pick up the knife by its midriff. From somewhere in his foliage, Salvage withdrew a twig and used the knife to slice it as if it were of no substance at all. Then, striking the lesson home, he lightly touched the knife's edge with his finger. Blood immediately welled up.

'That is sharper than any razor I have at home,' I said. 'I would have wrapped my fingers around it and perhaps cut them all off. I am truly sorry to see you bleed in order to teach me not to be so heedless.'

I lifted the knife by its handle of burnished wood. The blade was fashioned from a glassy stone like flint but more green than blue and not as dark. Its edge was formed by chipping as I could tell when I held it up to catch the light. It had the power to strip the flesh from a man's arm in a twinkling, although a robust knock with something hard, my steel blade for example, would shatter it. As I inspected and admired the weapon, Salvage put his fingers into another part of his leafy dress and withdrew a ball of moss which he applied to his finger, quickly staunching the flow.

'You will be hungry,' I said, feeling that I ought to make amends for his injury by serving him a meal. I rose, intending to fetch the platters of food back out again, but he followed me inside and so I had perforce to serve him there where his body smells rose from him and were trapped by my walls and ceiling. We had another silent meal during the course of which I placed the stone knife in my satchel firmly bound in its cloth. Salvage chewed more slowly than ever and there were long moments of stillness between mouthfuls. What thoughts was he wrestling with or was his mind simply a comfortable emptiness into which he was content to slip? On a whim, I decided to sing to him. The noise would probably make me feel better, or it might even drive him away. Either outcome would be a happy one as I was beginning to find his odour suffocating. I began with *Sir Thomas by the Lakeside* which is long-winded and amusing if you have an ear for puns. Then, and I do not know what possessed me to do this, I began to sing in French, a little song I had once overheard and liked. I had barely completed the first couplet

Doucement, doucement, doucement s'en va le jour,

Doucement, doucement, à pas de velours.

before he began to tap his finger to his lips in a highly anxious way. I stopped at once and offered him a piece of fruit which he knocked from my hand. And then he was gone, although his smell was not. 'So you may be French,' I said to myself. 'And you have tender memories.'

The next morning I was disturbed from my half slumber by the clacking of the two stones. I slipped on my fresh green breeches and stepped outside to see what Salvage was about so early. The grass was cool with dew and the air was distinctly fresh on my unclothed back and chest. Well at least he was not about to say, 'And as for your behaviour last evening.' I sensed that he had summoned me for an important reason and I stood there wriggling my toes in the dampness and waiting to see what he intended. He tapped me on the shoulder and pointed to the group of trees which were his usual gate of entry into the woodland. Then he imitated my walking movement with his fingers.

'*On va visiter la forêt?*' I asked, unable to refrain from the slight malice of speaking in French. My reward was to have my legs swept from under me with a swift kick and I lay damp and breathless on my back while he glowered above me. 'Who is the moody one?' I said, more bemused than angry. Then, to show that I was not in the least put down, I got up, walked into my lodging and lay on my bed. The clacking of the stones recommenced almost at once. At first I responded with silence and then I called, 'Master Edward Harry is not at home. Pray take your business elsewhere. Good morning and *au revoir.*' The clacking now became so furious I thought it would shatter the stones. He had no choice, finally, but to march in uninvited and adopt a *You are making me very angry* pose with his arms akimbo and his lower jaw thrust out. I smiled sweetly and said, 'You knocked me flat on my arse. My father says we should no longer keep company.' His response was wordless, naturally. He pulled a twig from my mattress and thrust it roughly into my side. His strength was double mine, and I am no weakling, so it was time to pay attention and cease my teasing before his anger overflowed and I found myself nursing a broken head. I sat up, folded my arms and looked him directly in the eye. In reply, he fetched me a plate of food and my toilet bucket. 'So I am to wash myself, eat a morsel and be ready for this new adventure in no more than two minutes? I shall be at your service promptly. *Allez-vous en.*' I flicked my hand in the direction of my doorway. He slapped the plate of food onto my lap and marched out.

I had grown tired of life by the waterfall and the prospect of further sight-seeing was an attractive one. Perhaps I should be taken to meet the Lord and Lady again. Perhaps I should be sent home. As I did not know whether we would be returning to our twig cabins, I made sure to sling my satchel across my shoulder. I had two knives now, the stone and the iron, and I was about to discover whether my new shoes fell apart when I trod on the first woodland pebble.

Once we passed between the trees, I was back in the true land of faerie and I at once felt a presence in the air about me. The woods sang and the very earth tingled. By some device, this had all been kept from me for the past few days and I experienced the shock of one who drops into an icy pool on a summer's day. From every bush and branch came the calls of unseen and unknown birds, or at least of flying creatures. Our path to the glade with its cabins had been swept clear of its eldritch life and now all that life rushed back over me in waves that initially delighted as much as they frightened.

My salvage companion had a place of honour there, or, at least, he was treated with complete acceptance. I was a novelty and, to some, an unwelcome intruder. Nuts soon began to drop on my head or were shied at me, my feet became tangled in roots and at least half a dozen times an unattractive face leered from a spot just out of reach. This sense of being the newly-come stranger was what I had been shown when first I went to school. It quickly became known that I had no father, that my grandmother was the village wise woman and that only a parson's good offices enabled me to learn my letters. The other pupils thought to make of me their whipping boy, one they could insult as the unkind fancy took them. I put an end to all of that within a single day by soundly beating as many of them as I had time to catch. In a similar way, I tired of the scraps falling from the trees and the pelted dungballs. Edward Harry would take the fight to them and see how they liked it. Having made my decision, I stood quite still and took a long breath. We had reached the little stream I recognised from our first journey. The figwort silently stank nearby in its moist bed. 'I am Edward Harry!' I called out yet again. Salvage, who was walking ahead of me and did not see that I had stopped, jerked violently at the sound. 'Edward Harry!' It rang from every trunk and branch. 'Take note. Your little vexations are over.' I withdrew my iron blade from the satchel and brandished it. 'Whatever magic you have, in whichever cleft or crevice you hide, remember that in my hand is the power of iron. You know this power and you fear it.' I slashed at the bushes around me and saw them wither. At once I had a sense of a tide withdrawing. The woodland became more ordinary, more silent. Those who had sought to annoy me now followed wiser council and let me pass. I do not know what Salvage made of my declaration, whether, indeed, he was aware that I had such a knife. He simply walked on, assuming I would follow.

Unexpectedly, we soon passed a number of beings walking along woodland paths which intersected our own. None reached my height and most were decidedly not fair. Humped and bristled as they often were, they were apparently going about the ordinary business of country-folk – carrying a loaded sack on their back, a bundle of wood or pushing a wheelbarrow piled high with squirrels' tails. Most avoided our gaze and quickened their step. One pair, dressed in voluminous garments of orange and red, and presumably females of an ugly sort, waved at me before scampering away. 'Goodbye, sweet ladies,' I called after them, at which Salvage was aghast. If it were dangerous to talk to beings here and to give my name to them, the damage had been done many times over. I thought I should sing to show how little I cared about such old tales. I have a deep store of songs. How else is a boy to amuse himself seated by a winter fireside with only a crone for company, after all? I knew three ballads about Robin Hood and sang them all lustily as being most appropriate to my present situation. Was I not like Robin Hood myself in my nettle breeches and armed with my good English blade?

We spent hours walking here and there, there and here, up and down and round and about. Salvage strode ahead with confidence as one who had wandered these paths all his life and who loved them dearly. He regularly drew my attention to objects which delighted him and in which I could manage little interest. He would press a soft leaf to his cheek or crush a stem and sniff the juice which dampened his fingertips. After he thrust his stained fingers towards my nostrils for the hundredth time, I pushed them away and turned my back on him. He was endeavouring to show me his home, his arbours and secret corners, and I made the most waspish of visitors. What conclusion was I supposed to draw from our meanderings, that this was a spot so soft and scented it must remain forever a world apart and unvisited? I could see little logic in such a view as all our faerie tales told us that the inhabitants of this world came into ours all too regularly with their tricks and spitefulness. Salvage and I talked to no-one, we saw no buildings, we learnt, as far as I could tell, nothing that we did not know that morning, and I eventually wondered whether he had been told to abandon me, exhausted, like a babe in the wood.

When my hunger and exasperation were at a desperate pitch, I simply sat down amongst the dead twigs and leaf litter and announced that I would travel no more. At first, Salvage did not notice my rebellion, but, when, after thirty yards or so, he understood that I was not at his heels, he came scampering back with a look of great puzzlement on his face. He threw himself down beside me and put his hands on both of my shoulders.

'Now is the time, of all times, for you to speak,' I thought. 'To ask me if I have become ill.'

Still not uttering a word, he patted me in many places to see whether I would cry out in pain.

'I am not hurt,' I said, unmoved by his concern. 'We have not stopped to eat or rest and, unless you explain to me why we have gone round about like the tribes of Israel, *Je reste ici!*'

Salvage took hold of me in an embrace and tried to lift me, but I hung as heavy as a corpse and could not be budged. He then wedged his hands beneath my armpits and tried to lift me to my feet. Each attempt to shift me meant that my legs hung the more limply. Although he could have draped me across his shoulders, he perhaps sensed how violently I would struggle and so he chose to squat beside me and wait. At first, I scratched around me to gather whatever I could that was light and dry. Thinking to humour me and to hasten the passing of my obstinate mood, Salvage added a leaf or two to my pile. Mayhap he thought that I had lost my wits. Any person seeing a grown man concentrating on building a heap of woodland gatherings as if his very life depended on it, would no doubt think the same. When I had held each item in the pile between my fingers to find which was the driest, I opened my satchel. If Salvage had realised half of what I was about, he would certainly have stopped me on the instant. When I removed the stone blade and the steel one, he obviously did not see the powerful connection between the two. Nor did he flinch when I bent forward and struck one against the other. It was not until the first spark flew out and buried itself in my tinder that he registered alarm. I had fluffed the tinder into the delicacy of a spider's web and it gorged on the bright sparks. I soon had a brisk fire and a weapon I intended to bargain with. Using a stick, I flicked portions of the fire all about us and threw handfuls of leaves and dry brush wherever the flames took. My companion was in a state of the deepest anguish now as was the forest itself. I felt an oppression in the air about me. If the fire were not put out very soon, the trees for miles around could catch fire which was not a thing I wanted. I had merely intended to make my point that I was being toyed with and that I would have no more of it. Then, of a sudden, the flames leapt upwards and were gone. The air around us began to spin and the woodland floor for a space of perhaps ten yards became wildly disturbed. Twigs, leaves and earth flew up and around us, pressing hard against our faces as they spun. I quickly held my hands to my face so that I should not be made to breathe, or eat, all this material that swirled around us faster and faster. As the power of the whirlwind grew, stones were lifted, larger and larger ones, and they now walloped me vigorously. Then we began to spin ourselves. The wind whirred us off our feet like a pair of spindles. I had never known a motion more sickening, not even on my sea journey to Ireland when Master Spenser and I suffered so much and turned so green. I pulled my limbs into my body, bowed my head down to my chest as best I could and accepted that I was to be blown hard at a tree trunk and left broken like a man of straw. Spinning so fast, I lost all sense of direction, up and down and athwart, but at least I had avoided the trees. When the physical motion ceased at last, my head and stomach spun on as if a perpetual spinning had been started inside me. I did not even dare groan for fear that my heart, guts, liver would fly out of my mouth and wrap themselves around me. I was lying on grass whose softness I adored after the assault with twigs and stones. I pressed my face deep into the grass and seized it tightly between my fingers as if that would stop the violent spinning that yet threatened to wrench me apart. I am sure I even bit the grass to give myself a better hold on stillness. Once, when a child, I stood and watched as two great millstones crushed wheat grains into flour. I now felt as utterly crushed as any handful of flour, nay even more so. I was a shapeless handful of fine powder without bones or orientation. Death, my friend, where were you at that hour? If I had known in which direction you stood, I would have reached out my hand to you gladly. But that would have meant loosening my grip on the tufts of grass which were all that kept my innards from spinning into my mouth. It was agony to lie there, although others might believe that once I came to rest upon the ground my discomfort would subside. Imagine eating an explosion or a biliously fermenting vat of beer and you understand my situation. At long, long last, something passed over me like gentle wave, from my head to my shoes and my turmoil was over. I shuddered and vomited. The sundry extremities of my body which had been spun apart joined together again and I was whole, if ravaged. I doubted, still, whether I would rediscover the strength to lift my head, let alone walk about as briskly as I was used to do. A second wave flowed, then a third and a succession of them. At last I was able to sit up with my grass-stained face and my Lincoln green shirt all spewed upon. Beside me sat the salvage man, his vines rent and scattered so that he was all but naked. We were a sorry pair indeed, but, though my companion might look abject with repentance, I had now recovered sufficient strength to rage. We were in the presence, once more, of the Lord and Lady of those woods, he stern and brown, she clad in light green and appearing, perhaps, more merciful. There were no attendants visible, so this was to be a private audience or judgement. My head still drooped, but I was determined not to have a conversation with their feet like some lackey of no importance. I flung my head back unsteadily and out-faced them.

'You brought fire to these woods,' declared the Lord.

'Indeed I did. And you have punished me for it. You have also punished this man which was unjust and, may I say it, typical of your kind.'

The Lady intervened. 'His task was to acquaint you with our ways before you are…useful. He allowed you to be headstrong.'

'Your kind are always headstrong,' added the Lord in much less gentle tones. His anger creased his face and made his eyes more alien and more unearthly in their colour if that were possible. 'You have an iron dagger which you think is a perfect…'

'Talisman.'

'A talisman against us. You are wrong.'

'Then you will not mind if I hurl it at your brown heart,' I countered. I wondered how often he received such threats. His eyes widened even further and I took delight in the pursing of his mouth.

The Lady now raised her arms in clear exasperation despite her smile. Two males squaring up to each other like schoolboys. She had had enough of it. 'Your punishment was fierce,' she said.

'Quite so. For my own part it may have been merited. For his (I pointed to Salvage) it was not. I believe him to be the most innocent creature I have ever met and you are tyrants. I shall *not* help you. Rather than do that, I shall slit my own throat with one of the two blades I carry in my satchel.' I unbuckled my satchel in accordance with my threat. My intention was to throw my iron dagger at his Lordship and then to fight using the stone one. As a last resort, I was sure I had the courage to end my own life.

'You are in our power,' said the Lord.

'But this blade is not,' I replied, now brandishing my knife.

They stepped back a pace or two for all their power of enchantment.

'You should not anger my Lord,' said the Lady. 'Everything around us answers to his will – the creatures, the trees, even the stones themselves.'

'I shall die fighting to prove that his power does not extend to me, Lady,' I said resolutely.

'Our punishment was severe, I concede. You brought fire into our woodlands which you should not have done. I ask you to respect that.'

'I prefer explanations to punishments,' I said. 'What sense does it make to have as my guide a man who does not speak?'

'There are secrets he must not tell you. That is why. And we thought you would learn more quickly.' There was a snub.

'If I prove useful, shall I go free?'

'No,' said the Lord in his most authoritative voice.

'But your life here may be a comfortable one. You do not need to be like him.' She pointed at Salvage who had sat with a bowed head throughout our conversation. 'He is silent by his own choice. We have not severed his tongue.'

'I shall consider your proposal,' I said. 'In the meantime I ask you to re-clothe us. I am not used to walk about dressed in my own retchings and my friend's nakedness demeans him.'

'So be it. Tonight you will sleep in this open place. You will forfeit all the comforts we granted you. Tomorrow he will show you certain sights and it is to be hoped you learn from them this time.'

'A pitcher of water, please,' I said. 'My mouth is utterly foul.'

'Water only, then.'

At this, they faded from view, no doubt an easy enchantment for them. Perhaps they were never really there and had been seated, all the time we spoke, in the branches of some tree fanned with bees' wings and the like. If the fading were meant to impress, it did not do so. I was quite beyond such tricks. I was to serve them and be a prisoner all my days. This they believed. For the moment, my only concern was to find a patch of grass as far away as I could manage from the space I had soiled. I wished to rinse my mouth and then lose myself in sleep, simple desires and ones I hoped I could soon satisfy. I picked up the scattered and broken vine stems that had, somehow, cohered to make my companion an outfit, and I tossed them towards him.

'I pray you, dress yourself,' I said. 'A man without clothes appears like a slave and we are neither of us that.'

He looked at me and achieved a suggestion of a smile before leaping up and throwing the vines as far away as he could. He then plunged into the woods and was gone. I did not have the strength to conjecture where he might have gone or what he might be doing as I occupied myself with my own small concerns. I walked around the clearing, almost certainly a different one from before, and selected my bedchamber, a patch of grass that was mostly flat but which provided a gentle slope for my pillow. I lay down at once, taking off my ruined shirt and tossing it aside. If my punishment were to lie in my breeches on a patch of perfect greensward, then there were many worse punishments in the world. The glade was scented and the sky azure. All I hoped for on the morrow were jugfuls of drink and a clean shirt. If I were, truly, to be of use to the Lord and Lady of the woodland, it would surely not cost them much to grant me another nettle shirt. Every damaged part of me began to settle and I was heading towards the comfort of sleep when the ground beside me took a great thump. I opened my eyes to see Salvage busily engaged with a gardenful of newly plucked vines and creepers. His mood was much brightened and he had, I was delighted to see, a bucket of clean water which I used to refresh my mouth and face. I then sat and watched fascinated as he made himself a sort of breeches and doublet by plaiting the stems and twining them round his body, biting off the extra lengths and even leaving enough for him to make a green cap which he twisted jauntily over one ear. Seeing my naked chest, he offered me the yards of greenery still remaining. I could accept a bed out of doors, every poor man in England has known this at some time, but I refused, for anything, to be clothed like a wild man. I would rather have died then and there. What would follow – an abandonment of speech and dining on rodents or carrion? They would provide me with a shirt in the morning or I should take out my iron and stone once more and set up such a blaze as would make them remember Edward Harry for ever. To reinforce my point, I shouted it at the top of my voice and then fell down dizzy. There was food left in my satchel, but I lacked the stomach for it.

'I intend a long and peaceful sleep,' I announced in my whiniest school usher's voice. 'You would oblige me by not rustling at my ear.'

In reply, Salvage clutched his arms about him to simulate feeling cold. Then he pointed to himself and to me and afterwards to a single spot on the grass. His intention to snuggle me may have been brotherly but it might also have had a more sinister purpose. And there was always the rankness of the air about him that never failed to put me in mind of a drain.

'Nay, lie further off, good friend,' I said and pointed to two places on the grass a good ten foot apart. 'You there. I here. All night long.' As there was no sword to place between us to preserve my maiden modesty, I took the remaining greenery he had gathered and drew it into a line that clearly shouted, 'This is an insurmountable wall!'

Salvage merely shrugged and lay down with barely a sound from his foliage. I wondered what to make of his last slow blink at me. Was it to say, 'You will be very cold, then,' or, 'Just wait until you are asleep.'?

Very soon I heard snoring and although, normally, this would have kept me awake, now I found it a very reassuring sound. I settled myself on the ungiving ground and felt sleep drift through me.

CHAPTER THIRTEEN

When I opened my eyes, I thought at first it was noon-tide. A radiance filled the glade that could only be the sun at its zenith. I sat up and saw at once that the light emanated from the centre of the clearing and not from the sky. Slipping my hand into the satchel, I removed both knives. With the stone knife in my left hand and the steel blade in my right, I made towards the source of the light. This was an enchantment and I would defy it, carving it to shreds with my steel blade if need be. Casting my eye towards Salvage, I knew him to be fast asleep and a scatter of flower heads over his hair suggested that I would not succeed in waking him.

It was the Lady alone, clothed more in light than green this time.

'Greetings to you, Edward Harry.'

I nodded but did not bend my knee.

'You are doubly well-armed.'

'Naturally.'

'I am here without my Lord who has night business elsewhere. Shall we sit?'

I did not necessarily believe her Lord was out of earshot and I failed to put away my knives.

'We in the forest do not seek closer contact with Humankind. You know that.'

I knew that her kind entered our world all too often with their tricksiness and malice, all on their terms and not ours. What she wanted to avoid was any meetings where men might have the upper hand. I simply nodded by way of reply.

'Our cousins, the dwellers in houses, think differently from us.'

'As I have seen.'

'In order to bring us to their way of thinking, they seek to overwhelm us. You prevented certain murders at their hands.'

'I was glad to do so.'

'I ask you to be our champion. You feel strong passions and you are resourceful. You also wield the power of iron. You would suit us well.'

'I should like to suit myself.'

'No doubt. That is not in question, however. We offer you a long life and all the comforts our home has to offer.'

'To be tongue-tied and wrapped in leaves?'

'No. That has ever been his choice since first he came to live among us. I know it would never be yours.'

'You wish to have me kill for you?'

She delayed giving her answer. I flattered myself that she knew only the truth would do.

'Perhaps yes.'

'I am not a killer put out to hire. I am a kind of wandering scholar who serves as amanuensis to a great poet and who teaches that man's son his letters. I believe you mistake my character, Lady.' I thought of the *Lios Alfar* I had stabbed to preserve Calvagh's life. I did not intend my days to be measured in such screams.

'If I can put your mind at rest. We do not seek to overwhelm. We seek balance. You would help maintain that balance. If we are strong, our cousins will give up their madness.'

'You appear, Lady, to think I have little choice. This blade in my right hand, which you cannot easily take from me, this is my choice. And I say perhaps I shall help you.'

She bowed her head and made a small gesture with her hand.

'But if you ever again serve me as you served me today, look to your woodlands. They make good tinder. I also came to Hy Brazil with a friend. I should like to know he is well. Better still, I should like to be with him again. Exile might be more palatable in his company.'

She shook her head, possibly in a gesture of regret. 'Your friend is kept prisoner by the others and is beyond my power. I believe that he still lives, however. Here.' She extended her palm on which at first I could see only a shadow. There was so much light on her skin, it was difficult to distinguish edges and shapes.

'You have a small blue follower who is devoted to you,' she said. 'You gave this follower an errand which he was able to fulfil although I could not. Take it.'

I looked closely at her palm and saw a small, black half moon. It was a lock of hair.

'Is this Calvagh's hair?'

'I believe so.'

'If this is no trick, I thank you.'

Her radiance shimmered as if in anger.

'I do not lie.'

'Yet you prevaricate.'

I put away the stone blade and took the curl. I had nothing in which to wrap it and so, dropping it into my satchel, which I now did, meant it would soon fall apart and be lost to me. It was enough, all the same, to have even this uncertain token that my friend still lived.

'Tomorrow that sleeping man will show you how we conduct our lives. He has been like a child taking you for aimless walks and wasting precious time. He knows that is over.'

'He is good-hearted,' I said. 'If you hurt him, you hurt me.'

'You are capable of great loyalty,' she said. Here was another of my virtues they hoped to put to their own use.

Where my deepest loyalties actually lay was a question I could not easily have answered. I was certainly an Englishman loyal to his Queen in a land that generally detested her. Yet I had chosen for my bosom friend one of those very men who should have hated Her Majesty the most. I was loyal to my humanity, to my name (God knows I had bellowed it often enough), to my feet which I always insisted were encased in shoes. I was loyal, the Lady said, to a mute swathed in columbines and ivy, and, last of all, to a blue mothman who repaid me with a curl of black hair. Ah, life. I embraced its extraordinariness, its confrontations and its abrupt changes of direction.

A hay moon had been shining above us all this while, a globe of dazzling, yet warm, yellow in its palest shade. The light came down and joined the brightness of the Lady herself so that a column of subtle gold appeared to stream from her into the sky. Although I managed to keep my answers resolute, I knew I was in the presence of the goddess of the place. I had wrangled with her as if with some minor female guest at Master Spenser's table and yet part of me wanted to kneel and worship. I was in her court, after all, a court that existed wherever she was. It was not a court of throne rooms and secret antechambers. Her presence was in every grassblade, every drop of dew. She spoke through the maggot and the fly, through the salmon and the wolf and now she had to call upon a man such as I to help her, a man who could not in truth call even his name his own. Yet I understood what she wished to preserve, the very self-ness of that place. It was *her* kingdom and she was *it*. This was its gentler principle speaking to me, offering me, perhaps, friendship, or, at worst, a bargain. The Lord, the thrusting, smiting element, she had banished for the moment as I could never respond to him as I responded to her. The Lord and I would have quickly found ways to enrage each other, to lock horns, so to speak. It was entirely probable that in his season he wore real horns; I certainly had mine and they were draped with a banner which declared, 'I am Edward Harry, a Man, and I do not easily stoop.'

'Lady, mayhap we have common cause,' I said. 'For you, these woods are all. You feel that such as I would profane them. My fear is that creatures such as you would profane my state of Man.'

'Do you know how old I am?'

I did not see that her question followed logically from my last remark and I was determined not to come off second best in a game of words. 'You are ageless and I am scarcely twenty,' I said. 'That is common knowledge to us both and beside the point. I shall accompany this salvage man tomorrow and then we shall see what follows. If I do not cross paths with your Lord, I believe we might rub along.'

'Once I trod the groves in your country too,' she said. 'I was regarded with fear and adoration. No one then dared to talk of rubbing along. That was lifetimes ago when the moon shone with a different colour. You should sleep now.'

'I believe I should. And if I am to continue to wear your livery, I would ask for another shirt and the necessaries that were provided when I lodged in the cabin.'

'So be it.' She was gone and most of the night's beauty with her. The moon was settling behind the treetops and an exposition of sleep came upon me. I felt enriched, although I only reluctantly admitted it, and I was unwavering in my determination to achieve my own ends, a reunion with Calvagh and our return to the world of Men. I dragged heavy feet to my sleeping place and was aware of nothing until the morning.

CHAPTER FOURTEEN

We lay side by side on our stomachs high up in the rocks overlooking an expanse of scree and then a plain flanked for miles by trees. The plain extended southwards in the direction of the territories of the Elven lords such as the one I detested most, Lord Ailill. We had been squinting for an hour at the southern horizon as a troop of horsemen cantered nearer. They were not Lord Ailill's men, although their liveries were similar. Their helmets and breastplates were brazen and the device on their pennants and quilted white surcoats was a green wheel. Hidden beneath their armour were almost certainly men like myself, ones who were quite happy in their new alien service.

A part of me wanted to admire the company. Their horses were fine and the soldiers rode them well. Man and beast were hale and confident and every accoutrement shone. Yet I could not smile or wish them well on account of the burdens they carried at their spear ends. Half of the riders, at least, clutched a raised spear with some creature's head on its point. Others had severed heads tied to their saddle pommels by the hair. What skirmish had led to all this beheading I could only guess. Had it been a fair fight, weapon against weapon? Some of the heads were tiny which suggested an ambush rather than a genuine battle between equals. Most of the heads were, to my eyes, ugly indeed, but I had seen how defenceless these creatures often were against a soldier's blade and I deplored what had happened to them. Their mouths gaped as if in outrage or at the shock of being so easily deprived of a body. A few of the heads were not ugly at all. They were as large and as evenly featured as my own and belonged to what I thought of as the Lord and Lady's higher subjects. The soldiers rode up to the edge of the woodland and flicked their sorry cargo in amongst the trees. There was laughter and cheering as they competed to see who could throw his head the furthest.

'I believe that was a woman's head,' I observed as the last one crashed amongst the branches. 'The lovely hair streamed out behind it. What kind of warfare is this?'

An answer came almost immediately, not from Salvage who maintained his silence as always, but in a hideous din that exploded from the wood and terrified the horses. A rabble of woodland creatures raced out, some astride hogs

163

or other antlered creatures which defied description, but most of them on foot. They wore no armour and carried only rocks or cudgels of wood set with lines of stone teeth. Their own teeth and claws were their best weapons and these they set about using on the soldiers and their mounts, oblivious to the vicious damage dealt to them by sword and spear. When two beings who are possessed of magic fall to blows, it would appear that the enchantment on each side renders the other useless. Their fighting comes to resemble the wrestling and hacking of any human conflict which sprays the earth with gore and fills the air with groans. I was as fascinated by this struggle going on at my feet as I was sickened by the sight of it. The soldiers were far fewer in number but more disciplined; the woodland creatures were often diminutive but driven by the courage of the possessed. It was an evenly-matched contest for some time until a number of young trees at the edge of the wood were smashed down by something emerging from the depths. Woodlander and soldier alike were crushed beneath the falling timber. And then there were cries of dismay and a silent halloo from my own lips as the fearsome beast which had taken me from Lord Ailill's manor issued forth. It was an assemblage of beasts, I could see that now, with the benefit of distance. Or was it? There were distinct trunk-like legs, several in number, beneath a vast of bole of branches out of which many kinds of arm wielding many kinds of weapon appeared. It reminded me of a man-of-war with guns ablaze as it flowed over the Elven and men from the south, trampling and overwhelming them. Soon there was not one left alive. What followed then was a gruesome aftermath which I indicated to Salvage I did not choose to witness. The horses were tied together and wholesale decapitation began. The heads of the fallen were to be sent home as an act of defiance or mockery. There was a dark irony in the fact that those who had delivered severed heads to the woodland were now to return as severed heads themselves. It was an irony that I did not wish to share and I did not care who caught sight of me as I rose and stumbled away, sick to my guts.

I did not feel even slightly more comfortable until we were walking beneath trees again and I had the scents of leaf mould and sap to fill my nose and distract me. True, I had pierced a man-like creature, one of the *Lios Alfar*, through the heart, but that was in defence of my friend Calvagh and I took no pleasure from it. In my breast there lurked a firm distaste for both factions in Hy Brazil, the

Men-welcomers and the Men-abhorrers, and I would never incline to either side while they beheaded their fellows with such glee.

It might seem a simple thing for me to have leapt astride one of those horses sent back home with a decoration of their owners' heads. 'Simple seems' is never the same as 'Simple is', regrettably. A cord of enchantment had been wound around my ankle and it was impossible for me to cross the border from this country of wild things. I would happily have run south the moment I glimpsed the open plain for the first time, but no amount of brandishing my iron dagger could break what was a most powerful spell. My blade glowed and my palm burned and that was all I got from it. I was chained, confined, tied to a stake. Now, I am not one to sing in my chains and my eye was always alert for a magic door half-open and the prospect of freedom beyond. The magic binding had not been mentioned by the Lady of the forest and I was unaware of it until Salvage and I approached the woodland edge. A sharp tug at my ankle warned me that I could not stray too far.

In Salvage's company I was daily taken to spy on forest dwellers at work and leisure. That is, we tried to spy on them and were immediately noticed and hissed at. We were never closer than twenty yards before they leapt up and away leaving their washing to billow in the stream or a small drum to roll where they had dropped it. The more times this happened, the more sheepish Salvage looked. My own expression must have been one of great puzzlement. I had been given a hero's welcome for saving their fellows from the sword, but they would not be peeped at. To trespass on their privacy seemed the worst of crimes and I quickly tired of their petulant stand-offish ways. So much for the Lady's hold over her subjects if they could think she would be pleased with their dung-pelting tricks. 'I shall injure you with a stool of my own passing, tomorrow,' I called after a particularly unwelcoming group and then I had to lean against a trunk and laugh at my own wit for many minutes afterwards.

Driven by a bitter sense of failure, all Salvage could do was to lead me to one of those vantage points where we might watch the great tree-beast go forth. Some days it stayed at home and on others it went to war in the company of a swarm of creatures who flitted in and out of its leaf-cover as the mood took them. Three times we saw it return with heads dangling red from its branches like succulent berries. I quickly decided I had no wish to see any more of such bloodthirstiness.

It was the sort of barbarism one expected in the Americas, not on England's very doorstep. I also harboured suspicions as to what might become of the corpses once so firmly attached to these heads. I knew that I should never be able to swallow another meal for the whole of my life if I were to catch a gaggle of eldritch beasties chomping on a raw limb hacked from a human or Elven soldier. I communicated all these thoughts to Salvage with, I believed, great clarity. I shouted in his ear in English and inaccurate French, 'You were commanded to show me how these creatures live, not how they butcher one another. Will this make me your Lady's champion? I think not!' While I raged, Salvage either covered his ears and turned his back on me or sought to placate me with objects he had found, a wing feather blue as lapis lazuli or a leaf with neat holes chewed out of it that gave it the appearance of a face. As a last recourse he put his hand inside his leafy coat and presented me with the smallest, daintiest and most brilliant bird's egg I had ever seen. I took it between my fingers and crushed it to nothing and then continued with my shouting although I was fully aware that there were now tears in his eyes. 'Will you be told!' I said. 'I have seen what havoc your living tree causes. I have watched it crush and batter and I wish to see no more. Pray pass that information on. It would appear the southern folk have no answer to this walking forest and my help is not needed.'

We slept in our former cabins and had returned to the pattern of fresh clothing, food and water being given to us each morning. My longing for meat was now quite sharp, despite the horrors I had witnessed, yet I could not bring myself to eat anything other than the cooked eggs and cheese.

So, on a particular morning, I sat still and would not budge. I heeded no entreaties for us to be gone, which is to say I ignored all Salvage's pouting and pulling and remained seated with my arms tightly folded. 'I know the woodland beast inside and out,' I said cheerfully. 'My education in that quarter is quite at an end. I am also an expert on the many kinds of faerie dung. Let us move on to other topics. Would you like to share your favourite book with me?'

In order to extract me from the glade, Salvage was obliged to use far more communication than he liked. He planted one leg firmly in front of the other and made thrusting movements with his right hand. 'You are fighting incompetently with a sword,' I said. Next he broke his invisible sword over his knee and with a ninny's smile walked forwards as if to …I know not what. I pondered. 'We shall not be witnessing a battle today. Is that your meaning?' I asked. 'I am greatly joyed to hear it. If you have some peaceful delight to show me that does not involve the hurling of dung, I shall go with you.' I took him by the arm to confirm my willingness because I had come to the conclusion that he had the facility to turn genuinely deaf ears to my words when he chose. In all honesty, I expected nothing more than to be taken to see a clutch of freakish acorns or leaves chewed into the semblance of lace. It was a shock, therefore, when, after an hour's walking, we came upon a gathering of the woodland folk around the base of an oak tree. My instinct was to retreat into the bushes and to protect my face from the first of the inevitable dung pellets. Salvage would not permit me to linger, however, and he pushed me forward until we stood at the outer edge of the woodland circle. The creatures were the usual mix of shape and size. There were the fanged snufflers who travelled on all four limbs, an assortment of manikins as green as their garments and two delicately featured beings my own size. There was some growling when I arrived which a female brownie put an end to by rapping the offending snouts with a stick. She, not the taller, lovelier ones, was evidently the mistress of ceremonies and she chattered away as if offering an explanation of why we were all gathered there. Her head was no higher than my navel, her face was lined and weathered, or perhaps simply very old indeed, and her clothing was a vague piece of drapery stained the deepest chestnut. She could have blended into any woodpile or heap of leaves and yet she held the attention of all, myself included. As the base of the oak tree was the heart of the gathering, I sidled around until I had an unobstructed view. We were there for a burial. In a hole dug between the largest roots of the tree lay not a body but a collection of limbs and heads. It was a warriors' grave, I imagined, yet this was no elaborate ceremony. There was no singing, no weeping and not a suggestion of a prayer. The brownie pointed to sundry of the mourners who offered a sentence or two or who, in one case, simply barked. Perhaps they were being invited to offer their opinion of the dead. Who knows. The schoolboy within me might have laughed at such a parody of our own churchyard formalities, but my eyes were lowered with the rest and I thought only of what cruel act had brought once living creatures to their resting place amongst tree roots. Where were their bodies, was my greatest question. When all that was due to be spoken, or vocalised, was done, the brownie set about dismissing us all. I now discovered that everyone there, except myself, had in their hand or paw something to drop into the grave. Usually this amounted to no more than berries or a tuft of sheep's wool and I was greatly vexed when even Salvage stepped forward with a handful of forest litter to sprinkle over the dead. We were the only two left by now and I felt a genuine pang that I had nothing to offer. In desperation, I slipped my hand into my satchel and came up with two brown and forgotten rings of dried apple. 'For whatever comes afterwards,' I said and added them to the other offerings.

Now the mistress of the occasion began to sidefoot the earth into the grave. Her feet were small and apparently lame and the task would have been a long one for her. Faerie etiquette was a subject about which clearly I had absolutely no knowledge and so I risked giving great offence when I said, 'Allow me, madam.' I said the words all the same and she stood aside as I quickly toppled the pile of graveside earth over the body parts. I did not expect a cross to be planted, obviously, but I wondered why there was no root of flowers to mark the spot as a special one. I certainly did not anticipate that madam would jump up and down to flatten the soil, clap her hands together as if to say, 'Well that's them seen to,' and stomp off. Earth to earth, I suppose and the tree would benefit from the decaying flesh. The personality of the mistress of the burial was so authoritarian and unsentimental, she put me in mind of many churchmen I had come across in England. Perhaps this was their secret, that beneath all the self-importance and absence of warmth for their fellow men there lurked a miserable little brownie woman who did not give a farthing for anything but herself.

I would dearly have loved to engage the taller, and, therefore in my estimation, higher, beings in conversation. There were thoughts I needed to share and many questions to ask. Pairing me with a mute salvage man who bore an aversion for the spoken word, and particularly for words spoken in French, had not been the best policy. The high folk disappeared in an instant after the funeral and I determined not to let such an opportunity slip through my fingers again. Were they dryads, I wondered, water spirits for their paleness, the dead, or humans stolen at birth in place of a changeling? If they were unwilling denizens of these woods, they might rejoice in joining with me and Calvagh to escape. It could not be such a hard thing to cross between our two worlds or there would not be so many stories of the faerie folk told to wide-eyed children. All the Elvenkind seemed to flit backwards and forwards as easily as we humans stepped out of our front doors. At the back of my mind, always, and interwoven into my every action, was the determination that I should discover this secret. If it meant I had to climb the tallest crag or swim a sea, I should manage it. When these thoughts came upon me like a passion, I was obliged to drench my face with cold water and slow my breathing lest I give myself away. At the moment, there was but a single magical chain around my ankle. I had no desire to give my captors an excuse to enmesh me in a hundred more.

Although I had stared fixedly at the tall beings, they never once acknowledged my presence. They had long pale faces and long pale hair, as if they avoided sunlight, and their garments were the same cloth as my own. Of their eyes I could not be certain as they kept their heads bowed, in my direction at least.

'This was an odd start to our day,' I said to Salvage. 'Where now? A wedding or a christening?'

He was already striding many paces ahead and so I followed. If an afternoon of slaughter were in prospect, I had a tempest of ill-temper to unleash on him. In fact, we walked back to our cabins, which was a considerable surprise. Even more surprising was Salvage's insistent mimicry which gave me to understand that I should sleep as much as possible during the day because we were bound on an expedition once darkness fell. There was much pointing to the sky and the forming of a circular shape with his fingers which I took to represent the moon. The Lady had asked to speak to me again, I was convinced, and so I determined to be at my freshest for the occasion both by sleeping now and also by paying great attention to my toilet. My beard was sorely in need of a razor and my hair was unkempt from the lack of a comb. How I wished I had stolen the one we found in lord Húon's bathing room. I would fain have sought the aid of a faerie barber, if such a creature existed, so that I might enter the royal presence with smooth cheeks and more of the appearance of a gentleman. I had to be content with merely a dampening and a patting down of my shagginess. For the briefest of moments, I thought of handing my stone blade to Salvage and asking him to shave me. The fatal flaw in this scheme was that I mistrusted his understanding of what I intended. I knew that Salvage would oblige me, his friend, but what if he believed I was asking him to cut my throat. He would carry out my request with his zany's smile and then the more fool I.

Daylight eventually quit us and the moon rose. I sat on my chair at the doorway of my lodging expecting that the Lady would appear before us in an aura of moonlight. I was unprepared, therefore, for a tap on my shoulder and a sign from Salvage that I was to follow him into the woods. I was intrigued and also a little concerned so I made sure to throw my satchel over my shoulder. It still contained the presents Calvagh and I had purchased in the Elven market and I wondered how the Lady would react if I offered some of them to her. She probably preferred a necklace of crab apples or jay feathers to the gewgaws we had purchased.

In darkness I am near blind. I blunder and stub my toes and curse. Salvage was as sure-footed as a cat, leading me by the hand deep amongst the trees. I still believed that I had been summoned to a secret assignation with the Lady, or, much less likely, with her Lord, and that I was to be entrusted with some embassy of great magnitude. I had come to believe that my value lay in the role of an ambassador delivering messages between the two contending factions. It was not the Lady and her trust that lay ahead of us; it was a meeting far more furtive and dangerous. It was, in truth, a spying rather than a meeting. I had crashed my way through the undergrowth up to this point and from now on, as was made clear by gentle blows whenever a twig snapped beneath my shoe, I was to be entirely silent. A good half-mile was traversed in this way and a very slow half-mile it proved to be. A glow amongst the trees ahead of us made our silence increasingly easier to maintain as I now had some idea of where I stood and where a branch was likely to snag me. We did not enter the glowing area, however, remaining instead in the shadows that skirted it. We could see and yet not be seen. Here was another of the smoothly-grassed forest clearings. We had walked across so many of them in our wanderings, I came to think of them as suites of rooms within the great palace of the wood itself. If one knew where to look, there were corridors running between them, woodland trails with waymarkers of particular stones or ancient, leaning trees. In the centre of this glade lay a low mound perfectly circular and a magnet for the moon's rays it would seem. Three figures danced atop the mound and a fourth, lesser, figure sat beside it playing a melody on a pipe. The dancers were all female and my shocked eyes registered that they wore little in the way of clothing. It hardly makes sense to say that they were clad in light, as if moonbeams can be stitched or taught to follow the shape of limbs. They certainly wore no skirts and yet, whenever one of them spun, something with a substance of cloud or cobweb flared out. Their dance meant that they intertwined with each other, their arms often extended upwards and their hair swirling and drifting in the air. I had never witnessed such an expression of pure joy and do not expect to do so again. They *were* the light and they *were* the music. I breathed in a deep contentment as if every part of my being were in a state of harmony or grace. The melody was not a single tune that you could learn and then sing along with like some 'Here we go a-gathering primroses' country ditty. It was snatches of sound, flutings, that made me think of, what shall I say, birdsong at dawn, bees in a meadow, even though the instrument also had the recognisable timbre of some kind of recorder. When I tore my gaze away and looked at Salvage, he had his hands clasped before him as if in prayer. Perhaps it was the regular feasting on such stolen delights that made his simple life bearable. I turned my head back and took a step in order to avoid an obscuring branch. This was my undoing as I trod in a hole and pitched forward. I fell with a noise that was all the rougher for its contrast with the music of the dance. At once, the music ceased and the light dimmed. Expecting an even greater whirlwind than when I had set the forest carpet alight, I hunkered down and made myself into a small and uncomfortable ball. Perhaps I heard a voice, perhaps a cry. I was struck, certainly, though by what I never knew. The blow spun me over several times and I made myself yet smaller hoping to avoid being blown from one end of the forest to the other.

I awoke in daylight, thrust under a bush, fortunately not a bramble, with an unpleasant ringing in my ears that took a while to dissipate. I sat up and found I was alone. Salvage had fled or had been taken away to be punished for his trespass. I was glad he kept no dogs for the punishment of Actaeon burst into my mind as it would for any schoolboy who knew his Latin. To be torn to pieces by his own pet hounds for peeping at a goddess! The parallel brought a sweat to my brow. I had made my situation vastly worse, of that there seemed little doubt and I was surprised not to be in pieces myself. I am enough of a countryman to believe that I can navigate my way out of any woods, no matter how dense. Yet these were not English woods and for all my perambulations with Salvage I did not feel at home in them. And I had clearly committed an offence. My first thought, as always, was to take my iron weapon and I duly opened my satchel.

'You have no need of a weapon. Your life is not at risk.'

I am sure that I rose inches from the ground for I had not been aware of anyone beside me. I hastily stood up and, notwithstanding the reassurances I had been given, held my knife out in front of me. A brown-skinned maiden was no more than an arm's length away from me but, such was her affinity with the woodland, my eyes had not seen her. She was, to all appearances, human, although I sensed at once that she was quite other. I looked at her ears, which were daintily pointed, and next at her feet and her back, wondering idly whether her beauty was to be spoilt by hooves or a tail.

'You played for the dancing,' I said, taking note of the pipe she carried in one hand.

I hoped for confirmation and received none which, even though my remark was of no consequence, was a mild irritant. It was an irritation I had soon to grow used to because it was never the habit of these 'people' to say 'Yes' when I had guessed some truth about them. The absence of the word 'No' generally told me that I was correct, but this was by no means always the case. Sometimes their silence signified that I had strayed onto topics that were not intended for the likes of me. She certainly never allowed herself to be drawn on the identity of the dancers.

We were still not far from the glade where I had watched the dancing and she walked into it, intending that I should follow. I first looked carefully about me, fearing to see the blasted remains of my salvage guide. As he was not dead, or, at least, not dead in this spot, I was glad to walk out into the sunshine and stretch my sore limbs. I had lain like some carcass trussed up for many hours and my body was letting me know its displeasure. I put my blade back in the satchel and walked up and down in long strides, swinging my arms and moving my back from side to side. When I was ready for conversation, or instruction, I marched towards the low mound and sat down on the very top of it. This was to make a point. The maiden sat a little lower down the slope, obviously without fear that I would use my position to harm her.

'The morning is beautiful,' I said, 'and would be even more beautiful if I knew that my salvage friend has not been harmed.'

'Why should you care?'

'Why should I *not* care? He wished to share a wonder with me, as friends do. I suspect it was forbidden and he is in disgrace.'

She turned away and looked out across the glade, making me wait, perforce, for her reply. As I waited, I took advantage of my seat to examine her closely from the top of her head down to her bare feet which I was so pleased were not cloven. Her hair was almost the hue of cowslips, a kind of moderated yellow, and it was kept neat by a plaited band of grasses. Her gown was nettle cloth like my own, if thinner, and gathered at the waist by a girdle of the same. Her bangles were of grasses and, wherever she could make them stay, there were flower heads of every colour, buttercups, daisies, ragged robins and bird's eyes. 'Flora,' I thought and *Flora* I would call her whatever her true name turned out to be.

'He is not hurt and will soon forget you,' she said slowly as if it were a casual thought and hardly worth the speaking. Her tone vexed me quite as much as if she had pointed to a few charred ribs and said, 'There he lies.' Perhaps her life moved at a different pace from mine, or perhaps she had been bidden to tantalise me. I decided that I would prefer to dictate the rhythm of our conversation myself and that I could not be doing with great silences, lovely as she was and delightful as I found it to sit beside her. I was reminded by the scent of flowers which rose like the gentlest of suggestions from her of how unsavoury the company of Salvage had been in one particular.

'Are you on an errand with regard to me?' I asked. 'Or shall we sit here pleasantly together for a while and then go our ways?' I stretched out and closed my eyes, not expecting an immediate response. 'You may warble on your pipe if you wish,' I said. 'I shall not mind.'

Perhaps ironically, she proceeded to play and I was lulled by the sweetest of melodies. Long after the melody was finished, she spoke again. 'You are to lodge with us now and we are to teach you properly. Then you will find a way to be of service.'

We? My curiosity was aroused, but I kept my peace. I luxuriated in the warmth and the ease and the thought that I might soon have regular conversation again. Just as I was beginning to slip into my regular melancholy conjectures, was Calvagh safe and how were we to get home, she said, 'We must go. My brother expects us.'

Her *brother!* I was to lodge with a family and could hardly wait to learn what lay in store. Flora led me, with no sense of urgency, along more of the woodland paths until we came to what I suppose amounted to a village, or at least a substantial hamlet. This was not a village of the English style that I had grown up in, with its church, manor and frill of cottages. There was a series of small clearings linked by well-trodden paths and in each clearing sat between one and three cabins of the kind Salvage and I once shared. A novelty was that there were fires, cooking pots and signs of manufacture. *Civilisation,* I thought, although it had none of the high living of London or the Elven manors. The nut-brown maiden had a living room of her own adjacent to that of her brother and smaller, more perfunctory accommodation had been reserved for me. The brother was, indeed, in the process of completing it as we arrived. Whereas for the walls of their own dwellings they liked to use living growth, saplings or thickets, my walls consisted of wattles planted in a small square like a sheepfold. *So, in their eyes, I am at the level of the cottage pig or Easter lamb,* was my immediate thought. A man leaning his full weight on my shelter could have flattened it in an instant and that it was the most temporary of homes was abundantly clear. They did not expect me to be amongst them long. The brother had placed a tall pole at each corner of my, what shall I say? – hovel, and then bent these over to form hoops. More flexible wattles fashioned of grass and creeper were being fastened on as my roof. I was invited to assist in the tying of my roof to the curved poles and this I accomplished most dextrously, if I may boast.

The brother was, like his sister and myself, clad in nettle garments, or weed weeds as I thought of them in a humorous moment. His skin was browner than his sister's and he had a sour face. Where Humankind were concerned, he harboured no generous thoughts and his demeanour towards me always let me know this. His ears were quite round and his eyes had very little of the slant about them. They were a kind of flecked brown and he could easily have passed for my brother, albeit one who was burnt by the sun and did not share my education. On a day when his sourness became particularly irksome, I pointed out to him how similar we were and rendered his manner even more rancid, as I expected.

So the house, I laugh at the word, was finished and Flora brought me a thin mat to sleep on, an insubstantial coverlet and a water bucket. I detained her when she had completed her errand as there were questions I needed to ask. Her immediate reaction was to stand in my doorway as if about to leave.

'I am not asking you to share great secrets,' I said and, reluctantly, she sat down. 'My last host would not speak to me and so I did not learn as much as I needed. Will I stay in this *hut* for ever?'

'I do not expect so. It is not built for winter.'

'Have you been told what to do with me?'

'My brother has.'

'Will he deign to tell me?'

'I do not know that word. He will tell you what he needs to tell you.'

Nothing was volunteered and I could have shredded my little home in annoyance. 'Am I expected to gather my own food?'

'Of course not. I shall prepare a meal soon which you will share with us.'

'Will that meal include meat?'

The look she gave me then was a most strange one, as if I were a cannibal and had asked for a juicy human thigh, preferably raw.

'Yes we eat meat, but many other things too.'

I explained that a few slices cut from an animal I recognised and roasted would be most agreeable.

'Some of us herd sheep,' she told me. 'My brother is fond of their flesh.'

This was good news as my bowels had begun to quarrel with me for my constant diet of vegetables and fruit.

Flora left to attend to her domestic duties and I lay on my very flat bed to collect my thoughts. I wondered which stage of my testing or education we had now reached. Was I supposed to conclude that the woodlanders' way of life could only be harmed by intercourse with men? Were the maiden and her sour brother really Humankind like myself who were simply blessed by better weather and the absence of the need to drudge? I could not think of it as an *Aevum Aureum*, a Golden Age, since I longed at times for the feel of a city street beneath my feet, for the camaraderie of a tavern, or for a silent moment with a book in my chamber. The woodland folk knew none of these and did not care for them or they would have come down to live with such as Lord Ailill and his father. 'Take as you find,' I said to myself and smiled when the fatty smell of cooking mutton eventually drifted through my doorway.

Outside, I found Flora engaged with a haunch of be-juiced meat turning over a fire in which she had also placed a number of earthenware vessels. So, they had potters amongst them, and mightily skilful ones too, to judge by the regular shape and smooth texture of her kitchen equipment. I imagined they possessed many skills and simply chose not to use them, an exercise in denial of which I knew I was incapable. Across the clearing, Flora's brother had a second cabin which I saw was a workshop. This drew me as I have always felt and shown respect for men who can fashion fine objects with their hands. I may be a scholar, but I do not place myself upon an absurd pedestal, I hope. I went and sat on the grass about six foot from the brother. He was engaged in making a bowl, which is to say that he had in his hands a piece of wood with a natural curve in it and he was simply encouraging a shape that was already there. Rather than create a bowl, he released it. What it lacked in symmetry it made up for in the individuality of its detail. Even apparent blemishes became necessary parts of the decoration. There were holes in it and the thickness varied and yet I would have treasured it. Around him lay his tools, a range of stone blades and pots of stain and polish and the rough brushes he used to apply them. I was happy to watch as he worked and he was very happy to ignore me. He had neither nodded me a welcome nor even cast the briefest of glances in my direction.

'My name is Edward Harry.'

'I know your name.'

'I do not know yours.'

'No, you do not.'

'You have the hands of a true craftsman. I should very much like to purchase one of your dishes.'

'We do not buy and sell.'

'Nor do you cultivate good manners, with your sour face and unfriendly tone. I would have thanked you for my cabin but I fancy you were commanded to build it and had no choice.' I left him before I gave in to the urge to kick his little pots into every corner of the glade. I felt the loss of Calvagh who had always been only too ready to share his company with me.

Our meal was mutton in gravy accompanied by peas and a nut stuffing. We dined off wooden platters mopped with squares of nut bread which I found most tasty. We followed the meat with a stew of summer berries and drank water infused with flower heads of a seasonal kind. I have always been a great one for gossip at mealtimes and I tried my hardest to engage the maiden in conversation. She either replied very briefly or looked at her brother as if to say, 'Am I permitted to answer this question?' and consequently said nothing. I found out little more than the meal already told me, that they kept beasts, made pots and would not soil their hands with coinage.

'After dinner, at Master Spenser's castle at Kilcolman, we are used to entertain each other,' I said brightly and caused a great glowering on the brother's face. I had decided to discomfit him as much as I could in recompense for his dog-in-the-manger-ness.

'Shall I tell you a tale or sing you a song? Both together, perhaps?'

As my hosts were confused by the generosity of my offer, I then and there opened my lips and launched into the sauciest ditty I could call to mind. I was loud, but perfectly in tune, and the expressions on their faces were soon ones of great consternation. I particularly relished the questions and answers in the song:

> O what is this so stiff and warm?
> It's only my old nag; he'll do you no harm.

> But what is this? It is a little well
> Where your fine nag may drink his fill.

'That is called singing for your supper,' I said when the last jolly notes of the chorus had died away in the trees around us. 'It was a splendid supper and I hope you thought it a splendid song.'

The brother stood up and walked over to his workshop for there were still hours of daylight remaining. Flora tidied up the relics of our meal and would not look at me. Unabashed I went to my lodging singing quietly to myself:

> And if she isn't gone, she lives there still.
> Ah ha was it so, was it so?

I determined not to bandy further words with Master Surly until he chose to speak to me but, as I had not yet been shown their woodland offices, I needed to walk over to him and put this important question. Without uttering a word, he took me to the enclosure with its soft mallow leaves and showed me the nearby stream. Above its little fall, the water was for drinking and, below that, one might wash.

'I thank you most heartily,' I said to his disappearing back.

On the morrow, we breakfasted in silence on fruit and bread and cheese and drank a hot infusion of leaves in water which I found most refreshing and palatable. I was then to be taken by the pair of them to see more of their lives, no doubt with a view to working out how I might set about preserving them from human taint. I learnt most of this from nut-brown Flora as her brother found it a point of conscience, almost, not to speak to me. She would have told me more, laughed perhaps, if that shrivelled presence had not stalked us with the cheerfulness of a death's head. We spent many hours out of the woods walking though what I would almost dare to call champaigns, fields with corn and other crops, sheep and a few cattle. There were no farmhouses or barns, however, as all accommodation was kept strictly within the trees. Even the gardens I was shown were like little woods themselves with the plants growing at all heights beneath the nut or fruit-bearing branches. As a country lad myself, I admired the neatness and efficiency of what I saw, although I soon grew tired of telling this to wilfully deaf ears. I never did discover how they managed their dairying in amongst the trees. Although, as a child, I had not needed to scare birds or clear stones from the fields, I felt a genuine interest in all that Flora showed me. There were questions to ask and comments I wished to make in which the brother, the nameless sour presence, showed not the slightest interest. I have, I think, a taste for objects which are beautiful and I would dearly have liked to accompany him as he searched the forest for pieces of wood he could shape. I made this request to him, twice as I remember, and was rebuffed with a snort. Heaven knows, I did not intend to steal his skills; I am a better audience than I am a fashioner of objects myself. He could, if he had possessed the wit, shared a knowledge with me that it would be good for men to know. Instead, he was aloof and tiresome and I longed to put my foot roughly to his arse. When he spoke to his sister, it was in their own tongue, too fast and too softly, and I was quite excluded.

Our day's journey ended with all three of us returning weary and somehow heavy of heart. Showing me the garden in which they lived should have been an occasion for celebration, not a grudging traipsing about.

'I feel you have not properly obeyed your Lady,' I said as we returned to the clearing in which they lived. 'I have spoken to her and she wishes to find an ally in me, not a reluctant guest who is slighted by you at every end and turn.' My words had an effect, as I could see from their widened eyes and whispered talk. 'Think on that,' I said as I entered my lodging. It was an imperious gesture which I carried off well.

CHAPTER FIFTEEN

The next morning we broke our fast awkwardly, although I made sure to eat my fill, and then we set off again.

'You are to see the battle lines,' said Master Bitterberry, the crabbed brother. 'There is more urgency now.'

'Do not show me beheadings,' I replied quickly.

'My brother regrets his coldness of yesterday,' whispered Flora.

'Does he regret it enough to answer my questions or tell me his name? That is how *we* dispel coldness.'

'His name is Fúam and I am called Éthaun.'

'I have already named you Flora for the goddess of the Spring.'

She laughed. 'You forget that this country is home to your gods and goddesses. Flora dwells here too.'

I chewed on this thought and decided that the fewer gods and goddesses I crossed paths with the better.

My feet dragged while we headed for whatever was meant by 'the battle lines'. As was my dread, we arrived at the edge of the woodland and looked out across the southern plain, much as I had done with Salvage before he tumbled into disgrace.

'I have been here before. It serves no purpose,' I said.

Not far in front of the trees there was a shallow but fast flowing stream. The banks were perhaps ten foot above the water and sloped down over sharp rocks which made the water itself all but unapproachable. It was a Rubicon, a boundary between two faerie worlds, the wild one which now held me and the world of city life and luxury. I had little time for either of them. There were no warring bands in conflict, I was glad to see, and I expected a day of gentle tedium with no scenes of bloodletting played out before us. My usefulness to my captors would be made no clearer it seemed. I leant against a tree trunk and nibbled some of the breakfast fruits I had placed in my satchel. Flora plaited grasses and the sour one, whose name I hardly troubled to remember, burnished a piece of wood with a handful of sheep's wool and a gobbet of brown grease. We were a peaceful trio, each in his own world and hoping that the fact of civil war, no less, would not impose itself upon us disagreeably. At intervals, there were chitterings and whistlings in the trees behind us and twice Flora slipped back to engage in conversation. I could not guess why she was called away and I little cared. The sun passed its mid-point in the sky and I began to wonder why we did not betake ourselves elsewhere. My silent question was answered when the brother leapt to his feet and moved us swiftly into the woods. There was movement on the plain due south of us and he did not wish to be seen by whoever it was that approached. We stood each behind his own tree trunk and watched as a small group came nearer at a snail's pace. Eventually the distant specks resolved themselves into two horses and three Elven, or human, figures, one riding, one lying across the second mount and the third stumbling behind. When they were closer still, I saw a soldier in a helmet and a breastplate covered over with a quilted cote-armure. He rode high in his saddle clutching the reins lightly with his right hand and holding the leading rope to the second horse with his left. They came to rest at the very lip of the bank and the soldier looked over his shoulder at the figure he had brought with him. I had not wanted to believe that it was a woman. She had been dragged all that way across the plain, tripping and stumbling and, no doubt, sobbing when she could seize the breath. She fell on her knees and then onto her face as exhaustion overwhelmed her. Her gown was torn at the shoulder and her dark hair spread out untidily around her head. I was reminded of the treatment I had seen meted out in London to vagabond women and those who had fallen into harlotry. I did not approve of the stripping and thrashing and I could hardly believe that an Elven female could be dragged so far for having put her body out to hire. Her foot nearest to me was unshod and caked with a black material that I imagined was as much blood as dirt. We all three leant forward as much as we dared, breathing hard. The soldier untied the body lying across the second horse and carried it the few feet to the edge of the river bank. He then threw it as far out above the stream as he could manage. We watched it drop from sight. He laughed loudly and addressed a remark to the woman which made the brother and sister wince. The pitiful creature realised he had removed the body and sat up, howling in dismay. Clutching at the horse's trappings, she struggled into a standing position and joined the soldier looking down into the stream. She cried out and tore her hair, perhaps confused as to whether she should beat the soldier or pay attention to the corpse in the water. I could not bear the howling which told of a grief far deeper than any I hoped I would ever know, although I was later proved wrong in this. I strode out from my hiding place and would not be restrained. A handful of paces took me to the near bank of the stream opposite the soldier and the frenzied woman. We were at the narrowest point of the little gorge and I could look both of them directly in the face, although I am sure the woman had no eyes for me. The soldier jeered as if my presence made no alteration in the situation at all. He had quickly registered that I was human, my round, shocked eyes giving me away, no doubt.

'Something green crawled out of woods!' he called. 'This is how we deal with you.' He looked down into the water, as did the woman and I. The dead man was turning in the current and being taken quite quickly away. On her knees again, the woman leant over the edge and stretched out her hands as if mere wishes or love could fetch the dead man back.

'Join him!' shouted the soldier gleefully and, with a mighty blow, he rolled her down the sharp rocks that flanked the watercourse. She landed on the first hard surface so awkwardly I was sure at least an arm was broken. This did not stop her crawling into the water where she hoped to catch up with the body which was by now many feet downstream. I could stand and watch and listen to the soldier's vile mocking or I could leap across the small chasm and assault a man with body armour and a sword. When I stepped backwards to give myself the chance to run before I sprang, I found that the invisible cord around my ankle grew taut and began to chafe and burn. Across the stream, the plain was another territory and the enchantment would not let me leap there. The soldier thought I had backed away for fear of him which hurt me deeply. He folded his arms at me which the boys at school had learnt to their cost was a mockery too far. He removed his helmet and shook his hair as if to show how little my presence troubled him.

'She was one of our kind,' he said, 'who dared tie herself to one of them, the savage woodlanders. That is why he is floating the devil knows where and she is scrabbling at the stream's edge like a goblin.'

'I am a man,' I called out to him. 'And I say this was unworthily done.' I slipped my hand into my satchel and took out the iron blade. The soldier knew at once that the space between us had changed. It was if my gripping the blade with a fell purpose in my heart somehow made me glow. He became still and looked at me with a fierceness that he believed would diminish me. As a boy, I had thrown sticks and stones with great accuracy and to throw a knife over that short distance came as easily as spitting. Perhaps iron flies faster and penetrates more deeply in that country because it is so alien. My blade certainly had far greater effect than I ever expected. I half feared it would be swatted aside, yet, instead, it flashed like a crossbow bolt and buried itself in the soldier's left eye. And then that scream, the agonised death cry of one who is pierced deep by a blade that corrodes and poisons even as it cuts. There was no time for him to put his hand to his ruined face before he plunged onto the rocks below him. By now, the woman had struggled into the water where, tired and injured, she had no strength to withstand the force of the current. Her clothing became heavy and she lost her footing. The stream first lifted her and then let her sink as she tried always to reach after the corpse that grew more and more distant. Her howls were wordless and incessant and echoed up and down the shallow ravine into which I now descended. I had three tasks before me, no four, because the unseen cord which allowed me to move downwards maintained its burning fingers around my ankle.

'For God's sake help us!' I cried to the brother and sister who were still cringing in their woodland safety. The ravine sides were steep and the rocks were sharp and my simple shoes offered little protection against cuts and bruises. I was, however, too distraught and, once in the water, too cold, to notice the number of injuries every part of my body received. My first thought was for the woman. She thrashed about and screamed and was intent on throwing herself downstream in the direction of the dead man. Her noise and wild actions and the fact that we were in fast-flowing water made it difficult to take firm hold of her, but save her I did. Somehow I managed to pin her arms behind her back and to push her towards our side of the stream. There was no use in my attempting to calm her with words as she had thoughts only for the dead body which soon passed around the first sharp bend and out of sight. All gentlemanly touches were set aside as I dropped her onto the nearest flat rock and held her there until Flora and her brother climbed down to join us, the brother taking as much care over the safety of his person as any girl, I noticed. Then I set off again downstream to retrieve the dead forestman if I could. I threw myself into the middle of the stream and, with the power of my strokes and the speed of the water itself, I soon reached the bend and shot past it. Even in the midst of my violent actions I found time to wonder whether I should swim right into a whirlpool and find myself a watery grave. It was simply more of the same, which was hard enough. The corpse now obliged me by wedging a leg between two rocks which rose out of the water and I was able to catch up with him. I took hold of his shirt and stood upstream of a large rock to recover my breath. If I could haul him back to the point where I had taken the woman out of the water, then I would do so. If the stream plucked him from my hand, then so be it. The least difficult way was to wade in the shallows and to lug the corpse behind me. The stream fought me and the rocks spoiled him, but what else could I do? My shoulders were burning from the effort by the time I arrived and the brother was able to help me lift the body up on to the bank. The lady fell upon it, this time weeping silently I am glad to say. She was near dead with exhaustion, as I was too, but I had my third task still to complete. I re-entered the water and crossed it to the rocks where the body of the second Elven man I had killed lay stretched on his back. There was an intense pain around my ankle once I stepped out of the water on the far side. I put my fingers on the handle of my dagger, closed my eyes and pulled. The blade came out cleanly with no attachment of eyeball or brain, which I had dreaded, although there was a trickle of black ichor down his cheek in mockery of tears. As I held the blade in the water for a minute or two to clean it entirely, the stream bubbled and fizzed, such is the power of iron on the elements themselves there. I took a farewell look at the creature whose life I had ended and could not find it in my heart to be sorry. This was a necessary death, not murder. These events had been forced upon me and my reactions, I trusted, were decent ones. The livery he wore was not that of Lord Ailill I noted. An embroidered shape of corn stalks gathered into a dolly sat upon his shoulder and the irony of his great importance cut down by my small knife was not lost upon me. I needed to beware in case I found myself puffed up with the conceit of what I had achieved. But I am Edward Harry; what use to tell me to mend my ways and show a little circumspection?

It was back into the water then and the climb up *our* bank which suddenly seemed very difficult. My limbs were heavy and aching and blood began to seep from many a gash. I stumbled along the grass to retrieve my satchel and lay clutching it as one stunned. Extreme discomfort wrenched every part of me and I felt as a man must feel who has fought several battles, climbed a mountain and swum far out to sea all in the same afternoon. How I longed for a long, long sleep. Cuts, bruises, scratches were all declaring themselves and they made even lying motionless on soft grass a desperate experience. Time passed, although I was never fully asleep. I was aware of conversation and comings and goings and of hands touching my feet. When I had recovered sufficiently to think more or less clearly, I rolled painfully onto my side and sat up. The lady had gone, as had the body of the soldier and the two horses. Flora and her brother sat together a little way from me, watching.

'Although I nearly drowned numerous times,' I said, 'I am very thirsty indeed.'

Flora handed me a cup of sweet drink which I downed in a gulp. The liquid had restorative powers because I felt my aches lessen somewhat. Being a little restored, I was also able to wonder why they had not poured the liquid into my mouth much earlier. The brother's spitefulness, no doubt, I thought, because I had accomplished what he did not dare. I now looked down at the sorry state of my feet.

'Once again I have lost a shoe,' I said. 'And that welt around my ankle, your magic has caused.'

'We owe you a debt,' said the brother in a voice near empty of indebtedness.

'That you do.' I wished to shout at him that he had barely dipped his dainty toes into the stream and that surely he had powers of enchantment which could have reduced my labours. The shouting would have to wait for another day when I did not require salves and a bed. But, rest assured, omitted was not quitted. 'I am in no state to walk home,' I said.

'You will be carried. They have been sent for.'

As we waited and I drank more of the cordial, I found I had to request information as none was readily given. 'The lady, who was she?' I asked.

'Ferdia, Lady of the Murth. She took as her husband a woodlander named Laeg. It was his body you rescued from the stream. In the past it was not unusual for men and women from the opposite ends of our land to marry. These troubled days you see what happens.'

'He was killed and she was exiled.'

'We shall make her welcome.'

'As I have been made welcome?'

The brother looked at me closely. Yes, my words were shot through with bitterness. He was not mistaken.

'Do you say that we have not treated you as our guest?'

'I say that I was taken by you against my will and that I am tethered by a chain I cannot see. I have killed for you and preserved the life of the Lady Ferdia of the Murth when no-one else would.' I hoped he was ashamed of being so tree-bound while I fought his battle for him.

'The Lady Ferdia thanks you,' said Flora.

'Which is most gracious of her. Tell her it was my pleasure and she may repay me by removing this chain and by presenting me with my passport home.'

I felt that on account of my exploit, my courage if you must, I now had the upper hand in conversation with this brother who had been so grudging with his words. I set out, if not to offend, at least to make him as uncomfortable as I could. 'Tell me something,' I said, 'that has been a cause of puzzlement to me. The eye into which I thrust my iron blade was of a violet colour and slanting, as are the eyes of the Lady Ferdia, as much as I could see them. Your eyes and ears and those of your sister are entirely like my own. Why is that?'

There followed a silence which perhaps ought to have embarrassed me, but I was determined to put in his place one who had regarded me with such an unacceptable sense of superiority. He could not bring himself to answer my question and so it fell to his sister. In a very quiet voice she said, 'Our mother was human, a merchant's daughter, during the time of the Rose Wars.'

'Aha! So a dog got over the wall and spirited the girl away. Think better of *me*, in that case.' I did not say this aloud.

'You are as much like me, as you are like your woodland neighbours,' I said. In what probably amounted to the worst insult I could offer them, I then pinched the lobe of the brother's right ear and wiggled it roughly. 'We could pass for brothers, I the scholar and you the artisan.'

He pushed my hand away and stalked off. I rejoiced that he was so mortified and his sister's expressions of distress did nothing to reduce my feeling of triumph. I swear I could feel my eyes sparkle with it. So, to be half-human in their world was the same disgrace as if I had to admit that my nearest relations were locked up in Bedlam.

If Master Surly had set upon me then, it would have been an unequal struggle. My natural vigour had nowhere near returned and I was still prone to shivering despite having lain for some time now in full sunshine. I reflected on the promise that I should be carried and hoped that my taunting had not put paid to this.

The eventual arrival of my escort was an interesting and noisy affair. I was to be carried shoulder high on a litter like some Roman or Persian dignitary. The difficulty was that the twenty or thirty creatures which had assembled to convey me were of such differing heights. The tale of my adventure by the stream had apparently filled them with an excess of animation and delight and they all wanted to hold a corner of the litter. If they had all had their way as they pushed, and even bit, to obtain a handhold on the conveyance, I would have been thrown to the ground after the first pace. The brother made no attempt to intervene to bring order to all the squabbling. He stood to one side as if this were the way that all co-operative tasks were undertaken. I also had serious misgivings about the litter itself. It had obviously been put together within the past hour and trailed loose ends of creeper like little miss's worst stitchery. Should I fall through it and break my neck? This was a serious concern.

The easy part was getting me to lie down on the litter which was an assemblage of greenery slung between two coppiced poles. I stretched out on it apprehensively and could not fail to notice what I took to be a smirk on the brother's face. He was longing for disaster and I condemned him for it. I am not a heavy weight and four of their man-sized creatures could have taken a pole apiece and carried me aloft with ease. It was not going to be so simple, however. Every being present seemed to have an opinion that was accorded equal importance. When a two foot high, wizened and be-tusked creature jumped up and seized hold of a carrying pole with its hand or foot, I could not tell which, it felt that it had no right to be dislodged. It was dislodged, of course, by something even smaller which defied description and which had sharper teeth. If the litter were jolted at all by reason of all the arguments raging, there was an immediate hush, copious apologies to my person (communicated by noises I could not directly translate) and then the fuss started all over again. For a while I was amused, then bored and, finally, angered beyond measure. I rolled awkwardly off the litter and shouted as loudly as my present strength allowed, 'Will you all stand still! At once! I said, "At once!"' The biting and chattering subsided and, where there was the odd pocket of reluctance at my taking charge, I glared in such a way as would have stared down any oddity on earth. 'You four,' I pointed to the four 'men', individuals dressed like myself and clearly capable of a strenuous task, 'will you kindly be my pole bearers?' There was an immediate hubbub which I stifled with a yell. 'My friends, I have a task for each and every one of you, have no fear. You are all valued. Each will be asked to contribute to my passage home according to his own special talents.' This seemed to go down well and there was a low murmur of what I took to be approval. I knew that every creature present needed to feel recognised and I hoped my vocabulary contained sufficient words for me to find tasks for them. The only four real tasks were those of the pole bearers. The rest would be decorative supernumeraries, although I should do my best to disguise this fact when I gave instruction. '*You* look strong fellows, so would you please clear the path for us? Would *you* agree to be my outriders? Will *you* kindly protect the pole bearers whose arms are not free? Will *you* protect us from behind in case there is danger in the rear?' And so on, almost interminably.

When my commands were all given, and I had looked about to see that no diminutive being was overlooked and resentful, I gave the order to set off again. The litter bearers raised me to shoulder height and we were on our way. 'Onward let us go, ye masters of the woodland,' I cried, delighting in the nonsense I was creating. The journey was surprisingly gentle. I did not pitch to the ground or rock from side to side in a way that unsettled my stomach. Had there been visible spectators along our way, I should have graciously waved my fingers ever so slightly to them like Her Majesty riding in a royal progress. I had never felt so applauded in all my life and the satisfaction was capped by the return of my little blue friend who flitted from the upper branches of a tree and rode on my stomach for a while. I was carried thus through the habitations of many of the woodland creatures. There turned out to be an extensive settlement a quarter of a mile from the hamlet where I lodged with the brother and sister. I leant on my elbow to take a better look at these places I had not been permitted to see before. In a succession of glades, I saw a range of habitations. There were a few cabins for those I always thought of as the higher Elven folk, the ones like myself, but there were also earth mounds, piles of sticks and nests even. On this special day, I was granted a privilege of access of which I knew I had better take full advantage. Strangely, there were few figures about and yet I could not believe that those who escorted me made up the whole of this local population. No doubt I was unpopular with some, being human, and I am convinced that a few dung balls rattled against my litter as we entered one of the smaller glades, the one with what I can only describe as a pig wallow. A great noise and agitation followed the appearance of the unsavoury missiles and the sheepish looks of two of my bearers convinced me that I was not wrong. The only figure missing was my earlier salvage guide. I would like to say that I caught glimpses of him behind trees as we passed, his leafy outfit merging into the bushes, but I believe my desire ran ahead of the truth. I had no idea how long his punishment for being a Peeping Tom would last but, if I had any present influence with beings in authority, I vowed to speak up for him.

I was deposited at last on the grass outside my modest lodging, the King having been brought home to his kennel, and the company melted away, every one, even the near-human ones I was fain to engage in conversation. I was still a thing to be mostly avoided, it appeared, and my celebrity was no more than a nine minutes' wonder. Fondly, I had thought there might be feasting or a suit of rich clothes as a reward for my rescue of the living and the dead. All that awaited me, however, was the stiffness of my limbs and the smarting of a thousand scratches. I staggered to my sleeping place bent double like the Ancient of Days. I knew then what it must be like when an animal crawls under a hedge to die, knowing that no comforting tongue will lick it or friendly companion lie beside it and offer warmth. I have to admit that I felt very sorry for myself. My celebrity had shone brightly and was now quite extinguished. Such are the ways of the world, human and Elven. We are ingrates all. Tasting these bitter thoughts, I lay with closed eyes remembering how welcome and soft a feather pillow would be at such a time. A disturbance in my doorway recalled me from the slough of self-pity and I opened my eyes. It was the brother with a basket and a substantial ewer from which steam arose.

'Pray enter,' I said, more curious to know what he brought than glad to see him.

'You must still be in discomfort.' I half expected him to follow this remark with a cackle.

'That is very true.'

'If you will allow me, I have brought hot water and salves. My sister has great skill in making them.'

'Can you not manage a magic wand and the instant relief of all these aches? I feel as if I...' I struggled for an apt simile. The truth was more powerful than any rhetoric. 'I feel as if I have climbed up and down sharp rocks and been in and out of fast flowing water and also as if I have killed a man by running a dagger into his brain.' I would not weep.

My words seemed to have affected him. 'You will be better helped by the magic of the woodlands,' he said. 'Magic shows are no more than show. These salves are made from the rarest herbs. We wander many days in search of some of them.' He took out of the basket a number of small pots and held up one for me to sniff. 'This will revive your spirits.'

I cannot describe that scent, that mixture of willow, lavender, mint, all the fragrance of the garden and miles of forest beyond. It took my tiredness and pinched it between its fingers. It separated all the sinews of my battered limbs and caressed them into a baby's ease. It was done in an instant and I fell sideways. I would have struck my head if he had not caught me.

'To make me sleep?' I murmured, still wide enough awake to ask myself why such an unguent had been kept from me until now. Perhaps I said the words out loud. I do not care either way.

'Not quite.' He helped me to lie back comfortably and I would happily have given in to sleep, but there was more to come. 'Here is water with certain leaves steeped in it. My sister has said I should bathe you if that is permitted. After that I will rub on the salves. My sister is usually the healer, not I.' He paused and swallowed. 'If there was to be bathing, I could not allow her... you understand. I beg your pardon if my hands lack tenderness. They are more used to smoothing the knots in wood.' I nodded in acknowledgement of his apology. My torn and ravaged backside needed the tenderness of an angel's hands if he did but know.

'If I am to be bathed, then I shall need to...' I struggled with my shirt and found that my arms now lacked the strength to remove it. He helped me undress and then brought up his ewer of water. As his wet cloth touched the skin of my back, chest and arms and found a graze or bruise in every place, there was an instant's discomfort and then the power of whatever had been infused in the water took the pain away.

'You have a soldier's body,' he said.

'I think of myself as a scholar,' I replied. 'I would never willingly go in search of a sword fight or the cannon ball.'

'How long will you have such strength? Five years?'

'Ten years at least, I hope,' I answered curtly. 'We true men are not such spring flowers that we droop so soon. And before you boast that you outlive us many times over and that you were a playfellow with my great-great-grandfather, let me tell you I do not care to hear it.'

'You misunderstand me. Today you outfaced that villain when life must be very precious to you.'

'All too often I act on a wild impulse and only give thought to what I have done a long time after the event. Some would call me foolhardy; others a buffoon.' All of this was true and not just spoken for effect.

My nurse now sat back on his heels and was silent. I wondered what I had said to cause such a reaction as normally when I render someone speechless it is because I have offered a deliberate affront and I know full well what my words will achieve.

'Your legs have suffered too,' he said. 'I should bathe them.'

'I have no objection to that.'

'You are wearing your breeches.'

'Oh, you mean that I should take them off?'

I unfastened the cord and prepared to slip down my shredded breeches.

'You will be naked,' he said quickly. So this was the reason for his awkwardness.

'There is a great rent in the seat,' I said. 'I have been a King carried in triumph with half his bum hanging out. Other men may have a maiden's bashfulness; not I. Wash away, I beg you. It is for my own good.'

I might just as well have kept the breeches on for he restricted himself to those sections of my legs below the knee, apart from a few swift forays to a bruise high up on my thigh. My little warrior might have been a glowing firebrand for all that he permitted his eyes or fingers near it. I should have to minister to my lumber injuries myself, which I did, and found sitting down much more comfortable as a result. After the bathing came the application of the salves, some to ease bruising and others to heal wounds. I dealt with my thighs and my backside myself and this time I did not hold back my chuckle. I looked the brother directly in the eyes as I spread the ointment behind me, urging him to laugh with me but he could not. He was more of a coy mistress than his sister, I declare. Or perhaps I have no breeding and am simply a village ruffian beneath the lacy frills of my education.

That night, brother, sister and I ate a simple meal together and then I was desperate to sleep. Next morning, I was delivered new clothing and, thank God, a pair of boots. I planned to ask for an audience with the Lady who had met me by moonlight, or with some other being in authority, but the brother forestalled me in this by announcing, as we breakfasted, that I was to be taken to meet someone of importance. I bridled at once. '*Taken*'? What had happened to *Would you be so good as to have a word with*? How many stricken women did I need to pull from the flood before they took my own wishes into account?

'Well let us be going, then,' I said before the meal was truly over. This meant I set off hungrier than I would have liked, but I needed to unsettle them.

'You are angry with us,' observed the brother as we walked through the wood together.

'These new boots are comfortable.' Now it was my turn to be distant as I was saving all my words for the important person I was due to meet. We came at last to a rocky hollow where the brother left me after the briefest of nods.

I could not help feeling at first like a man who has been taken up the steps to a scaffold by a treacherous friend who has then sped away. I was vulnerable and lost and this never brought out the gentlest responses in me. All I had needed was a few words by way of explanation, a sign that I was worthy of a modicum of respect. But they were who they were, and so I would be as thoroughly myself. I looked about me endeavouring to appear nonchalant as if I had a hundred and one other errands to run. The ground sloped down sharply from where I stood, almost in rocky steps with very little grass on them. At the foot was a low circular mound like the ancient ones I had occasionally seen both in England and Ireland. *Faerie mounds* they were called in both countries. How presently true. The novelty was that this one had an entrance, a doorway, whose lintels were carved with spirals and other patterns that I walked forward and traced with my finger. I did not for a moment think of going inside. As a child, I had let others be the first to wade in the pond or walk out on the fragile branch. I had to be sure of my ground before I ventured forth and now was most surely a time for being sensible.

My speaking out of turn was another matter entirely. Nothing, save the constriction of the grave, would ever stop my 'I am Edward Harry' moments. As always, I had my satchel and the protection of my iron knife. I walked back from the doorway, waited, and then, as nothing happened, I sat down on the lowest of the rough steps. I was on the verge of singing one of my 'Fol-de-rol, let us tumble in the new-mown hay' ditties, when a figure emerged through the doorway. I remained seated, thinking that I should either make an important point about my independence or be blasted into a sooty vapour. The woman who appeared was not my moonlit vision. Nor did she have a sunlit look about her. I imagined that I was expected to quail when such a fearsome presence strode out of her underground closet. If it had been my own Queen, Her Truly Formidable Majesty Elizabeth, Empress of the finest regions of the world and of every true Englishman's heart, my tongue would have shrivelled and my bowels opened. In London, if one trifled with authority, there were ear-trimmers and hooks on the gibbet which kept most of us in our rightful places. In this strange land beyond enchantment, I was pert to the point of recklessness and I did not choose this moment to change. She was a woman somewhat taller than myself with wonderful hair of every shade you could associate with copper, bronze or brass. The eyes were slanted, naturally, and with a flash of dark blue in their violet I noticed when she moved closer. I wondered whether they had ever known softness as none was directed towards me at that moment. Her clothing I found immodest and, to my mind, there was something of the courtesan about robes that plunged from the shoulders and were gathered up at the hips. Did she intend athletics, clad in that way, I could not help wondering. In Cheapside or The Strand she would have had 'Primping Queane' shouted at her as the magistrates took her into their keeping. I folded my arms across my satchel into which I slid one hand and I smiled.

'You try my patience, Edward Harry.'

'Just as you and all your kind try mine, Lady.'

'I could smite you.'

'And I could throw my iron blade at your inhuman eye. I did it yesterday to good effect, as you undoubtedly know.'

She walked towards me, barefoot, and stopped when only a couple of paces distant. Without the slightest ruffling of her garments, a chair appeared beneath her and she was enthroned. With a jolt, so was I, but I did not lose hold of my dagger. We looked at each other knowingly and I allowed her to be the first to speak again since she was the one with the important business.

'You pleased me with your determination yesterday.'

I inclined my head in gracious acceptance of the compliment.

'You are, what shall we say…?'

'Intrepid?'

'I like the word. You also managed the childish disorder when they could not carry you without falling over each other.'

I opened my mouth to offer a witticism, but she gestured at me to be silent. This was a meeting for negotiation and not entertainment.

'Know that I am Nemain and my business is warfare. I would recruit you into my guard.'

'Never!' I was so at odds with this suggestion that I half stood up to utter my denial of it. 'I am not a soldier by nature and if I fight it is in the cause of those I…value. You surely have been told, Lady, that the first death suffered at my hands was one of the *Lios Alfar* who intended to kill my friend. My allegiance is to my own, that is to say, to Mankind. I cannot be bought or co-erced.'

She hardened her expression and I took a tighter grip of my dagger. Our swords were drawn, you might say, and we were in a gladiatorial ring circling around each other, I and this Elven Queen of Battle.

'You know you may never return home?'

'That remains to be seen. I am, by nature, always hopeful of good outcomes.'

'Such ready answers.'

'The words are entirely my own, Lady Nemain. I have no need to rely on that dishonest power you call magic. What would you be without it? A thousand year old crone in a harlot's dress?' The bolt of lightning would come now, I was sure.

'Let me ask you again. You know that there are two factions at variance here, those who would remain what we have eternally been, and those who would do the unthinkable?

'By 'the unthinkable', you mean lowering your enchanted guard and inviting in such creatures as myself?'

'That is what I mean. If you do not share my relish for the battlefield, then I would ask you to consider another option. Will you listen to me?'

'I will do that.'

'You have seen, I know, that very few of our people in the woodlands are used to battle. They have been scattered by the discipline of the trained soldiers from the south.'

'I have seen that and regretted it. I have also seen the, what shall I call it, the tree go forth like a wolf after sheep.'

'One tree, no matter how vast, cannot take on ranks of spearman and archers who know their trade. You could give our people leadership, order. I would not expect you, necessarily, to shed blood, unless your own life were endangered.' She read a refusal on my face and her jaw tightened. 'You will do good of some kind for us or you...'

'Will regret it?'

'That is so.'

I knew full well that my single piece of iron could not offer me protection against such a witch for long and yet I would not simply slip into her livery and be her tool.

'If the taste of battle is so sweet to you, why do you not lead your troops yourself? Dare I say that you must have had centuries of practice?'

'Rest assured, my spirit is with them, but if I am seen at their head or it is known widely that I marshal them, others will enter the conflict on the opposite side. This would lead to consequences we dare not contemplate. We wish to win an argument, not see this land of ours given over to wholesale slaughter.'

'I pray you, allow me some moments' thought to myself.'

She made an impatient movement with her hand, an insect-flicking gesture, at which I stood up and walked about, weighing each alternative against the other. In truth, I had but one choice, to agree to run with these creatures while preserving the few freedoms I could. The *Lios Alfar*, the Elvenfolk to the south, I could not agree to kill out of hand as they too closely resembled myself, despite their tallness in the case of Lord Trim, their malevolent purple eyes and their despising of Humankind. My hand would falter and my stomach sicken if I endeavoured to make it my daily task to inflict bloody wounds on them. I confess that I would find it an equal difficulty to slaughter a score of Her Majesty's Spanish or French enemies on a daily basis which may be a reflection on the depth of my patriotism and so I shall not dwell on it. Naturally, these *Lios Alfar* would be bent on putting out my own spark and I could fall lifeless with an arrow in my throat two minutes after my first rash sortie. I would taunt and tease, I would leave mocking objects, pelt dung balls even, and, if Nemain and her minions demanded more, I should set about *them* until I was overwhelmed and all my options in this life were ended. There was one condition, however, which needed to be agreed upon if I were to be of use. The shackle must go. This burning humiliation around my ankle which I could not see pained me in every way imaginable.

I had stroked my chin and walked about, looked up at the sky, ho-hummed and 'If she says that, then I shall say this'-ed until I was sure of my words. 'Lady,' I said, 'my thoughts are these...'

When I had laid out my conditions, it was her turn to muse, although she did this seated and far more briefly than I.

'I am disappointed in you, almost to the point of anger,' she said, 'but the help you offer will undoubtedly be of some use. The chain is gone, rest assured.'

She pointed her finger at me and the world changed. That unsettling shimmer, the awareness of a frightening glamour all about me, returned. My skin chilled briefly and the nape of my neck twitched as if pinched by cold fingers. I swayed on my feet and gripped the back of my chair firmly for support. If I had not been sure that I was to be put to work as well as I could, I would have sworn that I had been afflicted with an illness, a poisoning.

'Welcome,' said the Lady Nemain. 'You are truly in my domain now. You will see and sense more than your thick human senses allowed you before. Walk slowly and breathe deeply. You have stepped over a threshold in a way that bodes well. Others will follow you now. Lead them strongly and do not think, for a moment, of betraying us or they will devour you, iron blade or no.'

I wanted to give her a mocking smile, but could not. I swallowed again. The sheer smell of the woodland ran its fingers down my throat. I had mistakenly believed when I dwelt with my salvage companion that I was admitted to the faerie world, but I was not even at its threshold. The air was now palpable and the ground pulsed with a slow rhythmic beat. I wondered how I should function as a leader if I were always to be in this state of feeling as if I had drunk a barrel of poor wine and a dishful of food on the turn.

The Lady Nemain left me, although I did not catch the moment of her leaving. Perhaps she fled into her underground chamber as a wisp of fretful, discoloured smoke. I did not follow her because a legion of small hands, seen and unseen, took hold of every quarter of my person and led me off amongst the trees. I was overwhelmed by the sense of touch, driven almost to the point of madness by it, the press of soft fingers and scaly ones, the brush of the vibrant air against my face, the assault upon my nose by all manner of rankness, animal sweat, dead plants, fungus on the tree bark. What a procession, what a dragging down to an even lower circle of Hell more like. I was truly, now, one of the damned. In my head, as I stumbled through the forest, there swirled the details of my career, each successive chapter less civilised than the last. From Master Spenser's goodly parlour at Kilcolman, I had passed through a great city as a prisoner and then tumbled through the branches of a vast tree, as it were, until I now sat on a block of stone surrounded by every grinning scrap of nightmare a painter with a vision of the infernal regions could have conjured. In the church of the village where I grew up, there was an area of the south wall decorated with pictures of such creatures as now wished to finger and crawl all over me. Even as a child, I had thought this depiction of the irredeemably wicked a poor piece of work, ludicrous in its grotesquerie – naked, screaming sinners being pitch-forked into gaping fundaments with sets of razor teeth waiting to shred them. What journey had the painter undertaken in olden times, I asked myself, for each clumsily drawn inhabitant of Hell's pit now danced or flew about me. How I longed for the opposite vision of Heaven, the salvation of angels, a loving hand reaching down, but it was not to be. Poor Edward Harry had walked too long in the paths of Pride and must now knock about as best he could. My habitations had changed too. Briefly, I was given use of a remarkable closet with hot water for bathing and a jakes that whisked my droppings away. Then there were cabins in delightful woodland clearings with a ready supply of food and clothing. Now, and how humbled I felt, I found myself stumbling into the back of a cave where I collapsed in a welter of tiredness and misery, fully expecting to wake up with one of my extremities chewed off.

CHAPTER SIXTEEN

I had not expected that my agreeing to serve, albeit much less than half-heartedly, in the Lady Nemain's war-band would drain me of all energy and hope when I first lay my head on the stone of that cavern floor. I imagined I should marshal a few sensible creatures of near-human kind and almost play at mounting little expeditions, like a boy with a fortress made of dirt and straws, which would not set my life at risk. Noddypoll. My journey hither, more a dragging and tormenting, had depressed my spirits to their smallest candle. I lay in a cave like a farmyard beast in its kennel, all dignity gone and all sense of having come off better in my bargain blown to the winds like this morning's mist. Hours must have passed before I could bring myself to open my eyes and start my acquaintance with this new 'home'.

In a near corner of the cave was a pile of old twigs or coarsely-furred animal skins; I was not sure until it scratched itself. Once, I might have cried out at such a scratching. Now, I only sighed and accepted my lot. I sat up and sneezed. My few hours of uneasy sleep had reduced my awareness of the earth's very heartbeat to no more than a gentle thrum. My senses were still sharp as a needle, however, and I recoiled from the pair of eyes located in the twigs or skins as I might from a foetid bubble which bursts on the surface of a pond.

'Grogoch,' said a mouth which I could barely see but which was, at least, set in the usual place beneath the creature's eyes and not in its backside.

'Well, Grogoch,' I said. 'Do you have any of the human tongues about you?'

'That I do, Master. For I have served...' He checked himself and blinked several times as if a secret had nearly escaped. I gave no sign that I had noticed his indiscretion, but, believe me, the information was set aside for later use.

'Are you here as my servant?'

'That I am, Master.'

He approached me and I stood up to establish my authority. What branches I had slipped through, I Edward Harry who felt he deserved to dine in the sun atop the highest tree in the orchard. I had first been given a human companion, a mute Wodwo, and then I was lodged with an ill-tempered half-man-half-faerie. Being allowed to sink to my own level, I had bounced from the lowest branch to a patch of nettles where a short brown creature, more hair than creature, bowed to me in a cave and addressed me as Master.

'So you have served men before?'

'That I have, Master.'

'With whom and where?'

'That I cannot tell you, Master.'

'I command you to clean yourself,' I said walking to the cave's mouth as I was in need of fresh air. Heightened senses are a poisoned gift when a noisome creature, a living fart, waits at your knee. 'I suggest you stand beneath a waterfall for a twelvemonth. Then you are to lie in a bed of flower petals until I command you not to.'

'Master?'

My words were simply a piece of my own cleverness and I had an immediate fear that the obliging creature might obey me to the letter and catch a fatal chill in the process. He had followed me to the doorway and stood expectantly as I scrutinised him. There was the shape of a stunted man beneath his overgrowth of a kind of animal hair, the coarse tufts one sees on cattle. My spirits rose now that I had someone with whom I could play the little lord. An ounce of authority does wonders for the soul, as they say.

'"Grogoch". Is that your name?'

'It is what I am, Master. We live in the houses of men and do their work.'

Such a body servant! I laughed long and loud. The Grogoch sank into a bundle beside me and I was moved to point out that I was bitterly merry at my situation and not at him or, God forbid, her!

'You will render me good service, I am sure,' I said. If he had been an obedient dog, I would have stroked his head, but I could not bear to touch even a single one of his soiled, matted hairs.

My cave opened into a grey cliff face with a rough stairway leading from it to a small, natural amphitheatre surrounded by trees. Much as I loved trees, I was beginning to crave a life in which I was not permanently hemmed-in by them. I could address my 'people' from my cave mouth like any warlord inspecting his troops from a garrison balcony which is, no doubt, why I had been led there. My spirits were reviving, the candle flame rose, and I am never one to repine for long.

I should take my situation firmly by the hand and make it serve *my* turn, if it could be made to do so in any way.

'Your first task must be to clean yourself,' I insisted. 'I do not wish to offend, but my nose can only manage sweet smells. Do you understand what I mean by bathing?'

'Yes, Master.'

'What is it?'

'It is what ladies do who have too much time to spare.'

I was encountering resistance at the very outset of our time together and I could not be doing with it. 'Let me correct you there,' I said in my firmest, *I am the Master*, voice. 'Bathing is running water over your limbs and it is keeping your hands always clean.'

These remarks gave rise to muttering and, possibly, the wringing of hands somewhere under cover of the matted hair.

'Will you prepare my food?' I dreaded the answer.

'No, Master.'

'Who will?'

'Others.'

'Then tell whoever has command of the pantry that I should like the cooks to be maidens or housewifes who keep their aprons white and who do not use to let fleas or dung fall into their meals.'

'It shall be done, Master.'

'It shall. Tell them, also, that I have no liking for things that crawl or slither, alive or dead. Every day I shall require a pail of hot water.' There came more mutterings which I ignored. 'And cloths with which to wash and dry myself. I have decided that my shagginess ill-becomes me and must go. Are you to be trusted with a razor?'

'Yes, Master, I am.'

'You will not draw a red line across my throat?'

'The Grogoch is wounded by the thought.'

'Then he may shave me every morning and tomorrow he may cut my hair and provide me with a comb.'

'The Grogoch will make Master as fine looking as a lord.'

'If you serve me well, be sure I shall reward you as much as is in my power.'

The Grogoch stiffened and drew himself up to his full height, about two thirds of my own. His hands were clasped in supplication and he repeatedly shook his head.

'Never reward me, Master, never never! The Grogoch who is given a reward departs. Never reward him. Never, never, never.'

With a sudden pang, I remembered a tale Calvagh had mentioned to me of a house spirit that worked tirelessly for many generations of the same family and then was driven away by the casual gift of a small square of cloth. 'I understand you,' I said. 'Do grateful words count as rewards?'

'No, Master. Thanks is not things.'

'We have our understanding, then,' I said. 'Your Master is hungry and has need of furniture and boots fit for a soldier.' The last was an unnecessary request, to be honest, but I felt duty bound to ask for some item which would put them to trouble.

The Grogoch ran down the staircase at a speed I would never have dared. As I was chair-less, I sat on the bare stone in my doorway and waited. Quite soon my 'man' emerged from the trees with a basket which he hurried to lay before me. As I leant over to see what repast I had been given, I was suddenly afraid that it might be beetles or mice still in their death throes. Joy. He had brought me soft white bread, a dish of butter, jam, cheese, berries and a pitcher of ale.

'Your circlet of flowers becomes you,' I said, 'but making a daisy chain is not bathing. Pay attention to me.' He resembled an untidy heap of horse dung and straw with daisies sprouting from its top. The fact that I had spotted his new decoration appeared to satisfy him as there was the possibility of yellow teeth revealed in a grin. His mane so be-tumbled his face that his expressions were mostly to be conjectured.

'Your chairs, Master!'

He scampered off again and made several journeys with the oddly-shaped yet beautiful furniture I had sat on before. He could pile objects to an extraordinary height and run with them in a way that defied belief and it was pleasant for me to watch his carrying tricks as I worked my way through most of the contents of the food basket. He brought up my bed of twigs gathered in a cloth and I heard the unmistakable sound of its being assembled. I had a table with an irregular top cut from a dark, burnished wood I did not recognise and, finally, he had an armful of besoms and switches which showed that my simple cell was to receive far more attention than his own person ever did. On the table-top was the comb I so badly needed. It was made of a pale wood and possessed fewer than a dozen teeth, but it would prove equal to the task of bringing my shaggy mane to order

And so to my task. These creatures had so little organisation, there was no chance, I felt, that they could ever prevail against the order and determination of the quilted spearmen and archers from the south. They reminded me, from my schoolboy reading of history, of colourful, frenzied tribesmen, the Casivellauni or Trinobantes, throwing themselves against the discipline of the Roman legions and being left to rot on the battlefield. My task, what exactly was it? To take them out and count them safely home, each little oddity amongst them? And there was to be no blood on my hands, not a drop, unless my own person were threatened. I had no lieutenants, no muster roll, simply the vague instruction that I was to create a nuisance. I might just as well have been given a rabble of schoolboys and told to capture Cambridge using toy bows and arrows and pebbles.

'Grogoch!' I called over my shoulder and brought him reluctantly from his household duties. 'I have an errand for you.'

He looked aghast, as much as a mound of hair hung with cobwebs and daisies can look aghast. 'But, Master.'

'You have your duties and I have mine, Grogoch. I am the chosen warrior, it would seem and I have need of lieutenants. There must be some provision for this. Indeed, I am convinced that they are lurking amongst those trees simply awaiting my call. You shall fetch them to me this very minute. A brace of them will suffice and I would expect them to be able to converse intelligently in English with me and to be obedient.' I hoped they would have a human form too; the exact nature of their ears and eyes was by the by.

The Grogoch carefully leant his besom against the cave wall and flew down the steps. Once again, I marvelled at the way his somewhat bowed limbs enabled him to skip over the awkward surface and not pitch him forward in a broken heap. As I anticipated, my 'officers' were hiding amongst the trees. No doubt, they had watched, and judged, how I conducted myself with my servant and how I fell upon my victuals. 'Like a gentleman born' is how I would have described myself in both cases. I expected servants to know their place, as I knew mine, but I spoke them fair. Nor did I cram my food into my maw and splutter half of it in a spray over the table and my fellow diners. My captains would have judged me well, I was sure, and I determined to maintain that state of affairs. I could wish, however, that I had not delayed the Grogoch's ministrations as my barber until the following morning. I felt untidy and somewhat diminished by this. There were two tall figures, no taller than I, thank God, or I should have felt uncomfortable every moment in their presence. So I would be commanding pure Elvenfolk and not even half-men. I knew I must comport myself accordingly and look for no kinship or sympathy. They stood in the middle of the grass plot and looked up at me, with a challenge in their eyes, I am convinced. They did not bow or show any of that shrinking into themselves one expects of inferiors in the presence of their general. A game toward? I would show them such presence and airs that their doubting of me would be cast aside.

'Gentlemen, ye are welcome,' I cried with my broadest smile and a gesture I mimicked from some play-actor King or other. It was to my advantage that I was many feet above them at my cave's mouth. They looked up and I looked down and I would endeavour to keep it that way. I decided to walk down amongst them after a suitable pause as a sign of my noblesse. An invitation to my private quarters would have to be earned. I also did not fancy strategic discussions carried out to the swishing of a besom and in air that had not been freshened with herbs or greenery, both of which I had forgotten to bid the Grogoch fetch me. Now for my descent. I am naturally light of step, but no fool, and I knew that I had to come down to them like a man of presence and not a goat-footed house faerie. I took my time, placing my feet each time with enormous care, and keeping my regard upon my two captains all the while. I managed not a single slip or stumble which delighted me enormously and doubtless disappointed the two Elven in equal measure. With my feet firmly on the grass, I could now stride with some authority and I placed myself directly in front of each and closer than he might have wished. The time I spent scrutinising their faces was surely a bitter moment for them and I knew they must feel as I would have done if some tavern rat had fallen upon me and exhaled his vomit-breath into my nostrils. My breath is generally sweet, I should add, but I could see the tightness in their jaws. They had sharp ears and slanting eyes, more green than purple in once case, and more blue than purple in the other. Both of the Elven men were slim and strong-limbed. They had comely faces spoiled by being over-written with the taint of disdain. If they had been Englishmen, I would have sought out their company and tried to make them my friends. I relish fellows who dance with life. We might have exercised together and jeered at a play in each other's company. As it was, they resented me entirely and I set my mind to crushing their biliousness without undermining our whole enterprise. Their clothing was the same as my own, loose green breeches, a green shirt and low boots. *Robin Hood's band of not-at-all-merry men,* I found myself thinking. Woodland dwellers set no store by the extravagances of fashion, I could see. There was no competition to set oneself apart from the crowd by using a different plant dye this year or by decorating one's shirt with feathers and berries plucked from the forest bushes. My scrutiny over, I seized their right hands in turn in a firm grip and accompanied this with a strong clap on each left shoulder. Let them see, and feel, that their person was mine to jostle if I chose. It was greatly to their credit that they made no sound and pulled no faces at such mortifying affronts as I was offering. I do believe that if I had taken hold of the nose of one of them and twisted it, he would have continued to stand thus passively.

'Be welcome again,' I said. 'Your names, please.'

There was just a moment's hesitation, but I noticed it. For two of the Elvenkind to have their names demanded of them by a human stripling and to know that they were obliged to answer him truthfully. How they must have wriggled inside, and how my smile shone.

'Cavad.' – he of the green-purple eyes.

'Follovin.' – the blue.

'Then let us sit here you and I, Cavad and Follovin, and discuss how we shall conduct our campaign.'

I thanked them for attending on me, using the Elven words for thanks, an expression which, translated, means that one is ever in their debt for the great gift they have placed in one's right hand. I also pronounced their names with an exactness which showed I had an ear for detail. As I have written them, the names seem as simple as a child's exercise, but the vowels were not simple and there was a good deal of trilling of the tongue behind the teeth which I carried off like a native. This was a further cause of insult too, I expect, the appropriation of their language by a saucy interloper. We sat cross-legged in a triangle, I at its point and they forming the base. I swung my satchel around my body until it rested on my stomach and placed my hand inside. 'This is a useful weapon,' I said bringing out my iron dagger with a speed that made them flinch. Their jaws were certainly tight now. I could not tell if the iron were a source of pain to them and so, after indulging myself with a brief flourish of the weapon, I replaced it and twisted the satchel until it lay against my back.

'I have been given authority by the Lady Nemain to lead you and others against your southern kin. Let me know your thoughts.'

They had not expected such a question. 'Our true thoughts?'

'Your truest ones.'

'We are ashamed to follow a human youth, but we bow to the Lady Nemain's will.'

I was not sure which of them spoke these words. The lips of either might have opened slightly or might have not. I sensed that I was meant to find such a game unsettling as if I were faced with two effigies and their voices were conjured from the air. No wonder they had failed to make their great point with their southern neighbours if all they were up to was to play a mountebank's tricks. I was their match, as I would show them.

'Your candour does you credit,' I said smoothly, 'but allow me to be equally candid with you. I am used to obedience (such lies!) and if I find that you work to frustrate me or plot behind my back, the Lady Nemain shall know it forthwith and you shall pay dearly. Tell me (I paused), individually, that you understand what I have just said.'

'I understand,' said Cavad.

'I understand,' said Follovin more quietly.

By snapping questions at them, by jumping to my feet and walking around them and, once, by fondling my iron blade with every indication of great relish, I got them to work with me towards a plan of campaign. At most, I had agreed to be a nuisance, the leader of a band of creatures who would make life uncomfortable for the city and manor dwelling Elvenkind. My intention was to draw this out as long as possible, to make a great deal of smoke with the minimum of fire, and somehow to effect my escape at the earliest opportunity. We would begin with a modest undertaking so that I might get the measure of my troops. It should also ensure that no blood was shed, in particular my own. I was given to understand that there were several manors a night's journey from the most southerly tip of the woodland. They were held by their owners to be inaccessible to predation by virtue of their location in narrow declivities or on top of rocky prominences. The great tree, the goliath of the woodland folk, needed flatter ground for its onslaughts and so had come nowhere near these manors, preferring to rampage and murder many leagues to the west.

'Do you have maps of these places?' I asked.

Green-eyed Cavad scoffed, one of his few expressions of feeling. 'Do men need maps because they fear places will walk away when their backs are turned?' His tone irked me tremendously.

'So you carry maps in your head?' I asked with a mildness that did me credit.

He smirked by way of reply and turned to his fellow, inviting him to do the same.

'Then call this map forth from your brain and place it on the grass before us. I hope it is marked with the strong and vulnerable points of these manors. There should also be our several possible routes there, so that we might approach them unseen, our likely points of entry, three of them I think, and the routes by which we might effect the most expeditious escape.'

The ensuing silence pleased me. At the same time, it showed painfully that they had miles and miles to go to match even a poor soldier like myself. I had never served in the field, and never intended to, yet here was I drawing on my misremembered gleanings from Caesar and other schoolboy reading to offer them a set of strategies. How the blind was leading the ignorant.

'I have no such map in my head.'

'Then the more fool you,' I shouted, wanting to slap him soundly about the head. 'What would you have us do? Run up to a locked door and shout curses or throw dung balls while arrows are aimed at our hearts?'

Master Blue-purple eyes nodded in my direction at this point which I took to be an important first step.

'I have a task for both of you,' I said, 'and I shall not speak to you again until you have accomplished it. You will draw me large, clear maps of each of the manor houses you have mentioned. On these maps you will write the information that I have said we need. If you do not have such information yourselves, you will tell me where I may obtain it. Now, be about your tasks. No, wait...' They had leapt to their feet, anxious, I am sure, to avoid further shaming from my tongue. 'You best know your people. Select a dozen, no more, of those you think will be most able to effect an entry into these houses. I do not care what size or shape these dozen are. I only insist that they are the fittest for the action I have chosen. Tonight I shall inspect your muster. Tonight I should also like to feast them. I have no idea who your cooks are, or your stewards, if, indeed you have such beings. But I intend to feast my men like great Harry before Agincourt. And there shall be music. I have heard much of the wondrous beauty of faerie music. You will please me greatly if you provide me with minstrels.'

As I issued my commands, I half expected mocking laughter to ring out all around us. Who was I, a callow twenty and a most unwilling guest, to swagger and demand? I had simply decided to overplay my part and see where it took me. It got me what I wanted for the moment because the two Elven men rose to their feet and made me a bow which probably sickened them to the guts. It was the stiffest, most arthritic bow I had ever seen. Then they ran off into the trees. To have immortals, possible immortals, dancing at my behest, would have turned a lesser head than that which sat atop the shoulders of Edward Harry who was not a gentleman born and whose main talents were his impudence and the fineness of his handwriting. I returned to my cave with steps that were six inches above the ground. The Grogoch was still hard at work wiping the irregular rock walls with a meticulous care that he must never, in his presumably long life, have used upon his own person. I had been deceived in the quantity of the furnishings he was able to bring hither. My bed was the springy assemblage of twigs and suchlike which I knew would be most serviceable. I also had three high-backed chairs with arms, two tables, a chest and a screen behind which I might with all modesty sit at stool. I need not add that each wooden item glowed in a way that made it a delight simply to behold, let alone make use of. The polishing gave the illusion of a tangible glow into which one could dip one's fingers. And yet there was not a straight line to be seen. All had been fashioned from lengths of wood that naturally lent themselves to being used in each peculiar way.

'Is the Master pleased?'

'He is very pleased indeed,' I said trying the largest chair for size and liking the springiness of its cushion. I say 'cushion' when each seat was in fact covered with a plate-shaped gathering of leaves and mosses that held together remarkably well. I ran my fingers along the arms of my chair and felt entirely like a king. What did it matter that my kingdom could be measured in yards and my entire court was gathered into the figure of a single grubby, but willing, Grogoch? The wood was a delight to touch, polished, yet not entirely hard like metal and it gave off a faint scent of, what shall I say, …of woodland. Oh yes, the Master was undoubtedly pleased. He was a cat drowsing beside a slow-flowing river of cream.

But there was more for me to do. 'Grogoch, will you stop your housework for a moment? The Master has some questions.'

At first he appeared deaf, as if I had spoken in a whisper which the vigorous scratchings of the broom he had just picked up quite drowned. The word 'questions' agitated him as I expected it would. His new Master was exactly the sort to demand all the secrets of the faerie land.

'Stop sweeping!' I called loudly and sharply. 'Sit on that furthest chair and attend to me.'

Drooping with reluctance, he obeyed. Unease always made him shrink into himself I came quickly to learn. His chin knocked on his chest and he drew in his legs like a dead spider. All that I was left with was a hairy bundle of reluctance muttering under its breath words I could not catch. I stretched out my legs and bade him look at my feet.

'Your Master is to be a soldier of sorts,' I said. 'These boots do well enough for my grassy area and for the smooth floor of my cave. If I am to clamber and run, I need footwear which is more robust. Have you a leprechaun in your acquaintance who will oblige me? I can pay him.'

Arms and legs shot out again from the mass of hair. This was a question he enjoyed. 'The Master is right,' he said. 'New boots for a new day. There is always a leprechaun passing through. I shall find him. And a jerkin, too, to cover the Master's heart.' He ran out of the cave and danced in his zany way down the staircase and into the forest.

I walked round my abode again, touching the various surfaces and opening the chest. It proved to contain many identical sets of shirts and breeches as well as handkerchiefs and the under-garments I thought only their city-dwellers wore. Small bags of herbs and dried flower heads gave the clothing a delicate scent. I opened the drawstring of one of the bags and recognised perhaps half of the contents, cornflowers, dog rose and lavender of course. I approved of such scenting and recalled the way my grandmother sprinkled pickings from the garden on her sheets when she laid them away. The faerie land had not yet provided me with sheets as perfect as those which were the old lady's pride. Childishly, I longed to point this out to someone. I allowed the chest lid to fall shut by way of emphasising this thought. I tried the bed for length and comfort and approved of the Grogoch's work. Finally, I poured myself a draught from the ewer of juice and sat down on my throne again to await my shoemaker.

The Grogoch arrived first, almost bouncing into the cave's mouth as he darted up the steps too fast for his own good. The Leprechaun followed, taking his time and wheezing in a way that I at once knew was theatrical. He stood with the light behind him, an ancient being clad in red breeches and a rumpled green coat. As a silhouette he was unintentionally comic as his rumpled hat was half as tall as himself and made his head look as if it were giving birth to a tree trunk. Although I was now a lord of sorts amongst these creatures, I determined to be gracious. I acknowledged his indistinct bow with a barely discernible one of my own (I had stood up) and bade him be seated. He avoided with a grimace the chair the Grogoch had briefly occupied and sat, instead, almost beside me in the other. He refused refreshment and failed to remove his hat. As I did not know whether this was simply a custom and not a slight directed at me, I chose to ignore it and proceeded straight to business.

'The Grogoch has told you that I require a strong pair of boots?'

'Why else would I be here?'

There was no sign of the words 'Sir' or 'Master' and I decidedly did not like his tone.

'Could you make me such a pair?'

'I could, but will I?'

If he had been a schoolfellow who prevaricated with me thus, I would have lifted him by both his ears and shaken him.

'Then let us understand one another,' I said. 'I do not know the cost of such boots but I am prepared to pay a fair price.'

'With orchalc coins that were a gift of Lord Húon 'l Dainn.'

All I did was blink, I am proud to say. I did not splutter into my drink or gape at him.

'We have met before?'

'Indeed we have, Master Edward Harry.'

'My friend treated you with more courtesy than I, if it is a market stall you speak of.'

'It is.'

'Pray accept my regrets for my actions that day.'

'I accept them.'

We settled on three orchalc coins as the price of my boots and, for a further coin, he knew of a 'person' with a quilted coat to dispose of. So he was a huckster, plying his trade in forest and town, mending and making shoes and knowing many a 'friend' with this or that item for sale at a special price. I had bought I cannot begin to guess how many odds and ends from such people on the corners of London streets.

The Leprechaun had with him a bag from which he now took a single thong of leather. I was asked to remove both of my boots so that he could hold the thong against my feet and measure them. He achieved this in the most ingenious way. First, he took the length of each foot which he marked with a piece of chalk no bigger than his thumb nail. He made a single mark for my right foot and then, reversing the thong and working from the other end, made a double mark for the left. In a way that was meant to impress, and most certainly did, he then measured the width of my feet at half a dozen points, each measurement being recorded on the thong with a single or double stroke. When he had finished, it was more white than brown and only a little perspiration would be needed to smudge and ruin all his information. With a final flourish, he coiled the thong into a tight circle with a snap of his wrist and made ready to go.

'I shall have your boots ready tonight,' he said. 'I trust you to pay me then.'

'Tonight we have a feast. I believe you would be a welcome guest.'

'I have heard of this feast and it will not be to my liking. I say this to you: many at the feast will not be to *your* liking. Feast at your own table and be slow to anger. The ways of the people of this forest are…what they are. They will never be your ways. Or mine.'

As I now, in a manner of speaking, owed allegiance to the woodland fold, it was a concern to me that the Leprechaun moved with such apparent ease between the two worlds which were at present in conflict.

'Before you go,' I said, 'I am obliged to ask you something that does not touch upon boots.'

'I dislike questions, especially ones that do not deal with boots and shoes.'

'Whether you like it or not, I shall ask it and you will oblige me with an answer.'

'Will I?'

'You will or I shall raise such a hue and cry about these woods.'

He furrowed his brow, possibly thinking of some kind of disappearance trickery, so I made sure never to take my eyes off him. As I must have already said, I can outface the sun himself if I am so minded.

'I met you in the market and now I meet you in the forest. How can I be sure that you do not repeat elsewhere what you see here? I am their prisoner and not their friend, yet I would not see them betrayed.'

'A worthy sentiment,' he said. 'We see much and say little. We swallow secrets and almost never bring them up again. There is a saying in this land: "Lucky to leave a leprechaun be". It goes well in the English. Rest easy.'

'I take your word on that,' I said.

'I did not give my word.'

'I take it nonetheless.'

I escorted him to the doorway with my eyes still on his face.

'Do not under-estimate me,' I said, 'though others make that mistake.'

I watched him down the steps and across the grass and into the forest. His shoulders twitched all the while feeling my human eyes upon them. If he wished to pop and be gone like a bubble bursting, then I thwarted him and gave proof of what I had just said. I was *not* to be under-estimated.

This encounter, the staring in particular, had made me weary and so I lay down, pulling the coverlet over me and closing my eyes. The Grogoch crept back in and had been dusting unnecessarily for a little while before I troubled to speak to him.

'So there *is* to be a feast,' I said.

He froze in mid dust, one of my wooden cups immobile in the air as he had been about to wipe the table top beneath it.

'I thought Master was asleep.'

'Since Master arrived in this cave, his ears and eyes have been much sharper. And his nose. I want whoever is preparing this feast to know that I am not to be tricked by some eldritch glamour into eating food I might consider loathsome.'

'There will be a table for Master and his own food. No creature else will touch it, unless Master invites them.'

I dreaded that he would go on to say he was preparing my meal himself. Such fingers dipping into my victuals and wiping themselves clean on his own hairy person I could not bear.

'A question.'

He dropped the cup onto the table-top with a sharp sound.

'The Grogoch does not like questions.'

'Like it or like it not. You have worked in the houses of men in my world, I believe. I do not ask their names, but this has been how you have spent much of your life?'

The curling up began, the mimicking of the dead spider, and he squeaked.

'The Grogoch has done this.'

'You could not have avoided the touch of iron in such houses. How did you overcome its power?'

'The Grogoch became more used to it. At first it made him cry out in pain. Now it just brings on the shits.'

He uncurled and pointed out some refreshment he had brought in while I rested. To give him his due, he never, as far as I saw, laid a finger on the food he offered me. Although he was careless about the squalor of his own body, he respected that I required cleanliness at all times. He even removed my stool bucket with enormous delicacy each morning, carrying it across the cave floor as if he held a great fragile egg which could be broken by the smallest vibration. Once on the stone steps, however, he was up to his usual leaping tricks and sped away into the woods with such liveliness I feared that he and all about him would be drenched in night soil.

CHAPTER SEVENTEEN

When I had attended feasts in Master Byfield's house in London or in the castle of Kilcolman, I had always been aware of a great business beforehand. There was much shouting, inevitably, impatience, the wondrous mixture of cooking smells and, if you were particularly lucky, the spectacular accident when a serving boy, scolded beyond endurance, tripped over his toes and threw the dish he was carrying far across the hall floor. There was none of this throughout a long afternoon. I nibbled and washed and nibbled again and ran my fingers through my hair and still, on all my visits to the door of my cave, I saw not a single sign of a feast preparing in the clearing below. It was hard not to humph like an impatient child who has been promised gingerbread and has yet to see it. I stood in my doorway too many times and gave secret watchers much merriment. Without question, I was observed continuously and sometimes I pointed to a bush or branch and gave a fraudulent sign of recognition although my watchers skilfully let me see not a single inch of themselves. The Grogoch was away on errands of his own, sweeping a fireplace in the human world for all I knew. This was just as well because, if he had been with me in my present irritable state, I might well have kicked my bed about the cave and raged at him for not re-assembling it fast enough.

The Leprechaun returned as the afternoon neared its end, his bag fat with the items he had promised. A human cobbler, knowing his station, would have helped me on with the boots and asked frequently whether they pinched Sir's toes and were to Sir's liking. This was not the way of the Leprechaun, perhaps because I was human, or because they are grudging personalities by nature. Uninvited, he drew up a chair and watched as I put on the boots and tried them by walking up and down. They were the finest boots ever made in the world, I am sure. They were of a light brown leather with a medium heel and they held my ankle and instep, every inch of my feet in fact, with just the right amount of pressure and never a chance of pinching. They were like a second skin to my feet and lower legs and I felt I could have climbed mountains or run miles in them.

'They are magnificent,' I said.

'I know that. I made them.'

'I have never had boots like these.'

'You certainly have not.'

He had also found for me a light quilted tabard speckled with yellow, brown and green which at first I took to be stains until I realised how well it would conceal me in the forest or undergrowth if any were to be found near the two manors we intended to assault. I paid him the orchalc coins, offered refreshment and then we fell into silence. My head ran with many questions, but I was sure it was not his way to give answers, truthful ones at least, to direct enquiry and so I was content to wait quietly for any titbit he let fall. That he felt comfortable in my presence was clear from the way he half closed his eyes and gave long sighs from time to time. 'Don't mind if I do,' he announced suddenly and thrust his hand into his bag. The performance that ensued was new to me. He took a good pinch of some dried herb and pushed it down into a bowl the size of a large thimble. This bowl had a hollow stem which he placed in his mouth. There was a spark or two from his finger ends and the herb caught light. The smoke was drawn with a pleasure-filled sucking along the stem into the mouth and out through the nose. He coughed violently at the first few draughts and then seemed to slip into a kind of dream.

''tis baccy,' he said.

The smoke had by now floated across to my side of the cave and mightily offensive I found it. Such a sharp stink, like a, I know not what, like an old privy on fire. So this was the tobacco that was the rage with the sharpest young gentlemen. It was a habit they should indulge on hilltops or far out to sea as far as I was concerned. I had heard Master Spenser recount how fond Sir Walter Raleigh was of it, almost as fond as he was of the mysterious potato.

'Come all the way from that New World,' said the Leprechaun. 'I have my sources in London. Boots for baccy. Not my best boots, but who are they to know?'

My eyes were watering and I thought I should smother. Master Spenser did not take tobacco and if he ever were to be offered it by Sir Walter, I would do my best to dissuade him. I walked to the cave mouth and drew in the clean air. I thought for a moment of throwing my pitcher of drinking water over this Leprechaun who had presumed to make my home uninhabitable but I was sure my Grogoch would have ways of rendering it sweet again. I wanted to call the

Grogoch and let him say all the *How dare you*s I had not liked to say. A hissing, berating skirmish between two such odd creatures must be an entertainment indeed. I was driven from this thought, however, by an odd stirring in the air about me. With my newly-wakened senses, I felt a ruffling of the hairs on the nape of my neck and an unsettling agitation inside me. I knew that magic was being worked or that there was a presence nearby. The hair on my head was winnowed almost and I took a step backwards, floating, I am sure. There was a great light which made me at once cover my face with my arms and, when I opened my eyes again, the grass was thronged with feasters.

'Not for me,' said a voice at my elbow, the Leprechaun wearing a look of great annoyance. 'Why can't they leave a body in peace? Will you this and will you that. I was just getting the full taste of my new baccy.' He dropped his lighted pipe into his bag and pulled his hat over his ears, as if any hat could keep out the din to which we were now subjected. 'Keep to your own table,' he said. 'Expect nothing and you won't be…you know what.' He danced down the rough steps almost as lightly as the Grogoch and was soon lost in the dark woods without giving the feast a moment of his attention.

Directly below me was a long table which I shall call the High Table, although that supposes there was order in the arrangement of the other tables, which there was not. Normally at a feast, the magnificent and mighty are seated on one side of a square or down the long stroke of the letter E, with lesser guests taking their meat while seated along the horizontal strokes. The tables this night were at every angle and height and those on the fringes of the clearing extended into the woods themselves as if the diners could not bear to be seen. Perhaps they were so unspeakable in appearance, even their brother forest dwellers would have choked on their meal when forced to look upon them. All the tables had appeared ready laden and the effect of such smells combined was as near as I ever hope to get to a cannon volley. I was buffeted by them. My every sense was shaken by its throat. Unsteady on my feet as all this made me, I looked down upon the scene wondering whether, since I had called for the feast, I was expected to offer a short address of welcome. Immediately, I knew this was a ridiculous idea. All the same, I was determined to give a good account of myself, to perform in such a way as would impress and make them say, 'He has done well for a man.' *I shall strut,* I thought. *I shall raise my chin and look about me as if I am superior to all.* It was also an occasion, I thought, when I might have need of my iron blade and I re-entered the cave to pick up my satchel and hang it across my shoulders. Then I walked down to greet the guests at what I was determined to call *my* feast.

A gaggle of Elven stood behind the High Table and I walked boldly up to them and pushed myself into their circle. They were dressed similarly to myself, but there were differences between them in eye and hair colour and even in stature. Nowhere in their expressions did I see the smallest indication that they were pleased to see me.

'Greetings,' I said and snatched at hands to shake them. I was faster to snatch than they were to pull away. 'Shall we sit and eat this remarkable feast?' How disconcerted they were that I should thrust myself amongst them as if their equal. But I was not their equal; I was their commander, their champion, and the sourer their looks, the more hailfellow I became.

'Gentlemen, you have the advantage of me in that you all certainly know my name and yet I only have the benefit of the names of Cavad and Follovin, my excellent map-makers.' No, I had certainly not forgotten the maps. As I spoke my last sentence, I kept hold of the hand I was shaking. Indeed, I tugged at it to compel the ungracious fellow to lift his head and at least make a show of looking me in the face. 'You, sir. And what do they call you?'

He mumbled at me so that I should not grasp his name at all.

'Nay, sir. Do not trifle with me with your mumble,' I said, still not relinquishing his hand although he was beginning to pull hard away from me. 'Give me your name clearly. I command it.'

There was a long silence during which I intensified my grip to the degree which had made enemies cry me mercy at school.

'Noisiu.' This time the word was audible and clear.

'I thank you, Noisiu,' I said, making sure to pronounce his name with all its slidings and trillings which were several despite its being so short. They would drain me of much energy and patience if they persisted in resisting my authority, but the Lady Nemain had given me dominion and underneath their obstinacy and fretfulness they must acknowledge this. I could now afford to be more expansive. 'In my village, as possibly in yours,' I said with the broadest of smiles, 'we have an expression: "The little men are nibbling at me". It means: "I am very hungry." Let us, therefore, take our seats.'

The table tops were highly burnished which made their appearance in the blaze of light a thing of great wonder. At intervals along each table and at a height of about six feet from the surface were golden lights, orbs of yellow which were not lanterns because lanterns are pendant and these globes simply floated in the air. For all I knew, they were living creatures, swollen glow-worms, because they pulsed ever so slightly and were not a constant shape. The light they cast brought out the deep polish in the wood's surface and it would have been an act of pleasure simply to enjoy the furniture for itself even without the delicacies which adorned it. There was no item fashioned of metal, I noticed, and none made from any kind of ceramic. There were irregular wooden shapes whose sides rose at varying angles, making them at their flattest a plate and at their steepest a dish. Our chairs had narrow seats and tall backs that spiralled or twisted into whichever shape the natural curvature of the wood took them. I cast my eye along the line of chairs to find the mid-point. Here I would place myself and the rest could then be seated on either side of me as my lessers. I pulled the chair away from the table and sat upon it as I thought a soldier or lord might, with decision. As I did so, I placed my hands on the table top firmly and with sufficient noise to be heard by those around me and to say *I have given you a sign.*

The moment my hands slapped this audacious slap, an immense hush came over the whole gathering. I was aware of the lines of heads in every direction dropping down. They had waited for my example before they took their seats. I fancy my head glowed at this knowledge as much as one of the globes that lighted us. In my movement towards the table, I had pulled Noisiu by the sleeve and he was obliged to sit at my right hand. To my left were Cavad and Follovin of the green eyes and blue eyes. There were no preliminaries to the eating. I had wondered about some kind of woodland blessing, an invocation of whatever powers they felt protected their home, but all about me I saw hands moving towards the dishes. There was conversation, a racket of Elven words and squeakings and squawkings, yet not a single word directed to my own person. That would have to change.

'In England,' I said to Follovin, who was the nearer of the two on my left, 'we are not used to playing this silent game at meal times unless we are in a monastery and they have been long suppressed. Silence is what Miss does when she has fallen out with her friend. You will include me in your conversation or I shall feed you your meat on my knife's point. You will not like the taste of your banquet then, I believe.'

'You enjoy threatening us, Edward Harry.'

'By no means. I behave as I find necessary. Is the Lady Nemain to grace us with her presence this evening? I should like to tell her how like a clutter of unsmiling children I have found you. Remember I no more asked to be in this place than you asked to have me your commander.'

'You are not our commander, Edward Harry.'

'I fancy that I am.'

Cavad leant towards Follovin and whispered a sentence or two at this point. Although the words were a secret to me, I hoped that their import was something like *Why do you make such foolish remarks when you know that we must obey him in all things? He is greater and more rational than we are.* My knowledge of the Elven adjective was in its infancy still and my conjecture could have flown leagues wide of the mark.

Littered between the containers of food were wooden spoons, each having its own individual shape, and slivers of the razor-sharp stone which were communal and allowed us to cut our food into manageable pieces. Arranged in a crescent in front of my chair was a selection of dishes untouched by any of the other diners. So they had expected me to sit here and this was the private meal the Grogoch mentioned. Not a soul had troubled to point this out to me. *May their trees fall in legions and crush them,* I thought until I tasted the first morsels of bread and a kind of omelette sprouting with sharp herbs. I insisted that my three neighbours explain all my dishes to me. I longed for meat, but, only after I had been promised that it was rabbit or fowl, did I cut a piece for my plate. There were vegetables and fruits I had never seen before and their smell alone was exquisite. They were purple and deep orange and crimson and they made my tongue fall in love with them. There were jellies and custards and creams, saffron-coloured cakes and almost transparent rose-scented wafers. And the bread! We had a constantly renewed supply of fine white loaves that seemed to be made only of air and a delicious yet delicate taste.

I made humorous remarks to my fellow diners and I thanked them when they pointed out a particularly tasty item to me, but never the trace of a smile did I receive in reply. They could not or would not unbend. This certainly did not diminish my pleasure in the meal, although it did fill me with a great desire to exact punishment. On the present occasion, this could only take the form of insult.

'Tell me,' I said, 'all three of you hearties (I was determined that the punishment should be general), why do the men in my world report such false stories about you?' They paid attention to this and rested from their meal and their conversation with each other. 'Yes,' I continued. 'We hear that you are joyful people, much given to laughter and merry japes, to dance and song. Yet, if there is a single faerie smile in my presence, it happens the moment I blink or turn my back. The truth is that I have found you most *un*smiling, humourless, ungracious, grudging, haughty, unmannerly, disobliging and self-regarding. I have many other words, but let it rest there.'

'You are pleased to slight us, Edward Harry,' said Cavad in the voice of one who is determined not to be roused to anger.

'Indeed I am, for I find that I do not like you at all.' I might have added that the only creatures whom I had found companionable were a salvage mute who could not bear me to speak French to him, a small blue, indeterminate creature that flew and my unkempt, besoming Grogoch. I mentioned none of these as I feared a spiteful retribution being taken against them. In children's tales, we are often warned of the spitefulness of the faerie folk and I am sure this has a good foundation.

I had discomposed them, but my reward was merely to see the slightest of twitches at the corner of Cavad's mouth and a tetchy word when he and a neighbour reached for the same platter of meat. I would have to do better, child that I was.

'Your table manners are delightful,' I next said. 'You do not overload your platters or elbow a fellow diner when he covets a delicacy you have chosen for your own. Your napkins are barely smeared, quite unlike my own.'

They looked at me uncertainly, not sure if my praise would be followed by more slighting words. It would. All along my own high table and at numerous others in front of us were seated Elvenkind looking much like myself and clad alike. There were women too, beautiful, slim creatures in light garments of the woodland green. I did not see Flora, although I especially looked out for her. None of the women was seated within many places of me, perhaps because it was their way and women were of lesser status. I doubted this as the woodland seemed a most free place to me but, then, I had not seen inside their families and it may have been that fathers and brothers exercised a tyranny over their wives, daughters and sisters. It was also unlikely that there was a fear I should spirit the women's hearts away. Who knows? Our pedlars have hawked many a ballad which tells of the love of the Faerie Queen for a handsome young man who is snatched from mortal fields to be Her Majetsy's paramour. I am far from being unpresentable and I did not consider the notion entirely ridiculous. There was a gravity in the demeanour of these women who looked no more than girls and who were, perhaps, ages old. They were conversing in their own tongue but, because of their distance from me, all I heard was a melodious whisper. Their gestures of arms and hands were slow and measured and lacked the excitable girlishness I expect from English maidens.

Now fell my time to wound, if they would not be convivial with me. 'I cannot help noticing,' I said as if about to embark on a remark of no consequence at all, 'that the further I cast my eye beyond our own table, the less like us the other guests appear. At the furthest reaches of the feast, they are smaller and, I suspect, much wilder.' I waited for confirmation of my observation and, of course, there came none. 'Is their repast the same as ours?' I continued. 'I would not like to think that they are invited here simply to dine on each other or on some poor human who has strayed into these godforsaken territories as reluctantly as I did.'

'You wonder much, Edward Harry,' said Noisiu. 'As you will not believe anything I tell you, why not visit those far tables yourself? Mayhap your welcome will be a warm one.' He had issued a challenge which he thought would silence my bothersome tongue.

The last word would be mine, however. 'If I visited them with my iron blade swishing right and left, I believe I should spoil their jollity,' I said and we left it at that.

No feast is complete without music and it was something I longed to hear. Faerie music, the stories have told us, is bewitching, maddening and, once heard, never forgotten. Of a sudden, the notes of a symphony arose as if in response to my wish. I could not see the players although I almost believed at times that they were in the air above me. Instruments were plucked and bowed, piped and shaken and they broke my heart. The most exquisite melancholy passed through me and

I felt that I wanted to listen to it forever. Tears quickly gathered in my eyes and I simply leant back in my chair and let them fall. The melodies seemed to be played on my very heartstrings and, when the voices were added, wordlessly, I thought I should not be able to bear their anguish. Perhaps the music spoke differently for everyone who heard it. For me, they sang of a human loss, my friend who had been parted from me weeks before and with whom I was determined to recover our way home.

Gradually the music died away and I was not sure whether, eventually, I was listening to its dying strains or to the sound of my own innermost grieving. The experience left me weak but yet not wretched. I was glad to be able to recover myself with a deep quaff from my wooden goblet. We had been served intoxicating wine that made me fear at first that I should end the evening in a stupor, my face buried in my dinner and all dignity gone. As a precaution, I slipped my hand inside my satchel and spent some moments gripping the hilt of my iron dagger. It was like bathing in icy water and I was almost myself again. When Follovin placed his hand on my right arm, indirectly, the touch of the iron was communicated through me to him and he snatched his hand away with a hiss as if he had tried to pick up a glowing coal. 'The feast is ended,' he said. 'You were best close your eyes as they may be harmed.'

I am not such a hothead that I do not admit there are times when I must be obedient. Even with my eyes closed, I was aware of a great blaze of magic as the feasters, tables, symphony were returned to the places whence they had come. My fingers touching iron ensured that I did not stagger, although my very seat was taken from me. It was as if the feast had never been. Not a bone or crumb was left behind on the grass. The light about us, however, remained greater than that shed by the moon. Cavad, Follovin and Noisiu remained in their places but now, facing me across the glade, were, what shall I call them, a terrifying eldritch assemblage. I had asked for twelve good 'men' and true in my company and a total of twelve creatures I had. In addition to the three significant Elven at my side, there were three more Elven of the human kind who proved determined to serve in my colours, but equally determined to keep their distance from me. I never learnt their names and was happy to leave them to their roles as anonymous infantrymen. For whatever reason, I was accorded not a single soldier from amongst my own Humankind. As for the remaining six members of my war-band, they could not have been more *other*. My eyes darted over them as I engaged in a fierce battle to keep myself from crying out. Imagine, if you will, that you are a poor benighted villager on a lonely country track at midnight. You are returning from a toilsome, honest day spent earning a few pennies for your family. You long for the warmth of your kitchen and of your wife and you hope there is bread and cheese and ale enough to satisfy the hunger that gnaws. And then, within a mile of your village, you see spread across the road to greet you every single faerie bugbear your grandmother ever frightened you with. Such was my situation at that moment. How I longed for a warm kitchen, however simple, and a solid oak door fastened with a lock of good English iron. To name them, I had directly in front of me a brace of tuskers, hog-like, four-footed dreadful beasts the size of year-old calves. They pawed the ground and slavered an offensive, glutinous drool. There was a stick creature, this was the closest I ever came to naming it, which was sentient and capable of actions like my own, but which could take on the semblance of a branch or sapling at will. The bones of its face, its ribs and limbs put me in mind inevitably of a skeleton, a death's head come to drag me to my grave. There were two winged beings. Insects they were not, yet they had an armoury of stings, claws, beaks. Their wings were a haze of speedy motion which meant I could never tell how many heads they possessed or even in which direction they faced. I was confident that they carried dreadful venoms about them and that the death they were able to deal was an agonising one. I caught glimpses of colour, yellow mostly and brown like dappled sunlight and a smell like leaf mould which was not unpleasant. And then, to my far right, was that being which Calvagh had sworn to me was the most fearsome of all – the Pooka. As if undecided which aspect of itself to present to me, it was never a single shape for long. I was least perturbed by the inky cloud and most in danger of screaming when it suddenly transformed to a huge black stallion with piercing yellow eyes and a sulphurous discharge form its nostrils. It is nigh impossible to put into words what my new woodland senses told me and it is unpleasant now to recall it to mind. I sensed their savagery, their capacity for destruction far beyond the competence of any human being with no matter what weapon. They were elemental and vile and yet they had an essence that held me in awe.

'These are the nine others who have chosen to accompany you,' said Cavad solemnly. 'Nemain of the battle song and the bloody hand, she who revels in the bright eye of the warrior and who brings the caress of death at an arrow's point, has bidden them answer to your will. Kneel before him.'

And kneel they did, all twelve of them, prostrating themselves before me, or, in the case of the winged ones, flying closer to the ground. The Pooka became an eagle with folded wings. At the exact moment of their kneeling, I sensed a drawing in of their power. It was as if I stepped back from a great fire which had been about to scorch the very skin from my face. My eyes saw nothing, but I knew they had accommodated themselves to me. They offered as much of their nature as I could be comfortable with, a space in which to breathe and collect my words. My desire was still to plunge screaming into the forest like Miss Muffet who has felt the first scratch of the spider's foot upon her hand, and yet words came and I spoke them resonantly.

'Arise and be welcome,' I said. Inside my head, another tiny, tiny voice, was running up and down squealing, *What now! What now! What now!* 'This night we shall spend in a council of war, I and my trusted band.' I thought grandiloquence might impress them and yet who is not to say that they saw in front of them a posturing manikin whom they would be happy to devour when he slipped into error. I was, myself, put in mind of a boy who clutches his father's sword, which he can barely lift, and who mouths a fatuous jumble of words which he thinks are soldierly. I did not believe in myself and assumed that it could be read in every inch of my body. 'I have commanded maps.' With that, I turned to Cavad and Follovin. As if by magic, I say laughingly, they had two rolls of parchment in their hands. They spread these on the ground and invited me to join them. I would wager many handfuls of orchalc coins that Cavad whispered the word 'Sir'. It was not distinct, and it was for form's sake only, yet he felt obliged to acknowledge that it was I who had commanded the drawing of the maps and it was I who would lead the discussion of how the band of twelve should proceed. I am no strategist, but I have been made to learn my Caesar by heart. That is the best that can be said of me in a way. I am the first to own up to it and I have pointed it out before. Cavad and Follovin had most certainly not read their Caesar or listened in any London ale-house to the rumours of how the Duke of Medina Sidonia was deploying his ships against England and to suggestions as to how he might be thwarted. As a non-combatant, I knew a great deal and, of course, I knew nothing. I did, however, appreciate the need for discipline and circumspection and I hoped I should be able to impart these qualities to Edward Harry's company.

Long into the night we talked, Cavad, Follovin, Noisiu and I, while the remainder continued kneeling with a degree of humility and patience which I found extraordinary. The Pooka altered its appearance several times as if simply flexing its fingers and finally subsided into a mound of darkness, perhaps signifying that it had fallen asleep. There was not a growl, a buzz or a question from them as we leaders came to an agreement over the details of our little campaign. I made most of the suggestions and they were countered with a few observations mostly from Follovin. I had no notion at all of which decisions were canny and which were likely to lead us all to a swift death or imprisonment. I trusted to my impudence and to Caesar's maxim that his enemies time-upon-time did not expect him to attempt the impossible. Our plan was shot through with impossibilities, yet I alone seemed concerned by this. Their trust was an exhilarating thing and I had constantly to remind myself that I now sat with a map of part of the faerie realm before me because I had insisted upon it.

There was much map-making as part of the English plantation of Munster and I had seen many a good and bad example of the cartographer's art in Master Spenser's study. I considered myself a discerning judge and I was well-pleased with the two parchment rolls Follovin had provided for me. Perhaps they appeared at the flick of a magic wand and I was being generous in my approval, but their occasional crossings-out and the fact that some names were pressed into spaces too small for them suggested that he had indeed laboured over them himself. I will always give credit where it is due just as I expect my own successes to be recognised.

'You have drawn excellent maps, Follovin,' I said when we were agreed that our plan was complete. 'Especially as you have never seen the use of them before.' I at once regretted my last sentence as it appeared to contain an irony I did not intend. He nodded and muttered a couple of broken sentences to the effect that I had been right when I ordered the maps to be made. I would have thought more of the man if he could have looked me in the eye when he told me he had been wrong to doubt their usefulness. I should never have mentioned it again, but this mumbling set my teeth on edge.

I was glad to stand at last and stretch my back. The maps were rolled again and securely in my hand where I intended to keep them against the day when I might need to plot a route of escape.

'Company,' I said, having run through a number of appellations in my mind, *Harry's War-band, Courageous Dozen* and so on, 'tomorrow night we sally forth for the first time. I intend to lead you to the manor of Lord Alanin, to tweak his nose, singe his beard and bring you all safely back. My three lieutenants,' again I had been very careful in my choice of the word, 'will remind you of the plan you have heard in the making tonight. Be bold and resolute, but not bloody, I pray you and meet me at dusk tomorrow beside the wood's far edge.'

Either they would meet me or they would not. I had little doubt that my every word had been learnt for anatomising later. For myself, I felt that I had carried off a piece of flummery outrageously well and that I deserved the twig bed that was now calling loudly to me.

'Farewell.' I contented myself with that single word and strode across the glade to the steps leading to my cave. I did not look back then or even when I reached the entrance to my lodging. I had done with them for one night and Edward Harry's present bodily comfort was all that mattered to me.

There was a small candle alight in the cave by the light of which I saw the Grogoch sitting on one of my chairs knitting. At my entrance, he jumped up and threw his knitting behind him.

'The Master has been kneeling in the wet a long time,' he said pointing at my damp breeches. 'Off with them.'

'All in good time. Did you listen to what was said down there?'

'Listen! The Grogoch listen! When I had cleaned away the dirty Leprechaun smell, I was busy with my needles. The Grogoch never listens.'

I doubted that, but I was too tired to tell him so.

He retrieved his knitting and began to work most violently at it. He was, as my grandmother used to say, 'vaporous'. 'The Grogoch sitting here worrying himself into a tremble while the Master talks and talks outside. The stink of a…,' he choked briefly before he could say the word, 'Pooka floating over the grass and into the Master's home. The poor Grogoch scattering apple-skins and pretty flowers to take away the nasty Pooka's presence and the Master not caring.'

I was by now undressed and ready for my slumbers.

'Will you desist,' I cried. 'The Master was brought here to lead a company and Sir Pooka chose to serve me.'

There came an anguished cry at this juncture and a veritable explosion of the knitting. In attempting to cover his head with the shapeless piece of textile which he had been making, the Grogoch simply lost it in the acreage of his hair and the needles dropped all their stitches. I roared with laughter which led to wordless pointing in my direction and an energetic bouncing up and down.

'The Grogoch cares,' he managed at last and fell sideways across the arm of his chair.

'The Master appreciates that the Grogoch cares, although he does not care enough to show the Master his way home.'

That brought him to his senses. He walked over and stood looking down at me in my bed, his arms folded and one knitting needle and a spiral of dropped stitches hanging out of his topknot.

'The Master knows how it is. The Master knows,' he sniffed in a hurt manner.

'Indeed, the Master knows all too well. A pox on this land and all who sail in her. Tomorrow I ride to war. Well, I ride to cause a nuisance. If I fail to return, distribute my possessions to the poor and set fire to the forest in my memory.'

The Grogoch tapped his foot and gave me a long, weary stare. 'The Master is full of the mocks and the Grogoch wonders where it will get him.'

'He hopes it will get him a hearty breakfast tomorrow morning. Until then, my thanks and good night.'

Although I now turned on my side and pulled the coverlet over my head, I was still aware of the Grogoch's heavy breathing only a few feet away from me. 'Will you be gone now!'

'The Grogoch is on edge.'

'It will do him no good. My course is planned and events may turn out as they will.'

'The Grogoch...'

'If the Grogoch utters another word this night I shall make him a gift of my fouled underclouts and that will be an end of it!'

He departed with a squeal, barely pausing to extinguish the candle which, to gauge from the sound, he merely knocked from its holder.

My mind felt quite trampled by this juncture. I had feasted amongst powerful creatures who resented me, I had planned a military campaign on behalf of nightmares and now my body servant was beset by moodiness. It was an overabundance of experience from which sleep was my rescuer.

CHAPTER EIGHTEEN

It is a singular feature of Elven beds that, constructed of twigs though they are, they afford one the sweetest repose possible. My head and body were much rested when at last I troubled to open my eyes. I had hardly sat up and taken my first yawn of the new day when a large wooden platter dropped onto my lap. On the platter was a dish of eggs with bacon and some bread and butter.

'Do not ask the Grogoch how he knows that Englishmen take great delight in eggs with bacon.' He stood over me in a pose that suggested he still felt some of last night's crossness, but also that he was very pleased with himself for producing such a breakfast.

'Tell me, Grogoch, how have you become so acquainted with the habits of Englishmen?' I asked in the spirit of sheer perversity.

He marched to the other side of the cave and began to make as loud a scratching noise as he could with his besom on the floor. I was put to shame because the eggs with bacon were perfectly cooked and perfectly seasoned. I took my time over each mouthful.

'Tell me then,' I shouted above his swishing and swashing, 'why you knit by candlelight when you could surely conjure a magical flame that would never blow out?'

After a number of particularly aggressive smacks of the besom against the cave wall, he deigned to walk slowly across to me. 'If the Master must know, the Grogoch feels homesick from time to time. He has his little corner in the house where he sits and burns the candle ends the family will not miss.'

Here was information indeed. The home he missed had to be in the human world and, all the time he spent with me, there was a family wondering why their house had become so ill-kept. I felt that I ought to make a peace offering rather than disturb him with more questions although, as ever, I had plenty. I caught a length of meaty bacon on my stone knife and raised it towards him.' Would you like…,' I began and then our eyes met. His eyes were wide with horror as I could plainly see despite his dense fringe. Thankfully, I at once realised why. If I had finished my sentence the way I intended, with the name of a gift, albeit only a few inches of bacon, our relationship would have ended forthwith. I recollected myself and began my sentence anew. 'Would you like to bring me a cup of drink? Bacon always makes me thirsty.' We had been a noun's length from disaster and we each needed time to recover.

I washed and had my hair trimmed and my beard removed with speed and dexterity by the Grogoch. I felt quite splendid and, in my clean shirt and breeches as well as the magnificent new boots, I sat idle as the heir to an estate in the cave's mouth while my housekeeper dusted and re-dusted and polished every surface. It was now that I felt the need of a book to while away the time, some extraordinary tale or history that would transport me away from myself, but, in truth, I was in as strange a situation as a man ever encountered within the pages of a book. In my time in the Elven city, I had seen no books and I wondered whether they went in for bookshops with their delicious array of printed poems, stories and plays. I relished the pleasure of opening a newly-acquired volume and I was eternally grateful to Master Spenser that he allowed me full use of one of the best libraries in Ireland.

Nothing happened in the glade below me. No pair of creatures stopped to gossip or quarrel; not even a bird landed in search of worms. Until mid-afternoon, my time was my own once the Grogoch was done and had gone on his way. I sat at my table with the two maps unrolled. It was important that, as commander, I understood the geography of the places we were to disturb at least as well as my troops who had dwelt nearby all their lives, which could mean since the days of great Caesar himself. I was astounded to discover that the Grogoch had left me pen and ink without my asking. I discovered them hidden behind my dishes and jug of water which suggested very strongly that they were forbidden. So I was now able to write strategies and notions all over the maps to my heart's content. Much of what I wrote was of little value and served only to keep my fidgets at bay. The alternative was to pace the cave or enter the woodland which I thought would be misguided. I removed my boots and took several long rests on my bed and made sure that I ate well (I was abundantly furnished with cold meats, bread and fruit) to provide me with the strength I knew I would need. I closely followed the passage of the sun across the sky and found myself drumming my heels and whistling many a tune as the day wore on. I had understood Follovin to say that he would accompany me to the other side of the forest and I instructed him to appear at about five of the clock. As a country boy, I have an accurate sense of how the hours are marked by the descent of the sun towards its western couch and by well after the appointed hour no Elven lieutenant had appeared. I was ready with my quilted tabard, my satchel and a rising temper.

At last, two figures entered the glade. Follovin was there, as ordained; the second figure was the Pooka. A tall, black horse, it walked slowly and yet with the utmost command as if to say *Who here is more to be feared than I?* The eyelids were three quarters down over the eyes and that dreadful gaze was muted, I was glad to see. I thought it significant that the Pooka led the way and Follovin walked meekly some paces behind. Such deference did not bode well and I wondered whether the first challenge to my authority had arisen before I even left my cave. Uttering my favourite curses, I went down to meet a possible rebellion.

Naturally I had my hand inside my satchel, my fingers grasping as fiercely as they could the iron blade which stood between me and dismemberment by a monster. I remembered the fear in Calvagh's voice when he told me of the might of the Pooka and its fabled malevolence towards Mankind. I reminded myself that it had knelt before me last evening and awaited my bidding. In daylight, surely I had the advantage?

'Is all made ready?' I asked in a voice that I thought was eminently soldier-like and barely undermined by any sort of quaver. If it had been a normal horse, I would have spoken the usual *Good boy* words. I knew that such behaviour would be an intolerable insult to the black demon pounding the ground with its right hoof and I had no wish to test its patience or loyalty towards me. The breath it expelled in sharp bursts through its nostrils had a most noisome savour, marsh gas, sulphur and long-dead corpses to name but three of its elements and it took all my composure not to cover my nose and mouth and run far away.

'The company awaits you at the woodland's end. It is some distance and the journey would tire you unnecessarily. The Pooka has therefore graciously consented to carry us both thither.'

'I thank him,' I said, my inward vision immediately bursting with pictures of being swept to Hell with never a chance of leaping from the Devil's back. The beast stood at least five hands taller than any horse I had seen in my life. It bore no saddle or reins and we lacked a mounting block. I confess I dreaded seizing hold of the mane and hauling myself onto the Pooka's back. 'Allow me to sit forward,' I said to Follovin. 'You may ride behind me and grip my waist.' Whate'er befell, I would not let *him* think he had me at any disadvantage. Uttering a silent prayer, I walked towards the Pooka's belly. I should add here that, while in the Elvenlands, I had uttered many such prayers, silent and out loud, and not one had altered my situation. The good words had broken no enchantments and sent no faeries running from us as their magic was overcome. Perhaps one was required to believe devoutly and all my life I had been a scoffer. As I lay my hand on the Pooka's shoulder, I now paid the price. 'Will you permit me to grasp hold of your mane?' I asked in a voice I hoped was not craven. The left eye opened fully and looked me up and down. I could return the look only for a moment, for I had never seen such ferocity. Within this black stallion, a whirlwind of rage, dislike, mischief longed for release.

'Do what you must.' The flat voice did not emerge directly from the animal's mouth. Rather, it was there in my ears from nowhere in particular, bidding me carry out my feeble human act..

'Your help, I pray you,' I said to Follovin who duly allowed me to step on his hand and spring onto the horse's back. He then clasped my own hand and leapt up behind me. No human legs could have managed such a flea's leap. Liking the comparison of the flea, I was tempted to express it, but thought it inopportune.

I would say that we then set off if such a phrase were not wholly inadequate. The Pooka swung round and arched its back so violently I thought my neck would snap. My body was projected forward even as my face, Janus-like, was twisted back into the nose and mouth of my fellow passenger. Over his shoulder I saw the entrance of my cave and the Grogoch sinking down with his arms wrapped about his head. It was the gesture of a man who knows his friend is about to lose his head and cannot bear to look. I was of the firm conviction that I would be knocked from my seat by the first substantial branch we met, particularly as my head was lolling so dangerously and I had not yet managed to bring it round to face the direction in which we were speeding. Strangely, not even the smallest twig made contact with us despite our hurtling forward as if possessed.

'Fear not,' came a voice at my ear. 'The Pooka will never unseat us.'

Although my head continued to loll and my neck to wrench at every change of direction, it is true that my legs remained closely fastened to the creature's sides. I was the commander of the man seated behind me and of the black steed on which we rode. For the moment, however, the black steed was Lord. He relished his strength and no doubt the apprehension my legs conveyed to him. I saw the woodland as he saw it, not in the diluted fashion with which it had generally been shown to me ere now. These were the true faerie woods with no trace of midsummer delicacy. There were thorns a hand's breadth long and pendant, leprous clusters of I know not what. The whole forest oozed nauseatingly sweet gums and the drippings from over-ripe fruit. If the Pooka's magic had not encircled us, I should have been torn and drowned in equal measure. Tongues and long arms were extended to us as we passed and the more they failed to touch me, the more the laughter gathered in my chest. I had been whooping for some time without knowing before Follovin tapped me on the shoulder and urged me to be calm. And yet I could not be so. I cried encouragement to the Pooka. I waved my arms and gestured at those we passed. It was the barest of woodland paths we used and creatures walking it threw themselves aside as we careered towards them. From time to time, Follovin urged me to show restraint, yet I would be shouting and reaching out to the fingers extended towards us. 'Do not do this!' he cried. 'They wish to unseat you and then you will be entirely lost to us.' Ask me not how a fruit resembling a small, scarlet apple came to be in my grasp and how I bit one lusciously sweet mouthful from it before Follovin struck it from my hand.

Our exit from the wood was a juddering thing. One moment we were fast amongst the lowest branches and, the next, the Pooka had leapt out into clear air and grassy footing. He stopped within a stride and both Follovin and I fell forward, he onto my back and I onto the Pooka's neck. At once, whatever bound our legs to the creature's flanks was gone. Our forward movement continued and I knew I should skim over the Pooka's head. I did not expect I would be allowed to break my neck, but I knew my landing was intended to be without dignity. Consequently I bent my head down to my chest and gathered in my arms. Once I had passed over the creature's ears, I performed a neat rolling in the air and landed upright with my feet apart. Tumbling was never a skill I expected to master and yet in this land of magic it had come to me as easily as walking. The Pooka and I were now face to face and, as horses cannot smile, I smiled for both of us, presenting this horror with my most gleaming expression. I offered him a second forest apple which somehow had found its way into my pocket. With a snort, he blew it out of my fingers and high into the air. When it fell earthwards again, he caught it and swallowed it.

'Those boots will not allow you to stumble,' said a voice that, once more, did not issue directly from the horse's mouth. 'You chose them well.' Follovin had not chosen his footwear so well for he fell onto his face when he touched the ground which vexed him greatly.

Our madcap passage through the woodlands was over. It was my time now. I drew in breath and looked about me. The edge of the wood was defined for miles into the distance by a fringe of mixed flowers and tall grasses. Ox-eyes, ragged robins and rosebays nodded amongst giant growths of the fly-trap sort that spoiled the air with their decaying breath. I was now like a dog in my new awareness of scents and deep breaths that were meant to settle me only served to fill my nose with a fiercer knowledge of this alien world.

All of my 'men' had obeyed my summons punctually. The tuskers lay on their bellies, their tongues hanging out eagerly. With each pant, they sprayed their noxious drool some yards, obliging the others to remain a good distance from them. The insects, or whatever the winged creatures were, fluttered between me and the declining sun and were rendered indistinct by its blaze. Not only did I not understand them or how to communicate with them, I rarely knew even whether their heads or rear ends faced in my direction. This is truly not the best situation for a commander and his troops. Our twiggy companion stood like a newly-planted sapling. Until it moved, I was afraid that I might have addressed an embarrassing number of remarks to a young nut tree. The Elven, Cavad, Follovin, Noisiu and the nameless trio, stood in a gaggle and waited for my commands. Waited for me to trip over my own feet, more like. The Pooka removed himself to a substantial distance and dunged fulsomely. Notwithstanding that he was down-wind of us, my new nose was mordantly offended by the acrid nature of the stink. Never put your hand in a wasps' nest and never stand within miles of a Pooka while he dungs. These are two of the greatest lessons my first twenty years of life taught me.

I took the map of our first journey together from my satchel and bade the company form a half circle while I reminded them of our strategy. I was thankful indeed that I had taken the trouble to write so many of my thoughts onto the map as I was now able to speak briskly and as if I were completely master of the situation. It fell to the stick-creature to stand next to the tuskers at this point and, when a snot-like tendril escaped from the maw of one of them and draped itself around a stick leg, the offending tusker received a blow from a fiercely whipped switch for its lack of consideration. The speed and ferocity of the blow took us all by surprise. A deep cut a good six inches long had opened across the tusker's, I hesitate to say 'poor tusker's', snout and it began to yowl inconsolably. Fearing that such noise would betray us and render the whole enterprise without point, I stood directly in front of the injured beast and shouted as loudly as I could, 'Your noise can be heard all the way across these hills. Shall I take out my blade of iron?' There was such magic in that short word, all of them were instantly subdued. 'Be sensible and move away from them. In that way you will not be soiled,' I said to the tree. 'I forbid you to lash out at any of us in that way again.'

The Pooka now joined us and I repeated our plan of campaign twice. After that, all that remained for us was to go to war. The words make it sound such a simple thing and yet I had already been struck by a dreadful misgiving. Our map gave little indication of distances and I realised I had not pressed Cavad or Follovin when they said places were 'not far' or 'only a little distance over the hill'. As I surveyed the territory to the south of us, I knew that a much longer march than I had expected lay ahead. Beyond the woodland, there was acre upon acre of meadow sloping gradually until it met a smaller continuation of the stream on whose banks I had recently put my dagger to its fatal use. On the far bank, the pasture was much coarser and rose in a series of steep steps for a distance of perhaps five miles when I had imagined it to be no more than one. Next there was a bleak plateau dotted with rock and furze which began near the horizon and was then lost to view. I knew that this terrain would be like the miserable, rain-drenched boglands of Ireland which the English all hated and that it was vastly more extensive than my map-makers had led me to believe. They shrivelled to nothing in my estimation. Miles of travel across this landscape that was uneven and spotted with muddy snares would eventually bring us to the head of the narrow valley which cradled the manor of Lord Analin.

'Allow me to give you instruction in the drawing of maps,' was all I could say. 'You have misled me grievously. For each of your miles, I fancy we shall have to trudge twenty. The devil take you for your incompetence and me for ever believing in you.'

The geography of the valley, if we ever reached it in the next sennight, would serve our purpose well. I, Cavad, Follovin and Noisiu would enter from the valley head while the tuskers and the other Elven approached from the two sides where substantial streams had cut deep beds. The stick-creature was to make its way through the orchards on the western flank of the manor while the Pooka, in fearsome solitary state, advanced from the valley mouth. The 'insects' were to flit wheresoever they wished. It had all sounded so flawless as a plan until I raised my eyes to the hills, as it were. All I could see from my present spot was a great panorama of virgin landscape and the more I thought of the miles we had to travel, the more I felt in need of a spell which could transport us to our destination in the blinking of an eye. Such a spell was evidently not in their possession, but I would not be defeated.

'Master Pooka,' I said. 'I crave a second ride on your back if we are to reach the manor before night falls. May I?'

'You may.'

'*We* shall run. It is not difficult for Elven legs,' Cavad told me. With that, they all set off at great speed, loping, bounding, flying. I have no words to describe the motion of the stick-creature. It neither ran on legs nor spun like a handful of dried weeds driven by the wind and yet its rapid forward motion savoured of both of these. I half expected it to fly apart with the effort and all its body parts to fall to the ground re-assembled as a gardening basket.

None of my company wasted a moment taking leave of their leader. 'Have you protected yourselves?' I called almost to the empty air. We had agreed that none would embark upon this enterprise until he had armed himself with whatever private magics he had at his command. I had no notion of what they were. I could imagine the stick-creature perishing in a column of flame or the winged ones being swatted as I would destroy a fly. They knew best how to protect themselves and I had enough to do to look after my own life. My Elven mounting block was now well on his way down the grassy slope and I knew I should not be able to mount the Pooka unaided. Thoughtfully he went down on one knee for me and so I was easily on his back after all. Before we set off on our adventure, there were some moments of conversation, not like that between friends of course, the light, playful kind that Calvagh and I were used to practise, but I found it one of the most extraordinary moments I ever knew in that land that a monster who filled the hearts of men with terror should exchange a kind of pleasantry with me.

'Few men who rode upon my back have lived to tell their story,' he said. 'Only that wily King, Brian Bóiromhe, and your puny self, in fact.'

'I am in good company, sir,' I replied.

'Were it not for the Lady Nemain and the witlessness of these forest dwellers, your sight of me would be your very last.'

'There is no need to say these things,' I told him. 'I know your power and you know mine.' I think he liked that.

'It is you who are to blame for my stink.'

'I?'

'You indeed. The Pooka does not behave like a farmyard animal for all the world to see. I am *not* an animal.' I thought my wisest course here was to remain very silent. He continued, 'The fruit you took in the forest and which I should not have eaten was not a honey apple. It was a dung apple in disguise. If you had kept your fingers to yourself, as you were told to, you would not have been punished when the fruit did its work upon me.'

We were both punished again when his haunches shuddered at the passage of a monstrous fart, the emperor of all foul winds, that could have toppled a windmill.

'There are those who have no love for me,' he said bitterly and then sped off in order to leave the unwholesome cloud behind us. No doubt it soon fell to the earth under the weight of its foulness.

We moved at a heady, but not break-neck, speed down the slope and passed the Elven runners soon after we leapt the stream and the other members of my company not long after that as they moved on their own paths towards the spot we had appointed. I had commanded that each of us would rest on the lip of the valley until darkness fell and then we would make our way down towards the lonely manor in order to wreak our various mischiefs. Throughout the ride, my legs were fastened to the Pooka's ribs and there was no danger of my being thrown from his back. As he traversed the ground in enormous bounds, my body rose and fell in a way which I would have liked to find exciting but which was, in fact, sickening and I was mightily glad when our journey ended. I slid from the Pooka's back and watched him begin his circuit of the valley's rim that would take him to its mouth a league or two thence. All I was required to do was to lie on my stomach and let it settle and await the arrival of Cavad, Follovin and Noisiu.

So there was the valley, narrow and neat, with Lord Alanin's manor half a mile below me, built on a natural platform resembling that of Master Spenser's keep at Kilcolman. The plan of the building was much the same as that of the very first manor I saw when I came into the Elvenfold. A tall structure of four storeys, it sat comfortably on its rise with a skirt of offices, barns and gardens spread out around the base. All was well ordered and spoke of a lord who was very pleased with what he had and who he was. I should have felt myself king if I owned such a house and was master of so many fertile acres that stretched along the valley bottom and sides for as far as my eyes could discern in the fading light. On the valley rim there was wildness and yet, once you slipped below it, you found yourself in a veritable bower. As the sun disappeared behind the western hills, and if only I were able to capture for you the colour of the sky at that moment of the day in Hy Brazil, I could not help thinking of the family in the manor going about their lives. Were they eating dinner or planning some activity for the morrow? Were there accounts to read or arguments to settle? My three major Elven companions, not the best word, arrived and Cavad, the least reserved of them, lay on his stomach beside me. I shared my musings with him and met with no response at first.

'I could wander a whole day in such orchards,' I told him.

He turned his disconcerting eyes towards me. 'You should know, Edward Harry, that Lord Alanin keeps human slaves and he does not keep them well. They put on chains at night. The meanest household tasks are done by our lowest woodland sort who can expect to die in my lord's service. Put these thoughts to your heart before you restrain your hand.'

It was always the Elven way never to tell me a whole story at a sitting. They delighted in tossing me a fragment now and then like a bone they had chewed for a while and then discarded. The presence of Humankind was sharp news and I was obliged to free them. We exchanged no further words and waited until the darkness had settled around us.

'Now is the time,' I said at last. 'Stand away for I intend to shroud myself in the power of iron.' They jumped back promptly as I waved my blade around each part of my person. I gave my head a double protection since I wore no helmet and feared the use of arrows against me. The knife's power was much diluted after so much time, however; I could feel this in the lack of resistance to the movement of my arm. An ordinary poison may be rendered harmless by constant washings with clean water and I wondered how long it would be before the dagger I saw before me lost all its venom and crumbled under the onslaught of Elven magic. Certainly, I had seen actors dance as nippily as my lieutenants jumped out of reach. I did not discount the possibility that they were humouring or even mocking me.

Cavad gave a sign, a wail as of some melancholy heathland bird, and the night's business began. The thing of twigs moved into the orchard and remained there for the whole hour we had allotted for our visit. It denuded the branches of fruit, no matter how small, and caused them to rot even as they reached the orchard floor. The tuskers and one of the Elven men set free the livestock and scattered them far and wide. I am sure that many of the smaller creatures escaped no further than the tuskers' jaws. Once the animals were gone, fluttering, squealing and setting up a frightful din, the tuskers and Noisiu moved on to the servants' quarters. Noisiu filled the rooms with unpleasant vapours and insects before the tuskers rushed in to complete the rout. It had been my intention, at first, to take Cavad and Follovin with me in at the back door of the house and to create terror and flame about us in equal measure. The new knowledge that I had Humankind to free diverted me and I spent some time roaring, 'Where are the human prisoners!' before I received an answer that helped me. One of my fellow men, a trusted servitor of many years' standing, was apparently waiting on Lord Alanin at table and two others had been put away for the night. I found them chained in a bare and windowless room, not quite a cellar, as I had been forewarned. My dagger weakened their bonds but no longer held the power to sever them and so I commanded Follovin, as the strongest of my band, to hammer them until broken.

'Where shall we go now?' pleaded one of the slaves I was freeing, an older man who looked quite helpless.

'Go where you wish,' I snapped. 'No Elven tyrant is your master now.'

This appeared to settle him, but I had no further time to listen to such, 'Oh dear, what is to become of me?' feebleness. I had to take command of our attack on the house itself. Our plan worked like a charm, an apt phrase if you consider where we were. My flying troops shattered the windows of the upper storeys, darting in at one side of the building and leaving from the other after a passage of nuisance and destruction. Those of us waiting below heard the screams grow nearer as the family were driven down the staircase towards us. Such a surprise they found – two thirds of our band, myself, six Elven and the tuskers all determined to expel them from the front door of their home and into the night before they had recovered their senses and were able to summon a useful quantity of magic or weaponry against us.

My Lord Alanin flew past me towards his great front door, not so much leading the exodus of his family as determined to reach a place of safety before them. He was tall and his eyes, darkened and more prominent as his panic had made them, rendered his face so inhuman-looking that I was spared the trouble of even a groatsworth of sympathy. He had obviously been dining at his complete ease in a suit of fine yellow satin that must surely tatter as he sped away from us. And his hair – no man deserved compassion who insulted his head with such long, tightly-rolled curls that bounced and sprayed like Medusa's serpents as he hurtled along. The lady of the house was hampered by the length of her gown despite its being made of one of those gossamer Elven fabrics. 'My lord, My lord,' she called in vain to the yellow satin back that grew further ahead of her with every step. 'My lord, your children!' These 'children' were not infants, let me add, helpless youngsters at the mercy of bloodthirsty heathens. They were young men, apparently of my own age but doubtless of my great-grandfather's generation at least. They had followed their mother down the staircase and now seized one of her arms each and hurried her through the door. One took time to gaze at my face as he passed. We stood eye to eye for a half breath, no more, and yet we spoke to each other in that instant of telling silence. His eyebrows rose as he perceived that I was human, or human-looking, and I offered him a delicate smile. I was not abashed or shamefaced to be about such work, I let him know. If he kept Englishmen or any other kind of man tethered below his stairs then he might expect far worse in times to come.

And so they were gone, not so much driven into the night by the iron blade I swirled about me as by the sheer disbelief that the lower orders, as they must deem all of us, should have the effrontery to forget their humble woodland station. The house was empty within a quarter of an hour, but if the family and servants attending them (we had stood unthreateningly aside to let these pass) believed that darkness was now their saviour, how wrong they were. Some half a mile in front of the house they had to face another terror. We shared with them the sight of the Pooka bearing down in all its nightmare glory. Two vast eyes like sulphurous moons, two orbs of horror that should have been saved for Judgement Day, floated in the sky. Even knowing their origin, I felt a chill come over me and took several steps backwards. I then jumped forward again as glass shards snowed down from the very top of the house. My winged soldiers had found even more windows to shatter. I moved in a third direction when a figure rushed out of the house and roughly elbowed me from his path.

'Master, they have set the house afire!' He ran past us, saw the angry eyes in the sky and turned uncertainly as if any amount of flame were better than what lay ahead. He was human but I never had chance to take him aside and reason with him. Fires were by now dancing in the upper windows and needles of glass continued to fountain outwards. I and my band stood in tight order across the doorway and the fearful man decided that his safety was more likely to be found off in the darkness despite those eyes growing ever closer. Lord Alanin, his lady and their two sons were driven back towards us only to find that our tuskers broke ranks and set about them, snarling without actually biting. The great eyes, so nearly upon us, now melted into a putrid cloud that carried every blight and murrain within it. Its heavy foulness swept up and down the valley causing everything beneath it to wither. When its first breath touched them, the manor's inhabitants fled stumbling towards the valley sides desperate to save their lives and yet unaware that I had insisted many times that there was to be no killing. The cloud thickened as it neared us and struck the ground like a wave breaking. It all but splashed over our shoes and then gathered shockingly to form the shape of the Pooka who pawed the ground with barely restrained excitement. I looked at my companions and saw bloodlust writ on every face. I had exalted them with my battle-plans and now I must lead them into a cooler place before savagery prevailed. I was happy to hear Lord Alanin shrieking in his curls and satin; I had no desire at all to have his head dropped at my feet like a football.

'Call back those hell-hounds!' I said to Cavad, punching him mightily in his upper arm. We could hear, with the unsettling clarity that the night air gives, a mixture of defiant shouts, animated howling and mayhap even the odd incantation.

Cavad shouted some instructions in a kind of beast-tongue which I had never heard him speak before, projecting his voice in a way that carried it far into the night. The howling quickly stopped and soon the tuskers skittered around the corner of a barn. They bounded at my feet looking for all the world like a pair of spaniels that were returning my stick. I saw no bloodstains about their jaws and, feeling that our work there was over, I ordered my company home. If my Lord recovered his breath sufficiently to work magic against us, I did not wish to remain in arrow-shot of it. Cavad's summons had alerted the stick-creature which joined us as we made our way to the head of the valley. I had quite forgotten it as it set about its no doubt enjoyable evening's work. The thought did pass my mind that I had allied myself with the instruments of Hell rather than agents of a civil war in the realms of faerie. Who else but Satan's own goodfellows would relish so warmly the plague and pestilence and whatever else the Pooka and that mockery of a nut tree had spread all around them.

As I stepped over the lip of the valley, I turned and stood for many minutes, staring at our night's handiwork. It delights me not to see wanton destruction. A fine house was on its way to becoming a charred ruin, the orchard grass must be calf-deep in a slurry of rotting fruit and field upon field had been visited by contagion. I had achieved nothing I could be proud of and it brought home to me that he is a very unwise man who involves himself in the quarrels of others, particularly when it is brother against brother, or an Elven lord of a manor pitted against his woodland siblings. I had touched pitch and been defiled, as many a writer has observed.

'Take me home,' I said to the Pooka. The rest of our band had scampered off into the night without a formal leave-taking of me, their captain. I was glad to see their disappearing backs, or foliage in the case of the stick-creature which I was increasingly coming to think of as an utter abomination.

'Yes, you shall sit astride me again,' boomed the Pooka's voice matching the thunders now assailing my conscience. 'And my thanks for such sport as we have had this night.'

If he had been a true horse, I would have lashed him. As he was, instead, a devil in a horse's skin, I had to endure the most violent ride a man has ever experienced on a four-legged beast. Such was his aroused state, he leapt fit to reach the moon and bucked and snorted for the sheer joy of his devilry until we had passed quite through the forest and reached the clearing which held my cave.

I was then allowed to slide heavily and uncomfortably to the ground, very ill-used but lacking the will to complain about it.

Hot water and a plate of food awaited me in the cave. The Grogoch was at his knitting which was a now a shapeless strip which hung down to his knees and was liberally sprinkled with irregular holes. He looked at me uneasily over his needles and knitted a slow stitch or two as he gauged my mood.

'Is the Master pleased?' spoken in a hushed voice.

By way of reply, the Master raised the pail of hot water over his head and emptied it, clothing or no. I felt calmer for being wet and I let the bucket drop. My skin smelt of burning and anguish, if anguish has a smell, which I now believe it does. I bade the Grogoch cast away his knitting and bring me as many fresh pails of water as he could manage. When he returned, I stood naked on the wet floor, having kicked my clothing far away from me. For someone who enjoyed an old dame's pastime in his quiet moments, the Grogoch was enormously strong. He had brought with him a shallow wooden bath, in which I was to stand, and three pails of hot water to pour over me as I directed. In all my time in that worthy creature's company, I never ceased to wonder at the objects he found so readily in the adjacent woodland. Was there some great pantry brimming with household goods and ovens and boilers to which he had instant access? If there were, I never caught sight of it. Perhaps he simply slid behind a tree trunk and worked a piece of magic which he was too secretive to want me to see. Whatever the case, I was now laundered and dry and I threw myself wearily into my chair. Being naked when not in the presence of women has never bothered me. My body, I am well aware, is comely in its shape and my little warrior could match the very best. The Grogoch, on the other hand, was most uncomfortable at the sight of my private regions and the you-know-what lolling at its ease. He tiptoed across and placed his knitting athwart my loins. 'I trust you have removed your needles,' I said, tickled by his modesty and the texture of the wool.

Taking my words seriously, he became all agitation and would have seized his knitting back except that this might have brought his fingers into contact with the parts he wished to hide.

'Have no fear, I am not skewered,' I said. 'Now, I pray you, take the food away. I cannot bear the sight or smell of it. Bring me wine or beer. Some drink that has the power to make a man forget himself.'

He offered me at first an end of bread and some sausage. The look which I gave him then, my eyelids half down and my lips drawn tight, made him retract the platter and walk slowly backwards with it until he reached the edge of the table. He at once sped out of the cave in his alarming way and soon returned with two pitchers of drink. I downed both of them almost without taking breath and I must confess I have no remembrance of what taste passed my lips as I did so. All I sought was sleep and forgetfulness. I fancy the Grogoch meant to deceive me by watering the drink so that, although I might believe I was drowning in it, I should suffer no harm. My stomach had heaved at the thought of the sausage, the pastries, the pared fruit which my brownie of a butler had prepared for me, but I thankfully felt able to go to my bed with the prospect of soon falling asleep. I laid my head on the pillow and willed the herbs stuffed into it to do their best. A gentle path to wherever it is that we go at such a time had opened before me when I was recalled to the cave and more bitter thoughts by the most hideous of sounds. Imagine a cat being skinned by slow degrees and you have some idea of why I sat upright in my bed, an appalled expression on my face. The Grogoch was crooning me a wordless lullaby, a distorted, sharp-flat, discordant, terrifying combination of sounds that would have made any boy refuse to go to bed in the dark for the rest of his life. His eyes were tightly closed and he was swaying from side to side with his arms folded as if around a child's form. I could not let this continue; the sound was boring into my head like an awl and I felt that soon my mind would bubble or liquefy under such an onslaught. I must act soon or I should find myself bludgeoning the speaker.

'Desist!' I screamed and, thankfully, he did so at once. 'I appreciate your… which is to say that I require complete silence if I am to sleep. My thanks.'

He looked down at his folded arms as if a, probably senseless, child still lay there and then with slow and haughty steps made his exit from the cave. I placed my head upon my pillow once again, but was overcome with such a fit of laughter I could not think of sleep for at least half an hour. Try as I might, I found it impossible to remove from my inner sight the picture of nursey Grogoch singing her young charge into his dreams.

CHAPTER NINETEEN

It has never been my custom, or my good fortune possibly, to entertain women from my bed, if you discount my grandmother with her occasional spoonful of bitter medicine. I had awoken and all but pushed the coverlet from me when I noticed a figure other than the Grogoch seated in a chair drawn close up to me. I always feel at a disadvantage, tetchy even, when I discover that I have been observed and have not known it. To have been naked under a thin coverlet merely sharpens the tetchiness. I collected myself, swallowed a sharp word or two and then looked at my visitor – the Lady Nemain with my new day's clothing on her lap. Of the Grogoch there was no sign.

'You have me at a disadvantage, Lady. Good manners confine me to my bed.'

She smiled in a way that did not weaken my resolve to stay beneath my coverlet. 'I am used to the company of fighting men who have no time for manners of any kind. And you will be clothed in a blinking.' She tossed the clothing onto my stomach and leant towards me. I refused to look at the tops of her legs which this movement revealed or at those other parts which tumbled forward. I pulled my knees up to my chest and surrounded as much of my body as I could with the coverlet which now seemed much smaller and inadequate for such a purpose. I also reached for my satchel which was always my bedfellow.

Some may wonder that my little warrior had not stood to full attention by this time. Perhaps he had, indeed, but let me explain myself. I do not frequent bawdy houses and I am not used to the sight of women clothed with the negligence of a Classical statue. Call me an insensitive bumpkin, if you like. It would have been all too easy to throw aside my coverlet and present myself as a vigorous young lover of twenty to this goddess, this half-naked woman with thighs and pretties as soft as any – as any young man's fancy. Years before, I had promised myself that I should be the father of four strong sons and so create the family I had never known. To that end, I would not scatter my seed like a wasteful sower in a field of tares. I would most certainly acknowledge the mother of my children and it would be no faerie lady, no matter how entrancingly she inclined herself towards me. I am no Eve's minion. And the Lady Nemain was, I guessed, a thousand years or more in age and in all likelihood as crooked as any midnight hag in the privacy of her own bed-chamber.

'Lady,' I said gathering the coverlet, my clothing and the satchel to me and stepping from my bed with great awkwardness, 'allow me to dress behind the screen and my attention is yours to command.'

Soon we were seated on either side of my table in a mood of entirely false amiability. The Grogoch made a brief appearance with a platter of sweetmeats and wooden goblets of cool drink and then fled. I would happily have fled with him as I felt that I was about to embark on yet another of these tiring games, a politic word followed by a stolen glance to see its effect and a slight movement of the body to confirm what you have said. But, if a game were to be played, then Edward Harry would play it to win. I partook of both the sweetmeats and drink to show that I had all the time in the world and that such a powerful presence as the Lady Nemain's in no way unsettled me.

In the world of men, that is to say in London, I have observed that the greater the personage the more they are bedecked in costly stuffs and jewels. Only twice before this had I been privileged to catch a glimpse of Her Great Majesty Queen Elizabeth as she sailed past her adoring subjects like some argosy laden with all the riches of the world. I was at many yards' remove and leaping all the while to improve my sight of the spectacle. Her skirts, her coat, her great arcing farthingale extended to such distances from her body that no man could approach her closely, even if he dared. Her face, as white as, what shall I say, as unblemished ivory, glowed frigidly in its nest of ruby, emerald, pearl and other stones of whose names I am ignorant. Such is the proper appearance of majesty, almost too resplendent for the eye to manage. In the Elven wildlands, quite another rule was their by-word. I was seated at a small table with a being who had the power to strike her servants down with a gesture or a simple thought. It would be no indirect threat as in, 'I shall have you beaten.' Her word, her look, brought real pain at once. And, to my mind, she was unacceptably unclothed. Her red hair, almost in ringlets, and yet not quite, lay along the bones of her shoulder and then fell forwards or backwards wherever it would as if pointing at those beauties we should not have the courage to peep at. I heard the voice of my schoolmaster, John Partridge, buzzing at my ear: 'And which of the goddesses bared her perfect arms the better to shoot her bow?' 'Diana, *Magister*.' 'Whose naked legs and feet could leave the fastest athlete a mile behind?' 'Atalanta, *Magister*.' Both of these figures I thought of as virginal manifestations of the female form despite Master Partridge's all too obvious savouring of them. The Lady Nemain, with her delight in the spray of blood as a sword bit home, was no such being. The loose folds of her brown upper garment and skirt could in an instant be thrown aside the easier for her to be at her seduction or murder.

'This is a council of war, Edward Harry,' she said breaking off a corner of one of the sweetmeats and touching it lightly with her tongue.

'Council of *whore*, more like,' I thought and disgraced myself by giggling.

She could not know the source of my humour and so she continued. 'Your task was performed like a true soldier. We are well pleased with you.' She extended her arm as if to lay her hand upon me and I edged away. Again, she let my behaviour pass without comment. 'Success and failure are like weights in a balance. Last night, the balance moved both ways for us. While you and your band taught Lord Alanin his lesson, our great tree suffered an unforeseen reverse. It returned to us despoiled of many of its branches and of those who live amongst them.'

'I cannot manage your tree, Lady. I am no woodland spirit.'

'That is not what I ask. The others must be taught a more painful lesson. Last night you did little more than spoil a garden, after all.'

'I have said I will not shed blood for you!' I did not care if I shouted and she did not seem to care that I strode away from her and drew my dagger.

'In three nights' time, the tree will go forth again and so will you and I, together.'

I remained standing where I was and listened to the plan of campaign that perhaps I should follow and perhaps not.

'Leagues to the south there is a great manor. Its Lord and Lady have dealt insultingly with our people and need to be taught to behave better. No, we shall not end our night's work with their heads on a stake. That may be for another time.'

'Simply fear and humiliation?'

'Simply that.'

'You would make a brute of me, lady.'

She did not care to answer this charge which I thought most telling.

'You also said, on another occasion, that it would be injudicious for you to be seen taking up arms yourself.'

'I know what I said! Circumstances change.'

'In three nights' time?'

'The tree has been sorely mis-used. It will take much healing from our Lord and Lady.' She placed her hand firmly on the table at this point and looked so fiercely into my eyes I was sure I had committed some grave offence. 'They used iron. They used iron! Such a thing is never done. It cannot be done. They have too many men like yourself at their command already.' She paused and once again looked at me with great concentration. 'I have a gift for you. I almost forgot it.'

I hoped it was not the gift of herself.

'We have given you a name.'

'Lady...'

'Cal-a-pin, which in the Elven tongue means *Rider to victory*.'

I surprised us both with the vehemence of my reply. It put paid to her slight smile at once.

'My name is Edward Harry. I have no need of your childish title. I throw Calapin back at you.'

To have accepted that Calapin would have been to accept that I should never go home; I would be theirs for ever. Let them understand that they must always watch me for I was determined to break open the door of my cage and take my friend with me as I stepped out of captivity. It would have been more politic, I know, to go along with this Calapin, which was probably an honour, and to keep my own counsel. Well, I said *No* loudly and strongly and made it all too clear that I still struggled against them. My name is the very heart of me because I chose it myself. Take away my name and I became an orphan brat made away with by the faeries, a changeling, a Hobbinol.

'If you call me Calapin, the Pooka rider, I shall not answer you. Not at all. Not in the most dangerous of circumstances, be assured of that.' I said it slowly and in my deepest voice, an actorly gesture which I did not carry off well.

She flicked me away with a gesture of her own and there ensued a long silence.

'Will you run with me on this enterprise, then, Edward Harry?' she asked eventually.

'I will, Lady, but I have conditions.'

She stood up with a suddenness that brought me to my feet also. I looked on with shock when she cast the table aside and made as if to rage at me. Taking a long breath, she said, 'Name those conditions, which cannot include your return home.'

I marked each of my points with a tap of my knife blade against the palm of my left hand. I began by saying, 'I have neglected my studies of late and I grow fretful with the tedium of dwelling in a cave. My prison yard is the greensward yonder and such is my whole world at this moment. I do not like containment, Lady, and with my newly-opened senses, I have no desire to penetrate your woodlands. I have seen the creatures they truly hold and they are not for me. To expect me to sit here for three long days and not descend into madness is an absurdity. Find me books to read and a tutor in your Elven tongue. That is what I ask.'

My request surprised her and she must have been glad indeed that I had not demanded my freedom with a threat to take my iron blade to every living thing about me. She sat down again and rested her foot on the overturned table. 'Books, you say?'

'Are there such things in the forest or in your great metropolis?'

'Not in the forest. We prefer to commit our songs and tales to memory. In the city I have seen whole shops full of books. Books scribed in the Elven tongues and printed volumes we obtained from the human world.' She snorted unnecessarily at this last piece of information.

'You rely on us for much, then?' I felt obliged to say. 'I would appreciate an armful of books in English, Latin or French and I would like them tomorrow. As for the tutor, most of what is said to me and about me I cannot understand because it is spoken in the language of the place. I need to remedy that state of affairs and I ask that you send me, this very morning, Cavad or Follovin, either one of that humourless pair, who can make good my ignorance. That is what I ask and so you may leave now.'

She could not help smiling at my forwardness. I was of use to them and so she would grant me my toys. My last words to her were ones I called from the top of my steps. She had already moved into the forest, or disappeared by some magical contrivance, but I trusted that she would hear what I said.

'We have need of a map and you and I must discuss our strategy, Lady, before the third day comes.'

My first visitor was the Grogoch who set about restoring order in the cave. He looked with great disapproval at a scratch made on the table when it was thrown to the floor and he spent a good half-hour tut-tutting as he swept and gave me my breakfast. His nerves were clearly in a state of disarray as he confused his duties, sweeping a little, then offering me an end of bread, flicking the air with his duster and then filling my goblet to overflowing.

'The Grogoch does not like her visits,' he told me several times and made me wonder whether she hurt him on her way out. My interview, or confrontation, with the Lady Nemain had covered my hands and neck with perspiration, although I was not aware of it at the time. Once she had departed, I decided to refresh myself and therefore placed the dagger I had been holding not back in its satchel but on the seat of my chair. I was still drying my face when the Grogoch entered and began his interminable *Oh my my*s. At one point, caught between whether to attack a dusty corner or give my breakfast further un-needed attention, he spun in a slow circle wringing his hands and backing into the furniture. His leg jolted my chair and knocked the dagger onto the floor. Although my head was still mostly enveloped in my drying cloth, I have sharp eyes and I saw him, in an instant, pick up the blade and return it to the chair. He had used his fingertips and he gasped slightly as he did it, but he had most certainly laid hands on a piece of iron. I believed this to be a very important piece of information, one he did not wish me to possess, for he had thrown a glance in my direction and was satisfied that the drying cloth obscured my view. At first, I said not a word about the matter. I let him plump up my twigs and fold the bed's coverlet twice. I let him cut me a piece of fruit and investigate the fullness of my goblet and then I struck. His back was turned towards me at the time as he leaned over my table and I had the cruel satisfaction of seeing a fountain of red juice rise high in the air before splashing all down his hairy front. I doubt that it was ever washed off. Perhaps he sucked at his fur in thirsty moments. Who knows? The ewer clattered away from him and his knees sagged.

'You saw what the Grogoch did?' His voice was hushed with disappointment.

'Indeed I saw him pick up my iron dagger and replace it on my chair. The Grogoch did not scream or shrivel so he must now give an account of himself.'

'The Master was drying his face.'

'But the Master is not blind, by any means. Have your years in the human world hardened you to the touch of iron?'

It stood to reason that this is what had happened. How did these house faeries ever survive in kitchens and pantries if they could not bear to touch the metal from which we make so many of our utensils? He walked to the nearest chair and sat across it, gripping its back. From what I could see of his face, I might as well have just told him that he had an hour to live.

'The Master is right. Over many years, many human lifetimes, the touch of iron becomes less of a poison. At first I screamed because of it. Then I had the shits and now I only have the trembles. Some of my mates in Yorkshire died of it, but that was years ago and they never were up to much.' He extended his right hand so that I might see how he shook, and also the two pink blisters on his fingers.

'In a big kitchen I wear gloves so that I get the trembles and not the marks.' He sucked his fingertips and gave me his most piteous look.

'This must seem like a holiday to you, then,' I said, not taken in by his performance which became more of an exaggeration by the moment. His fingertips were now beneath his armpit and his trembles made the chair legs clatter on the floor. He would have me believe that iron was to be avoided at all events and now I knew better. If he could grasp any skillet or carving knife while wearing gloves, he could steal my dagger when my back was turned, or even out of my very own fingers. I was glad of the information. He soon made it clear, however, that it was not my knowing his secret that worried him; he was frightened I might reveal it to others.

'Please,' he said. 'Please, Master.' His hands were now joined in supplication and he fell to his knees. 'They think the Grogoch is the hairy beastie who cleans the floors and empties his Master's bucket. If they knew I could bear the touch of iron, they might use me in their fights. The Grogoch dreads that.'

'Have no worries,' I said graciously. 'Your secret is safe with me. I would be foolish if I said a word that lost me such a careful servant. You make my cave a palace.'

My promise revived him entirely and, as he completed the remainder of his household duties, he sang to himself, at first under his breath and then with painful gusto. Not everything in the land of faerie is beautiful and the song of the cheerful Grogoch is best avoided by miles.

'In return for my promise, you must solemnly swear never to sing in my presence again,' I said. 'There are some sounds beyond the tolerance of the human ear. If you sing one note more I shall have the shits and trembles all at the same time and you will have much to do to clear up after me.'

He nodded at this and continued with his besoming, so happy that he needed to find an outlet for his feelings. If singing were prohibited, he experimented with skipping and found that it upset the rhythm of his sweeping. His final method of rejoicing was to mime the words of his song while he kept the melody firmly locked up in his head.

His duties done, the Grogoch scampered away and I was left to await my tutor, if the Lady Nemain kept her word. I had informed the Grogoch that I expected a visitor and would require double the quantity of victuals for my dinner so at least I should eat myself to bursting if I still found myself alone.

In the mid-morning, as I lay in irritable listlessness on my bed, a shadow appeared in my doorway. It was Cavad come to give me my lesson. No schoolboy who has pissed maliciously on my lady's slippers and who awaits his thrashing could have approached his master with such an ill grace as that with which the Elven man now entered my cave. He waited to be invited across my threshold which I did with a bonhommie I decidedly did not feel towards him. He had shown me his slapped-arse face before and I had tormented it with cheefulness and little touches and prods that must have seemed utterly distasteful to him.

'Shall we sit either side of my table as though we were in a real classroom?' I said. 'I promise to learn my lessons well and you must promise not to tan me when I am in error.' My playful words were entirely wasted and brought no response from him. He sat down at the table as if he had thought of the action himself.

'What do you know of our Elven tongue already?' he asked, confident that there was very little of it lodged in my brain and that, if he made feeble efforts at instructing me, there would be not much more after three days. I had other ideas. We both knew that he who has words has power and I had studied enough of languages to know when I was being deliberately misinformed. When he played tricks, I would spot them and I was quite prepared to kick him for it. I truly believe it was the strangest classroom in the history of education – the normal battle of wills being entirely reversed; the *Magister* was determined to be slow and confusing and the discipulus was intent on total mastery of the subject. I trilled a few Elven phrases, the sum of all I knew, and had the pleasure of seeing my tutor's eyes widen. How out of countenance it made him. We began by naming the items around us in the cave and then we went to work on our bodies, moving from hair to toes. My little warrior was not left out of the inventory which occasioned an extraordinary level of annoyance on Cavad's part. He refused to speak the word above a mumble. It is *ta-ag-in,* if you must know. I will not say that we passed our time pleasantly or that there was shared amusement when I struggled to make certain sounds with my lips. I had not smiled during my lessons at school, so I was not bothered now.

The Grogoch brought us a tasty hot dinner which I fell upon with relish, as I tend to fall upon all food when my mind has been busy. Cavad was hungry and yet reluctant to enjoy my hospitality. The few pieces of meat or vegetable he could bring himself to put in his mouth must have inflamed his hunger painfully and I thought him the biggest fool for such a performance. We worked hard throughout the afternoon until I felt my head would burst with so many new words and sounds.

'We have toiled enough,' I said. 'So now you may take your leave.' I escorted him to the cave's mouth where I was able to speak to him as I would never have dared speak to schoolmasters who were ungenerous to me and whom I hated.

'One day, believe me, I shall boot your arse from here to the horizon for your milk-curdling demeanour,' I said. 'It may not happen in your world, but it will certainly happen if ever you set foot in mine.' As he descended into the clearing I could not refrain from calling childishly after him, *'Ha-an-a!'* the Elven word for buttocks. I wished that I also had the word for nettles and a command of their future tense. However, the action lifted my mood and, I trust, depressed his.

My modest library of books arrived by Grogoch, which is to say that he hurled himself into the cave with a basket in which the volumes bounced so violently I feared they would be reduced to a few tatters of leather and paper in a state fit only for my jakes. He placed the basket on my table and seemed very pleased with himself.

'Books!' he said as if I were in need of an explanation.

They were possibly the first printed volumes ever seen in that forest and I was so eager to examine my present that I did not enquire after its provenance. The Grogoch told me nonetheless.

'It was the town *here* or the town *there*,' he said looking about him guiltily as if the cave walls were hung with ears. 'Because they know me better, I went *there*.' He was bursting so to let me know the lengths to which he had gone to find me the books that it overcame any injunction concerning secrecy. I feigned to be entirely caught up in my titles, but my ears were singed. By *there*, he could only mean the human world, perhaps London itself. One day, when my occasion served, I would make him tell me how it was that in the space of a few hours he had travelled to the realm of Humankind, looked over a bookseller's stock, haggled with the bookseller even, and returned laden with such treasures. He had obtained the armful of books as easily as if he had slipped into another room to fetch them. It was that simple for him to pass into the human world and yet I was utterly prevented from doing it.

'Some Caesar,' I said. 'His *Gallic Wars*. A good choice. My childhood favourite almost.' I realised, of course, that he could hardly have presented himself as a customer amongst the booksellers of St Paul's churchyard looking as he did, a good-hearted fright, but a shaggy fright all the same. They would have thought some demon had come amongst them for their sin of turning the Lord's house into a shop and counters. 'Did you help yourself to these without their owners' knowledge?' I asked and was met with what I took to be a wink although the sheer quantity of hair tumbling across his face made any expression difficult to read accurately.

'A set of French whim-whams,' I said, continuing my inventory. 'Not such a happy choice. I shall save them for a very idle moment. North's *Plutarch*. Excellent. Ah, Master Ovid's *Metamorphoses*. An old friend greets me in this place of strangeness. No devotional works, I see. A pleasing omission. You have chosen well, Master Grogoch. Were they your own choices?'

He simpered at me and made a deprecating gesture with his hands. There were depths to my Grogoch if he could understand my reading habits from the few observations I had let fall. For all I knew, he kept a substantial library of his own to which he devoted all those spare moments he did not spend a-knitting. I clutched each book to my breast and showed every appearance of uncontrolled and unthinking delight. The Grogoch positively capered to see me so pleased with the world, little thinking that another, invisible, Edward Harry was even then building so many schemes.

'I shall take my chair and sit in the cave mouth with my old friend Julius Caesar,' I said innocently and did as I promised. I was perhaps a dozen chapters into the first volume when a platter of cakes and drink appeared at my side. This was one of the best evenings I spent in all my time as a prisoner in Hy Brazil. All I needed to make my life complete was my freedom and, God knows, that was a thing to ask!

The next morning, Cavad was on his guard. Did it not occur to him that I was always on mine, too? The *discipulus* had peformed too well in his previous day's lessons and the *Magister* set about a campaign of confusion. My questions were not to be answered directly and, if I made errors, they were to be reinforced rather than corrected. It occurred to me more than once to pare a slice of the devil's ear with my blade to show him the extent of my displeasure. Did he think I came to the schoolroom so naïve and trusting that I could be sold any mis-featured pup he fancied? I had worked long into the night rehearsing my lessons. Now that I was possessed of paper as well as pen and ink, I wrote all my Elven words in English spelling and asked the Grogoch for correction whenever I doubted my recollection.

'You may stay here with your knitting all night long,' I said. 'I have need of your advice.' He obeyed my behest and I repeated my new vocabulary over and over until my ears rebelled and the Grogoch moved to the furthest corner of the cave to be away from it. I truly believe he thought my reason hung over a precipice and that, any moment, I should plunge into the idiocy they say befalls those who have been locked in a windoweless cell without benefit of conversation for untold years.

I have a naturally retentive mind and the added mixture of anger and desperation ensured that all my drills and lists were still in place when my unsociable tutor arrived to misinform me. I was exhausted, yet smiling. There is nothing in the world so disconcerting as a smile. I had guessed, ahead of Cavad's arrival, that a hobble might be put on my progress, and the Grogoch was under the strictest orders to be near at hand and to take his time over his household duties as we studied. By certain signs, a cough or a clattering of his besom, he was to inform me when I was being led into the by-ways of error. Oh, how well it worked! In the first quarter of an hour of our lesson, we might as well have been at school inside a windmill with all its grinding and grating. The Grogoch's besom battered floor, wall and crevice time and again to indicate the lies I was being told.

'Shall I ask that question again?' I said perhaps twenty times before Cavad gave up on his deceptions and adopted, instead, a policy of slowness to hinder my mastery of his language.

'Let me present you with a small analogy,' I said, smilingly. 'Imagine that a Spaniard has found his way to England with, let us say, the purpose of mapping all of the country's defences. He needs to move about the country to do his work, but he is, unfortunately for him, at once recognisable. They are swarthier than Englishmen, you will know, because their homes are closer to the sun. This said Spaniard finds himself in Cambridge and wishes to take the road to Bristol. He falls into conversation with a man who directs him eastwards to Norwich. And when he arrives in that city, he is told to journey due North and soon finds himself on the windy shore of a cold sea. It is not Bristol at all. It is nowhere near it. I am not that Spaniard. Do you understand me? If I wish to be taken to your Elven Bristol, then go there I shall. Norwich holds no interest for me. And, as I am young and more than usually vigorous, I do not need to proceed at the pace of a cripple!'

We sat in a long silence, I staring and he avoiding my gaze.

'The geography of England has never been my concern,' he said at last. 'There are three kinds of future tense in the Elven tongue. They denote differing levels of probability. Do you believe you are able to learn all three?'

'Let there be thirty-three. Let there be a new dialect in every street or under every tree. I wish to know it.'

The Grogoch's broom had been near inaudible during this last exchange as he strained to hear what we said. From the corner of my eye, I saw him moving with a preternatural, dreamy slowness, the twig bristles caressing the floor with the softest of touches. The smile this brought to my face, when added to my look of satisfaction that I had flattened Cavad's game, must have been immensely infuriating.

'Three future tenses call for special measures,' I said and collected one of my books which, up to now, had been out of sight. 'As you instruct, so shall I write. Is not that the best method?'

Now the *Magister's* expression changed. He had come across the turd left in his desk. His eyes widened and his lips half disappeared in a scowl. Turning abruptly, he shouted, 'Is this *your* doing!'

In response to this attack, the Grogoch clutched the broom handle to his chest where it mostly disappeared in the hair. His head fell below the level of his shoulders and I observed to myself that he always looked a foot shorter when he adopted this wounded pose.

'These books are the gift of the Lady Nemain,' I declared in an even louder voice. 'Let us stand together at my cave's mouth and summon her so that she might give an account of her actions. You may tell her to her face that this act of kindness was in error.'

'There is no need.'

'I insist upon it. She needs to be told.'

'There is no need.'

I dismissed the Grogoch, who was happy to be gone, and the lesson could now begin on a proper footing.

Thus far, I had been merely feeling my way around the Elven language, touching its walls and finding doorways through which I lacked the knowledge to pass. As the morning's instruction proceeded, I entered some of those doorways and became dimly aware of rooms and furniture. Very soon many pages of my book were filled with writing and my inkwell much drained. I had quickly covered the blank end pages with the tiniest writing I could manage and moved on to despoiling the printed text itself. I had chosen the book of French sonnets as I have never been fond of the sonnet form, finding its intricacies affected and effeminate. I have pointed out before that I enjoyed a kind of celebrity for the fineness of my handwriting and I took pride in the orderliness with which I was transcribing my lists of nouns and verbs and the rules governing their use. My study of sundry European tongues, dead and living, had suggested to me that languages arise in much the same shape as each other and I found the Elven tongue not greatly dissimilar in this regard. It had its quirks, do not they all, but when Cavad darted here and there in his attempt to bewilder me, I could always ask the question that enabled me to fit any piece of information into its correct place in my unfolding scheme.

'Sometimes your Elvenish reminds me of the Greek,' I said, 'and sometimes

I hear echoes of my own robust native tongue. Did your scholars set out to copy them?' I knew this would nettle him and that he would feel compelled to contradict me.

'You have no notion of how ancient is the Elven tongue. It is the first of languages in every way.'

'That being the case, I shall expect many sales of the Elvenish grammar I intend to publish when I am next in London. Would you like me to acknowledge your help at the front of the volume?'

'You are *fir-a-pag*! That is our most insulting word for a fool.'

'No doubt it is connected with the voiding of the fundament.' I made a point of writing down the word and repeating it. 'When we are even better friends, I hope you will show me how to write your script. I confess I find our Roman letters somewhat plain in comparison.' My request was a sincere peace offering after our snapping at each other and it fell to the ground disregarded. I had seen and admired a few examples of the Elven hand and planned to take at least one book written in it with me when I returned home.

At this point, a pie was brought in for our dinner. It had a rich golden crust and would have satisfied a hungry family.

'The boar's head in hand bear I,' I cried when the Grogoch set it down. He appeared very proud of it and I hoped he had not been much involved in the preparing. The smell was rich and heavy and gripped my stomach with hungry pangs.

'The Master and his teacher must please to make room while the pie is hot.'

A pastry crust can hide many a dark tale, many a frightening piece of offal that would cause diners to blench if it were held up for close inspection. I prised up a corner of the crust suspiciously.

'Please assure us that our eyes will not recoil from what is chopped up small in here,' I asked.

'Beef and things,' the Grogoch insisted. 'Tasty things. Not crawly or wriggly things. I gave them the recipe myself. From a lord's table.' He tapped the side of his nose and then so busied himself with our plates and knives and the serving of the pie that he was able to ignore my question as to the name of the lord in question. It resembled an English pie, you see, with its substantial crust, its pinchings at the edges, its pastry shapes and, most particularly, in the thickness of its gravy. I had a low opinion of Cavad's character already, to be sure, but when the pie was cut and succulent mouthfuls of beef washed across our plates, I despised him for his utter indifference. Perhaps he hankered after some titbit more refined, much as Her Majesty Queen Elizabeth would have turned up her nose when offered an acorn or an onion for her dinner.

Our afternoon lesson continued much as it had in the forenoon: the *discipulus* fastened eagerly on every single crumb of grammar and the *Magister* was as much of a grudging hindrance as he dared make himself. I took faltering steps down the corridors of the Elven tongue, shutting myself by accident in numerous cupboards along the way, but, by five or six in the evening, I was able to slip in and out of their three future tenses like a dancer. It gave me more pleasure than I can say to be able to put into the words of that land the thought that remained uppermost with me: 'One day soon I shall leave this place. I shall return home. Note well,' I said, 'that I have used the most definite and categorical form of the future tense. I allow not a fraction of a doubt into that statement.'

Naturally, Cavad did not respond to my declaration, although I fancied I saw a twitching of his shoulders when I stood at the cave mouth and bawled the words to his disappearing back and to all others who cared to hear.

The Grogoch returned almost as soon as my teacher had left. 'The Master will be tired,' he said.

'Tired as a man who has been pushing a plough single-handedly for a week. But also very pleased with myself.' I repeated the two short sentences about returning home and he smiled with approval. Perhaps he was pleased with how much I had learnt or, possibly, he believed my words would eventually come true. I refreshed my face and changed my shirt and then lay on my bed singing the two sentences over and over. I made them fit a tune I had enjoyed in London and looked forward to singing it when next in my classroom. It was bound to grate. I dozed through the early evening and might have slept interrupted had not the cave suddenly been filled with a shockingly bright light. I sat up only half awake, wondering if I were in the throes of execution by some magical blast. Or was a divine figure visiting me in their full glory which was too painful for human senses? I rubbed my eyes and willed my vision to clear. In front of me, seated on my best chair, was a figure who made gestures to the right and left, drawing my attention to something I did not understand. Was I being offered choices?

'Nemain?'

'No,' replied the Grogoch.

I could think of nothing to say. If he had proved turncoat and I was about to die by fire, let it be swift.

'The Master sat reading so late yesterday. His eyes will suffer if he does that again. Look. A thousand candles.'

I breathed in deeply and was pummelled in the nose by the quantity of bees' wax in the air. At least, I now understood what had happened. A candle stood in every spot that would take one, and in many spots that should not have done so, the hinges of my privy bucket, for example. Some of our leavings are best left unrevealed. I had never known such brightness indoors and certainly no room in Kilcolman Castle ever blazed in this way. Master Spenser's apartments were full of shadows and dark corners where any Irish assassin might have lurked to his heart's content. Although the Grogoch's boast of a thousand candles cannot have been right, I am sure there were three or four hundred. Nor were they of the kind I knew at home which burnt down to a stub all too soon and whose flames were at the mercy of every errant draft. These were Elven candles whose flames burnt tall and whose length never changed. I complimented the Grogoch on finding so many niches for his candles and said I hoped I was not to be given the bill for them. Damn him; if he cared that much for my eyesight he would not have set out to dazzle me thus. He giggled at my pleasantry in a curling-up and twisting kind of way which amused me and I did not have the heart to say that so many flames were beginning to prick my eyes. As I ate my supper, I yawned many a time so that I could quickly take to my bed and be covered in darkness. I believe he hoped we would sit and gossip well into the night but such a plan would have taxed my eyesight beyond endurance. I had intended to read over my lessons but I knew it would be a nonsense to attempt this in such a sun's glare. I had to be content with reciting what I could from memory while the distracting pinpricks on my eyeballs gradually died away. I displeased the Grogoch by insisting on taking to my bed so soon after supper and he let me know this by removing the candles from their niches one by one once he had snuffed them. A snap of his fingers would have swept them all away, I am sure, but he had his point to make.

The morning brought me no teacher. I had breakfasted and was seated at my table with pen and book before I noted how self-consciously the Grogoch was going about his duties. He cast one too many apprehensive looks at myself and the cave entrance for it not to rouse my suspicions that a plan had been made to which I was not a party.

'You know something I do not,' I said. 'Pray tell.'

His reply was to investigate invisible dust beneath the chairs where my glare would not reach him. I believe he would have crouched there for an hour, shaking his head while I fretted, if our visitor had not arrived and enabled him to escape. The Lady Nemain.

'Are you to be my teacher this day, Lady?' I asked brightly.

'Your lessons are over for the present.'

'Are they so? I understood I was to have three full days at my studies before we turned our thoughts to military considerations.'

'These decisions are not yours to make.'

'As I have come to understand. Would you care to see the tables I wrote yesterday? My handwriting is a wonder, I am often told.'

'Stop this!' Her words were delivered in a hiss which she accompanied with a slap on the page I had held out for her inspection. I took the hint and waited quietly for what she had to say.

'Tonight the tree will go forth. We have salved its injuries and found eager warriors aplenty to inhabit it. While it rampages amongst the encampments to the south and west, we shall assail the manor of that certain lord I mentioned. His is a house full of insolence and I wish to put an end to it.'

'Tonight?'

'This very night.'

'And am I to be accompanied by the tribe of Hell once again?'

'They chose to run with you. Be honoured. Each considers himself your creature now. Their lives are yours.'

Well, there was news. I had seen no such devotion and my raised eyebrow showed how little I believed her. We did not dwell on this difference of opinion, however, as she had a scrolled map of the chosen manor and its environs which she spread across the table. She, who had been waging campaigns for a thousand years past, wished to discuss her battle plan with a lad who was still not twenty one. There was no sense in this and yet she was quite determined.

A measure of the lady Nemain's present seriousness was that she was dressed for conversation rather than seduction or enticement. She wore a long garment of a shifting tawny colour which contrived to show far less of any of her limbs than was usually the case and her arms were wrapped in a shawl of some silken stuff dyed in a darker tone. Her hair tumbled as free and as ruddy as ever and she was lightly shod. Yet I still believe that Parson Fitzjohn would have gasped at the sight of her and shouted, 'Fie on thee woman for thy immodesty.'

We sat together at my table and looked at the position of the manor house on the map, noting in particular the easiest points of entry for felons such as ourselves, but I was so struck by the absurdity of our relationship that I am sure I spoke no more than half a dozen sentences which made sense. I gathered that the note of caution I had introduced, the idea of mapping beforehand and not rushing in without a moment's forethought, was considered a great advance. They should have stolen more volumes of Caesar from our booksellers and studied them well. I insisted once again that I would shed no blood, whatever threats she might lay against me.

'I know your thought,' said she who must have done to death whole battalions in her time and relished every moment of it. 'Fear is our aim. Lord Tar-a-puin and his lady have offended us deeply. I wish to see them kneel and beg as you hold your iron blade to their throats. If I stood there, I would surely behead them.'

'So I must chase them about their own house like a ruffian and a bully? Perhaps they have children who can be made to hide under their beds.'

Human children frightened by tales of unseelie faerie folk and faerie youngsters shrieking at the sight of a wild boy with an iron dagger. It would have appealed to my sense of irony if I were not to play such a sneaking part in the game.

'This manor is far to the south, you say?'

'Half a day's journey at good speed.'

'Perhaps you intend me to fly, then, lady.' This was not a serious suggestion, but the notion of sitting on a dragon's back had suddenly come into my head. I was taken aback when the Lady Nemain gave it serious thought.

'Our flying beasts are small and spined. You would tire them even if you managed to find a seat upon their backs.'

'So it is to be the Pooka once again?'

'He says you ride him well.'

'Do I?' I wondered what other discussion they had about me. I had never felt so interesting in all my life. The ride through the forest was not a journey I looked forward to, although I now knew better than to take any of the fruit which might be offered. I could not help but laugh inwardly at the memory of Sir Pooka troubled in his bowels because of my gift of an apple. I was to have no escort this time and would meet the Lady Nemain and all our crew on the far side of the forest about the middle of the afternoon. This meant that, once the Lady left me, I lay down to rest until dinner-time when I partook only lightly despite the Grogoch's determination to keep my plate heaped with food. My quilted surcoat was still most presentable and I did not wish to disgrace myself by puking a hearty meal all down the front of it.

At about three of the clock, the Pooka appeared in the clearing below my cave snorting and stamping for all he was worth. He obviously had far greater relish for the enterprise than I. Without my asking, he went down on one knee and I was able to get up and astride his shoulders. And so away we went. More than ever, I was resolved to ride, fly or crawl my way home and away from such skirmishes as the one which lay ahead that night.